AVIATRIX

AVIATRIX

DON OAKLEY

 Eyrie Press

Eyrie Press
Gainesville, Virginia 20156-0805

Library of Congress Cataloging-in-Publication Data

Oakley, Don 1927-
    Aviatrix / Don Oakley
    p. cm.
    ISBN 0-9619465-4-7 (hardcover ; alk. paper)
    1. Women air pilots—Fiction. 2. Air pilots—Fiction. I. Title

PS3565.A42 A95 2002
813'.54—dc21   2001054530

Printed in the United States of America

AVIATRIX

The Recent Present

T HE NURSE'S aide wheeled the old man out onto the terrace,
as she did every nice afternoon.

"He's sleeping again," she whispered to the young woman
walking beside her. "Poor old Willy's pretty much out of things
most of the time these days. But he'll wake up later."

She shrugged one shoulder and made a mouth and looked
at the other knowingly. "As much as he ever does."

The girl nodded curtly, irritated at the woman's reference to
her great-grandfather, even though Willy was what he'd always
told everyone to call him. It should be Mr. Reynolds, not "poor
old Willy." But they spoke as familiarly and condescendingly of
all the patients at the nursing home, treated them like children—
which, distressingly, most of them were. Shakespeare had it right,
she thought: the last stage of life was a return to infancy.

Yes, poor old Willy. What did he have to do but sleep? He
was so old, so incredibly old. They'd celebrated his hundred and
fourth birthday a few months ago. Or, more accurately, they had
observed it, her mother and she. Willy had been pretty much
"out of things" then too, only nibbling at a piece of the cake her
mother had baked and seeming almost annoyed at this interruption of his daily, eventless routine.

How much longer could he have? she wondered. He was

clearly failing. One of these days he wasn't going to wake up at all. Well, what could you expect, what with his age and two major heart attacks in as many years and recently a series of minor strokes? "Transient ischemic episodes," the doctors called them.

Every time she had visited him lately he was more "out of things." She wondered how many more visits were left. She hoped, for his sake, not too many. It was sad to have your life end like this, just slipping away a little more each day.

The aide locked the chair in position, back from the edge of the terrace so that it was within the shadow of the canopy, and tucked the blanket around the old man's legs. "You be a good boy now, Willy."

She cocked her head at the girl and shook it sympathetically and went back inside.

The girl pulled a metal lawn chair next to the wheelchair. She smoothed the few wisps of snow-white hair on Willy's head before she sat down.

He had been a robust and handsome man in his day. Movie-star handsome. That was long before her memory began of course. He had always been an old, old man to her: a dour and distant and somewhat forbidding one to a child's eyes, and, now that she was grown, just a pathetic, worn-out, helpless fellow human being. She could hardly remember when he hadn't been in the nursing home. But she had seen photographs of him taken in his youth and young manhood, when he was a college professor of English literature. That was eons before her time too; he had retired before she was even born. There was still character in his face though, despite the wreckage of the years.

Poor old Willy. He had outlived his wife by more than twenty years now. She'd never known Great-grandmother Reynolds. They'd both outlived their two eldest children for longer than that, a son missing in action in World War Two, never found, and a daughter killed in the Fifties in a car accident. The rest of the second generation, another daughter and son, growing old themselves, and their children and their children's children, were scattered all over the country, living their own lives.

It was sad. Of all his dozen-some descendants, the only ones who were near enough or cared enough to visit him or do more than make perfunctory inquiries about him once or twice a year were one granddaughter—her widowed mother—and herself.

Really only herself. Her mother rarely came anymore. What was the point, she said, when she couldn't be sure if he even knew who she was or cared that she was there?

The doctors said it wasn't Alzheimer's disease. If it had been Alzheimer's it would have killed him years before, they said. Willy's mind was still intact as far as they could tell. He simply seemed content to exist in his own world, wherever that was. It was just extreme age, they said, just natural wearing out. Senility. What could you expect?

It was sad, to grow old and be all but forgotten, even by your own children. Almost as sad as growing old and forgetting everything yourself, everything you'd done in your life, everyone you'd known.

Or was that a blessing of old age—your own forgetting?

She opened the magazine she had brought with her and started to browse. An airplane was passing overhead. There was a small grass-field airport nearby and planes frequently flew over the nursing home. The building was right in line with the runway. There had been complaints about it, although the airport had been there first. She glanced up, but the plane was hidden by the canopy.

The little airport's days were probably numbered, she mused, just as Willy's were. One day it would be replaced by another housing development. It was the booming Nineties. Every city in the country was growing ever larger, their suburbs gobbling up the surrounding countryside.

Willy wasn't asleep, yet not entirely awake. He was aware that he had been hauled out to the terrace for his daily "sunning," like an old lizard, by that horse of a nurse or whatever she was. He merely pretended to be asleep when she was around to spare himself her inane, solicitous chattering. Most of the time, though, he was asleep. It was hard to tell the difference some days. Not that it made any difference. What was that damned racket?

He opened his eyes and turned his head and saw the girl.

He looked vaguely confused, disoriented. "Hi there, Gramps," she said reassuringly. She leaned closer to him. "It's me, Marilyn. How are you today?"

His watery eyes seemed to clear a little and he nodded at her.

"You're a very pretty girl, Marilyn. You remind me of someone I used to know."

All at once he began staring at her so intently that she was startled. She had never seen him look so alert.

He turned his head again and saw the airplane that had banked around over the building and was coming in low for a landing at the airport. It was an indistinct blur to him. He fumbled for his glasses. They were back in the room. But it was a single-engine private plane; he could tell that from the sound of the engine.

"Probably a Cessna," he said quite lucidly. "A 150 or 152 if it's a student. Probably practicing takeoffs and landings. That's the Blériot trainer of today. They don't use Cubs much anymore."

Did those people up there appreciate what it was they were doing, flying through the air? he thought. Not likely. It had become such an everyday thing, so ordinary. All instruments and radios now. No longer a miracle. Not for decades and decades had it been a miracle.

He turned to her again. "They used to call us 'aeronuts,' Marilyn. Did you know that? No . . . of course you didn't."

He smiled at her and chuckled and she realized she had never heard him do that before. Nor had he ever engaged in what could be called conversation with her; he had always been only half-there, part of him in the present, the rest . . . somewhere else. She closed the magazine and let it lie in her lap.

"They did, Gramps? Who did? Why?" But his grasp on—or interest in—the present already seemed to be slipping.

"It's all buildings and shopping centers now, Hempstead Plains," he said, more to himself than to her. "That's where

Lindbergh took off from, you know. Not our field. Another one they built next to it later. They named a boulevard after him, Lindbergh. Ovington too."

He was still staring at her—no, beyond her, at something only he could see. His eyes veiled over again. The moment of lucidity was fading. She tried to bring him back.

"Go on, Willy. Tell me about the old days. I want to know. Do you know something about airplanes?"

Airplanes, he thought. When did we start calling them that? He couldn't remember. The English never did. They still used the old spelling: aeroplane.

"They're all gone of course, long ago," he said. "André. Matilde. Leo. Hamel. Beachey. Harriet. She was the first."

He spoke each name slowly, as if calling off a roll, and made a kind of chuckle again, more like a raspy *huhn-huhn* sound in his throat. "Carole too, no doubt."

Carole. He hadn't thought about her for—he couldn't remember how long it was. Why did he think of her now?

Was that last name the "someone" she reminded him of? Marilyn wondered. It wasn't his wife's name. None of the names he mentioned were family names.

"Yes, Willy, go on," she encouraged again. "I'm listening."

But now he was only talking to himself. "All of them gone, every one, years and years ago. I'm the only one left. There's no one else to remember anymore."

She put her hand soothingly on the thin, frail hand that had gripped the fold of the blanket in his sudden-seeming awakening, still gripped it, shaking feebly.

Hamel, he thought. For all his experience with the channel, to be lost in the end over the North Sea. When was it? 1914. Did he love her too? If so, he was lucky. He only had to endure two years without her. And if he didn't love her . . . that was even luckier.

Old Beachey, a year later. 1915. Came back to flying when he heard that a Russian and a Frenchman had looped the loop. Couldn't stand to think anybody could outfly him. Beachey—

crashing down into San Francisco Bay, his wings broken, giving his final, ultimate thrill to the crowd.

San Francisco. *She* had lived there once.

His hand stopped shaking. Marilyn patted it. His eyes were closed again. He had left her. It was so pleasant and peaceful out here she felt like dozing off herself.

"Go back to sleep, Willy, if you want to. I'll be here."

Did he dream? she wondered. What did he dream?

Willy dreamed, but his mind was not asleep. It churned.

All of them gone. Into the past. But what is the past? A bucket of ashes, Sandburg wrote somewhere. True enough, but no more than that?

The past is a noun, a grammatical convention. But there is no such *thing* as the past. You can't hang "the past" on a wall and look at it. It has no substantive, objective existence outside the mind that recorded it, apart from the memory of the person who lived it. The past is nothing but a jumble of memories of experiences in the mind of the person who experienced them, and mind and memory themselves are nothing but the reiterative dance of trillions of flashing nerve synapses in the two pounds of raw meat we call the brain.

So when the brain dies and the dancing ceases and the person is no more, is "the past" he experienced gone as well? When I am no more, will *she*, who exists only in my brain, then truly be no more, even less than ashes?

Oh yes, a shadow of her "lives" in the collective memory— in history—and will as long as the collective memory endures, as long as anyone cares to look her up. But history is not the past, not the real past. History is only secondhand memory, the fragmentary public residue, false and true, of the interactions of all our billions of private pasts.

Oh God—how long ago it all was, how long ago. Yet so real, so real, every day still real.

Is this my final punishment then, to be the last one? To live so long . . . remembering . . . always remembering . . . sifting a bucket of ashes . . .

Prologue:
New York City
1909

1

NEW YORK had been in a festive mood for days. The city was in the throes of the Hudson-Fulton Celebration, jointly commemorating the three-hundredth anniversary of Henry Hudson's exploration of the river that was to bear his name and the one hundred-second anniversary of Robert Fulton's duplication of Hudson's voyage, from New York to Albany, in the world's first practical steamship, the *Clermont*.

The planners of the celebration had decided against holding a traditional world's fair in a single, centralized location. Instead, the entire city was to be one huge fair for a period of two weeks. There were to be at least three major parades, one on water and two on land; fireworks displays on the Hudson; sports events; banquets for foreign dignitaries; special historical exhibits in the city's many museums; innumerable pageants, lectures and commemorative exercises in the schools and colleges and universities of all five boroughs, and dedications of plaques and monuments to Hudson and Fulton and Giovanni da Verrazano, the Italian discoverer of New York Bay.

And something else, something no city had ever sponsored before: aeronautical exhibitions, not merely by airships and balloons but demonstration flights in the newfangled invention called the aeroplane.

In preparation for the latter, the U.S. First Army drill field on Governors Island had been enlarged to an area of ninety-six acres with dredgings from Buttermilk Channel between the island and Brooklyn and converted into a flying field for Wilbur Wright and Glenn Curtiss, both of whom had signed contracts with the Aeronautical Committee of the celebration. Hangars were erected to house their machines and obstructing telephone and telegraph poles relocated.

It was intended to be the greatest celebration in the history of New York City, and no one who was there to witness it could doubt that it was. An estimated one million visitors were in town, augmenting the city's own vast population of five million and filling every hotel and boarding house and private lodging available.

Flags flew everywhere, both the good old Red, White and Blue of America and the orange, white and blue Dutch tricolor under which Hudson had sailed in his tiny *Half Moon* and which, with the addition of the letters "H-F" encircled by a golden laurel wreath, was the official flag of the Hudson-Fulton Celebration.

Back from its epochal voyage around the world Teddy Roosevelt had sent it on, America's Great White Fleet—sixteen battleships and six heavy and light cruisers along with their tugs, tenders, supply and other auxiliary vessels—had come for the celebration. Joining them were warships or training vessels from seven other nations: Great Britain, France, Germany, Italy, the Netherlands, Mexico and Argentina. In all, some forty great ships were anchored in the Hudson River for a stretch of ten miles from Forty-second Street northward.

At night the four great bridges across the East River—the Brooklyn, the Williamsburg, the newly completed Queensboro and the soon to be completed Manhattan—were transformed into fairylike things by thousands of light bulbs outlining their spans (13,000 on the Brooklyn Bridge alone), and searchlights atop tall buildings played against the sky. Fifth Avenue on Manhattan, the main line of march for the land parades, was lit up like day from Fifty-ninth Street to Washington Square by extra lights on both sides of the street especially installed for the occasion.

In another twice-nightly display at East One hundred-fifty-fifth and Riverside Drive, an enchanting invention called the Ryan Scintillator played beams of colored lights against clouds of steam, creating a manmade aurora borealis.

Hudson-Fulton was, in short, the grandest public event in New York City since the opening of the Brooklyn Bridge in '83, still fresh in many minds. Certainly the grandest since Admiral Dewey's triumphal return from the Philippines in '99, fresher still.

It was unquestionably the most exciting thing that had ever happened in Willy Reynolds's young life, although it was impossible for him or anyone else to partake of more than a sampling of the events. He was a smart, tall, good-looking lad—attributes he was not unaware of.

What more could you ask of life than to be almost 19 and smart, tall and good-looking; to be lately liberated from high school and recently matriculated at New York University; to have cigarettes and spending money in your pockets, and today to be in the company of three fellow freshmen as full of themselves as you were as you wandered the impossibly thronged streets of the greatest city in the world savoring as many as you could of the endless attractions that had been arranged just for you?

Willy (nobody but his mother called him William) doubted if there had been a fully attended class at the university since the celebration had begun the week before. All normal routine was in more or less a state of suspension. In any case, there was simply too much going on in the real world outside the campus on University Heights in the Bronx to waste one's time in a classroom. Missed lectures could be made up somehow or crammed for later; the sights, sounds, ceremonies and especially the parades of the Hudson-Fulton Celebration would never be repeated.

On the morning of Saturday, September 25, nearly sixteen hundred vessels of all sizes had assembled in the Kill van Kull between Staten Island and Bayonne, New Jersey, to escort replicas of the *Half Moon*, the gift of the Netherlands, and the

Clermont, built on Staten Island, in the Inaugural Naval Parade to the Water Gate at One hundred-tenth Street for the official beginning of the celebration. Willy and his mother and father had watched the start of the parade as well as they could from Borough Hall on Brooklyn Heights, then hurried over to Manhattan. By the time they arrived at the Water Gate they could get no closer than the top of the slope of Riverside Park, and from there had a distant view of the ceremonies as the *Half Moon* and the *Clermont* docked and men dressed as Hudson and Fulton disembarked to be received by celebration officials and special guests waiting on a large platform projecting into the river.

As darkness fell that evening, at a prearranged signal the dark hulks of the mighty ships anchored in the Hudson were suddenly lit up in a blaze of lights, and fireworks were set off from barges along the Jersey shoreline.

On the following Tuesday the first big land parade, the Historical Parade, had been held, assembling at One hundred-tenth Street and proceeding down Central Park West and Fifth Avenue for six miles to Washington Square. Willy had marched in this parade as one of two hundred and fifty NYU students accompanying a float on which blunderbuss-carrying men dressed in seventeenth-century military uniforms reenacted the transfer of the city from Dutch to English rule. "New Amsterdam Becomes New York" was Float No. 21 in a total of fifty-four floats depicting three centuries of New York City history.

They had marched proudly past the Court of Honor, the official reviewing stand on the west side of Fifth Avenue between Fortieth and Forty-second Streets where the old Croton Reservoir had once stood and where an imposing new public library was being built. The Court of Honor was itself worth coming to New York to see: thirty-six towering Roman columns flanking Fifth Avenue, eighteen on each side, connected by looping festoons and surmounted by golden spheres sixty feet above the pavement. On each side of the street were bleachers accommodating more than six thousand spectators. Every seat was filled, as indeed was every seat in private stands lining Fifth Avenue as well as behind upper-story windows of buildings facing the street.

(There had been complaints that the city was violating its own ordinances by permitting the owners of buildings and shops along Fifth Avenue to put up viewing stands on the public sidewalks and to charge people as much as ten dollars for the right to use them. But there they were, everywhere you looked. Nor would New York City have been New York City if there hadn't been a few scandals involving the misappropriation of bleacher tickets by aldermen and other officials, not to mention at least one instance of wholesale counterfeiting of tickets, which led to a number of interesting disputes between holders of reservations for the same seat.)

The Historical Parade had been witnessed by fully two million people, the papers said, the largest crowd ever assembled on Manhattan.

As a participant in that parade Willy had seen only his own small portion of it. But now he intended to see as much as he could of the next big parade, the Military Parade, held over the same route two days later, on Thursday. Yet it was turning out that he was seeing even less of this one. Not only did it take the marchers, who included the soldiers and sailors and marines of eight nations, the New York National Guard and Spanish-American War veterans, along with those veterans of the Civil War who were still spry enough to join them, nearly three hours to pass a given spot but it was impossible to find a vantage point close enough to watch them. (The next day's papers were to agree that the viewing throngs had surpassed the previous record by half a million.) For another thing, his companions were too restless to stay put in one place.

He was with three chums. Not really chums, just new acquaintances from NYU, two of whom he knew only by their first names. As a commuting student making the daily trip from his home in Brooklyn, and because classes had begun only a few weeks before, he had not yet made any real friends.

He was also a year older than the typical freshman, having been held back to repeat the first grade due to a prolonged and near-fatal bout of pneumonia at the age of six. Though no fault of his own, all through school this had been a source of private embarrassment to him and as a result he had developed a certain shyness or reserve in his demeanor.

Today however he was as infected as were the others with the excitement of the bright warm late-September day and with a carefree abandonment engendered by virtue of being young and agile and irresponsible in the midst of jostling, milling crowds of people everywhere they went. All along both sides of Fifth Avenue for the entire route of the Military Parade there was nothing but a sea of humanity.

And the noise. Not only the cheers and applause of the multitude but the blare of bugles and the music of countless bands, competing with the shouted commands of drum majors and sergeants and the rhythmic sounds of booted heels and horses' hooves striking the pavement. Willy would not have been surprised if the din was heard all the way over in Brooklyn.

It was intoxicating.

Two of the boys — Willy knew them only as Ernie and Rick — were the leaders. Followed reluctantly by a more circumspect Willy Reynolds and Frank Adams, they darted across Fifth Avenue past policemen who were trying to impose some sort of discipline on the crowds that spilled off the sidewalks in front of the bleachers, dodging through ranks of paraders, doffing their caps elaborately to the marching troops, shouldering their way through people on the opposite side and then repeating the performance at another point along the parade route.

A block above the Court of Honor Willy and Frank got separated from the boisterous Ernie and Rick. Willy was just as glad. Those two were acting like a couple of adolescent show-offs. It was lucky they hadn't all been collared by the cops.

"Let's go down to the Court of Honor!" he yelled at Frank's ear. Mayor McClellan and Governor Hughes and a bunch of other bigwigs were supposed to be there again. They might as well give them a huzzah.

Frank was willing to try, but they quickly found it was impossible to press through the crowd on the sidewalk. They might have been able to take a side street around to one of the stands along the sidewalk above and below the Court of Honor but they wouldn't have paid the tariff being charged for a seat. Not that any seats were available anyway.

"It's hopeless," Frank said. "I bet we could see more at Washington Square."

Willy had caught a glimpse of a contingent of strutting Prussian sailors and marines from the cruiser *Victoria Luise* doing "the Kaiser step" and wanted to see more of them. Frank's idea was as good as any other, he thought. The crowds might be smaller where the parade ended.

They made their way along Forty-third Street and across Sixth Avenue and Broadway, both of which were congested with carriages and automobiles that had been diverted from the parade route, over to Seventh Avenue. The elevated station was even more congested with people; you couldn't even get up the steps to the platform. They decided to walk to Washington Square.

If anything, it was worse there. The crowds were not only as thick as uptown but more unruly, their numbers increased by the paraders breaking rank as they reached the end of the route. People surged off the sidewalk into the street. Outnumbered and frustrated, several policemen linked arms and charged against them. A woman fainted and the cops stepped right over her. One of the policemen reached into the crowd and, for no good reason Willy could see, rapped his billy club against the head of a perfectly respectable-looking Italian gentleman, knocking off his hat, which was quickly trampled underfoot.

"*Police brutality!*" Frank shouted.

The crowd fell back, Willy and Frank with them. It had been a mistake coming here. They found themselves being propelled toward Seventh Avenue again.

"Let's forget about the parade and go down to the Battery and see if we can get over to Governors Island," Frank now suggested. "Maybe Wilbur Wright'll fly again today. Maybe he'll go around the Statue of Liberty again."

"Huh? What are you talking about?"

For all his intelligence Willy Reynolds was uninformed about the larger world outside himself. A seldom reader of the newspaper, all he knew or cared to know about politics or the state of the economy or the latest crisis in the Balkans or Morocco was what he chanced to hear people talking about. With no career goal in mind he had enrolled in NYU as a business administration major to please his father.

John Reynolds was a prosperous real estate broker who had sagely pulled out of the stock market just before the Panic of Aught-seven and only recently got back in and was currently involved in developing a new section of Brooklyn called Mableton. There was still open land in the borough and John Reynolds considered every unbuilt-upon lot a personal challenge.

Willy however was more preoccupied with girls and their mysteries than concerned about real estate and business or the urgencies either of world affairs or of academic study.

He had heard of Wilbur and Orville Wright of course; even he could not help but have heard. The two brothers from Ohio were said to have realized the age-old dream of "conquering the air," or at least that they and other men were in active pursuit of conquering it. A Frenchman named Louis Blériot had flown across the English Channel a few months before. But along with many people of the day, the fact that mechanical human flight had been achieved had not fully registered with Willy. It was not that he did not believe it (as many still did not). The fact simply had not impinged upon his own personal concerns.

It was excusable ignorance, for like most people Willy Reynolds did not appreciate the distinction between aeroplanes and balloons and airships. He did not know that there was a vast and fundamental difference between what the Wrights were supposed to have accomplished and what other men had been doing for years and years with balloons. He'd already seen the balloon tethered to the ground near Grant's Tomb in which somebody named Leo Stevens took people up to view the city and activity on the Hudson, and he'd heard that the *World* had offered a prize of ten thousand dollars for an airship flight from New York to Albany and that a man named Captain Thomas Baldwin had tried it and failed.

"Yeah? One of the Wright brothers flew around the Statue of Liberty?" It wasn't like flying all the way to Albany but it was rather impressive.

"Where have you been, Willy? He did it yesterday. Flew right over the Lusitania, for Christ's sake, or he could have. It was in all the papers today."

Willy shrugged. "So what? People have been flying in balloons for a century."

"It wasn't a balloon, you dope. It was an *aeroplane.*"

Willy did not want to betray his ignorance further and said nothing.

It was Frank's turn to shrug. "Do you have a better idea?"

Willy didn't. But although he'd seen hardly anything of the Military Parade he'd had his fill of the crowds. And while he was dubious about Frank's idea, even if it was just another airship on Governors Island it might be worth going to see. Especially if, unlike the Stevens balloon, it was free-floating and steerable.

"Well, all right, why not," he said. "Let's give it a try."

2

THIS TIME they managed to squeeze onto a packed elevated train to lower Manhattan and found the Battery almost as bustling as midtown had been. But most of the people were just strolling about or gazing from the seawall at the myriad boats in the harbor or waiting in a long line to visit the Aquarium, one of New York City's most popular tourist attractions even before the celebration. There was hardly anybody on the ferry to Governors Island. Evidently there weren't going to be any airship flights today. It was another waste of time to have come here, Willy was already convinced.

A guard at the ferry dock at Governors Island wouldn't let them off the end of the gangplank.

"Do you have passes, boys? No one is allowed on the island without a pass."

This was news to them.

Frank was nervier than Willy. "It's all right," he said nonchalantly. "We're here to see Wilbur Wright fly."

The man shook his head. He motioned to them to stand aside to allow several soldiers and a few civilians heading for Manhattan to get on the ferry.

"There's no flying today, boys. See that flag?" He pointed toward the flagpole atop the round shape of Castle William in the distance. "That black flag with the white square means no flying today. Either too windy or some other reason."

The man was not surly or impatient like some people given a little authority tended to be. He was even friendly.

"When they put up a white flag with a red square in the middle, that means the weather's favorable. When you see the same flag with a red flag under it with a white square, that means there'll be flying within the hour. And when they're reversed, with the red flag on top, that means within fifteen minutes.

"Watch for the flags, boys. You can see everything just as well from the Battery."

Willy was more than ever convinced that they had come on a wild goose chase and was ready enough to retreat back onto the ferry. But Frank didn't give up easily.

"If there isn't going to be any flying today why do we need a pass? We'd just like to walk around a bit. No harm in that, is there?"

The man shook his head again. "Sorry, son. Those are the rules. This is government property, you know."

"Come on, Frank," Willy said. "There's nothing to see here."

And there wasn't, just the field and two big wooden sheds at the far end of it in front of Castle William. It was almost four o'clock anyway and would start getting dark in another hour.

"What's the problem, George?"

Two men were approaching the gangplank. The one in the lead who had spoken was middle aged and well dressed, wearing a bowler; the other was about their own age or maybe a couple years older. Pinned to the first man's breast pocket was an orange, white and blue ribbon with the official medallion of the Hudson-Fulton Celebration suspended from it. The bar at the top of the ribbon said "Commissioner."

"Afternoon, Mr. Beck." The guard touched his cap. "I was just telling these two they need a pass to get on the island."

"Are you boys interested in aeroplanes?" Beck said.

"Yes, sir!" Frank piped. "We're New York University students."

"Are you indeed. Well, if you're really interested in aeroplanes you ought to transfer to Columbia and join Mr. Loening here who is taking the first course in aeronautical engineering in the country."

The younger man grinned modestly and nodded at Frank and Willy. For some reason Willy liked him immediately.

"We'd like to *see* an aeroplane first, Mr. Beck," Frank said. "How do we go about getting passes?"

There was a blast from the ferry's horn, signaling its imminent departure.

"I'd be glad to show these fellows around, if it's all right with you, Mr. Beck," Loening said. "I'll take another ferry."

The older man shrugged. "If you want to, Grover. Mr. Wright has gone back to the city but you can give them a peek into his hangar, if the guard'll let you."

He started up the gangplank, then paused and looked at Willy and Frank.

"If you boys are really serious about seeing Wright or Curtiss fly, give Mr. Loening your names and I'll write out passes for you. You can pick them up at my office. He'll tell you where that is."

"Thank you very much, sir!" they said in unison.

The three youths introduced themselves as they walked across the field. Willy and Frank laughed when their newfound friend

told them his full name—Grover Cleveland Loening—and
Grover chuckled when he heard Willy's last name.

"Do you know, your name's already famous in aeronautical
circles, Willy. Have you ever heard of the Reynolds Number?"

Willy thought Grover was ragging him.

"It's a dimensionless number used in designing airfoils, a
mathematical formula invented by an English scientist named
Josiah Reynolds in the last century."

Mathematics was not Willy's long suit and he was lost when
Grover tried to explain what a "dimensionless number" was. He
wondered if he might be distantly related to old Josiah.

Grover hoped to be awarded the first graduate degree in aeronautical engineering in America next year, he said. One of his
professors had written a letter of introduction to Mr. Beck for
him and he had been coming to the island every day since Wilbur
Wright had arrived with his machine the previous Saturday. The
first day Wright had handed him a rag and told him to wipe up
the oil under the engine.

He chuckled again. "When that was sopped, I used my handkerchief. Mr. Wright is not an easy man to get to know, but when
he saw me do that he knew I was serious and he loosened up a
bit. He's a genius. Orville Wright too, of course."

Planted on the ground in front of the Wright shed was a
wooden monorail, maybe eighty feet long, pointing toward the
Statue of Liberty across the bay.

"This is what Mr. Wright takes off from," Grover said.

"Uh-huh," said Willy.

There were two large sliding doors hanging from a track on
the front of the shed—locked. There was no guard. They went
around to the back to a smaller door. It was also padlocked but
there was a window and the three of them peered into it.

"There it is," Grover said. "Isn't it something?"

Whatever "it" was Willy could not have said; the interior of
the shed was dark and only a little light entered through the window. There seemed to be a conglomeration of cloth-covered
shapes—some kind of wings, he assumed—connected by all kinds

of wires and lengths of wood. He couldn't see any gasbag. But then they probably filled it and attached it to the airship when it was outside, he guessed.

Grover started to describe what they were looking at but a gruff voice interrupted him.

"You men! Get away from that shed!"

The boys jumped back from the door. An Army officer was striding toward them. The bill of his cap was pulled down so far he had to hold his head up unnaturally to be able to see, causing his jaw to jut out in a commanding military manner.

"I'm Grover Cleveland Loening, one of Mr. Wright's assistants," Grover said, his voice a little unsure.

That cut no ice with the captain. Willy recognized his rank by the double silver bars on his shoulders. The man thrust his jaw out even farther and peered at each of them in turn.

"We were just looking at the aeroplane," Grover said. "We didn't go inside."

That was obvious, but the captain gave a hard yank on the padlock to make sure.

"Good thing you didn't try. No one is allowed in Mr. Wright's hangar when he isn't here. Except his mechanician. I don't know what you boys are up to but you'd better go about your business or you'll find yourselves in trouble. *I mean right now.*"

He jerked his head toward the ferry landing and they took the hint.

"I'm not really Mr. Wright's assistant," Grover whispered to Willy as they walked back across the field. "Not officially, that is."

They waited for the ferry near another group of soldiers headed into the city. Grover wrote down Willy's and Frank's names and told them where to find Mr. Beck's office. "Arnold Beck is the chairman of the Aeronautical Committee for the celebration. I'll make a note on this to remind him about the passes and drop it off on my way home."

He added almost matter-of-factly: "On his next flight Mr. Wright is going to fly up the Hudson to Grant's Tomb and back to Governors Island. You don't want to miss it."

Willy thanked Grover sincerely, although he could not quite credit his last statement. Grant's Tomb was nearly all the way up to the northern end of Manhattan. Yet a number of things that he had heard at one time or another but had not paid much attention to were starting to come together in his mind. It was beginning to dawn on him that what the Wrights were doing must be importantly different somehow from what other men had been doing for decades with balloons and airships and gliders. Talking with Grover and looking at—or almost looking at—the Wright machine had suddenly conjured up in him an intense desire to find out just what it was.

"Watch for the flags, boys," the guard on Governors Island had said. There were enough of them, depending upon where you were. Besides Castle William, Grover had told them that the same flags were flown from Signal Corps stations atop the Singer and Metropolitan and Times buildings, the Brooklyn and Williamsburg bridges and the *Brooklyn Eagle* building. In addition, when Wright's attempt up the Hudson was to begin, the message would be flashed by Marconi wireless from Governors Island to the warships in the river.

The flags on the bridges and skyscrapers were too far away to make out from his house on Brooklyn Heights and Willy couldn't remember all the flags the guard had described anyway, except that the red flag with a white square was the important one. But he could clearly see the flagpole on the Eagle building over the rooftops of Brooklyn. He checked it first thing in the morning both Friday and Saturday.

Black. No flying. Both days were either rainy or gusty all day. He didn't bother checking on Sunday. That was *dies non* for Mr. Wright, Grover had told him. Neither of the Wright brothers ever flew on Sundays.

Early Monday morning, October 4, the black flag was still flying. But the day looked promising, a little overcast but hardly any wind. He decided to take a chance. Armed with the pass he had picked up on Friday he rode the Brooklyn Bridge trolley and then the Third Avenue elevated to the Battery. This time the park was relatively uncrowded but there was a line of people boarding the ferry. Word of Wilbur Wright's ambitious plan had been announced in the newspapers.

Now there were tandem flags on Castle William as well as on the Singer building looming over Wall Street: white with a red square over red with a white square. If he remembered correctly, two flags signified there was going to be a flight, sometime that day!

He spotted Frank on the deck near the gangplank and waved. "I had a hunch you'd be here," Frank said when Willy joined him. "Did you pick up your pass?" Willy pointed to his pocket.

By the time the ferry docked at Governors Island two soldiers on the castle roof were changing the flags. As Willy watched, the flags were hoisted in reverse order. The red with white square was now on top and the white with red square was below it. Did that mean the flight was imminent? If it did, they were just in time. He looked at his watch. It said eight forty-five.

"Morning, George," they said jauntily. The guard remembered them and merely glanced at the passes they waved.

A rope monitored by soldiers had been strung up to keep the spectators—there were already several hundred of them, Willy estimated—away from the Wright shed. Willy and Frank pushed as close to the rope as the crush of people would allow. Even as they did so the hanging doors of the shed were rolled aside. A small group of people emerged, including Army officers, Grover Loening and Mr. Beck and others Willy assumed were also celebration officials or other bigwigs.

Then, behind them, several soldiers began moving a fantastic-looking contraption out into the open, trundling it across the ground on single-wheel trucks under its wings. Willy could now see clearly what he had glimpsed only dimly before.

It was a huge thing, the most impressive feature of which were its two broad, slightly drooping wings, some twenty-five feet in span, one above the other, covered in white cloth and connected to each other by vertical wooden struts and a complex network of wires. Attached to a framework extending out in front were two smaller wings, similarly connected one above the other. In the rear was another boom with two more small wings at the end, but unlike the others these were in a vertical position. Just behind and between the main wings two long, thin propellers were affixed to wing struts on either side of the rear boom. The propellers were connected by chains to an engine that rested off-center on the lower wing. Next to the engine and slightly forward of it was the driver's seat, with long vertical levers on either side of it—evidently the steering controls—and below and in front of the seat was a footrest mounted across the forward boom.

There were no wheels but instead a pair of runners at the bottom of the machine, like a sled's runners.

Willy did not know it but this was the Wrights' latest improvement on their original 1903 design, the culmination of a decade of dreaming, researching, constructing and trial-and-error sweat and testing, and then redesigning and reconstructing by the two brothers, yet already being rendered obsolescent by aeroplane pioneers in France. But he did guess that the lean-faced and lean-bodied, hawk-nosed and firm-jawed man in civilian clothes directing things, unhurriedly but purposefully, must be Wilbur Wright.

Yet if Wright was going to fly the machine he would hardly be dressed the way he was in a business suit and high starched collar and tie and an ordinary cap on his head, would he? It seemed to Willy that if you were going to fly through the air you should be in some sort of special outfit, or at least wear a duster and goggles like an automobile driver.

There was something else. Under the bottom main wing, strapped between the runners, was, of all things, a red-painted canoe, its top sealed over with canvas. Willy supposed it was intended to help keep the machine afloat in case it landed on the water; he couldn't think of any other purpose. Fastened and covered like that, you couldn't very well paddle away in it.

Were it not for the proven fact, whose import he was belatedly beginning to comprehend, that the Wright brothers had unlocked the secret of flight—and indeed that other men were flying aeroplanes of their own design—Willy would have laughed if someone had told him that this unlikely structure he was gaping at was capable of leaving the ground. He didn't laugh but he was still skeptical. He still half-expected them to attach a gasbag to it, if only to help lift it into the air. It was simply too much to believe that this thing could actually rise off the ground under its own power. With the engine and all it must weigh hundreds of pounds, not counting the weight of the driver. Yet it certainly looked as if it was designed to fly. The men hauling it along the ground certainly intended doing something with it.

The machine was positioned over a little trolley sitting at the rear end of the monorail, which was still aimed at the Statue of Liberty, though this was not supposed to be Wright's goal this day. Then the trucks under the wings were removed so that the chassis of the aeroplane rested on top of the trolley.

People around Willy were jabbering. He listened as one man, who had either seen the Wrights fly before or otherwise had reason to know what he was talking about, gave everyone within hearing the benefit of his knowledge.

"Wilbur and Orville and Charlie must have developed a more powerful motor," he said authoritatively. "That's Charlie Taylor there, Wright's chief mechanician. They're not using a catapult, even though the wind's not more than a few miles an hour."

As the man obviously expected, someone asked him what he meant. It seemed that in their experiments at Dayton, Ohio, following their initial success at Kitty Hawk, North Carolina in 1903 (actually the Kill Devil Hills, about four miles from Kitty Hawk, the man clarified) the Wrights had devised a catapult launcher and monorail system so that they didn't need to start into a wind to give them lift but could take off from level ground even on a calm day. They would drop a weight from a derrick at the back end of the rail that pulled a rope attached to the front end of the trolley to give the aeroplane a boost along the rail.

Even in Wilbur's demonstrations in Europe, the man added, and in Orville's recent trials for the Army at Fort Myers, Virginia, during which a Lieutenant Thomas E. Selfridge had been killed in the first-ever fatal aeroplane accident, the brothers had used a catapult.

All of this was a revelation to Willy. The Army was testing an aeroplane and somebody had been killed in it? He was as skeptical of the man, who spoke of "Wilbur" and "Orville" and "Charlie" as if he knew them personally, as he was of the machine he was looking at. He vaguely recalled hearing or reading that some German named Lilienthal had been killed in a glider or something years ago. Anyway, with enough force you could catapult anything off a rail. What did that prove?

There was an awful lot of fussing around going on. Wilbur Wright was checking over everything, running his hands along the rear edges of the wings, saying things to his helpers, testing the tension of wires and Willy did not know what all. Finally everything seemed to be to Wright's satisfaction. He took his seat on the bottom wing and gripped the two long levers in his hands and moved them back and forth. Willy saw the small horizontal wings in the front point up and down and the two vertical ones in the rear move from side to side. At the same time an ingenious arrangement of wires and pulleys bent the rear tips of the main wings up and down. When one side went up, the other side went down. Except for their tips though, these wings were rigid.

Willy couldn't imagine what all this was supposed to do. Just working the wingtips and the other wings up and down or left and right wouldn't be enough to lift the ponderous thing. Obviously, of course, the propellers were what made it go. But what were the flexible wingtips and the movable wings for?

What a complicated mechanism it was. Before, Willy had thought it ungainly and weird. Now he was beginning to think that it was the most wonderfully impressive looking machine he had ever seen.

But could it actually fly? It just didn't seem possible.

Satisfied that the controls were working properly, Wright primed the engine and then took a position behind one of the propellers and grasped the end of the blade. The man the knowledgeable spectator had identified as Wright's chief mechanician, Charlie Taylor, put his hands on the other propeller. Two soldiers stood on either side of the aeroplane holding the ends of the lower main wings. At a nod from Wright both he and Taylor pulled down slightly in unison on the propellers, as if feeling the resistance of the engine, and an instant later pulled down hard.

The propellers became a blur as the engine roared deafeningly, sending out a cloud of blue exhaust. Everyone was startled by the noise. The wash from the propellers blew a piece of paper swirling into the air and back toward the shed.

Wright then took his seat again and fussed some more with the spark or throttle control, letting the engine warm up. Then, as Willy and Frank and hundreds of others held their breaths, Wright gave a final signal and gunned the engine. The soldiers at the wingtips began pushing the machine along the rail.

For the first few seconds Willy maintained his skepticism, his doubts about the whole thing warring with the hope that it really was true, that this amazing contraption could actually fly. And indeed in the first few seconds his doubts were reinforced. The machine moved forward—as it could not help but do—and quickly gained speed until it was moving faster than the men at the wingtips could run. It left the end of the rail—again as it could not help but do. But at first it just skimmed along a few feet above the ground, not really flying, just responding to the momentum imparted to it by the engine and propellers—as any object would do.

But then ... But then ...

3

A SPONTANEOUS and universal gasp arose from the onlookers as the flying machine—*yes, it really was a machine that could fly!*—climbed into the air, exposing the full area of its broad white wings to the pale October morning sunlight as Wright tilted it in a sudden ascending arc. Then there was almost silence, except for the diminishing clatter of the engine and the toots and whistles of boats in the harbor. People were stunned.

"My god!" an elderly man cried. *"He's flying! He's really flying! I've lived to see it!"*

The aeroplane no longer looked ponderous and ungainly. As it continued to rise and then started heading out across the seawall and over the waters of the harbor it was transformed into a bird, a beautiful great white bird, yet unlike any bird ever seen before.

Then for a moment it was obscured by a black cloud of smoke from a steamer and Willy felt sudden alarm. But when it could be seen again it was soaring past the Battery and turning up the Hudson. Wright seemed to have his machine under flawless control. He had to be over a hundred feet in the air. The motor could no longer be heard above the din of blasts from all the boats.

Willy and Frank punched each other's shoulders.

"Did you see that! Did you see that!"

In another minute the marvelous machine was out of sight, but Willy remained stunned. Transfixed.

In that wondrous instant when the great white beautiful bird had risen into the air, not only had his skepticism vanished as instantly but the realization had hit him with the force of absolute certainty that his life—*everyone's* life—had been changed forever by the amazing Wrights. He was a witness to just about the most stupendous thing it was possible to conceive, and he was suddenly possessed by a consciousness of the pettiness of his own concerns in the face of such a miracle.

It was true, it was really true! How had the Wrights done it? Grover Loening hadn't exaggerated. What geniuses they must be, the greatest inventors the world had ever known!

What must it be like to be up there—to be actually flying through the air, high above all the boats in the harbor? Someday, somehow, he must find out for himself. If he never did anything in his life, someday he would find out.

People were recovering, beginning to babble to each other. Willy listened to them, loving them.

"It's about twelve miles to Grant's Tomb," someone said. "If he makes it there and back it'll be the greatest aeroplane flight in history."

"What about Blériot?" someone else countered.

"That was over open water, in a straight line. Wright is going to fly over the warships, then turn around. He could get hit by their smoke or hot air from their funnels, or even drafts from the side streets, and be tossed all over the place."

"If he had a bomb he could drop it right down their stacks!" said another astonished voice. "Why, this could be the end of navies. And fortresses. *Maybe war itself.*"

No one had thought of that. The sudden implication rendered them all speechless again.

People stood waiting. Willy had never seen such a large crowd so patiently expectant. After about twenty minutes passed there was some worried speculation that Wright might have run into trouble. Willy began to worry.

"He had to fly against the wind upriver," someone said reassuringly. "Give him time."

Sure enough, a few minutes later the "'plane" (people were already shortening the word, as if an aeroplane had already become a familiar, everyday object) came into sight again, rounding past the Battery.

"He's coming back! He made it!"

As wonderful as had been the takeoff, even more beautiful was the sight of Wilbur Wright banking over the harbor, mere feet above it, and seemingly floating down to a smooth graceful landing near the middle of the field. The aeroplane's runners positively kissed the ground as the craft skidded on the sand until, its momentum lost, it stopped, tilted up a little on the curved front of the runners and then back down, and then was still, a captive creature of the earth again.

As the soldiers and Wright's mechanic ran up to the aeroplane, a great cheer burst from the crowd. Soldiers lined along the roof of Castle William waved their arms and hats.

"Wilbur Wright is king of the air!" someone shouted. And who would dare say nay?

Wright walked along beside his machine as it was trundled back toward the shed. He grinned in modest acknowledgment of the cheers and applause and lifted his cap to the people, briefly exposing his bald dome.

A rumor spread through the crowd that the flight, magnificent as it had been, was only a preliminary trial. Wright was going to make an even more ambitious attempt, flying this time up the East River over the bridges (or even under them, some said), rounding over Spuyten Duyvil and back down the Hudson for a complete circuit of Manhattan Island. Others said no, he was going to fly up the East River and back and then over the harbor to New Jersey before returning to Governors Island.

Nobody knew when any of this was supposed to happen, however. Wright had gone back inside his shed along with the Army officers and celebration officials. But his mechanic and the soldier helpers had repositioned the aeroplane on the starting rail and were refueling it. That indicated that the rumors must be true: there was going to be another flight.

The two boys waited. And waited. More and more people continued to arrive on the island. Willy guessed there must now be at least a thousand spectators milling about. They couldn't all have passes.

"I don't think he's going to fly again," Frank said. "Let's go back to the city. I'm getting hungry."

Willy was hungry himself; he had skipped breakfast in his dash from the house that morning. But he didn't want to risk missing anything.

"You go ahead if you want to. I'm going to stay."

"What for? It could be hours yet. We've seen him fly. What is he going to do different next time?"

Willy looked sharply at his friend. Frank had been exuberant before. Now the way he talked he made it sound as if seeing a man actually soar up into the sky in a huge machine had just been an interesting oddity. We've seen him fly; what'll we do next for entertainment?

"You go ahead," Willy repeated.

"At least let's get a sandwich or something," Frank said. He jerked his head toward the nearest of several food vendors who had been allowed to bring their pushcarts onto the island.

Willy hesitated. If they left their places by the rope they might not be able to get them back again. But then he saw that everyone seemed to have the same idea as Frank. The vendors were doing a land-office business.

Eventually they were able to get through to one of the carts and purchase hotdogs. Taking advantage of their opportunity the vendors were charging ten cents apiece, double their normal price.

It was hardly worth the trouble. The food only sharpened Willy's appetite and he wasn't aware of tasting it anyway, he was still in such a suspended state of mind.

They went back to the rope, which was now pretty much abandoned by spectators. The aeroplane resting on the rail was itself abandoned except for a few soldiers, who motioned away anyone who tried to approach it.

The doors to the shed—the hangar, Willy corrected himself—were open and no one was inside it. Mr. Wright and the celebration officials had probably gone into Castle William to have lunch at the officers' mess.

Frank waited with Willy a little while longer and then began urging again that they go back to the city. Finally, unable to persuade him, he said so long, see you at school tomorrow maybe. Willy merely nodded. He felt sorry for Frank. The fellow obviously had no true appreciation of the historic event he had witnessed.

He wished he could get closer to the aeroplane, but the soldiers kept everyone at a distance. The nearby Curtiss hangar was not roped off, however. He started to work his way around to it.

The front doors were partially open. Inside, a couple of mechanics were doing something with the Curtiss aeroplane, either putting it together or taking it apart. The tail section rested on the floor, detached from the wings.

At first glance the machine appeared nearly identical to

Wright's: two main wings and a boom in front and rear, each with smaller horizontal and vertical wings. But then he began to notice the differences. There was only a single small wing on the end of the front boom instead of paired wings. Also, there were two little auxiliary wings between the main wings on either side, and there was only one propeller in back, with four blades. The Wright machine had two propellers with two blades. And the engine was behind the driver's, or pilot's, seat, not alongside it. But the major difference was that the Curtiss machine rested on wheels rather than runners: two wheels under the main wings and one under the front boom. And instead of levers to control it the craft had an automobile-type wheel mounted on a column in front of the pilot's seat.

The wheels struck Willy as a more practical arrangement than runners. With wheels you could take off from any field. You wouldn't need a monorail like the Wrights used.

"Did you see the flight, Willy?" said a voice behind him. It was Grover Loening.

Willy had trouble finding the words to express what he had seen, and still felt. Grover nodded. "I know what you mean. Even though I know how it's done, it still seems like a miracle every time it happens."

"Is Curtiss going to fly too?" Willy asked.

Grover shook his head. "He made a short flight of twenty-six seconds early last Wednesday before Mr. Wright flew around the Statue of Liberty, and another one of forty-five seconds yesterday evening. But he didn't leave the island. It's a new machine and underpowered. I don't think Mr. Curtiss trusts it over the water. He can't handle the wind like Wright anyway. This machine's smaller and lighter than the one he flew at Rheims."

"Rheims, France?"

"Yes. He won the Gordon Bennett cup there in August. Hit more than forty-six miles an hour. It's the first aerial meet that's ever been held and Curtiss beat out Blériot and Latham and all the Frenchies. The machine he used is on display at Wanamaker's."

Willy was embarrassed by his newly realized ignorance of what was going on in the world.

"Is Mr. Curtiss here? Which one is he?"

Grover pointed him out. Glenn Curtiss had a bushy mustache and appeared to be some years younger than Wilbur Wright. He had a sour look on his face.

"Is there any chance he'll fly later today?" It was a dumb question. Even as they were talking the front section of the aeroplane was being taken apart.

"No, they're packing it up to ship to St. Louis. Mr. Curtiss has another contract to fly at an exhibition there."

Willy was a little disappointed to hear this, yet secretly pleased. Having decided that Wilbur Wright was the greatest man in the world he did not want to hear that someone else might be able to compete with him. Unless it was Orville Wright of course. The brothers had invented the aeroplane together. That much he knew.

Yet it was not without awe and admiration that he looked at Glenn Curtiss. You would have to be either very brave or very competent—or both—to leave mother earth in such a complicated and really fragile-looking craft.

"What are those two little wings between the big ones, Grover?"

"The French call them ailerons. Curtiss uses them instead of warping the wings like the Wrights do to bank in the air."

"Oh." Now Willy understood what the flexing of the wings on Wright's machine was for, or was beginning to understand. He had no idea how it actually worked.

"It hasn't stopped the Wrights from lodging a patent infringement suit against him though," Grover said. "The Wrights and Curtiss aren't exactly on the friendliest of terms. They claim he stole their basic discovery of how to turn in the air. I don't know if he did or not, but when he won the Scientific American trophy last year for a one-kilometer flight he could only fly in a straight line."

Willy was learning a lot about aeroplanes. And the men who flew them. What luck that he had met Grover the other day.

"But I think both of them are going to be overtaken by Blériot and others," Grover went on. "Even though Curtiss won at Rheims in a pusher biplane, I think the tractor monoplane is the design of the future. The pusher is inherently hard to control, especially with the forward elevator, which causes a lot of longitudinal instability. It's also safer to have the engine in front of you rather than behind you in case of a crash."

Willy nodded in agreement, as if he thoroughly understood. As an aeronautical engineer, or soon to be one, Grover Loening obviously knew whereof he spoke. Maybe he should go into the field himself. After all, his name was already famous in aeronautical circles, wasn't it? But though he found business arithmetic a breeze, he doubted if he could crack the higher mathematics that must be involved in aeronautical engineering.

He hoped Grover was exaggerating about the enmity between the Wrights and Curtiss. The aeroplane was the most wonderful invention in history. It belonged to the whole world. It would be a shame if the men who flew aeroplanes could not be friends.

It was nearly four o'clock in the afternoon when, at long last, Wilbur Wright and his entourage appeared again, walking from the castle toward his hangar. The soldiers had relaxed a little during the long wait and a number of people had wandered past the rope. Now everyone was ushered back behind it again. Willy refused to allow himself to be displaced from the front line of spectators, even if he had to be rude. Most of these people were newcomers. They hadn't witnessed the first flight.

Once again Orville Wright went through the checking-over and fussing-around routine. Finally he joined his mechanic at the rear propellers, and again they pulled down in unison on the blades.

Once. Twice. Again and again they tried. The engine wouldn't start.

Then at the ninth pull (Willy was counting) there was a muffled bang and something shot up from the engine and went through the upper wing, tearing a gash in the fabric. It was a black piece of metal that flew into the air for twenty feet and then fell to the ground close to where Wright was standing.

"She's blown a cylinder head!" someone said.

Willy knew enough about motors—his family had a car—to guess that that was probably what had happened.

Oh damn it all! He was as disappointed for the other on-lookers as he was for himself. But it was fortunate the piece of metal hadn't fallen on Wright. It was even more fortunate that the accident had happened on the ground and not when he was in the air.

Wright looked at the smoking object at his feet and shrugged and extended his arms apologetically to the crowds, swinging his hands down.

He said something Willy couldn't hear, but the gesture expressed it plainly: there would be no more flying today. Worse, maybe no more flying at all for the rest of the Hudson-Fulton Celebration if Wright needed a whole new engine.

Willy did not wait around after that, much as he still wanted to stay. The aftertaste of mustard from the hotdog had turned bitter in his mouth and he was stiff from being on his feet for eight hours, as well as in need of going to the toilet. But most of all it made him too sad to stand there looking at the crippled aeroplane knowing what it was capable of but that without a working motor it was just a conglomeration of wood and wires and fabric, no more able to rise in the air than he could by flapping his arms. He felt sorry for those who had come too late.

But his mood brightened as he rode the ferry back to the Battery. It was too bad Wright hadn't been able to make a second flight, yet Willy was really glad he hadn't. Even if he had outdone his first one it would have been anticlimactic somehow.

He was almost in a daze. He had to tell himself over and over that, yes, he had actually seen a man fly through the air.

And he was going to do it himself, he resolved again. Someday he would learn how to fly. Even if he had to build his own aeroplane.

He laughed at the thought. That was even more fanciful than the idea of learning to fly. Nevertheless he promised himself that he was going to learn as much as he could about aeroplanes, and it was not impossible to think that maybe someday he could learn to fly, and maybe someday even buy his own aeroplane.

Why, it wasn't impossible at all. The aeroplane was at the same stage the automobile was ten years ago—a rarity. But today anybody could buy an automobile. You could get a brand-new Ford Model T for as little as five hundred dollars. His father could buy an aeroplane when they became available, even if they were expensive. His father had money. If not, Willy certainly could when he reached 21 and came into the inheritance his grandmother had left him.

Aeroplanes definitely had to be the coming thing. Everybody would have one someday.

What must it be like . . . to fly through the air?

4

THE BATTERY was thronged again when Willy got off the ferry. With visions of the miracle he had witnessed that morning still before his eyes, he began wandering uptown, away from the crowds, hardly conscious that he was doing so.

It was only five o'clock. He didn't want to go home yet and neither did he want to get on another packed elevated or street-car or subway. He kept on walking up Broadway; he was young, the miles went by unnoticed. The farther he walked, however, the more people he encountered, not just civilians. Groups of sailors and soldiers in a variety of uniforms, foreign and American, were everywhere, strolling about to take in the sights of the city or sampling the innumerable saloons New York boasted.

How many of these people knew about the stupendous thing that had happened today? Had any of them seen it? If they had, why weren't they shouting and yelling about it, telling everyone who didn't know about it what they had seen. Why wasn't he?

He'd told his mother not to expect him home for supper and was now acutely conscious of just how hungry he was. He went into a saloon near Union Square and ordered the big fifty-cent meal and a bottle of Knickerbocker to go with it. The place was surprisingly uncrowded considering all the people on the streets. He ate slowly, killing time while the city's lights came on. Too bad Wanamaker's department store was closed. Maybe he could go there tomorrow to see the Curtiss aeroplane. After the meal he had another beer and a cigarette, then a third beer.

He started walking up Broadway again. As dusk embraced Manhattan the Great White Way began living up to its name and the festive air of the city began to infect him again. He felt restored by the meal, and a little lightheaded from the last two beers.

This was the place to be—on Broadway, at night. For perhaps seven blocks between Thirty-eighth and Forty-fifth Streets the sidewalks were a mass of people and the streets themselves clogged with vehicles as far as you could see. Many of them were what had been dubbed "rubbernecker" wagons, open-air buses filled with tourists gawking and waving at people on the sidewalks and being gawked at and waved at in return. The dinnergoers and theatergoers, the women elaborately dressed, were arriving now too, mingling with the sightseers from out of town and the poorer-class denizens spilling out of the city's tenements: Hebrews, Italians, pigtailed Chinamen in their native costumes, ragged street urchins. Willy caught the sounds of half a dozen different languages, as well as accents from the Midwest and South. What a mosaic of humanity America was, and especially New York.

It was like another parade. On both sides of Broadway a stream of people strolled unhurriedly in one direction on the sidewalk, passing another stream strolling unhurriedly the other way, all of them determined not to miss a thing, even if it was merely to look at all the other people, all of them smiling, all of them having a good time.

He was passing another saloon near Times Square when a

sailor, a Britisher, having quite obviously bent the proverbial three sheets to the wind, staggered out of the door and right into the path of two other sailors sauntering along. There was a snarl from the jacky and exclamations in German from the two he had bumped into, themselves not too steady on their feet, as they grabbed him by his arms and turned him around. Willy saw the name *H.M.S. Intrepid* on the first sailor's cap. Out of nowhere several other sailors, a couple of them American, a couple of them Frenchmen, joined the tussle.

Willy stood to one side on the curb. It looked like there was going to be a fight, if not a veritable international incident.

"Now, now, boys," said a policeman, waggling his stick and starting to approach the group. "Let's conduct ourselves like gentlemen."

But the sailors weren't fighting. They were hugging each other and slapping each other's backs like long-lost friends.

"Hurrah for King Edward!"

"Hoch der Kaiser!"

"Vive la France!"

"Here's to President Taft!"

People had stopped to watch and they laughed as the two Germans steered the Britisher who was still in their grip back into the bar to bend yet another sheet, accompanied by the other sailors who had joined them.

This is great, Willy thought. Sailors from four different nations getting along so well together. But that was the spirit of the whole celebration, wasn't it? How ridiculous for countries to fight each other, for men who would under other circumstances be friends to try to kill each other. Those sailors didn't know it, all these people looking and laughing at them didn't know it, but like that fellow on Governors Island had said, the world might very well have seen its last war, thanks to the Wrights. Wilbur Wright might very well have flown over those sailor's own ships that day.

He thought about following them into the saloon. He wanted to get drunk himself. He was already more than a little on the way, both from the beers and the intoxication of Broadway at night.

Someone was tugging on his sleeve.

"Those boys are having a good time, aren't they?"

He turned and saw a girl smiling up at him. She was short, hatless, had pale, washed-out hair, and wasn't very pretty. By no means homely though. In fact, even moderately attractive as he focused on her.

She squeezed his arm. "Are you looking for a good time too?" Her smile was pleasant. Her brown eyes looked boldly into his.

He knew about such girls—the guys talked about them all the time. He'd seen them on the street too, or assumed that was what they were, but had never let himself be stopped by one, much less ever . . .

"If you are," she said, "I know a place we can go. How about it? Come on."

She tugged at him and he let her lead him over to Sixth Avenue and down a cross street a short distance to a seedy-looking hotel. He resisted at the entrance.

"It's all right, honey. They know me here. Come on. You won't be sorry. That's the boy."

She was not much older than he was but he felt like a child being led by its mother as he let her pull him into the dim and grimy lobby. The girl nodded at a hard-faced man behind the desk, who nodded back knowingly, and then led him up the stairs. The treads were covered with dirty, well-worn linoleum with holes that exposed the wood in places. They went up two flights, then down a hallway with stained, frayed carpeting between dingy walls to a door that hadn't seen a coat of paint in years and looked so ill-fitting that he was sure he could have pushed it right open without unlocking it.

If he could, so could a copper.

She sensed his fear. "Don't worry. No one will bother us."

She took a key out of a pocket in a light jacket she was wearing and opened the door. She reached around and switched on the light, pulled him inside and closed the door.

The room was as shabby as the rest of the hotel: a broken-down-looking bed, one chair, an old dresser with a wash basin on top of it and a streaked mirror above it, faded wallpaper peeling in places, patches of plaster hanging down from the ceiling from the middle of which a solitary bare light bulb hung on a wire.

She looked at him appraisingly as she began removing her jacket.

"You *are* a beauty, aren't you? Are you a college boy?"

He nodded uneasily, wondering what he was expected to do. He put his hands on her forearms and bent his head to kiss her but she turned away, saying, "None of that now."

Puzzled, he dropped his hands.

"What's your name, handsome?"

"Willy," he mumbled before he thought that he should have told her a fake name.

She smiled again, so pleasantly that some of his fear began to leave him. Then she giggled.

"I bet you've got a lot of girlfriends, don't you, but none of them'll do what I'll do, will they?"

He didn't respond and she continued eyeing him.

"You've never done it with a girl before, have you? Well, Willy me boy, tonight we're going to complete your education. There're some things I'm sure they don't teach you in college. Why don't you sit there on the bed and watch me take off my clothes. Then we'll take off yours."

One time in high school one of the guys had passed around a French postcard he'd gotten somewhere with a photograph of a nude woman on it, a rather Rubenesque woman with ample breasts reclining on a divan with a potted palm at one end of it and a rural scene on the wall as a backdrop. By the time the card had gotten to Willy it was creased and smudged but it actually showed the dark patch of her pubic area. That was what made it different from classical pictures of nudes he had seen, that and the fact that it was a photograph, not a painting, and especially the fact that the woman was so frankly displaying herself, smiling right at the camera. It was the closest he had ever been to a nude woman.

Now a real woman, a girl, was standing in front of him totally unclothed, except for her stockings, which only accentuated her nudeness. He looked at her body shyly, pretending not to. She was not as well endowed as the woman in the photograph but better looking. Certainly younger. Yet, strangely, not as erotic as the photograph.

The girl helped him undress. She fondled him briefly, laughing softly, expressing admiration, then pulled him onto the bed alongside her. He put his arm around her waist and tried again to kiss her but she wouldn't let him. The single bulb above their heads was glaring.

"Let me turn the light off," he said.

"No. Leave it on. Close your eyes if you want to."

As she fondled him some more the illicitness of what she was doing began to excite him. She could have been one of any number of girls he knew and with whom one was never supposed to have sex before marriage, or even think about it. He dared place his hand under one small breast, cupping it, touching the nipple with a fingertip, feeling it stiffen to his touch, exciting him more, and this she permitted. She still wouldn't let him kiss her on the mouth but she let him do anything else. He was puzzled anew by her unwillingness to allow him to demonstrate anything like affection toward her.

Satisfied that he was sufficiently aroused, she showed him what to do next. He rested himself on his elbows in position above her, and did close his eyes then, imagining it was a different girl, a prettier one, not a prostitute. Someone he loved.

It was over surprisingly quickly, and when it was she jumped off the bed and went to the dresser and began cleaning herself with a washcloth and water from the basin, in full view of him. He lay there watching her. He wanted to spend some more time with her, really make love now that he knew what it was like. Or at least talk with her. How had she fallen into this way of life? Did she actually live in this room? What a dreary life if she did.

"Come on," she said as she began putting her clothes back on, not smiling now. "That's it. I have to go back to work. Unless you want to do it again. If you have the money."

"How much do I owe you?"

"Ten dollars."

"*What?*"

He sat up on the edge of the bed, disgusted. It hadn't meant a thing to her. He meant nothing to her. Well of course, it was just a job to her. But she was trying to take advantage of him. He had always heard that two dollars was the standard fee. Or three at the most.

"That's rather steep, isn't it?"

"Are you going to give me trouble? You don't want me to call the man downstairs, do you?"

Then, ingratiatingly, "I'm worth it, honey. I'm not one of your common street whores who do it in the alley. I have to pay for this room. And I'm clean. You don't have to worry about catching anything from me. I don't do it with anyone who isn't clean too."

"How do you know I am?"

She laughed. "I'm a pretty good judge." Her voice hardened again. "Come on. Get dressed."

He did as she said and gave her the last ten dollars he had. It was more than she usually got, he was sure. She was taking advantage of him so she wouldn't have to "work" so hard the rest of the night. But he didn't mind. She had been worth it. Or the experience had.

She smiled as she took the bill and ushered him to the door.

"Thanks, honey. You're a nice boy. Maybe we can get together again sometime. If you don't see me around just ask for Charmaine downstairs. I have special rates for regulars."

It couldn't be her real name. Her real name was probably something plain and unexotic, like Betty or Mary.

He didn't think he would ever want to see her again. He nodded, saying nothing. She closed the door behind him.

The unsavory character at the desk glanced at him uncuriously as, with face averted, he quickly left the hotel. He was relieved to be back out in the open air. Not until he was well away from the place did he lift his eyes from the sidewalk for fear that people passing might know where he had just come from, what he had been up to. He felt dismally sober, faintly ashamed. What would his parents think if they could know?

So he was a man at last—supposedly. He had completed the rite of passage. He would have something to tell the guys, if he wanted to tell them. But he wasn't going to tell them, not even Frank. Guys only talked about it if they hadn't done it. Frank had disappointed him anyway, the way he had acted in the end like Wilbur Wright's flight had just been a curiosity. Yet if it hadn't been for Frank he would have let the guard on Governors Island turn him back that day and he would never have met Grover Loening and never have seen Wilbur Wright fly. He would always be grateful to Frank for that.

Why wasn't he elated? It had all happened so fast with the girl. It had been so mechanical, so . . . *clinical*.

But his mood brightened again as he rejoined the throngs of people and headed home to the tranquility and gentility of Brooklyn. During the ride he went over and over what he had seen that day on Governors Island and pitied everyone who hadn't seen it.

He had stood on his feet for eight hours to witness a miracle that had lasted less than one hour and of which he had seen only the first and last few minutes. But that old gent on Governors Island had waited his whole lifetime to see it.

God, what a day. He had got out of bed that morning like he did every morning, and in the space of ten hours had not only discovered the one thing he wanted to do in life but had lost his virginity on top of it. On top of her, that is.

He grinned to himself and turned his head toward the window of the streetcar, as if his fellow passengers might guess just by looking at him the reason for the self-satisfied grin, but glad that it had happened with the girl. Almost as glad as having seen Wilbur Wright fly.

Yes, it had been quite a day. He was nearly 19, and now a man. A man who knew what he wanted to do with his life.

Hempstead Plains

1

I N LESS THAN two years nearly a dozen flying fields had sprung up amid the lush meadows of middle Long Island, but Willy had no trouble locating the one he wanted; it was just east of Garden City via the Hempstead Turnpike.

It was a fine Saturday morning in early May 1911. He was passing through farm fields on either side of the road when he heard the sound of an engine coming up fast behind him, its roar competing with the clattering of his father's new Chalmers "30" pony tonneau.

He immediately assumed it was the traffic cop who had been poorly concealed behind a bush just over the Kings County/Nassau County line and who had given him a rather surly and suspicious look when he went by. The cop had been sitting on a motorcycle, not a bicycle, so Willy had been watching his speed. The speedometer showed he had crept up a little over the prescribed limit of twenty-five miles an hour. He dropped down to a cautious twenty, just to be on the safe side. He'd heard they were strict in Nassau County. His father would not be pleased to learn that he had gotten a speeding ticket. His father was not pleased about the reason Willy was using the car in the first place.

The tonneau's top was down. He turned his head and was relieved to see it was only another touring car.

The car, a big Stevens-Duryea, whished past him. Its top was also down. There were four people in it. As the machine cut in ahead of him, a woman and a man sitting in the elevated back seat turned and waved, laughing, the woman clutching a wide-brimmed hat with one hand. Fortunately the highway was mac-adamized or he would have been eating a cloud of dust. As it was, the driver cut in so close that a small stone thrown up by a rear wheel bounced off the hood and sailed past his head.

Damn fool.

Only a moment later he heard the barking of another motor approaching from the rear. This time it *was* the motorcycle cop, who zoomed past Willy in obvious pursuit of the other car that had clearly been exceeding the limit. He smiled in satisfaction.

A little farther on the Stevens-Duryea that had passed him so recklessly had pulled to the side of the road and the officer was standing with one foot on the running board having a discussion with the two people in the front seat. Willy saw now that the person behind the wheel was a second woman. She was wearing a duster buttoned up to her neck and her face was mostly ob-scured by goggles and a scarf covering her head and tied under her chin. She looked all nose. Who did she think she was—Barney Oldfield?

As he sedately motored on by he waved at the people in the car and touched the bill of his cap. They did not wave back.

Now that the patrolman was occupied, and probably would be for some time, he pushed down on the accelerator and sped up to thirty until he reached the village of Hempstead, where he turned north onto Clinton Road. The Hempstead Plains aero-drome was supposed to be somewhere along this road.

"Seven hundred and fifty dollars!" his father had exclaimed—two times. "Seven hundred and fifty dollars! That's nearly as much as your entire college tuition!"

Willy had prepared himself and had waited until after sup-per one evening, when his father was sitting in his favorite chair and had gone through the ritual of cleaning, filling and lighting his pipe and was finished with the evening paper, in which Willy hoped there had been no unduly disturbing business news.

John Reynolds was shaking his head. "And for what? To learn to fly a fool aeroplane? What would you do with it, even if you didn't break your neck in the process? No, no, use your head. Finish college first. You're almost halfway through. Get your degree. Then if you still have this fool notion . . ."

He shook his head again and applied another match to the pipe, which had gone out, and puffed on it vigorously.

Soft touch though his father usually was, Willy nevertheless had omitted telling him that while seven hundred and fifty dollars was the cost of flying lessons (payable in three installments of two hundred-fifty), that did not include the cost of breakages to the machines the students were responsible for and which, if you smashed up a machine badly enough, could conceivably cost thousands of dollars. But Willy did not conceive that he would have any breakages at all; from his reading of aviation magazines he already knew everything you could know about flying an aeroplane without actually having flown one. Anyway the school only required a breakage deposit of another two hundred-fifty, and he had a little more than that in his own savings account thanks to a money gift from his parents at Christmas and the extra spending money his mother pressed upon him from time to time.

"I'm only asking for a loan, Dad. I'll pay you back from the trust fund. I intend to learn to fly and it just doesn't make sense to wait two more years."

At her death several years before, Willy's maternal grandmother had bequeathed him the heady sum of seven thousand dollars, collectible on his twenty-first birthday, plus interest compounded from the date of deposit. That birthday was only a matter of months away, but he wouldn't graduate from NYU for another two years.

After seeing Wilbur Wright fly he had reconciled himself to postponing his aviation ambition at least until he was 21. But in February he had seen an advertisement in *Fly* magazine placed by the Hempstead Plains Aviation Company, a manufacturer of aeroplanes in Queens, announcing the opening of a flying school in the spring. He had immediately written for the company's "handsome, illustrated booklet." The president of the company was Alfred J. Moisant, the older brother of the well-known flier John B. Moisant.

The Moisants had been involved in some sort of soldier-of-fortune adventures in Central America before going into aviation, according to rumors Willy later heard. Alfred was not an aviator but John had won fame in August 1910 by flying himself and his mechanic from Paris to London, only to have his career cut short four months later when he was killed in his Blériot monoplane during an exhibition in New Orleans (another item of information Willy neglected mentioning to his parents).

His enthusiasm fired by the booklet, Willy had visited the company's office in the Times Building. Mr. Moisant was not there but an associate he talked to had been most enthusiastic and encouraging. As a minor, however, Willy needed his parents' permission to enroll in the course, he said. After leaving the office Willy had confidently purchased a motorcyclist's leather helmet and goggles at Abercrombie & Fitch.

"What do you need a license for in the first place?" his father asked. "You don't have to have a license to fly an aeroplane, do you?"

"No," Willy answered. "But you need one from the Aero Club of America if you hope to fly professionally. You wouldn't be considered a real pilot if you didn't have one."

He quickly reinforced his argument. "The field is moving fast. According to the man I talked to the school has been flooded with applicants. I'd be left behind if I waited two years, or even six months. I could start earning money after I got my license and pay you back from that. Why, Claude Grahame-White, the Englishman, was paid fifty thousand dollars to fly at a meet in Boston last year. Fifty *thousand!*"

The celebrated Grahame-White was an exception of course. Few aviators earned that kind of money, not from just one meet. Still, meets were being held all over, with thousands of dollars offered at each one. Wilbur Wright had been paid fifteen thousand to fly at the Hudson-Fulton Celebration.

His father was both impressed and alarmed. He aimed the stem of the pipe at Willy. "You're not thinking of going into competition flying, are you? It's much too dangerous. Your mother and I would never allow that."

John Reynolds glanced at his wife sitting on the davenport with her hands folded in her lap. The look of concern that had come on her face when Willy had broached the subject of taking flying lessons had deepened. Even more indulgent than her husband of their only child, their dear sweet William, who had come back to them from the verge of death in childhood and to whom thereafter she could deny nothing, Ellen Reynolds inclined her head pleadingly at Willy.

Willy realized he had overreached and he pulled back a little.

"Well, I don't know about competition flying—I haven't even learned how to fly yet!" He chuckled and gave his mother a reassuring smile. "But there are all sorts of other possibilities," he said with all the earnestness and assurance he could muster. "I could become an instructor myself. Flying schools are opening up all over the place. Or do exhibition flying—not competition, just flying in front of people. Promoters pay you good money for doing that. Or you can earn a lot of money just giving people rides. Aviation is really still only in its infancy, Dad. There are all sorts of opportunities.

"This would all be after I graduated from college of course," he added. "But by then I'd have earned my certificate."

"You'd have to have your own aeroplane to make any money," his father said. "How much would that cost?"

The answer was five thousand dollars and up, for a Moisant monoplane, depending upon the powerplant. Willy didn't want to go into that. Although his ultimate dream was to own his own aeroplane, the immediate goal was to persuade his parents to let him learn to fly.

"I wouldn't necessarily have to have my own plane," he said. "A lot of aviators are being paid to fly by aeroplane manufacturers, like Wright and Curtiss, to demonstrate their machines, the same way automobile companies pay racing drivers to drive their latest models."

But they were talking about theoretical possibilities that might or might not be feasible. He decided to emphasize the safety issue, which he knew was what was really worrying them.

"If you'll just read the brochure I got from them, Dad, you'll see it's going to be a very thorough course. You have to take two weeks of ground school learning all about aeroplanes before they even let you get in one!"

"We've always hoped you might go into business with your father," his mother said.

"I still could. I could do both."

All three sat in silence for moments. Willy could tell his parents were debating with themselves: perhaps if Willy got this flying nonsense out of his system . . . maybe if we let him start lessons . . . it might be worth the down payment just to let him find out it wasn't for him . . .

He did not need to offer any further arguments. He knew he had won. He was a spoiled only child, and he rejoiced in the fact. But someday he would make his parents proud of him.

In the end his father said he would advance Willy the tuition down payment, and the rest of it if he decided to complete the course, but only on his promise that he would not let his flying lessons interfere with his studies and that whether or not he got his license — and didn't break his neck — he would finish college. As for what Willy wanted to do after that, well, that was a long time in the future.

Ellen Reynolds was still distressed, but if this was what William really wanted, and if he was sure it was safe . . .

God yes, it was what he really wanted. He could think of nothing anyone could want more. *To fly. Actually to fly.*

He was crossing Stewart Avenue on the outskirts of Garden City, still heading north on Clinton, when there was another roar behind him. Good lord, not the cop again, or another one. They certainly were dedicated fellows.

But this was a different sound, and before he could think to brake a shadow passed directly over him, followed an instant later by the cruciform shape of an aeroplane. It was no more than fifty feet in the air, going at least sixty miles and hour, exempt from the limits imposed on ground-hugging vehicles. It was going so fast he couldn't identify its make, only that it was a monoplane.

He almost went off the road as he watched the plane make a steep bank, losing height with its engine now cut off, until it was obscured by a row of trees. It had to be going in for a landing because it was obviously under complete control. The flying field must be just beyond those trees.

God, how beautiful! What must it like to be up there? Willy could hardly believe that at long last he was going to find out, not today of course but in only a few more weeks, and he was sure that once he got up in the air the way that aviator had been he would never want to come down again.

MOISANT FLYING SCHOOL, the sign said. Underneath those words: HEMPSTEAD PLAINS AVIATION COMPANY.

He drove past the sign at the roadside entrance to the aerodrome and pulled up alongside several other cars parked behind a small metal-roofed structure, evidently the aerodrome office or administration building. At one side of it a short distance away and abutting each other in a line were the school's five hangers that had been pictured in the booklet, and on the other side a little viewing stand with a number of people sitting in it.

The flying field proper and the whole area around it was immense, nearly perfectly flat, stretching to the horizon. A vast alluvial plain, the gift of the last glaciation, it had been waiting ten thousand years for the advent of the aeroplane. Because of the perfect terrain, three aerodromes had been located in close proximity to Garden City: one on Nassau Boulevard on the west side of the town; one on the east side near Washington Avenue, where Glenn Curtiss had opened a school, and, a mile east of that, the Hempstead Plains-Moisant School field. Curtiss was also manufacturing aeroplanes in a plant on Stewart Avenue on the southern perimeter of the latter.

The Hempstead Plains field, Willy's field, was by far the largest, however: nearly three miles long and three-quarters of a mile wide—a thousand acres unobstructed by tree or bush or fence, with an additional five thousand acres of open land surrounding it that students had permission to fly over. And the company had ambitious plans for the aerodrome, according to the brochure, including dozens more hangars, a clubhouse, a grandstand for sixteen hundred people and even a racing course for contests between aeroplanes and automobiles.

Willy walked around the office to the entrance facing the field. A monoplane was parked in front of the first hangar, apparently the very one that had flown over him on the road. Two mechanics were attending to it, one standing on a short stepladder behind the engine pouring gasoline into its tank from a large can, the other doing something under the cowling.

He had left the house in Brooklyn well ahead of time on this the first day of his scheduled training but there were already five other men in the office. All of them were older than he was by anywhere from a few to perhaps a dozen years, but three of them, the younger ones, were evidently new students like himself, judging both by their ages and by the eager expectation on their faces as they glanced at him when he entered, the same expression he felt must be on his own face.

They immediately directed their attention back to the two older men around whom they were gathered. One, sporting a healthy black mustache, wore a collarless and tieless white shirt buttoned at the neck, the sleeves rolled above his elbows, pants tucked into knee-high boots. The other was dressed in oil-stained coveralls and leather helmet and goggles, the latter perched rakishly on his forehead.

He edged up to the group. The second man had to be the pilot of the plane he had seen landing. This supposition was confirmed as he listened to the questions the others were peppering him with and the answers the pilot gave with obvious pleasure and noblesse oblige:

". . . trained in France at Issy . . . it's a Queen monoplane,

basically like the Blériot Model Eleven . . . fifty-horsepower Indian rotary . . . fly out of Nassau Boulevard on the other side of
Garden City . . .”

The questioners reacted with noises of admiration at every
answer and Willy looked at the man with the same awe that he
had looked at Wilbur Wright and Glenn Curtiss that day on
Governors Island.

He made a quick survey of the office. Against one wall was a
large rolltop desk, the top rolled up, with a telephone and clutter
of papers on it. On the wall above the desk was a poster advertis-
ing the January 1910 Los Angeles meet, the first international air
tournament held in the United States. A table standing against
the opposite wall held a coffee urn and a profusion of newspapers and magazines. Near the front door was a rather worn-look-
ing sofa. Several straight-backed wooden chairs and pictures of
aeroplanes on the other walls completed the furnishings.

The mustached man came up to Willy and offered his hand.
He identified himself as André Houpert, the chief instructor of
the Moisant School. He was in fact the new school's only instructor at this time. He looked to be in his early thirties. Willy
told him his name.

“Welcome, Mr. Reynolds.” Houpert reached for a paper on
the desk and made a check mark on it with a pen. In heavily
accented but excellent English he said, “We are all here now
except for Miss Quinlan, who seems to have been delayed for
some reason.”

Willy wondered what he meant. Surely there wasn't going to
be a female student, was there? That would be something to see.
Maybe “Miss Quinlan” was a secretary and there was some kind
of paperwork to go through. But he'd already sent in his application and down payment.

“Earle,” Houpert said, catching the flier's attention. “Here is
one more of our budding birdmen.”

The other men drew aside so that Houpert could introduce
Willy to the pilot. “Earle Ovington,” he said. “Willy Reynolds.”
It sounded like *Weelee*.

Ovington looked at Willy appraisingly and extended his hand.

Earle Ovington! He had flown at the second Harvard-Boston meet the year before, the same one Grahame-White had been the star of. Speechless, Willy grasped the man's hand, a self-conscious grin on his face.

Still grinning like an idiot, he stuffed the hand that had shaken the pilot's hand in his pocket as if to save it, then withdrew it as the three other men began introducing themselves and offering their hands. They were: Harold Kantner, who said he was from Chicago; Shakir Jerwan, a New Yorker, whose name, if not appearance, suggested he was of Near Eastern extraction, and Ferdinand DeMurias, who had come all the way from Havana, Cuba. The last named was a small fellow whose thin little inverted "v" of a mustache reminded Willy of pictures of the Brazilian Santos-Dumont, the first man to get an aeroplane off the ground in Europe, however briefly.

The students resumed asking Ovington questions and Willy casually picked up the paper Houpert had replaced on the desk. Typed down the left side in alphabetical order were five names, with checks after four of them: F. DeMurias, S. Jerwan, H. Kantner, W. Reynolds. And above his own name, unchecked: H. Quinlan.

Five students was a large enough class as it was. Why did one of them have to be a female who would hold them all back?

One of the mechanics stuck his head in the door and announced in a French accent, "Your machine is ready, Monsieur Ovington."

"Gentlemen," said Houpert. "Shall we watch Earle take off?"

The students needed no other invitation. They trooped outside enthusiastically.

The monoplane had been turned around to face the straightaway, or getaway. Like a good pilot, Ovington did not take the mechanic's word for it but checked every part of the machine thoroughly. He seemed to pay particular attention to the alignment of the wings and the tension of their bracing wires, standing at the tips and sighting along their lengths. Finally he climbed into the cockpit and pulled his goggles down. Willy and the three other students rushed up to assist Houpert and a second mechanic in holding onto the wheels and fuselage as the mechanic who had announced the plane's readiness flipped the propeller. The people in the viewing stand stood up.

There was a throaty roar from the rotary engine and a blast of wind from the propeller and the odor of the castor oil used for lubrication. Willy felt the fuselage vibrate like a live thing under his hands.

At a signal from Ovington the men let go and the craft leaped forward, gaining takeoff speed in a matter of seconds. In a minute it was a hundred feet in the air and banking west toward Garden City.

"That, gentlemen, is how it is done," said Houpert.

The students all stood open-mouthed as they watched the monoplane shrink in the distance.

2

BACK IN THE office Houpert invited the four students to sit down and make themselves comfortable. Hardly had they done so and the chief instructor had started to say something to them when there was the noise of an automobile stopping behind the building and the sound of chattering voices. A moment later the door opened and two young women entered, followed by two men.

The first man was also fairly young but the other was a portly middle-aged gentleman who had gallantly held the door for everyone. As gallantly, the students rose from the seats they had just taken.

They were the people who had passed him on the road. Willy recognized the woman who had waved at him from the back seat. So the other had been the one driving. But now she was entirely feminine and demure. The duster had been removed to reveal an ankle-length dress with a frilly-fronted blouse and high collar, and the scarf and goggles replaced with a large flowered hat. She even carried a folded parasol. She was tall for a woman, slender and willowy, brunette. And quite pretty.

"Ah, Alfred," Houpert said. "And Miss Quinlan?" The pretty one dipped her head. "Now we are complete." Then to the male students: "Allow me to present Mr. Alfred J. Moisant, the president of the Hempstead Plains Aviation Company."

Houpert recited the students' names and the portly man advanced and shook hands vigorously with each of them in turn. He didn't appear to recognize Willy from the encounter on the road. "Good to meet you, Mr. Reynolds."

Willy shook Alfred Moisant's hand. Lucky thing he hadn't thumbed his nose at the car when he'd passed by, as he had been tempted to do.

Moisant extended an arm toward the two women. "May I introduce Miss Harriet Quinlan, who will be joining your class, and her friend, Miss Helen Vanderbilt, who"—he smiled genially at her—"I am sorry to say has declined."

The second lady nodded and smiled and, as if not wanting to steal the limelight from her companion, stepped back to stand next to the younger man who had not been introduced. She was attractive also, but nowhere near as good looking as Quinlan.

Willy grimaced inwardly. A Vanderbilt, no less. Obviously Harriet Quinlan was some rich and pampered society debutante, or former debutante, who had decided to take up flying as a lark to fill her useless days. Why had the school enrolled her? It certainly wasn't desperate for pupils.

He had barely formed the thought when Moisant's next words forced him to revise it.

"Miss Quinlan is the dramatic critic and women's editor for Leslie's Illustrated Weekly magazine," he said proudly, lifting his eyebrows as if this was some kind of remarkable feat and an honor for the school.

A career woman was just as bad. She had enrolled in the

school as some kind of journalistic stunt, to get publicity for her magazine . . .

"She will be writing a series of articles for Leslie's describing her experiences in learning to fly as a student of the Moisant Flying School."

. . . and the school had enrolled her for publicity purposes of its own, Willy completed the thought.

He was disillusioned. He wondered if his resentment of the woman showed on his face.

The expressions on the faces of the other men, however, were those of sheer admiration as they eyed Harriet Quinlan. Willy couldn't blame them. She was more than merely good looking; she was striking, all fetching femininity without the motorist's trappings he had first seen her in as she stood leaning forward slightly, with her hands, encased in elbow-length gloves, resting on the handle of the parasol whose tip she had placed on the floor like a cane. For another feminine touch she had tied a bright bow around the stem of the parasol.

Her undeniable attractiveness made him resent her all the more. What did she think she was doing here, trying to force herself into a domain that belonged to men? No doubt she was a suffragette as well.

What Harriet Quinlan said next did not enhance Willy's appreciation of her unexpected appearance.

"I must apologize for being tardy," she said to Houpert. "We had a little problem on the road with a constable. It seems we were driving a bit too fast for his liking, but he was very nice after we had a long discussion explaining our mission. 'Oh,' he exclaimed, 'you're some more of those *aeronuts*. Well, all right, I'll let you go this time. Just remember to obey the speed law when you're on the ground.'"

She chuckled amusedly, as did Willy's three fellow males. "Aeronuts," they repeated, grinning at each other. It was already a bond they had in common.

"Of course I didn't tell him that I think the speed law is ridiculous. Ten or fifteen miles an hour in the city may be one thing, but twenty-five in the wide-open countryside? *Really.*"

The men made noises of agreement and Willy had to admit the woman was right on that score.

"Miss Quinlan is already an expert automobilist," said Moisant. (Yes, she nearly ran me into a ditch, thought Willy. She doesn't even know it was me.) "She has driven a Pope-Toledo racing motorcar at one hundred and twenty miles an hour!"

Willy's three fellow males exchanged glances and exclamations.

Quinlan flushed slightly and rocked the parasol from side to side and tapped it up and down. The color in her cheeks and the nervous action with the parasol made her even more fetching.

"I was driven *in* one," she corrected, "as a passenger of Mr. Herbert Lytle, the Vanderbilt Cup racer, a few years ago. I wrote an article about it for Leslie's. But I'm afraid our top speed was only a hundred, although"—she laughed modestly—"at the end when Mr. Lytle asked me if that was fast enough for me I said, "Twasn't very. Can't you make it go a hundred and twenty?'"

Willy did not join in the general laughter, but in spite of himself he was as impressed as the others were. No aeroplane had ever yet hit the one-hundred mark—not in level flight, not intentionally. The adventurous Miss Quinlan would probably find herself quite bored in an aeroplane doing a mere sixty.

Mr. Moisant wasn't done enthusing over the school's prize catch.

"Miss Quinlan will be the first woman in the United States to be licensed as an aeroplane pilot," he declaimed. "And as I said, she will be writing a series of articles describing her accomplishment."

Quinlan flushed again and tapped the parasol some more. "That is my hope." Then, speaking to Houpert but with all the man hanging on her words, "I'm also having more appropriate attire for flying designed by Mr. Alexander Grean, president of the American Tailors' Association. It was supposed to be ready by this time. I'm assured it will be next week. But I must tell you that in any case I will be unable to participate in flying on the Sabbath. I have promised my mother. I do, however, apologize again for my tardiness."

Her mother? And did the silly woman actually think they were going to fly today, or even tomorrow? This Saturday meeting was only an orientation session. Willy could not credit this Quinlan person. He sensed that the Frenchman too was not exactly over-joyed at having been presented with a female student, though his reply was one of Gallic tactfulness.

"Not at all, Miss Quinlan," Houpert said. "We were just about to begin the preliminary orientation. You are arrived in good time."

Willy had begun tempering his initial harsh opinion of Harriet Quinlan just a little. She *was* an unusual woman. And although she obviously enjoyed being the center of attention, her man-nerisms—the self-effacing laugh, the dropping of her eyes, the nervous fiddling with the parasol—betrayed an underlying em-barrassment.

But then, as if she had not already charmed everyone enough, she said, "Monsieur Houpert—"

"André."

"André. I can't tell you how thrilled I am to be under your tutelage. I have read of your career in France and I am impressed that even though the aeroplane is an American invention how the French have taken the lead in aviation. There are some eigh-teen hundred aeroplanes in use in the world today—isn't that the figure you mentioned, 'Fred?" She looked briefly at Mr. Moisant, who nodded. "And fifteen hundred of them are in France. Just consider the terms we use. Like fuselage, for example."

Houpert added with a pleased look, "Yes. Fuselage . . . em-pennage . . . nacelle . . ."

"Volplane," suggested the student named Jerwan.

"Yes, the glide," said Houpert. "That is definitely something you will have to master."

"Speaking of terms," said Moisant, "I've often wondered, André, why we use the term aero*plane*. A plane is something flat but a wing is curved. We should really call them aero*curves*, it seems to me."

Or simply "airplanes," Willy thought. He had read in one of

his aviation magazines that some professor in England had suggested that word. But he said nothing. That would have meant interrupting Miss Quinlan.

"The French word is 'avion,' is it not, André?" she said. "I went to finishing school in France but I'm afraid my command of the language is a bit rusty. Perhaps we should call them that since it stems from the same root as aviation and aviator."

"And aviatrix," said Alfred Moisant, beaming again.

"Why not 'máquinas de volar'?" put in the Spanish-speaking Ferdinand DeMurias, and everybody laughed.

That only slowed Quinlan down a little bit. "Not only French words," she went on, "but the many outstanding French designers and fliers—Blériot, Farman, Voisin, Paulhan, Vedrines, Conneau, Garros—and the records they are setting for distance and altitude and so on, not to mention the funds the French government is devoting to aviation. I'm afraid the United States has fallen far behind. Our Signal Corps has purchased two Wright Model B Flyers, I understand. *Two* aeroplanes. France has unquestionably become the world's leader in aviation."

Houpert nodded. "Ah, but it is not just the French. There are outstanding fliers in other countries. Grahame-White and Gustav Hamel of England. Here in this country Harry Atwood, Glenn Curtiss, Lincoln Beachey. The Wright fliers Brookins, Hoxsey and Johnstone—until, *hélas*, Mr. Hoxsey's unfortunate death. Oh there are many others. If you were arrived but a few minutes sooner you would have met our local aerial star, Earle Ovington."

"And another American, John Moisant," said Quinlan soberly. "Until *his* tragic death."

She turned to Alfred Moisant. "I saw your brother fly at the Belmont Park meet last fall. Actually, as you know, it was watching him perform and speaking to him later that inspired in me the ambition of learning to fly." Then, brightly, "But this also proves my point, for Moisant is a French name, isn't it?"

"French-Canadian," said Moisant.

Willy knew all the names that had been mentioned, and others that hadn't. Why no reference to the records set by the Wrights, long before anyone else had ever flown? Although they may have been eclipsed, it was the Wright brothers who had shown the way. But he felt uncomfortable and subdued among these older people. His fellow students as well seemed to be virtually tongue-tied under the spell cast by this obviously well-bred woman who was not only exquisitely feminine but commanded — or pretended to command — a knowledge of the aviation world not to be ex-pected in a female. Or even most males, for that matter. Willy resented her as much for that knowledge, and the way she was dominating the conversation, as for her intrusion into the class.

Harriet Quinlan was quite stuck on herself. Was it necessary for her to let them all know she had been educated in France? "I'm having more appropriate attire designed by blah, blah, blah," he mimicked in his mind.

He wondered how old she was. He guessed 25. And her be-ing so young and already so accomplished added envy to resent-ment, resentment that was only increased by what Harriet Quinlan said next.

"I attribute much of the blame for the present situation in this country to the Wright brothers. Their incessant pursuit of patent infringement cases against Curtiss and others has greatly impeded the progress of aviation in America, I sincerely believe."

Alfred Moisant vigorously nodded his agreement with this and Willy wondered if he had also heard from the Wrights' law-yers. The Moisant machines were built under license from Blériot, but Blériot himself was the target of a suit brought by the Wrights in France. Much as it pained him, he had to admit that the woman might have a point. The aeroplane was such a basic machine that it was like trying to patent the lever or the wheel. He wished the Wrights would simply make a gift of their invention to the world and devote their genius to perfecting it.

Yet he could see their side. They had done something no one else had ever been able to do. Why should others come along and copy them and reap the financial rewards? They were entirely willing to let anyone use their discoveries royalty-free to build an aeroplane for sport or pleasure, but not for business.

One of the students, however, then asked Mr. Moisant a question about the machines they were to train in and Quinlan at last withdrew from center stage. There were not enough places for everyone and there was a minute of shuffling. Miss Quinlan was offered a seat on the sofa between Jerwan and DeMurias, and Miss Vanderbilt sat down in a chair some distance from the class she was not to be a part of. Willy stood next to Harold Kantner against one wall. The unidentified male from the car perched himself jauntily on the table and lit a cigarette. Willy wondered if he was Quinlan's boyfriend or Vanderbilt's.

Moisant seemed to have welcomed the question, for when everyone was settled he began speaking expansively.

"As I wrote recently in an article for Leslie's magazine, the modern flying machine, crude as it may be compared with the types that are certain to be evolved in the next decade, or even the next two or three years, is utter simplicity. It has infinitely fewer working parts than the automobile, the locomotive or the steamship and is far less complex in operation. On a weight-to-power ratio, no other conveyance is as efficient. Last December Henri Farman remained in the air continually for eight hours and twelve minutes, covering a distance of three hundred fifty-four miles, in a fifty-horsepower machine. No other conveyance has ever equaled this kind of sustained performance, even though we have had railroad trains for seventy years and automobiles for twelve years. This is not to mention the aeroplane's ability to travel uninterruptedly over cities and countryside and rivers and so on.

"Think of it—to become a companion of the birds, to search the skies and from great heights to look down upon the flattened earth while one's monoplane bears him where his whim directs. To realize, to the throbbing of the motor and the song of the propeller, the dream of man throughout the centuries. All of these and more are what flying means. And there is none, except the mentally or the physically unfit, who may not taste its delights."

Mr. Moisant hadn't really answered the question that had been asked and spoke as if reciting from memory what he had written in his article, but Willy wished his father could have heard him. He wondered what issue the article had appeared in. Maybe he could look it up in the library.

The man would gladly have gone on talking but Houpert was showing signs of impatience. With a few more words of welcome and encouragement, the president of the company turned the floor over to the chief instructor.

This was, Houpert began, telling them what they already knew, the first class at the Moisant Flying School.

"We shall begin the training as a group, but because some of you may be able to come only on the weekends—that is, on Saturdays, as we do not have lessons on Sunday (a nod to Miss Quinlan)—and perhaps not always once or twice during the week, we will not all finish at the same time. We wish as much as possible, however, for all of you to go through the training at the same pace, for one learns as much from the errors of others as from his own. Much of course also depends upon the weather, as well as upon individual progress."

Harold Kantner spoke the question that was on everyone's mind: "How long will it take for us to qualify for our licenses, André?"

Harriet Quinlan turned to look at Kantner, then her eyes moved and lingered on Willy for what seemed longer than necessary, he thought. She smiled at him and then turned back. His face felt suddenly hot.

"The average in other schools has been about two hours, or a little more, sometimes a little less," Houpert answered. He grinned somewhat mischievously as the male students exclaimed and whistled.

"But of course," he quickly added, raising a forefinger, "you must realize that those two hours will be made up of many segments of no more than five or ten minutes each over a period of perhaps three months. In France no student is permitted to practice longer than that in any one lesson. We also advise at least one day of rest between each lesson."

Willy was dismayed. According to the booklet the entire

course was only supposed to last five weeks, including ground school. He did some quick figuring. If the actual flying time was two hours, or a hundred and twenty minutes, and you were only allowed five minutes in each lesson, that came to twenty-four lessons. If the course was really going to be spread over three months—twelve weeks—that meant you could only take two lessons a week.

He wanted to ask, what if a student was so proficient that he could practice every day, as he would be able to do once the semester was over? Even at only five minutes a lesson he could get his certificate in a month, before the end of June. Would he have to be held back because the others were slower?

The others had been doing their own figuring, for in answer to the next immediate question Houpert assured them that, weather permitting, they would certainly be ready for the Aero Club of America's licensing tests by July, or August at the latest.

He answered Willy's unasked question. "But in any case not sooner than five weeks. That is the minimum length of training we consider adequate. However, as you know, this school, unlike other schools, permits you to take as long as you need without extra cost."

The other students were as unclear about things as Willy. One of the men asked, "Does that mean we will start flying lessons immediately? What about ground school? Or will we take both at the same time?"

"Yes, well, our ultimate intention," Houpert replied, "is that students must successfully complete our ground school first. Unfortunately, we are not as yet completely set up for that. We are hoping to engage Signore Albert C. Triaca of the Aero Club of Italy to conduct these classes. But yes, you will receive laboratory instruction in aircraft and engine construction and mainte-nance as you undergo flight training. Perhaps not the full two weeks, but entirely adequate."

Willy didn't think it was unfortunate at all. He wanted to learn everything the school could teach him about the mechan-ics of aeroplanes of course, but that could just as well be done at the same time you were learning to fly.

Houpert emphasized again the importance of the weather, especially when they began making short flights in the machines. Then they would have to be at the field no later than six or seven in the morning, before the wind built up. Even better, five in the morning so that they would be ready as soon as it was light.

"It must be early in the morning in the beginning because that is when it is almost always calm. After you advance somewhat it may be possible to fly in the late afternoon or early evening when the wind dies down again. We consider any wind of more than six miles an hour to be too dangerous in the learning stage."

He let that sink in for a moment, then said, "But now, at long last, let us all proceed to 'An*gair* Number One to begin to familiarize ourselves with the aeroplane."

And to begin to separate the men from the girl, Willy thought, casting a sidelong glance at Harriet Quinlan.

3

THE MOISANT Flying School boasted six training craft, two of which were in the first "'an*gair*." Like the four other hangars it was a large concrete-block structure, some forty by fifty feet, with steel curtain doors and serviced by plumbing and electricity. Along with the aeroplanes there was an array of other things aeronautical: a detached, uncovered wing against one wall, its skeletal spars and ribs exposed; an undercarriage without wheels; a partially dismantled engine on a stand; spare propellers and other parts of aeroplanes; benches with blueprints, and a profusion of tools and equipment. In one corner was a large blackboard on a stand with wooden chairs grouped in front of it. Willy's heart stirred as he took all this in, especially the two flying machines, both of them monoplanes of the same apparent design.

André Houpert bade the four men and Miss Quinlan gather next to one aeroplane that faced the open doors of the hangar. It

looked the same as the other machine, but it had some important differences, as they were to learn. Alfred Moisant and Helen
Vanderbilt and the younger man who had apparently just come
along for the ride remained in the office.

The mechanic who had spun the propeller of Earle
Ovington's plane was standing nearby. Houpert motioned him
over and introduced him as the school's chief *mecanicién*. He
was another Frenchman named Hardy and he headed a crew of
two or three other men. "'Ardy" presumably had a given name,
but Willy was never to hear anyone use it.

Hardy bowed to them and then went off to work on something in the rear of the hangar. The orientation session began.

All of the school machines were Moisant monoplanes, André
told them, assembled on Long Island at the old Singer sewing
machine plant in Winfield, Queens, and based closely on the
design of the now-classic Model XI in which Louis Blériot had
conquered the English Channel not quite two years before. The
machine they were looking at, however, was the initial trainer
and although it was capable of flight, it was designed mainly for
learning to steer on the ground. For this reason it was both heavier
and less powerful than the school's other aeroplanes.

The chassis, or fuselage, was a rectangular, tapering framework open its entire length from nose to tail. The uncowled engine was also completely exposed. There was a bucketlike seat in
the pilot's compartment, or cockpit, formed of stiff sheet metal,
with holes cut in its back for lightness. It was fastened to the two
lower members of the frame by steel supports on each side.

They walked around the machine as André identified each
component and explained its function. Willy, who knew all this
from his dedicated reading of *Fly* and *Aircraft* and every other
aviation magazine he could get his hands on, wondered how
much of it was new to the other men. Surely it had to be a revelation to Miss Quinlan, whose demonstrated knowledge of aviation was probably confined to French words and the names of
French aviators. Every time they stopped to examine something
she leaned forward with both hands on the knob of her parasol,
looking and listening intently.

They returned to the front of the aeroplane and André began to go into elaborate detail. The fuselage was supported at its head by two bicycle-type wheels, but smaller than a bicycle's, at the ends of two vertical bedsteadlike struts fashioned of stout hickory supported by Shelby steel tubing, with shock absorbers and sliding collars of manganese bronze. The landing cradle was of bamboo and the axle of Krupp chrome-nickel steel.

Another feature of the undercarriage, uniquely Blériot, was that the wheels were on casters. This made it easier to push the machine about on the ground, as well as being an advantage when maneuvering in a crosswind, André said.

Despite the shock absorbers and the extra strength built into the struts, the undercarriage was the part most subject to breakage by learners, he informed them cheerfully. That and the propeller.

They started another circuit of the machine. The rear of the fuselage also rested on a wheel. Because the back end was closer to the ground than the front, the aeroplane slanted upward, giving it the appearance, it seemed to Willy, of being eager to cleave the air in flight even as it was static on the ground.

The rear wheel, André explained, was to facilitate driving back and forth across the field and to minimize stress on the airframe. The machines used for flying were equipped with skids at the tail.

"Thus when you begin to fly," he said, nodding toward the other machine in the hangar and anticipating what all of them were anticipating, "it will be important to elevate the tail as soon as possible in order to avoid dragging the skid."

More about the fuselage. The four long wooden members of the framework were made of second-growth ash and were called, appropriately, longerons. Spaced at intervals at right angles to the longerons on each side and on the top and bottom of the fuselage were Oregon spruce members. Each of the "boxes" formed by the cross members was crisscrossed on all sides by reinforcing wires of the finest piano wire with chrome-nickel turnbuckles of Moisant design, making a pattern of Xs. This gave the airframe both flexibility and strength.

The whole aeroplane in fact was a network of bracing wires or cables, the most prominent of which were those attached to stress points on the upper surface of the wings and connected to a trapezoidal mast ahead of the pilot's compartment. These were of the finest Roebling stranded cable. (Willy wondered if the others knew that the Roeblings, father and son, had designed the Brooklyn Bridge.) Other wires, including the wing-warping wires, were connected from another mast under the pilot's seat to the undersides of the wings and to the undercarriage.

The spars of the wings and the framework of the empennage—the rudder and rear stabilizing planes—were also of second-growth ash, reinforced with three-ply Oregon spruce. The undersides of the horizontal stabilizer, where it was attached to the fuselage, were supported by straps of chrome-vanadium steel. The covering material of all the flying surfaces was of French three-ply rubber-impregnated silk.

Since this machine would be used for primary training, André said, it was fitted with only a thirty-horsepower Gnôme rotary engine but suitable for learning how to steer an aeroplane on the ground—"grasscutting" or, as some phrased it, "trimming the daisies." The now thoroughly bewildered students laughed appreciatively.) They would also use the same machine in the next stage to make short hopping flights—"kangarooing," this procedure was called. (Laughter again.) For initial kangarooing, a special device would be installed on the elevator to limit its movement to prevent them from hopping too high.

The aeroplanes used for actual flying were equipped with fifty-horsepower Gnômes developing a thrust of three hundred and sixty pounds, enabling these machines to achieve a normal speed of sixty to sixty-five miles an hour. When the students graduated from grasscutting and kangarooing and were ready to leave the ground in true flight they would of course employ the more powerful machines.

Anticipating again, André explained that another reason they used the low-powered machine for initial training—besides preventing a student from suddenly finding himself in the air before he was ready—was because rotary engines, by virtue of their rapidly revolving mass, developed a great deal of torque. The torque of the engine, combined with the gyroscopic effect of the propeller, tended to pull an aeroplane in a direction opposite to that of the revolving engine and propeller.

He beckoned them to the front of the machine and demonstrated by moving the propeller back and forth through partial revolutions. As he did so, the five cylinders of the engine, which were arranged in a radial, star-shaped configuration, also moved in unison with the propeller.

Observe, he said, that unlike a conventional engine, whose cylinders are stationary and whose propeller is mounted on the end of a revolving crankshaft like the flywheel on an automobile engine, the cylinders and the entire crankcase of the rotary engine revolve around a stationary crankshaft, with the propeller being fixed not to the crankshaft but to the spinning crankcase. Hence the term "rotary."

Since the engine and propeller revolved to the right (when viewed from the pilot's seat), the gyroscopic effect caused the fuselage to want to revolve strongly to the left around the axis of thrust. Thus experience had proven it advisable that students first master steering in a straight line with a low-powered machine before advancing to the more powerful ones.

Houpert looked at them to see if they understood. Everybody was nodding.

"And that tendency to turn is countered by using the rudder," Kantner stated.

"That is correct. But there is an additional means of controlling the torque, if necessary. That is by controlling the running of the engine."

The students were informed that there was yet another difference between rotary engines and conventional engines: rotaries had no throttles but ran at full blast continuously as long as the spark was on.

"That is why you gentlemen had to help hold Mr. Ovington's machine—to permit 'Ardy to get out of the way." (Another laugh from the men.) "But also for taking off in the shortest distance by allowing the engine to develop full revolutions before the machine is released."

Although there was a fuel lever on a quadrant mounted on the right side of the cockpit and an air lever on another quadrant on the control column that were operated together to achieve maximum r.p.m., the only effective way of governing a rotary— and by consequence its torque effect—was by "blipping" the engine off and on by means of an ignition interrupter switch or button. But that was something they would go into in greater depth in subsequent sessions.

André then said that each of them would now take turns sitting in the pilot's compartment and told Ferdinand DeMurias to climb in first. As the Cuban mounted the fuselage the aeroplane started to shy away on its castered wheels on the smooth concrete floor until André and the others steadied it. (Just like a skittish young colt, Willy thought.)

Savoring his anticipation of the moment when he would actually sit in an aeroplane—*he had not expected it would be so soon!*—he let the others go ahead of him. If he was the last one maybe he would get to sit in it longer. Poor Miss Quinlan was forced merely to watch; she could hardly be asked to try to get into the plane in her long dress and possibly expose her calves. While the men crowded around the cockpit, she stood by herself a few feet away, looking rather subdued, he thought, as if conscious at last of how out of place she was.

Maybe it was also dawning on her just what she was letting herself in for. Driving an aeroplane was not the same as driving an automobile. He himself was finding out that an aeroplane, in its structure at any rate, was more complex than he had appreciated. It was not the epitome of simplicity that Alfred Moisant had made it out to be. He felt a little sorry for Quinlan. Didn't she know you could get hurt in these things if you didn't know what you were doing?

As he waited, he gingerly touched the fabric of a wing, pretending to test its tautness but secretly just because he wanted to touch it, and slid his fingers along one of the bracing cables. Such a beautiful thing the craft was, even if only a groundhopper at best.

When his turn in the cockpit finally came he nodded impatiently as André told him to place his feet on either side of the rudder yoke, a pivoting bar which caused the rudder to move right or left, and to observe the action of the rudder as he worked the bar.

Houpert suddenly realized that Harriet Quinlan was being neglected. He asked one of the men to fetch a stool from a corner of the hangar and place it next to the cockpit.

"Miss Quinlan, perhaps if you would stand on that you will be able to watch as Mr. Reynolds performs the control operations."

The woman's face brightened. She removed her large hat and gave that and her parasol into the keeping of one of the men and another assisted her to step onto the stool. She gripped the side of the cockpit with her slender hands and peered inside. Her face was very close to Willy's.

André, balancing on a lower longeron on the other side of the cockpit and with one hand on the overhead mast, had Willy operate the rudder yoke again, then said to both of them, "Now observe the control column."

"*Regardez-vous, mademoiselle. C'est très important,*" said Willy, rolling the first "r" exaggeratedly and showing off his high school French for Harriet Quinlan's benefit. She made a giggle, but it was not an appreciative sound.

"*Oui*, Monsieur Reynolds," André said with a touch of testiness, or perhaps of weariness at repeating himself yet again. "This is most important. We employ the cloche system, which, in addition to the tractor monoplane, is the great contribution of Blériot to aviation."

Willy knew all about this too. He had also heard the man explain it three times before. But now it was his turn to handle the control and he listened carefully, both because it *was* important and by way of making up for his flippancy.

At André's direction he placed his hands on the wheel. It was not only smaller than the wheel of an automobile but, unlike an automobile's wheel, couldn't be turned because it was fixed on top of the column. The bottom of the column ended in a universal joint just above the cockpit floor, surrounded by the "cloche," a piece of metal shaped somewhat like a flattened bell. (*Cloche* meant bell in French, he knew.) Control cables were attached to the flared rim of the bell at north, south, east and west positions and were led over pulleys to the control surfaces: one pair to the elevator and the other pairs to each of the wingtips. Since the cloche was also a fixed part of the column, when the column was moved the wires attached to the cloche were pulled in one direction or another.

As he had done with the other students, Houpert explained that pulling the wheel (and column) back or pushing it forward made the rear elevating plane go up or down, in flight causing the aeroplane to pitch up or down; that is, to ascend or descend. To execute a turn, moving the wheel (and column) to one side or the other flexed, or warped, the wingtips, causing the aeroplane to heel over or roll right or left around its longitudinal axis.

But—and this was most important—the upraised wing, because of the greater resistance it presented to the air, tended to drag, creating an adverse yaw. If not compensated for, this would result, at best, in a skidding turn or, at worst, in a dangerous slide toward the lower wing if the angle was excessive. Thus the rudder must be employed to overcome the drag of the higher wing by forcing it around in the direction one wished to go. For example, for a left turn both wheel and rudder were moved to the left. Naturally, for a right turn the opposite was true. It was this simultaneous combination of wing roll and rudder yaw that enabled an aeroplane to make a graceful banking turn in the air.

The essential problem of learning to fly, André emphasized, was simply learning how to combine the three elements of pitch, roll and yaw by the use of one's feet and hands in a smooth and coordinated manner.

Willy again watched the action of the plane's surfaces as he executed the different movements by moving the wheel to the extreme left and extreme right: how the right wingtip flexed downward and the left wingtip flexed upward when he tilted the column to the left for a left turn, and vice versa when he tilted it to the right for a right turn. He was actually sitting in an aeroplane, actually working its controls, and even though its heavy chassis and small engine made it barely capable of flight, it was an *aeroplane*. Indeed, Blériot's channel plane had only been powered by a little three-cylinder, twenty-five horsepower Anzani engine.

He almost forgot the woman, who all the while was nodding and saying, "Oh yes, I see. Uh-huh." It was with reluctance that he climbed out of the craft when Houpert was finished.

Their instructor then directed a number of basic questions at the group in general: what would they do to raise the nose of an aeroplane in flight; how would they lower the nose; what happened when the wheel was moved right or left; what was the function of the rudder in a turn, and so on. The pupils chorused the answers and Houpert nodded in satisfaction.

He then said that would be all for that day; they had been exposed to a great deal — indeed, perhaps too much. But at the next session they would go through it all again, and again in succeeding lessons, until they were thoroughly familiar with the aeroplane and its controls. If they all did well, and if the weather cooperated, it was entirely possible they might begin their grasscutting lessons by the end of the coming week.

Everyone made enthusiastic noises, and contrary to what André had assumed in the office all of them said they would be able to come to the field on weekdays and Saturdays. So it was mutually agreed that the initial lessons would be held on Tuesdays, Thursdays and Saturdays, with one of the three days devoted to laboratory lessons in the hangar. Which day it would be would be determined by the weather.

Still in a state of excitement, talking and gesturing, the students started back to the administration building, from there to go their separate ways. Miss Quinlan walked beside André, no doubt turning on the charm again, Willy thought. He lingered behind; he wanted to look at the other aeroplane in the hangar. He had it all to himself, for Hardy had also gone elsewhere and no other mechanic was around.

Although essentially identical to the primary trainer, this machine was by virtue of its larger engine and lighter structure a true high-performance aeroplane, in which, or in one like it, he would eventually go up in the air.

Unlike the primary trainer, the fuselage was covered with fabric from the nose to just behind the cockpit and the fifty-horespower engine was partially cowled with sheet metal. It was the engine he was especially interested in.

It was also a rotary but with seven cylinders instead of five, arranged in a circle around the crankcase. He read the words stamped, without accent marks, on the front of the crankcase: SOCIETE DES MOTEURS GNOME.

He had read about the Gnôme and what a marvel of engineering it was. Its paper-thin cylinders were each machined from a solid block: eight pounds of metal milled down to four and a half pounds; and one hundred pounds of crankcase casting milled down to thirteen and a half pounds.

Harriet Quinlan had been right about one thing: the French had taken the lead in aviation. Not only would he learn to fly in an aeroplane of French design but the rotary engine, the most dependable and efficient aircraft engine yet developed, was the achievement of two French brothers, Laurent and Louis Seguin. Even the propeller, fashioned of highly varnished laminated walnut, had been made in France, by the Chauvière Company.

Yet as Harriet Quinlan had said (give her that much), the aeroplane was an American invention. Whatever the strides lately made by the French, they had been going nowhere until Wilbur Wright had amazed France and all of Europe with his mastery of flying. Every aeroplane that flew, or ever would fly, had the Wright brothers to thank for their monumental and historic discovery of the elements of pitch, roll and yaw and the invention of wing-warping. Curtiss may have improved on the Wrights with the use of wheels instead of runners and monorail (which the Wrights themselves had abandoned), and monoplanes with the engine in front might be supplanting the pusher biplane, but Curtiss hadn't been going anywhere either until he ferreted out the Wrights' secret of how to turn in the air.

(Was there some connection between being brothers and having mechanical genius? he mused. The Montgolfier brothers had invented the balloon; the Wright brothers had invented the aeroplane; the Seguin brothers had perfected the rotary engine for aircraft use, and brothers named Farman and Nieuport designed and flew aeroplanes in France. Even on the ground, it was two brothers, the Duryeas, who had built the first automobile in America.)

It occurred to him then that when he had watched Wilbur Wright's machine emerge from its hangar on Governors Island on that day that now seemed so long ago he had been so totally engrossed in trying to guess what its different strange-looking parts were for, how they were all supposed to work together, that he had not really perceived the aeroplane itself as a whole mechanism, even when it rose off the ground before his eyes. Now, paradoxically, having just examined an aeroplane in the minutest detail, he was struck with what a unity it all amounted to, how logically designed were its various parts for utilizing the laws of physics to achieve the end result of lifting itself and its driver into the air.

Mr. Moisant had said that today's machines were crude compared to what would come in future years. Willy could not imagine what that might be. Bigger, faster, more powerful of course. Yet unless someone discovered some as yet unknown laws of aerodynamics the aeroplanes of the future would only be a refinement on the basic perfection of these machines.

He finally forced himself to leave. It was only three days until the next lesson, but he had final exams nearly every day next week and it would be a problem getting back and forth between Hempstead Plains and the Bronx. He would have to talk his father into letting him use the car on mornings when he didn't have an exam and went to the field early. When they started flying in the afternoons he could take the Long Island Railroad. There was a new stop at Clinton Road and Stewart Avenue within walking distance of the aerodrome.

Thank God the semester would be officially over in a couple more weeks. Then he could come to the field every day to fly if he wanted to. And, unlike the elegant la Quinlan, he would not need a special costume to do it in.

Miss Harriet Quinlan. She might think she was going to be America's first female aviator, but she was going to have to eat *his* dust this time because he would easily win his license long before she did.

If she ever did.

4

WHEN WILLY'S alarm clock woke him at four A.M. on Tuesday he looked out the window and saw by the light of the nearest streetlamp that the rain that had begun the previous evening was still coming down—lightly, you couldn't hear it on the roof, but steadily, descending like a mist.

He'd had to go through another slight argument with his father the evening before. His father did not want him to drive the car if it was raining in the morning. The car had a top, Willy said. The streets would be slippery, his father countered; the tires already had nearly a thousand miles on them. What if the spark plugs got wet? He didn't want to get a call from Willy informing them that he was stranded somewhere out in the middle of Long Island.

"Well, I'd just wait until they dried out, Dad. But the car sits out in the street in all kinds of weather. We've never had any trouble with it starting."

It was true enough, ever since they'd had a new Remy-Magneto ignition system installed by Bruns Auto Company in Brooklyn, with electric lights in place of the original gas-fired ones. Although they did little driving at night it was so much more convenient not to have to fumble with matches to light the lamps, not to mention keeping the inside of their glasses clean and the acetylene tank full and pressurized. All automobiles would come with electric lights eventually, Willy was sure. Next would be some kind of self-cranking mechanism, and then even his mother could drive anytime she wanted.

"The papers predict rain all week," his father said. "What if it pours?"

Everybody else would be there, Willy said. (He hoped they wouldn't; he hoped he would be the only one.) The first lessons were very important, he said reasonably. If he missed even one he might not be able to catch up with the rest of the students. He didn't want to be left behind.

"They will have to be as crazy as you are," his father said in a resigned tone which, together with the usual shaking of his head, told Willy he had prevailed again.

He arrived at the field a little after five, proud of himself for having negotiated the deserted rain-slick streets of Brooklyn and the country roads of Long Island without incident. He had never driven at night on unlit roads before, but the headlights cut swaths that illuminated the way and the sun was coming up by the time he got to the field. The Chalmers had perked along with no hesitation at all. Automobiles were so reliable these days, thanks to the improvements the industry had made in only a few years. It would probably be the same with aeroplanes.

Everybody *wasn't* there. In fact the office was empty. It hadn't been necessary to come so early after all. He went outside and around to Hangar One. The front sliding doors were closed. He pushed open the side door.

He had been beaten again. They were all assembled around the trainer, which sat in the same position it had on Saturday: Jerwan, Kantner and DeMurias, along with André Houpert, plus, to his surprise, Harriet Quinlan. He hadn't given her a thought since Saturday and even if he had given her a thought would not have expected her to be there so early, if she came back at all.

He thought it was a boy at first and was not sure it was she until she turned. She was dressed in a strange costume, the most striking aspect of which were billowy pantaloons or knickerbockers that ended in knee-high laced-up boots. The suit was of one piece, made of shiny material like satin, with a hood hanging down the back. The whole outfit was mauve or plum colored, except for the black leather boots.

So this was the flying "attire" she had commissioned the president no less of the American Tailors' Association to design for her. To make it all the more ridiculous, she had a helmet and goggles in her hand, to accommodate which her hair had been done up in a tight bun. As if they would be "cutting grass" today, much less doing any flying.

She smiled at him, and he granted her a curt nod.

Sawhorses had been placed under the tails of the two machines in the hangar to raise their fuselages level with the floor. This was to accustom them to the attitude an aeroplane would be in during normal flight, André explained as the lesson began.

But first, as they had during the orientation session, they walked around the training machine and briefly reviewed what they had learned about its structure and various parts. This time André went into greater detail about the engine.

The rotary type lacked not only a throttle; it had no carburetor either. It was fueled and lubricated by a mixture of gasoline and castor oil feeding from separate tanks that were mounted side by side just forward of the pilot's compartment. The gasoline provided the power of course and the oil the lubrication. Castor oil was used because it was not readily diluted by gasoline. The gasoline and oil entered the revolving crankcase through the hollow, stationary crankshaft, where centrifugal force sucked the gasoline into the cylinder heads to be exploded by the spark plugs. Unavoidably, the oil was also thrown into the combustion chambers, where some of it burned but most of it escaped through the exhaust ports.

Thus it was essential, André said, anticipating again, that when one is descending for a landing, which can only be accomplished by shutting off the engine with the ignition interrupter, one must "blip" it on again frequently to clear the cylinders in order to prevent the spark plugs from being fouled with oil.

"It can be most embarrassing, if one has come down too short, to reopen the ignition and have the engine fail to respond and find oneself landing in a potato patch."

The students all laughed again appreciatively, and not a little dubiously, exchanging looks.

"We will not start the engine today, of course," said André. "That will come in a future session when we will have the trainer bolted to the floor so that each of you may see what it is like to sit in an aeroplane with the engine running and practice how to govern it."

He then told the four men to take turns sitting in the fifty-horsepower machine and practice with the controls and directed Harriet Quinlan, this time unencumbered with a dress, to climb into the trainer. In the two machines, both of which had the same system of controls, the students went through the motions of raising and lowering elevators, turning rudders and warping wings. André went from one to the other, again questioning them as to what this control was for, what that control did, how they would manipulate them to accomplish this or that maneuver in the air, what they would do under such and such a circumstance.

It really *was* simple once you had gone through the motions for the hundredth time and Willy found himself becoming bored with the reiterated questions. But he knew this procedure was important. Mastery of the controls had to become automatic, almost second nature, before a person could venture into the air, for once off the ground there would be no instructor to turn to for assistance.

He remembered something his father had said after he had looked over the Moisant literature: why didn't they use biplanes with side-by-side seats and duplicate controls for training? Some of the other flying schools on Long Island did, he understood. Wouldn't that be safer, having an instructor right alongside you to correct any mistakes you might make?

Surprised that his father knew that much about aeroplanes, Willy had been unable to answer right away. The question did seem to make sense. But he had turned it around to his advantage by saying, "Well, Dad, dozens of people have learned to fly in one-person monoplanes. That just goes to show how safe and easy it really is. Actually, you learn faster that way. By the time they let you take it up you know all about how to control it."

Yet for the first time he felt a chill of apprehension. Sitting in the powerful aeroplane, he felt a faint stirring of doubt about his ability to guide a thing like this up into the air, as he would eventually be required to do.

He looked at the plane's two instruments mounted on the crossbrace in front of him: a tachometer, or engine revolution counter, and an altimeter, the latter's two pointers resting on zero. He imagined them moving to ten to twenty to a hundred feet and more as, perhaps in this very plane, he climbed away from the earth . . . *alone*.

He shrugged it off and redoubled his concentration on the controls. If a woman could learn to fly an aeroplane—and Harriet Quinlan wouldn't be the first to do that for there were several French female pilots—certainly he could too.

He turned around and looked at her in the trainer. Her back was to him as she sat ramrod straight in the cockpit. Did the woman have any appreciation at all of what an amazing thing it was for men—*men*—to fly? In machines that were the invention of men?

Not likely. It was just a lark for her, a suffragette's aping of men to prove (as if anyone cared or as if it made any difference in the world) that women could do anything men could do, that they did not have to be confined to home and children. That, and a stunt calculated to increase the circulation of *Leslie's Weekly*.

When André was satisfied that the five students had demonstrated that they understood the function of the controls as much as they ever would in a stationary machine he had them gather around the trainer again.

"You have all done very well," he said. "It is a pity it is so miserable outside, otherwise I believe we could skip the lesson running the engine with the trainer bolted down and actually begin the cutting of the grass today. But, *hélas*, the ground is much too soggy and we must not rush things. It is difficult enough to guide a machine in a straight line when the ground is dry, as you will discover. Next time for a certainty, if the rain ceases."

Willy wondered if André meant to include Harriet Quinlan in his statement that they "all" had done well. She had had only one session operating the controls while everyone else had now had two. But she was definitely more at ease than she had been on Saturday. If she had any doubts about her ability to handle an aeroplane, and to do it as well as a man could, it was not apparent in her manner.

Cursed rain. What if it really did last all week? He was as annoyed by the thought of that prospect as he was by Harriet Quinlan. She was already bringing them bad luck.

It was still early, not yet seven o'clock. The men went into the office and poured themselves coffee from the urn on the table. Harriet Quinlan had gone into a lavatory/dressing room that had been reserved for her in the back of the second hangar. When she rejoined them she was all femininity once more. By some clever arrangement of buttons, the pantaloons of her "uniform" had been transformed into a walking skirt.

Willy was thinking about the next lesson on Thursday and trying to remember what his exam schedule was when Quinlan exhibited her aeronautical expertise again by initiating a discussion about the relative merits of the biplane and the monoplane. All the men again hung on her words.

"It seems to me, André, that if man is to fully conquer the air"—the "man" was not lost on Willy—"it will have to be as the birds do it. I have made somewhat of a study of bird flight and the monoplane is the closest thing to a bird in design. The biplane is really nothing more than a box kite with a motor on it."

"Yes," agreed Houpert. "As you know, all the Moisant machines are monoplanes. The aeroplane of the future, I am sure, will be nothing more than a tube with but rudimentary wings on either side. It is speed which really makes flight possible. A slow airplane needs large wings with which to generate lift from the air passing over them. Thus it is but logical that as more powerful engines enable us to attain greater and greater speeds, smaller and smaller wings will generate the same amount of lift. One has only to observe that it is with monoplanes that aviators are setting new speed records every day. About all that can be said for the biplane is that its wings are perhaps more strongly braced and that it may be somewhat more maneuverable at slow speeds."

What André said seemed quite reasonable and unarguable, yet Willy was not so sure. Although he agreed with what Grover Loening had said about the tractor monoplane being the design of the future (in fact, that was one of the reasons Willy had chosen the Moisant school), Wilbur Wright's flight up the Hudson had been pure perfection. Glenn Curtiss and Lincoln Beachey and Glenn Martin and Harry Atwood and others all flew biplanes and were doing some amazing things with them and their speeds were as great as monoplanes. "Box kites" indeed. He was debating with himself whether he should mention this when Harold Kantner redirected the discussion.

"What is your opinion of ailerons, André? I've read that the aileron is really a more efficient means of turning an aeroplane in flight than warping the wings."

Houpert gave a little snort. "Those who are promoting ailerons, how much is it a genuine advance in design and how much an attempt to get around the Wrights' patent? It is possible of course that in time ailerons may prove to be the superior method. I have never flown a craft equipped with them so I am not that familiar. The aileron may be a feasible alternative to wing warping, but for the moment it seems to be a violation of the principle of simplicity, which is of the essence in aeroplane design.

Consider: which is the simplest structure—a wing of one piece with no moving parts but flexible at its tips, or one with hinged vanes on the trailing edges, or between the wings as on Curtiss biplanes? And as Miss Quinlan just remarked, we must look to our feathered friends in our conquest of the air. Who has ever seen a bird with ailerons?"

There was good-humored laughter at this.

"But André," Willy spoke up. "Who has ever seen a bird with a propeller? Or an aeroplane that rose into the air by flapping its wings?"

He did not mean to challenge André and surprised himself a little with his interjection. It had been prompted as much by intense interest in anything having to do with aeroplanes as by the wish to take a little wind out of Quinlan's sails.

"*Touché*," said Houpert. "A very good point. Of a certainty human flight cannot be modeled perfectly on that of a bird, any more than the propulsion of a ship is modeled on that of a fish. Birds are organisms and the aeroplane is a machine, and much effort has been wasted, and is still being wasted, in attempts to build ornithopters that imitate the flapping wings of birds. Even so, there is much that we still have to learn from the birds. Consider those that are able to soar effortlessly for hours, rising and descending without perceptibly moving their wings. We have yet to understand how they do it."

Willy was conscious that Harriet Quinlan was looking at him with seeming great interest, smiling at him pleasantly.

He avoided her eyes and gave his attention to the coffee cup cradled in his hands and took no further part in the discussion. He was annoyed with himself now. Had he wanted to take the woman down a peg, or was it really that he had wanted to say something to impress her?

It was his own doing of course. She talked and kidded quite easily and naturally with the others, and they with her, but except for the moment on Saturday when she had been leaning into the cockpit and he had made his dumb French remark he had avoided her and tried to pretend she wasn't there.

But why should he care whether Harriet Quinlan was impressed by him or what she thought of him? He wished again that she weren't so pretty.

Before going home to do some overdue cramming for his next exam, Willy went back into the hangar for another look at the fifty-horsepower machine he had practiced in.

He still found it hard to believe that this inert assemblage of wood and wires and silk was capable of moving across the ground, lifting into the air and entering the realm that had been the sole possession of the birds since time began. How lucky he was to have been born and come of age at the precise moment, out of all the thousands of years of human history, that man had begun to conquer the air. Why couldn't his father understand that?

Lovingly, caressingly, he ran his hands over the smooth surface of an exposed longeron behind the cockpit.

Then, closing his eyes, he bent his head and pressed his lips to the varnished wood.

He looked up. Harriet Quinlan was standing by the side door of the hangar only a few feet away, looking at him. Embarrassed and flustered, he pretended to be examining something on the fuselage.

Maybe she hadn't seen. At least she wasn't laughing or giggling at him. Her expression was sober as she walked toward him. She had a long coat on over her costume.

No—she *had* seen, for she said, sweeping her glance over the aeroplane, "It *is* beautiful, isn't it? I'm looking forward to going up in it. Or one like it."

She laughed then, but playfully, and looked frankly into his eyes. Her eyes were a beautiful grayish-green.

He could no longer pretend otherwise: her whole person was beautiful.

He cleared his throat. "Orville Wright says that the most fun about inventing the aeroplane was lying in bed at night trying to imagine what it would be like to fly."

"Yes." She moved her beautiful head up and down several

times. Maybe she did understand after all. Yet she was merely "looking forward" to flying. He had dreamed of nothing else for more than a year and a half.

He walked around to the side of the plane where she was standing. "I thought everyone had left."

"I'm waiting for a car from the Garden City Hotel. I live in Manhattan but I've taken a room there. Since we have to be at the aerodrome so early, I plan to come out to the hotel after work on the days before the lessons so I can get a good night's sleep and not have to get up too much ahead of the crack of dawn!"

She really had a friendly, self-effacing laugh. She really was not at all affected or condescending. Her voice too was beautiful, so softly modulated. For the first time in his life Willy was conscious of, and embarrassed by, his Brooklyn accent.

"You live in Manhattan?"

"Yes. On lower Broadway. And you—I understand you're attending New York University?"

How did she know that? He was flattered that she had even the slightest interest in him. He told her where he lived and about his studies. He was majoring in business administration with a minor in English.

"Business administration," she repeated. "That's very smart. Are you going to go for your M.B.A.? Even if you don't, English and the humanities will always help you. With that education and your pilot's license you should be able to get in on the ground floor in aviation. I mean, with so many companies starting up in the field—flying schools . . . aeroplane manufacturing . . . aerial photography . . . eventually, I'm sure, aerial package or passenger services. Is that your intention?"

He shrugged. It was still too far in the future to think about what he might do with his license; his immediate goal was just to get it. He disliked business administration. He would rather be majoring in English. But his father wanted him to come into the real estate business with him.

She was waiting for an answer.

"I could drive you to the hotel, Miss Quinlan. I could go through Garden City."

"Why thank you, Willy, but I've already called. In fact, they may be here. I'd better see."

She turned to go, then turned back and fixed her eyes on him again. "Is your name Willy or is that short for William? I've been wanting to ask you because Willy is also a proper name."

"It's William."

"Is it? I was wondering about that because Bill, or Billy, is usually the nickname for William."

She had wondered about his name? And wondering why she had wondered, he said nothing.

"Nicknames are funny, aren't they?" she went on. "I've always thought it curious that the usual or customary nicknames for William should start with a 'B'. But then we use Bob for Robert, don't we? Not to mention Betty for Elizabeth. Must be some arcane law of linguistics involved." She laughed pleasantly again.

He was so surprised at her apparent interest in him that he couldn't think of anything to say.

"My I call you William? Or is that too formal? I know there's a great spirit of camaraderie in the group since we're all in this adventure together, but William is such a nice name and seems to me to suit you better than Willy. William is also my father's name."

He didn't quite know how he felt about that. His mother was the only one who ever called him William and he certainly didn't want this woman to feel motherly toward him.

"Whatever you like would be just fine," he said.

"All right. William then, if you don't think that's too formal. And please, no more 'Miss Quinlan.' I'm just Harriet."

She paused a moment and he thought she was waiting for him to say something, but before he could think of anything, she said abruptly, "Well, this has been an interesting discussion and we must continue it sometime, but I really must be going. See you on Thursday? William."

He didn't want her to leave. "Some other time? I mean about giving you a lift?"

She didn't answer but he thought she nodded.

He waited in the hangar a while longer, then went out to the car and set the spark and throttle levers and cranked it up. The rain had stopped and the sky was clearing.

He drove down Clinton Road with a feeling of high anticipation inside him, and was not sure if it was because in just two more days they might begin practice in the trainer under power or because, in just two more days . . . he would see *her* again.

5

THURSDAY BROUGHT both good luck and bad luck. The good luck was that Willy didn't have an exam until that afternoon and the weather forecast had been wrong: the morning dawned bright and windless. With no rain and no wind and no need to hurry to school, he would be able to stay all morning to begin ze cutting of ze grass, as André had promised.

And that was the bad luck.

He went directly into the locker room in Hangar One to don the coveralls the school provided and hurried out to the front, wondering if he had missed anything, for everybody had preceded him again. They were sitting on the apron in chairs they had brought out of the hangar, talking animatedly among themselves as they watched the trainer being readied by Hardy and another mechanic under André's supervision.

A third mechanic was carrying a tall pole with a red flag on top of it out to the far end of the aerodrome. There was a kind of broad, shallow dip in the middle of the field, hardly noticeable even when you were right in it. But because of the foreshortened perspective from the hangar the mechanic began to disappear as he crossed the depression and for a minute all you could see was the moving pole and the flag.

Willy was a little bothered to find that his fellow students seemed to be as dedicated to learning to fly as he was. One of these days he was going to get there first. Not that that was important; he would soon enough surge ahead of them. He was more bothered with himself for being so glad to see Harriet Quinlan. On the way home on Tuesday he had been struck with the full force of his embarrassment at her having caught him . . . *making love to an aeroplane.* She had been too polite to laugh, but what had she really thought?

Harriet smiled at him quite warmly though, and the others lifted their hands in greeting. Before he could begin to feel awkward standing there—he hadn't brought out a chair for himself—André waved them over to the trainer. Everyone jumped up, and Willy suddenly felt his stomach tighten.

"I think it should be ladies first," Jerwan said. He winked at Harriet. Kantner and DeMurias agreed. "Yes, you show us how, Harriet."

"Oh no. I wouldn't want to set a bad example. Please, one of you go ahead of me."

His fellow males' gallantry (or, Willy hoped, their own sudden qualms masked by gallantry) was unnecessary. André had already decided and told DeMurias to climb into the cockpit. The Cuban gave the others an oh-lucky-me look with raised eyebrows and set lips and did as he was told. He fastened his helmet and goggles over his head while André crouched behind him on top of the fuselage. Hardy was priming each cylinder with gasoline from a squirt can.

Jerwan and Kantner and the other mechanic held onto the after part of the fuselage. At DeMurias's word Hardy swung the propeller and the rotary engine spurted smoke and exploded into life. A blast of wind drove Willy and Harriet away from the rear of the aeroplane. They looked at each other, sharing their mutual startlement at the immense racket put out by the engine. It was actually a staccato series of roars as André, reaching into the cockpit, showed Ferdinand how to "throttle" the engine by blipping the ignition on and off.

That was another characteristic of a rotary—the intermittent roaring. Yet another, which Willy had first experienced when

Earle Ovington's machine was started and which he would forever associate with aeroplanes, was the odor—the pungent odor
of half-burnt castor oil.

André had Ferdinand practice with the ignition button for a
minute to accustom himself to controlling the engine and then,
after adjusting the settings of the fuel and air levers, climbed
down. When Ferdinand indicated he was ready, André signaled
to the men holding the vibrating frame to release their grips.

The trainer began moving forward very quickly, straight ahead
at first, then toward the left. DeMurias attempted to correct that
with the rudder and by interrupting the spark, but the machine
kept veering to the left. He gave it more right rudder. Too much.
The machine abruptly swerved to the right. Left rudder—again
too much; the machine swerved back to the left. Right rudder
again.

The result was a meandering, bumping course across the field
toward the distant flag. When DeMurias reached the low area in
the middle he and the entire plane, except for his head and the
overhead mast, vanished for a few seconds the same way the mechanic carrying the flag had, like a ship going over the horizon.

It was a funny sight, repeated when Ferdinand made the return trip, and everyone laughed. Willy would have laughed too,
had he had not been gripped in an almost paralyzing state of
nerves. He hoped he would not be next.

DeMurias held the ignition off until the engine died and the
craft came to a stop about as far away from the hangar as it had
been in the beginning but yards to one side. He climbed out,
shaking his head. His goggles and face were smeared with oil
sprayed back by the engine.

André gathered the group around him.

You have now seen the torque effect of the rotary engine, he
said. Because it spins to the right, he explained again, the body
of the machine turns to the left—as Mr. DeMurias has so amply
demonstrated.

(Newton's third law of motion, Willy thought. For every action an equal and opposite reaction. Or something like that.)

In addition, André said, when the machine is forcibly turned in a new direction it wants to continue in that direction — as was also demonstrated by Mr. DeMurias.

(The first law?)

Anticipation and correction, said André. Correction and anticipation. One must keep one's feet alert on the rudder yoke every instant.

"But Ferdinand did very well for his first time. Now . . . Miss Quinlan?"

Willy watched the trim figure climb into the monoplane. Harriet's costume, which he now thought most practical and becoming, was protected by a duster instead of coveralls. She pulled the hood up over her head and helmet and adjusted her goggles. The engine was restarted, with André leaning again into the cockpit as Harriet worked the blip switch.

Then she was off. At first her performance promised to be a duplication of Ferdinand's, for the machine veered left as soon as it started rolling. Then, as DeMurias had done, Harriet overcorrected and it veered to the right. But unlike him she did not overcorrect again. There was only a slight amount of meandering as she progressed across the field.

On the return trip she had obviously gotten the hang of it. Her course was nearly an undeviating straight line. Not only that but, to everyone's amazement, about three quarters of the way back she lifted the machine up on its two front wheels for a second or two and came toward them with tail raised and fuselage almost parallel with the ground. She stopped the machine nearly on the spot in front of the hangar where she had started from. She made it look so easy.

André was enthusiastic. "Excellent, excellent. That is how it should be done."

The others showered Harriet with accolades as she climbed out and removed the goggles. She grinned at Willy (at the others too, but mostly at him, he thought) and made a circle with her thumb and forefinger. There's nothing to it, she seemed to say.

Willy gave her a strained grin. His stomach was in knots. As he was hoping, André next chose Jerwan and after him Kantner to make their first essays at grasscutting. Neither of them did any worse than DeMurias had done, but neither did nearly as well as Harriet.

Finally there was no getting out of it. It was his turn.

He sat in an aeroplane again, but for all the practice in the hangar it suddenly seemed completely foreign to him. This time he would not be merely playing with the controls; this time he would be expected to use them. And this time the machine would not be sitting still; this time it would be moving.

Leaning over his shoulder, André reviewed the use of the ignition interrupter to prevent the Gnôme from building up more than a thousand revolutions, reminding him that the ignition was otherwise always open, reminding him of the importance of constant alertness with the rudder. All he had to do was merely— merely!—keep the machine going in a straight line to the other end of the field, where the patiently waiting mechanic would turn him around, then come back to the starting point in another straight line.

If by chance he found himself in the air (not likely, Willy thought, not if he could help it!) he was to cut the engine immediately and allow the machine to settle back onto the ground. But always he was to continue his straight-line progress across the field.

Also on this first venture Willy was not to concern himself with trying to lift the tail wheel off the ground, even though Miss Quinlan had done so (Willy had not even considered it). That would come after he mastered straight-line driving. André spoke with an optimism that Willy did not at all share.

André clapped him on the shoulder and abandoned him to his fate. Willy pulled his goggles down and gripped the wheel with one gloved hand and put the fingers of the other on the all-important ignition interrupter. Everything—the wheel, the column, the quadrants, the rudder bar, the edges of the cockpit— was slippery with oil. He pressed his feet against the rudder bar, took a deep breath, and braced himself.

Hardy stood by the propeller. Willy turned to look at André standing beside the cockpit and the chief instructor bobbed his head at him. This was it. Everybody was watching.

"Ready!" Willy said. It sounded like a hoarse gasp to him. He peered around the side of the cockpit to see Hardy at the front of the machine. The mechanic gripped a blade of the propeller, then swung.

The engine did not start.

"Ignition off," Hardy said calmly.

Willy held the button down. *"Off!"* Not quite a gasp this time. Maybe something was wrong with the engine, he almost hoped. Maybe he wouldn't have to —

Hardy pulled the propeller through a revolution and poised his hands on the topmost blade. "Ignition on," he directed.

"On!"

The cylinders spurted smoke as the engine caught. Hardy darted out of the way. A blast of air and a fine mist of oil struck Willy's face as the propeller swirled smoke and oil spray up over the wings and back into the cockpit. The noise of the engine and the violent shaking of the machine alarmed him. He blipped the engine off, then on again before it stopped. Each time he switched the power on, the tachometer needle danced crazily and he could feel the entire fuselage twist to the left with a jerk and could see the wings shake.

André slapped the upper longeron and moved away. Keeping his fingers ready on the button, Willy allowed the engine to rev up. He had not anticipated so much noise and vibration, so many things to think about. All of a sudden he was moving. He cut the ignition off, then on. The machine was rumbling slowly over the ground, crawling. He let the engine run a little longer. The machine pulled toward the left. He immediately cut the engine and pushed the rudder yoke hard — too hard — and the machine suddenly turned sharply to the right. He was starting to turn in a circle. The fact that the wheels were castored made it all the worse; the machine wanted to go everywhere but where he wanted it to go.

He cut the ignition again momentarily. He could not make the thing steer straight. It seemed to have mind of its own. He had moved all of two dozen feet from his starting point. But veering now to the left, now to the right, power on, power off, he described a crazy, zigzag path across the grass, moving not much faster than walking speed. He lost all sight or even thought of the flag. He could hardly see out of the goggles anyway because of the oil spray. The mechanic had to leave the flag and run for yards to meet him when he finally managed to reach the end of the field. The mechanic pushed the tail of the plane around and pointed Willy toward the distant school hangars some two miles away.

Willy took another deep breath and let the engine run. As he had done in front of the hangar, he almost immediately started to turn in a circle to the left. The mechanic, who had unwisely stayed too close to the plane, had to run a second time — to avoid being chased down!

Now he was heading in the wrong direction, and now of course the stubborn thing wanted to go straight. André had warned them that there was a gully at the end of the flying field and then a slope upward of about twenty feet to another field beyond. He was still a good distance from the gully but in fright held the ignition off until the engine died.

Totally disgusted with himself, Willy sat uselessly in the cockpit while the now cautious mechanic turned him around once more and restarted the engine. He then moved well to one side and flung his arm up and down in the direction of the hangars.

Yes, yes, I know, Willy mouthed. That was the whole idea.

By this time thoroughly cowed by the little engine (who would have thought it could put out so much power?), he again demonstrated the ground-turning capabilities of the machine (it could hardly be called an aeroplane, the way he was using it) as he slowly made his uncertain zigzag way back across the field until finally, thankfully, he could again hold the ignition off until the propeller stopped turning. At least he had ended up within shouting distance of the apron in front of Hangar One.

André hurried over and stood beside the cockpit. Willy started to get out but André motioned him to stay put.

"*Reposez-vous une moment, Weelee.*"

Willy released his iron grip on the wheel and took his feet off the rudder bar. The muscles in his arms and legs were aching, his fingers were cramped. He lifted the goggles and wiped his oily, sweating face. The treacherous engine was now innocently still. Heat waves rose from it.

"You are too tense," André was saying. "You are trying too hard. It is not necessary to force the aeroplane. Do it once more. You have already learned much. You have learned how *not* to do it. This time try to anticipate the movements and correct them gently, gently. And let it go a little faster. It is more easy to control that way."

He grinned and patted Willy's shoulder again and went to stand near the tip of one wing, where he gave Willy encouraging nods. Willy was not encouraged. The others had been allowed only one round trip across the field. Had he done so wretchedly that André thought he needed an immediate second one?

He tugged his gloves up at the wrists and pulled his goggles back down, and indicated his readiness to Hardy. The engine started at once and picked up revolutions. This time as the machine responded to the gyroscopic effect of the spinning cylinders and crankcase and propeller he was prepared. He tried to maintain a light and steady pressure on right rudder, willing his tense legs to relax. *Gently, gently.* He craned his head to one side and saw that the nose was pointing at the flag. He was going straight.

A little too much rudder. The flag shifted to the left of the nose as he began veering to the right. Ease up on the rudder, he told himself; the engine will pull you back to center.

Relax, relax. The nose was again pointed at the flag.

With only a moderate amount of weaving, mostly with his head as he shifted his view from one side of the cockpit to the other, he progressed in a more or less straight line toward the flag. He was moving more rapidly than the first time, but still barely faster than a man could trot. All three wheels were firmly on the ground. No matter. He was beginning to get the hang of the thing. The flag was just ahead. In fact if he kept on going he would run right over it. It was easy after all!

The return trip started out well. He didn't have to keep moving his head from side to side to keep his objective in sight; you could see the hangar peaks over the nose. An American flag hung limply from a staff on top of Hangar One.

Locking his eyes on Old Glory, he let the engine run. *Anticipate*. A little more right rudder. The machine picked up speed and he could feel it wanting to turn to the left, but with constant pressure on the rudder the nose remained dead-center on the hangars.

He was elated!

Now he was moving as fast as a man could run, and still going straight. André was right: it was easier to go straight if the plane went faster. The rudder gave more leverage, with less effort of his feet, because there was more wind pressure on it. That would be true of the elevator too, wouldn't it?

He still had more than half the field to go. Plenty of room. He would show Harriet Quinlan how it was really done.

With the engine running full speed, he eased the wheel forward. The tail lifted immediately and the nose dipped until he could see the entire shape of Hangar One looming straight ahead. He was racing across the field on both front wheels, just as Harriet had, but much faster then she had.

His speed suddenly frightened him . . . the rumbling and shaking and roaring . . . the blast of the propeller wash . . .

As he entered the shallow spot in the field his speed gathered even more. In panic he pulled the wheel back with both hands to get the tail back down, forgetting the ignition button entirely. The nose of the machine instantly shot up into the air and the tail wheel bounced hard on the ground. His hands were so rigidly glued to the wheel that the jar made him involuntarily push the wheel forward. Now the front wheels slammed against the ground and the tail bounced again and all at once the machine careened violently to the left. The left wingtip nearly scraped the turf. All he was aware of in the next few seconds was that he was heading full tilt toward the side of the field—on only the left main wheel he was later told—and before he could recover enough presence of mind to cut the engine . . . disaster struck. The machine stopped abruptly as if it had run into a wall as the left wheel hit something and the nose dug into the ground. The rear of the fuselage shot up at a forty-five-degree angle and leaned to one side. His forehead banged against the front crossbrace and the wheel jammed into his chest. Then . . . silence.

By the time he was able to climb out of the upended machine on the side that was leaning and could see what had happened André and the mechanics and the male students had reached him. He would never have thought he would be so glad to get out of an aeroplane.

The left landing gear strut was cracked, its wheel broken loose from the axle and twisted. Both blades of the propeller were shattered. Fortunately, the wingtip resting in the grass didn't appear to be damaged, or not badly so.

André looked at Willy anxiously and saw that he was unhurt. (He was, except for a severe headache he would become conscious of later.) Then André sadly surveyed the wreck.

"Congratulations, Mr. Reynolds," he said reproachfully. "You have succeeded in finding the only hole in this entire field. I will see that it is filled at once."

His fellow students voiced their sympathy.

"What rotten luck, Willy."

"You were doing great until you hit the hole."

"It wasn't your fault. You couldn't know there was a hole in the field."

As sadly as André, Willy looked at the abused machine in its unnatural position. It was definitely *hors de combat* for the rest of the day, and probably for several days. The only consolation was that the accident had happened after the others had had their lesson in it. That and the fact that the school could not very well charge him for the repairs. The hole wasn't his fault. And if they did charge him it didn't matter. They could deduct it from his breakage deposit and unused tuition and refund whatever was left, if anything.

He wouldn't be taking any more lessons. His parents would be happy.

But in the final analysis it *was* his fault. It wasn't an "accident." He had completely lost control. The hole shouldn't have been there, but he should have kept the damn thing on course. He should have cut the engine as soon as it careened. He shouldn't have tried to lift the tail off the ground in the first place.

As he walked back to the hangar—crept back, it felt like—stronger even than his chagrin over the accident was his mortification that it had happened in full view of Harriet Quinlan. She was standing by the chairs and gave him a concerned look as he approached. She made as if to say something but he kept his eyes on the ground and shuffled past her. He didn't want her to see him crying. All he wanted was to get the hell out of the coveralls and the hell away from the place.

Three times he had come to the aerodrome with high expectancy and anticipation, and twice now he was leaving it in acute embarrassment.

Well, it would be the last time.

6

HE HURRIED into the lavatory—just in time, before he humiliated himself completely in front of everyone—and threw up, then stripped off his coveralls, praying that others were still looking at the wreck and that he could leave without encountering anyone. He hung the helmet and goggles on a peg in the locker room, for the last time. He would leave them there. The school could have them.

In the minute it had taken to make the shamefaced walk from the scene of his fiasco he had solidified the painful decision. Whether or not the school charged him for the repairs to the plane, and even if they let him continue with the course, he was going to quit. He was not meant to fly. It was not at all like he had expected.

What an understatement! From the instant Hardy had spun the propeller the first time he had realized that he had absolutely no feel for the aeroplane. Oh, the second time he'd thought he had, when he was moving straight over the ground toward the flag, but he was only kidding himself. Coming back he hadn't just lost complete control of it; he'd never really had control to begin with. If the hole hadn't stopped him he would have gone clear off the field and possibly smashed the trainer up even worse. His first time in an aeroplane under power and he had wrecked a beautiful machine and made an utter fool of himself in front of his classmates.

Most telling of all: he had been plain scared—*plane* scared—, sick to his stomach, even before he got in the damned thing, and in the end terrified. The stirring of fear and doubt he'd briefly experienced when he was practicing in the hangar was nothing compared to what he felt now. He was still shaking. If he couldn't handle the primary trainer on the ground, how could he possibly control an advanced trainer in the air? The thought of going up alone in one of those powerful machines—assuming he could even have gotten that far—almost made him vomit again.

When he emerged from the dressing room Harriet was standing in the hangar beside the fifty-horsepower monoplane. It was as if she had been waiting for him.

"Are you leaving?" she said.

She was the last person he wanted to see him slinking away.

"I think I'd better, don't you?"

She frowned and searched his face. "You were really doing quite well, William. You—"

"Oh yes, hah-hah."

"Honestly you were, until it got away from you for a minute.

You just tried to do too much. Perhaps André shouldn't have made you practice a second time, so soon."

If anyone had told him the previous Saturday that this woman—girl, really—who had flounced into the office with her flowered hat and parasol would less than a week later be consoling him for his ineptitude in an aeroplane, instead of the other way around, he would have laughed in their face.

He thought he heard voices approaching the hangar.

"I have to go. I have an exam this afternoon and I should do some studying at home. Excuse me."

"Listen—could you wait a minute? We obviously won't be able to do any more today. Uh . . . I was thinking I might take you up on your offer of a lift into Garden City. I can catch the train there. It's still early enough to put in a full day's work at my office. I brought my things from the hotel. I can be ready in a jiffy."

His mind was still in a fog of self-recrimination. "Well . . . all right," he said absently. "If you want. I'll wait for you in the parking lot."

Any other time, under any other circumstances, he would have been thrilled by her request. But she had only made it because she felt sorry for him. He didn't want her solicitude.

He had the engine started and the car backed around when she appeared in the walking-skirt version of her costume and with a scarf tied around her head. She got into the front passenger seat and placed her purse and a small overnight bag beside her. Without looking at her he pulled out onto Clinton Road.

Any other time, under any other circumstances, he would have driven slower than the limit, to make it last, but he sped up until the noise of the car and the wind precluded any attempt at conversation. He didn't want to hold a conversation and Harriet didn't try to initiate one, until he pulled up to the Long Island Railroad terminal in Garden City.

She removed the scarf but made no move to get out of the car. "Listen, William. I know you feel bad about what happened. But you mustn't let that—"

"I'm quitting. Before I smash up another aeroplane." He stared at the steering wheel.

"You don't mean that. Don't you know that some of the best fliers have been the slowest to learn? Almost every student has some kind of breakage. I'm sure we'll all have our share, maybe even worse than yours. And yours wasn't really that bad. I'll bet Hardy will have it repaired by Saturday."

He fervently hoped so, for the others' sakes. But she hadn't seen the wreck up close.

"Even Louis Blériot had crash after crash at first, William. In fact he got so good at crashing he used to throw himself out onto the wing every time he landed!"

She laughed and he allowed himself to meet her eyes for the first time since she had given him the "O.K." sign after her grasscutting run. Her face became sober and she peered at him frankly, genuine concern in her eyes.

He looked away, hating her concern; it made him feel even more useless, and acutely conscious of the gap in their ages. Why should it matter to her what he did? At the same time he was grateful to her.

"I don't know. Not everybody can fly. Maybe I'm one of them."

"Isn't it just a bit premature to make that conclusion, William? You've hardly had time to give it a chance. All you need is to gain confidence in yourself. Once you achieve confidence in yourself, and in your machine, you'll be able to do anything."

She laughed again. "That's not original with me. I got it from Alfred Moisant. André says the same thing. It's true."

"I don't know," he repeated. "I don't want to be the . . . class clown."

"Come on, you don't believe that. Are you going to go home and mope and feel sorry for yourself, William? I wouldn't have thought that of you."

"Look . . . Harriet. I appreciate your—your trying to . . . I don't know why you're bothering."

"Because I think you're a very nice boy and because, well . . . I happen to know how you feel about aeroplanes. I think you may have expected too much. From the aeroplane, or from yourself. But I also think you have the makings of a fine aviator. Maybe better than all of us."

She didn't have to go that far. But he was no longer quite so disgusted with himself. If she had intended to try to make him feel better, and obviously she had—why, he didn't know—she was succeeding. He allowed himself to look at her again. God, she was so terribly pretty.

She started to lift her bag. "Well . . . I'd better see about my train. One should be about due. They run frequently."

He came out of his gloom.

"Hey—I just thought. It's silly for you to take the train when I'm going in the same direction. Why don't I drop you off at the Brooklyn Bridge trolley stop? It's not too far from where I live."

It wasn't a very good idea; the train would be much faster and take her directly into Pennsylvania Station on Manhattan. A better idea occurred to him.

"As a matter of fact, why don't I drive you to your office? It's only across the river."

"Oh no," she protested. "That would really be out of your way. It's nice of you to offer but it isn't necessary at all."

"I've never driven in Manhattan traffic," he said quickly. "I need the practice." He had never driven in much traffic at all, to tell the truth.

She looked at him dubiously. "A weekday morning is hardly the recommended time to do that."

She sat holding her bag in her lap. She was actually considering the suggestion.

"Well, we *could* go through Queens instead of Brooklyn and take the Queensboro Bridge over to Fifty-ninth Street," she said. "That way you wouldn't have to fight the traffic all the way up to midtown and back again."

He was already fishing in the pouch under the dash for an old League of American Wheelmen bicycling map of Long Island. He unfolded it and they both studied it. It wasn't much good, so many new streets and roads had been laid out on Long

Island since the map had been published. He didn't know why they didn't get a new one from the automobile association.

He couldn't see anything on the map anyway. Harriet's face was so close to his that all he was aware of was how clear her skin was, how soft her dark hair looked.

"I know the way," she said. "All we have to do is get onto Queens Boulevard and that will take us to the bridge. Then over to Fifth Avenue and straight down that. My building's at Two-twenty-five. The Leslie-Judge Building."

He started the car moving before she could have second thoughts.

Traffic became increasingly congested as they progressed through Queens toward the Queensboro Bridge. Automobile ownership was proliferating in the New York area at a tremendous rate. There were supposed to be half a million automobiles in the United States, at least sixty-five thousand in New York State alone, and most of those, Willy would have bet, must be going in and out of Manhattan Island at any one time. They'd clocked as many as four hundred automobiles a day on the Long Island Motor Parkway alone, and that wasn't even near Manhattan.

New York must be the most motorized city in the world, he thought, although there were still a lot of horse-drawn vehicles.

As far as he was concerned it couldn't be too soon when horses were supplanted entirely. Their drivers seemed to consider themselves exempt from any rules of the road, charging through intersections, pulling out from the curb in front of you in blithe confidence of your ability to stop on a dime, plodding along and hogging the way, making U-turns right in front of oncoming traffic. Not to mention the animals' droppings, whose flattened residue dotted the pavement.

Not that automobile drivers were all that courteous or considerate or law-abiding. They were equally as unconcerned with their precipitate maneuvers and constant jockeying for advantage. There was a steady blast of horns, both at other vehicles and at crisscrossing pedestrians, who seemed to be as confident of your ability to avoid them as the horse drivers were. Everyone thought the road belonged to him alone. Fortunately, at the major intersections there were policemen imposing some sort of discipline on the traffic. Otherwise it would have been sheer pandemonium.

There was talk of requiring everybody to get a license before they were allowed to drive an automobile, like professional chauffeurs had to, even making them take a proficiency test. It might be a good idea.

Yet it was exciting and exhilarating and it really seemed like no time before they were across the bridge and he had worked them along Fifty-ninth Street to Fifth Avenue, where he turned left. They passed the recently opened public library at Forty-second Street, on whose wide steps and plaza the Court of Honor for the Hudson-Fulton Celebration had stood, and started sailing and bumping over the pavement down the long grade to Twenty-sixth Street, and for once that day he was not annoyed when a horse-drawn wagon lunged out from the curb just ahead of him and he deftly slipped into the vacated spot, directly across from Two-twenty-five Fifth Avenue.

He set the brake and blew out an exaggerated *whew* through pursed lips and grinned at Harriet.

"Well now," she said. "Anyone who can negotiate a car through Manhattan traffic should have no trouble handling a monoplane."

Not true, but he was rather swelled by his accomplishment. "If this is what it's like in midmorning I'd hate to see it at rush hour," he said.

"You ought to see it around five o'clock. There's nothing but a steady stream of cars and trucks going past our building."

He looked across the avenue. The Leslie-Judge Building was a very square and very solid-looking structure squatting on the entire block above Madison Square Park. Of stone the first two stories, pale red brick above that, it was about ten stories in all, with a lot of ornamental stonework around the upper stories. Quite imposing.

"It's nice that you have the use of a car to go to the aerodrome," Harriet said. "Or is it yours?"

"Oh no. My father's."

He belatedly remembered a codicil of his agreement with the Chalmers's owner: his promise to have the car back in Brooklyn on his flying lesson days by nine o'clock so that it would be available if his father needed it. He could still make it. And if he didn't, well, his own need had been greater this day.

"How many horsepower is it?"

"Thirty. Just like our trainer."

He was sorry she'd asked. It only reminded him of the accident, which he'd almost started to forget in the excitement of the drive, and of the fact that the machines used for actual flying were nearly twice as powerful.

"I used to have a little runabout when I lived in San Francisco," Harriet said, "but I wouldn't have one here. Not only the traffic but where can you park anymore? Garages want an arm and a leg."

She seemed to be in no hurry to go. He turned the ignition off. It was a relief to have the noise and vibration stop. Now all they had to contend with was the clatter of cars and wagons going past.

"You lived in San Francisco?"

"Yes. I was born in California. I wrote dramatic criticism for the San Francisco Dramatic Review and later did reporting and features for the Chronicle and Call-Bulletin. About two years all told. I've been with Leslie's going on seven years."

"You missed the earthquake then."

She smiled soberly. "I missed the earthquake. Unfortunately a portrait of me that used to hang in the old Bohemian Club wasn't so lucky. Both it and the club were destroyed."

He said, "Oh . . ?" but she didn't offer to elaborate. Then he thought: seven years with *Leslie's*? And a couple of years in San Francisco before that?

"Ah . . . may I ask . . . how old are you, Harriet?

She turned her head away, observing people passing by on

the sidewalk, then turned it back and, phrasing it somewhat oddly, he thought, said, "If you were to check my employment record at Leslie's you'd find I turned twenty-seven on the first of May."

Twenty-seven. Two years more than he had guessed. But he should have realized. It was surprising she was not older than that. She would have been barely 17 when she had started her career nine years before, in 1902, when he was still in knee britches. What an exceptionally talented person she was.

"And you're what, William. How old?"

"Twenty-one. In October."

"Oh . . . I thought you might be somewhat older. But of course you said you were only a sophomore in college. You seem very mature for your age."

He was flattered, but it did nothing to ameliorate the fact that the gap between them was more than a matter of their ages.

"You must lead a very exciting life, Harriet. Seeing all the latest plays, hobnobbing with theater people. People like the Vanderbilts."

"You mean Helen? Listen, William, there are *the* Vanderbilts and then there are Vanderbilts. Helen isn't in the Commodore's line. She's also not the type to trade on the name.

"I guess it is exciting, although it's not always as glamorous as it may appear on the surface. I've only been the regular dramatic critic since Nineteen-eight and I still write articles on many other subjects besides the theater. I've been privileged to take two trips overseas for Leslie's and I've even freelanced a few screenplays for a man named D. W. Griffith, who makes motion pictures for the Biograph Company. But yes, I really love my work, especially now in being able to combine it with learning to fly, which I'm beginning to believe I'll eventually love most of all. Someday, though, I'd like to retire and write books."

"That's a long way off, I'm sure," he said. "I mean retiring."

She smiled and looked away again and seemed to be thinking of something for a moment. Then with a quick glance and another smile at him, "I guess I'd better be going."

"I've never seen a play," he said suddenly. "I mean, not a Broadway play."

He intended nothing by the statement. It was spoken only out of the consciousness of the ordinariness of his own life and his own person compared to her life and her person, and because he didn't want these moments with her to end.

"Really? We must remedy that sometime. I often get complimentary tickets to plays, in addition to my critic's privilege. But it's the summer doldrums now. Perhaps in the fall when the new season opens."

He could hardly believe his ears. "That would be wonderful, Harriet."

"Well, I really must go. I want to go home and bathe and change my clothes before I go to the office."

"You live near here?"

"Just a block over, at Twenty-seventh and Broadway. The Hotel Victoria. Very convenient."

She opened the door and got out. She glanced down the street, then closed the door and looked at him.

"If you're going to Brooklyn, William, probably the best way is to take Canal Street to the Manhattan Bridge. Broadway runs into Fifth Avenue at the Flatiron Building." She pointed toward the famous landmark at the other end of Madison Square. "Just stay on Broadway to Canal Street."

He knew that, but nodded his thanks.

"Well, thank you for the ride, William. I hope you'll think over what I said and that I'll see you at the aerodrome on Saturday. I'm not going to let you quit!"

He watched her walk away until she disappeared around the corner, then got out and restarted the car.

The Chalmers had wings.

7

WILLY REYNOLDS was a hopeless case from then on as far as Harriet Quinlan was concerned. He was in love with her, and the realization that he was both exhilarated and stunned him.

How fast it had happened! How much he had learned about her in the space of a morning. He almost wished he hadn't. All he wanted to do was learn to fly; he didn't need this kind of complication in his life.

Why did she have to be 27 or he only 20? Of course, he would be 21 in October, but six and a half years' difference was hardly any better than seven.

Yet it wasn't the actual age difference that mattered so much. Six years (he was already disregarding the five months between their birthdays) was not all that great; it was where you started counting. If he were 27 he would be established in life, be in a position to consider a serious commitment to a girl. The fact that Harriet would then be 33 would be inconsequential.

She'd said he was very mature for his age. But he was still only 20, still only a college sophomore. She'd called him a nice "boy."

She'd mentioned the possibility of getting tickets to the theater sometime. But there had really been no implication that they would go together, however much he replayed her words searching for such an implication. They had merely been spoken on the spur of the moment.

What an amazing person she was. It was almost unbelievable how much she had accomplished in her young life, rising to a top position with one of the nation's leading publications at

24, if she had been made dramatic critic for *Leslie's Weekly* in 1908.

He wondered how she had been able to squeeze in finishing school in France. Did one go to finishing school after high school or in lieu of high school? It had to be the latter, otherwise she couldn't possibly have started her journalistic career as early as 18. She had even driven her own car in 1902—hardly anybody had a car in 1902—and apparently had been the toast of San Francisco with her portrait in what he assumed must have been some kind of businessmen's club.

Harriet Quinlan was not only six years his senior but was so far beyond him in every other way that it was patently ridiculous to think she would remotely consider a romantic relationship with him. (Nor, truth to tell, would he ever have thought he would want to have one with an older woman.)

Yet, he argued with himself again, six years wasn't such a tremendously great difference, was it? Even six and a half, if you insisted on being exact. If he was mature seeming for his age— she'd said he was—and she young looking for hers—which she certainly was—it was not completely outside the realm of possibility, was it? But that only brought him back to the question of why such a beautiful and accomplished woman would even for a minute consider having anything to do with him, other than as a fellow flying student. What did he have to offer her?

He wondered why she wasn't married already. She must meet all kinds of similarly accomplished and probably wealthy men in her work. The certainty that she must, the fact that Harriet Quinlan must have any number of far more eligible men to choose from, would have left him in abject hopelessness—except for one other fact, and he dwelled on it: the undeniable fact that she had extended herself much, much more than would have been necessary to make a clumsy, disconsolate "boy" feel better.

After all, she could have simply taken the train from Garden City.

~ ~

He'd gotten a call from André Thursday evening, on the fatal yet wonderful day, a call he had dreaded even as he basked in thoughts of the ride with Harriet.

But the damage had really been fairly minor. Willy had cracked the undercarriage and the propeller but had done no damage to the Gnôme's delicate cylinders. And although Willy had precipitated the accident, the school had taken into account the fact that he had run into a hole that shouldn't have been there, André said, and had decided to split the cost of the repairs. Willy's half would be a hundred and fifty dollars. That would still leave a hundred in his breakage deposit. André not only made no suggestion that Willy give up the idea of flying but took some of the sting out of his humiliation by telling him that Hardy was confident he would have the trainer repaired in plenty of time for the Saturday lesson.

That was comfort. At least he wouldn't be holding the others back. Indeed, you could even say he had done his fellow students a favor by giving them a good object lesson.

Hardy needn't have hurried. Another rainy, windy day was dawning when Willy awoke on Saturday, and he was glad; they wouldn't be using the trainer in this weather and he could stay home in good conscience. He would miss a laboratory session but he could catch up on that somehow. It would give him three extra days to think about Harriet, and to persuade himself that no one considered the accident to have been his fault. Before the weekend was over he was almost able to believe it wasn't his fault, and his eagerness to learn to fly had returned.

Fair weather was back by Tuesday. Willy took his time getting to the aerodrome, not worrying if he was the last again. The trainer was parked in its usual spot in front of the first hangar, appearing to be as good as new. Harold, Shakir and Ferdinand were standing near it, watching André and Hardy "preflighting" it for the day's lesson.

He approached them diffidently, wondering how they would react at seeing him again.

To his relief they greeted him without surprise, as if nothing had happened. None of them referred to the accident.

He had just begun to wonder where Harriet was when he saw her figure emerging from the second hangar. She smiled at him as she came up to the group, but not particularly brightly, no more brightly than she smiled at the others; certainly not in the *special* way that in his daydreaming he had hoped she might — with some subtle indication of acknowledgment that his decision to continue the course had anything to do with her (*"I'm not going to let you quit!"*), that it was a "secret" they shared.

Well of course. She could not know that he had really rejoined the class because he could not contemplate never seeing her again.

He could hardly tell her that, not in so many words, not right now, not right here. He tried to hint at it though, with looks and smiles and with the hope that she might give some sign that she might want to hear such words. And when in impatience he decided to say the words anyway and at the first chance when none of the others was near them, planting himself directing in front of her and giving her his most engaging smile, started with, "Well, I came back . . ," she merely nodded and said, "Yes, I see," and then pretended that something had caught her attention and moved away and started talking to somebody else.

He had another chance, a better one, a few minutes later, when André started a test run in the repaired trainer and the noise of the engine gave him an excuse to come up close to Harriet again.

"Do you need another ride today?" he said casually and lightly. "I've got the car again."

"No," she replied, her eyes following the trainer's progress. "Thanks anyway."

"I really enjoyed the one we had on Thursday. I'd like to do it again. I still need practice in Manhattan traffic."

He laughed, also casually and lightly. She was still looking off into the distance. He took the plunge.

"I thought about you all weekend, Harriet. I'd like to see you — away from here, I mean."

It would be too brash to suggest an evening date. "I was wondering . . . perhaps we could have lunch sometime? I'm in the city nearly every day . . ."

She shook her head, still not looking at him.

"No, that wouldn't be possible. Thank you, William, but I'm either too busy to do more than grab a bite from the cafeteria in the building or if I do take time for lunch it's usually with someone I'm interviewing."

Some handsome actor? he wondered.

"Well, perhaps dinner then? I owe you at least that much. If it weren't for you I wouldn't have come back at all. You know that, don't you?"

No response. He plunged the rest of the way.

"You're extremely attractive, Harriet. You're the most attractive woman I've ever met. Are you, uh, going with anyone?"

She turned then and the look she cast at him was not unfriendly, but frosty enough.

"Look, William. I merely thought you needed cheering up. Don't read any more into it than that. I'm glad you decided to come back, but we all have a lot of work ahead of us. Please don't spoil things by . . ."

She didn't need to finish. She gave him a tight-lipped smile and walked away.

He stood there, instantly sobered. What had he been thinking of, to make such a clumsy, blatant overture to a woman like Harriet Quinlan? Yet he was more than a little perplexed. Even before his bungled approach her manner had been definitely cool, and her reaction to his forwardness seemed all out of proportion to whatever offense he had apparently given her.

It was crazy, but it was as if she were retracting the graciousness she'd shown him the day of the accident. It was almost as if she regretted having told him so much about herself. In any case, she was making it rather clear that she welcomed no advances from him on a personal level. Everything he'd let himself think she might have been telling him with her concern for him and interest in his plans had all been only in his imagination. All his thinking and thinking and thinking about "possibilities" had been . . . *stupid*.

Well, he'd had to try; he wouldn't have been able to live with himself if he hadn't tried. But he had never forced himself on any girl, and he certainly wasn't going to do so again with Harriet Quinlan. She obviously considered herself out of his class. And, as his better judgment had told him at the outset, obviously she was.

He was crestfallen and abashed and, a little later when he watched Harriet complete another perfect (in his eyes) run across the field and back, jealous.

After all the others had finished their turns at grasscutting, each of them this day making at least two trips back and forth between hangar and flag, André came up to him and said, "Why are you not dressed, *Weelee*? You wish to learn to fly, do you not?"

Willy ran to the locker room.

After directing him to get into the trainer, André told Willy sternly not to attempt so much this time. Do not permit the engine to speed too fast. Do not attempt to run on the front wheels only. It was not necessary to remind this particular pupil what could happen if he did, whether or not there was another hole to run into.

"The—what is the word?—the cockiness has been knocked out of you. Yes, that is the word. That is good. Now think of the aeroplane as like a woman. She wishes to be courted, to be treated gently. Not, uh, manhandled."

André's forgiveness of the accident helped ease Willy's mind, though he still was filled with apprehension and self-doubt. André had pegged him aright: he had been cocky before, and it had most emphatically been knocked out of him. But André didn't know that he was here now only because of Harriet. But she'd merely felt sorry for him. It really meant nothing to her if he was here or not. Harriet Quinlan was interested only in Harriet Quinlan. So the hell with her.

He did feel a little more at home in the pilot's seat this time.

He had a better idea of what to expect. He knew what he had done wrong and was resolved not to make the same mistake again. He had been too rough with the machine. No inordinate strength was required to control an aeroplane. Harriet's performances were proof of that.

The Gnôme was started. As it revved up he willed himself to rest one hand *lightly* on the wheel, the thumb of the other hand *lightly* on the ignition interrupter, his feet *lightly* on the rudder yoke. He tried to forget that people were watching him, tried to ignore the intimidating roar of the engine, the vibrating of the frame, tried to forget Harriet Quinlan, although he thought that she might also be watching him. Out of the corner of his eye he saw her standing beside a car parked next to the administration building, chatting with its occupants and once or twice glancing toward the field.

André signaled the mechanics and students who were holding the plane back to let go and the craft leaped forward. Willy's progress was still more or less erratic, the machine still wanted to wander off course, but he trimmed the daisies at a respectable pace, and the man waiting to turn him around did not have to run to meet him.

As he neared the hangar on his return André advanced into the field and was churning his hand in a circle and pointing toward the far end. Willy understood: he was to turn the machine around himself and make another trip.

It was easy enough to do. After all, he had almost made a complete circle the very first minute on the first day!

He handled the machine even better on this attempt and at the end of the field waved the mechanic away and turned himself around. Coming back he was sure he could have gotten the plane up on its two main wheels and kept it straight and under control, but he obeyed André's warning.

He cut the ignition and rolled to a stop in front of the hangar. He had accomplished four round trips across the field—two today and two on Thursday. Well, three and a half; he hadn't completed the second one. But he had aggregated at least fifteen minutes' time at the controls of an aeroplane to record in his logbook.

He was so elated he wished he could have tried yet another cutting of ze grass. He felt he had begun to achieve a degree of skill, if scarcely as yet anything approaching real competence. But the tenseness in his arms and legs told him he had been in the machine long enough for one day.

"Excellent, *Weelee*," André said to him as he climbed out. "It is not so difficult, *n'est-ce pas*? You are learning true confidence. A few more times like that and you will be ready to try the kangarooing."

Willy accepted the praises of his fellows as he walked over to where they had all been watching. Had he really once thought himself superior to them, knowing all about aeroplanes? Now he was happy just to be their equal, although still the laggard of the class.

He looked around for Harriet but she was nowhere to be seen. The car was gone. His elation drained away. Couldn't she have stayed just a few extra minutes to say a word of congratulation to him?

For the next few lesson days Willy deliberately avoided close proximity to Harriet, as he had at the beginning of their training, standing at distance from her whenever the students were in a group, pointedly ignoring her at other times. Now he did it not out of resentment at her presence in the class but from injured feelings. "*Don't spoil things*," she'd said. He had been rebuffed by a girl once or twice in his life but never the way Harriet had put him down. If she was going to accord him nothing more than casual, polite and unavoidable acknowledgment of his existence, well then, he thought, he wouldn't even give her that much.

It was absurdly adolescent of him, he knew, and he could not keep it up for long. He was only punishing himself.

He wondered if he had simply moved too fast with Harriet, coming on too strong and too soon. At the same time he felt a growing need to confront her (as if he had the slightest right to confront her) and tell her point-blank that he was in love with her (as, he had to admit, he still was, and was more and more each time he saw her).

But that would be much, much too strong. Better just to tell her he was very attracted to her and would honestly like to know what chance he stood, or didn't stand, with her.

No—not that either. Just start being friendly and nice to her as if nothing had happened, he decided. Just show her that he liked her a lot, and see what happened after that.

But there never seemed to be a good opportunity to speak more than a few words to her. There were always people around her, if not their classmates then Helen Vanderbilt and other friends of Harriet's who motored out to the aerodrome in gay parties to watch her practice.

And in the final analysis, he was afraid she might repulse him again if he said too much. So he continued to more or less keep his distance from her.

Hélas, as André might say, and did say more than once, the weather seemed bent on spoiling nearly every succeeding lesson day in the latter part of May and beginning of June, either with rain or mist or excessive winds. And as their mentor reminded them more than once, he considered any wind over six miles an hour to be too dangerous for his fledglings at this stage.

The unfavorable weather greatly diminished the number of spectators at the aerodrome, reducing them to a handful of curious souls who had nothing better to do than hang around even when it was announced that there would be no flying. The students were confined on the worst days to blackboard sessions inside the hangar, where they reviewed and reviewed an aeroplane's controls and were instructed in proper field procedure and were introduced to the theory of aircraft engine operation and airframe maintenance and watched, and sometimes assisted, Hardy with disassembling and reassembling an engine or learned how to rig an aeroplane's wings.

Willy didn't care. Despite his misery over Harriet, these were the happiest days of his life, the days when they were all still groundlings. He tried for a while to nurse back his resentment of her, but that was childish. He would have admired her even if he weren't in love with her. Eventually he was almost able to laugh at himself and the fantasies he had woven—still wove—around her and was content just to be in her presence, as painful as her presence was to him, to steal long glances at her, looking away quickly if by chance her eyes turned toward his. Content in his discontent.

Once or twice he didn't look away. Once or twice their eyes met, for a moment, and he thought (wishful as the thought was) that there really was something in the way Harriet looked at him, and then looked away, that was different from the way she looked at anyone else.

On one rare day he was able to get in another grasscutting session and Harriet began kangarooing in one of the fifty-horsepower machines. A week later, on another good day, DeMurias and Jerwan and Kantner tried their hands at it. They were all ahead of him and he eventually began to get a little impatient. But there was no hurry. A few weeks' delay didn't matter.

Except to Harriet, especially when they heard near the end of the month that a woman named Blanche Stuart Scott, a student at the Curtiss school on Washington Avenue, had just made a short solo hop in a biplane, although without leaving the boundaries of the aerodrome. Harriet was more than ready herself, but André insisted she must wait for ideal conditions.

The sun came back again. First thing on every lesson day André would go out into the field with an anemometer and hold the device above his head to measure the wind. If the cups didn't move, or turned slowly enough, they would practice.

Harriet began making flights across the entire length of the aerodrome in what were essentially long kangaroo hops, staying in the air in a straight line at ten feet above the ground, allowing the plane to settle back down at the end, and then returning in the same manner. Ferdinand, Shakir and Harold also perfected their kangarooing and Willy, still confined to the low-powered trainer, polished his grasscutting technique.

One day he sat down beside Harriet in their little circle of chairs outside the hangar, only because there was no other vacant chair and it would have looked odd if he had merely stood there. Ferdinand, returning from a kangarooing trip, muttering in Spanish, regaled them with the tale of how he had run into an "air hole" and only by dint of expert manipulation of the controls had managed to bring the craft safely back to earth.

He described it so vividly and so earnestly that they all broke up with laughter. And when Harriet squeezed Willy's arm and looked at him with sparkling eyes his blood rushed.

Why had she done that?

This provoked a discussion with André as to whether there were such things as holes in the air, or "pockets," as the famous pilot Charles Willard claimed. André said he had never encountered one—*certainment* not at ten feet above the ground!

Harold Kantner then topped Ferdinand by relating how he had been attacked by a vicious sparrow during a kangarooing run. This made them laugh again.

"I'm going to use these stories in my next article," Harriet whispered to Willy. She leaned so close that he felt her breath on his cheek.

He soared. He had never seen her speak so confidentially with any of the others.

The same day Harriet made her first true flight. No more straight-line flying just above the ground. Now she was not only to reach a greater height but to make a one-hundred-eighty-degree turn in the air at the end of the field and come back and land.

Willy watched with consuming interest, as did everyone, as Harriet performed the assignment, the first of them to do so. She lifted off quickly and reached an altitude of perhaps sixty or seventy feet by midpoint over the field, then banked around neatly at the end in a left turn and came back toward the field again, landing almost exactly in her takeoff path. It took no more than five minutes.

André had her do it again, but this time telling her to make a right-hand turn in the air and fly back to the hangar end of the field and make then another right-hand turn to land in the same direction she had taken off.

She did not do so well this attempt. There seemed to be a little uncertainty in the first turn, the way the plane dipped and hesitated until she got it turned around. Then when she flew back, along the south side of the field, her second turn was too wide, causing her to come in at an angle to the getaway. Even so, it was an achievement none of the men had made, and fully deserving of the praise they heaped on her when she rejoined them.

Willy made exclamations along with the others but hesitated to voice his admiration directly to Harriet. As the most bumbling of all the students he did not think his congratulations would amount to very much. But he still felt the pressure of her squeeze on his arm and the breath of her intimate whisper on his cheek. He caught up with her as she walked toward her dressing room.

"You did just beautifully, Harriet."

She paused. "Thank you, William. It really wasn't as diffi-cult as I had expected, although I had a little trouble with the right turns. I don't know why."

"It's the torque. It makes the plane want to turn left."

"Umm, maybe. But I don't think that's the entire reason. It just seems more natural to turn left. I think probably because I'm right-handed. If that makes any sense."

She smiled at him, then resumed walking. And he proceeded to ruin everything.

"I thought you worked for a reputable magazine," he said bluntly, so bluntly that she stopped again and gave him a startled look.

He had read an article in *Leslie's*, which he'd begun looking for at the newsstands every week: "Who Invented the Aeroplane?" The article implied that but for a snag in his launching mecha-nism, Samuel Pierpont Langley's tandem-wing "Aerodrome" would have been the first aeroplane in history to carry a man in flight. The so-called "snag" had in fact occurred during two attempts by the director of the Smithsonian Institution to launch his machine from a houseboat on the Potomac River below Washington, the second occurring December 8, 1903, only nine days before the Wrights' first powered flights at Kitty Hawk. Langley's mechanic and would-be pilot, Charles M. Manly, had nearly drowned both times.

The article had incensed him. Why this attempt to take credit away from the Wrights, to make their glorious achievement seem like merely their good luck and Langley's failure merely his bad luck? The writer did not know what he was talking about. The Wrights had discovered that the tables of air pressure and wing designs used by Langley and Lilienthal and Chanute and everyone before them were all wrong. It was the Wrights alone who had discovered the principles of flight. Langley's machine, even though powered by one of the most advanced engines ever built up to that time, by Manly, had simply been incapable of flight.

Harriet listened impatiently as he spouted all this.

"I saw that article, William," she said evenly. "I can't say I read it—I really didn't pay any attention to it. We print a lot of articles on aviation. If you feel this strongly, write a letter to Leslie's. We try to be as accurate as possible. But in spite of what you apparently think, I am certainly not responsible for everything we print."

She was offended, and he was disgusted with himself. "Oh I didn't mean you were responsible. It's just that I thought that since you work for the magazine . . . Listen, I'm sorry. I—"

She wasn't listening. "Write a letter, Willy," she flipped over her shoulder.

He should have gone after her. He might have, if she hadn't called him Willy. Somehow, by dismissing him as mere "Willy," she could not have told him more plainly that neither he nor his opinions were of any interest to her.

8

I T WAS THE freely voiced acknowledgment of the four male students of the Moisant Flying School that Harriet Quinlan was the star of the class. If any of the other men had harbored doubts about having a female among them, or if any of them might have shared Willy Reynolds's first prejudiced suspicion that her participation was nothing more than a suffragette's exploit or a journalistic stunt, such reservations had long since been forgotten. They were proud to share in her reflected celebrity.

And if André at times displayed a degree of favoritism toward his female student, it was in Willy's eyes fully warranted. It seemed to him that Harriet had a natural flair for flying. By July she was making continuous circuits of the aerodrome and practicing the figure eights and precision landings that under the latest international rules were the basic requirements for the Aero Club of America's license, while he was just beginning to learn how to keep a fifty-horsepower machine in a straight line on the ground.

Word had spread that a woman was flying an aeroplane on Hempstead Plains. At dawn even on weekdays the parking area started filling up and by seven A.M. cars and carriages were lined up on both sides of Clinton Road. It was even worse on days when Harriet flew in the afternoon. Latecomers who could not find a seat in the small viewing stand crowded against a newly installed fence at the hangar end of the field behind which André restricted them, craning for a glimpse of the daring female.

Some would later say, as was said about the Wrights' early experiments, that Harriet Quinlan had learned to fly in secret. Yet not only did dozens and sometimes scores, if not hundreds, of people watch her as she perfected her skill, and not only were there stories about her in the newspapers, but as far back as late May *Leslie's Weekly* had published the first in her series of articles: "How A Woman Learns to Fly."

Willy had of course bought a copy of the issue and devoured every word of the article. It was illustrated by seven photographs taken by *Leslie's* photographers at the field one day.

At the top, the width of the page, was a narrow and rather indistinct picture of a monoplane in low flight. Centered below that was a full-length photograph, with the background cropped out, of Harriet in her now famous aviatrix's togs (*Leslie's* used the French *aviatrice*) standing with her right arm archly bent and the hand on her hip as she looked at the camera. To the left of that was a small picture of her climbing into a monoplane and to the right one of her sitting in the cockpit as "Monsieur Houpert (the caption said) illustrates the warping of the wings." Two more small pictures showed Hardy about to flip a propeller and, opposite it, mechanics holding a plane back "until the propeller reaches sufficient velocity to start the monoplane at a brisk pace."

Finally, centered at the bottom of the page, was another picture of "Miss Harriet Quinlan, Leslie's dramatic critic and the first woman in the world to fly with a monoplane."

This was a formal studio portrait. Dressed to the nines, beaded and behatted and begowned, her right hand resting on the arm of a chair, her left hand limp and open in her lap, Harriet looked unsmilingly at the camera lens.

He showed the article to his parents and told his father he was going to enter a subscription to the magazine in his name as a present. His father seemed pleased. "I'll read it," he said. "This is a good magazine."

"She's very attractive," Ellen Reynolds said when her husband passed the copy to her.

If a woman was capable of learning to fly an aeroplane, then it could not be all that difficult or dangerous. His mother didn't say that but Willy hoped that was what she was thinking. It was the reason he was showing his parents the article. He had never told them about his accident.

He stood behind his mother's chair and leaned over her shoulder as she looked at the pictures and told her what an amazing person Harriet Quinlan was, not realizing how much he told her.

"She must be quite a bit older than you," she said.

"A few years."

It was not a good picture of her, he thought. Too formal, too somber. But after his parents had read the article he carefully clipped out the picture and mounted it in a little frame and put it on his dresser. Later, *Leslie's* printed another photograph of Harriet to accompany the third installment of her flying adventure. This was a much, much better picture. It showed Harriet in a light summer gown and large hat, sitting sideways to the camera with her face turned toward it, smiling, and her hands on the end of a parasol. It might have been the same dress she'd worn and the same parasol she'd carried the first time Willy had seen her at the aerodrome.

Luckily, it was about the same size as the first photograph. He cut this one out and put it on top of the one already in the frame on his dresser.

He pored over everything Harriet wrote for *Leslie's*. Nearly every issue had an article by her about the New York theatrical scene. Her play reviews bore the general heading of "Through the Opera Glass" and she was forthright in her opinions, favorable or unfavorable. There were "not a dozen really good actors in the country," she stated in one article. Theater managers were "the most timid people in the world," caring only about the box office, she decreed in another.

He was a little disturbed to learn that she was a bit of a prude, or maybe more than a bit. In one article she savaged a play in which a female impersonator pranced about in women's clothes. She called it disgusting. In another she praised the city of Evanston, Illinois, for banning plays with profane or "suggestive" language and performances on Sunday. At the end of her reviews she always gave a list of wholesome plays "one may take his wife or daughter to."

Yet on the other hand she took to task subscribers who had complained about her running a picture of an actress named Gaby Deslys who had, or was having, a notorious "connection" with the king of Portugal. Why discriminate against Gaby, Harriet wrote, when equally notorious actresses such as Bernhardt are "received with acclaim in the homes of America's most aristocratic citizens?" She stopped short of calling the complainers outright hypocrites.

Harriet was a good writer, although, had infatuation not dulled his critical faculties, Willy would have admitted that her style seldom rose above, well, adequacy. But he was blind to any deficiency in her.

Hopelessly in her thrall, Willy Reynolds would not have brooked the slightest disparagement of Harriet Quinlan, had any been made. She was the bravest and most beautiful woman who had ever lived. She was an adornment to the world. Each time she flew he gazed at her with admiration, not unmixed with envy, and—it was a continual ache in his heart—with longing.

And now there was not just one aviatrix for the spectators to goggle at but two. Harriet had been joined by Alfred Moisant's younger sister, who had persuaded her brother to let her take flying lessons.

The day Willy first saw her upon his arrival at the field she was standing with André beside the primary trainer at its usual starting position in front of the hangar. For a second he thought it was Harriet. But while the female figure was dressed in knee-high boots and knickerbockers, her costume was brown instead of plum, and she was shorter than Harriet.

He watched as the woman began a grasscutting trip across the field, to his chagrin far better than he had done the first time. He didn't know when she'd had her hangar sessions but she demonstrated the same kind of natural aptitude as Harriet.

When she came back he was introduced to her. Matilde Moisant was a bright-faced, pretty woman of about 33 who wore glasses. He was to come to know her as a very friendly, likeable and unassuming person. That day, however, he was almost as resentful of her as he had once been of Harriet. Despite starting her lessons after him, he had a feeling that she was going to leap-frog over him.

She did. "'Tilde" soon entered the kangarooing stage and the other students advanced to actual flights and one-hundred-eighty-degree turns. Matilde used a plane with the number "13" painted on the rudder. She had been born on Friday the thir-teenth, she said, and that had always been her lucky number.

But the day eventually came when André decided that his youngest pupil had accumulated enough experience at keeping the grass and the daisies neatly cropped to aspire to higher things, if only a few feet higher.

André removed the elevator-limiter on the tail and gave Willy his instructions. He was at a most critical and important point, the instructor stressed, for once he lifted the aeroplane into the air it would be subject to tipping and it would be necessary to employ the wing-warping control to maintain its balance.

Try two hops at first, he said, perhaps three coming back. Feel the effect of the warping control. But on each hop do not permit the machine to rise more than a few feet.

"*Comprendez-vous?*"

Willy nodded. He comprehended all right. It shouldn't be all that difficult, he reassured himself. During his last few ses-sions in the fifty-horsepower Moisant he had felt the powerful machine reaching the point where just a slight pull back on the column would have put him in the air. But he was glad when he lowered his goggles and the trepidation inside him could not be seen on his face.

In his nervousness he began inauspiciously, swerving from side to side almost as badly as he had weeks before in his initial grasscutting attempts. He was nearly halfway across the field be-fore he had the machine under good control and up on its front wheels.

He was moving fast, going straight.

Now . . .

He pulled back gently on the wheel—or thought he did. The

nose abruptly shot up at a steep angle and he felt a jar as the
tailskid slammed against the ground. The impact bounced the
plane into the air, leaning toward the left. In another second he
would be heading toward the same kind of catastrophe he had
engineered that first day in the trainer. But he immediately
blipped off the ignition and the machine dropped back onto the
ground in a rocking "landing," the left wheel touching an instant before the right.

By this time he was too close to the end of the field to do a
second hop. He taxied to within a few yards of the edge of the
slope that led to the field beyond and turned around and sat for
moment, blipping the engine on an off, feeling the oily sweat
running down his cheeks. The mechanic waiting in case of need
started to approach but Willy waved him off with a motion indi-
cating that everything was all right, he was just resting.

He instructed himself: pull back on the wheel even more
gently this time, then as soon as you lift push it to neutral to level
the fuselage. Be prepared for the leftward tilt, counter it with
right warp. Remember to cut the power before you get too high.

This time he was up on the wheels in short order, the fuselage level with the ground, going straight. Ever so gently he pulled
the wheel toward him and the nose angled up slightly. He was
still running on the mains but the skid was not dragging.

A little more speed. Keep it straight. Okay, a little more angle.

He was up! He immediately neutralized the elevator and at
the same time moved the column to the right in anticipation of
the lean — overanticipating, for the right wing dipped sharply and
almost scraped the ground.

Heart pounding, he overcorrected again and the left wing
dipped, but not as much. A touch of right warp again.

He was so preoccupied with getting the wings level that he
was not aware that he had allowed the nose to rise and that he
was gaining too much height. When he realized this he eased
the wheel forward, trying not to introduce any sideways movement that would unbalance the wings. He saw with alarm that
the hangars were rushing toward him at a frightening pace and

he was much higher than he was supposed to be, at least twenty feet in the air. Panic seized him as it had the day of the crash and he cut the switch.

If that was all he had done, if he had let the fuselage remain parallel to the ground, the plane would have glided smoothly onto the wheels as it lost momentum and have landed itself. But he attempted to control the landing by pulling the nose up. The result was a three-point landing, but a hard, slamming, bouncing landing as the plane dropped to the ground. He was sure he must have damaged something. He was so unnerved that he let the engine die. Somehow he had drifted well to one side of the path he had started out on. The mechanics had to come up and push him to the apron in front of the hangars.

"Congratulations again, *Weelee*," André said. "You have just demonstrated what we call the stall, the loss of flying speed."

André meant no sarcasm, for he added immediately, "You took off very well your second time. You unbalanced but you recovered. You allowed the machine to rise too high, but you will not do so again, *n'est-ce pas*? Do you wish another turn? You must do more than the one hop in each direction. You must be able to rise and descend at will."

Willy shook his head. The few minutes in the aeroplane had seemed like hours and he was exhausted, physically as well as mentally. He was shaking.

"No . . . perhaps not," André said, observing him as he climbed down from the cockpit. "Think over what you did until the next lesson. You have learned much today."

So at last he had been in the air, for a few seconds. But it hadn't felt like flying, certainly not like he had always imagined it would feel.

He wanted to take off his oil-stained coveralls and slink away again, but it would have been rude of the class clown not to allow his fellows the chance to express their remarks about his performance.

"How high were you anyway, Willy?" Harold said. "Hit any birds?"

Willy grinned crookedly for answer. But he knew that behind their good-natured joshing there was encouragement. They
were all better than he was, but he was progressing.

On one sunny day near the end of July the class posed for a
group photograph on the field. Harriet and Matilde stood in the
center. The others crouched down on either side of them while
André squatted in front pretending to be pointing at something
as part of a lesson. Willy knelt at one end with one knee on the
ground, well away from Harriet.

He had tried even harder to avoid her after making his un-
called-for remarks about the article in *Leslie's*, although she
seemed to have forgotten it or dismissed it. At least she was as
pleasant to him as he had always been — no more and no less —
acknowledging him with a smile and a hello, for which he was
grateful. It was all he had to be grateful for.

On another day in late July he and Ferdinand and Harold
and Matilde were sitting in the chairs on the apron. As they
watched Harriet walk to her plane for another practice flight,
Matilde remarked to no one in particular, "I think she's the pret-
tiest girl I've ever seen. Those eyes of hers."

Yes, Willy thought, and wished he could be as relaxed and
natural with Harriet as he was with Matilde. But then he did not
entertain romantic fantasies about Matilde. He wondered if any
of the other men was in love with Harriet, and if not, why not.

When Harriet landed André called for Ferdinand to take a
turn at figure eights. The Cuban had caught up with Harriet
thanks to the bad weather that had grounded her so long. Harriet
sat down in the chair Ferdinand vacated and began chatting with
Matilde. Suddenly Harold, who had already flown that day,
jumped up. Muttering "Excuse me," he dashed toward the hangars.

Harriet giggled. "Don't tell anyone, 'Tilde, but I think Harold
must have ingested some of the castor oil the engine sprays over
everything."

Both women hunched their shoulders and giggled with their
heads close together.

The phenomenon had in fact been a running joke among the men, though Willy had attributed his own occasional need to run to the toilet more to nerves than to the emetic properties of the engine lubricant.

"Well, " Harriet said to Matilde, "even though it's rather late for a dose of the cod liver oil the doctors always recommend in the spring, the castor oil seems to have the same effect of keeping us all very regular, doesn't it?" Both women giggled again.

This unexpected earthiness in Harriet surprised Willy.

"Harriet . . ?" he ventured.

She turned her head. "Yes?"

"I want to—"

But he couldn't say anything now, not with Matilde there.

"I wonder if I could talk to you," he said softly. "Not here. Privately."

She frowned and pulled up a satin sleeve and looked at her wristwatch.

"Well, as a matter of fact I was thinking about getting ready to leave. Why don't you walk with me to the hangar."

He spoke quickly; it was only a few steps to Hangar Two. "I want to apologize for the other day. I didn't mean—"

It wasn't what he wanted to say. It was a weak way of backing into what he wanted to say, of delaying what he wanted to say.

"Apologize? Whatever for?"

"What I said about that article in Leslie's. The one about Langley."

"That? Don't be silly."

"I didn't mean to imply that you had anything to do with it."

"I know you didn't. I went back and looked it up. You were quite right. It did seem to cast doubt on the Wright brothers."

He wasn't done, but they couldn't talk here either, outside. The always-present contingent of visitors was watching them. He took Harriet by the elbow and steered her inside the hangar, surprising himself by his boldness.

"It's not just that," he said. "Before—for trying to put you down."

"Put me down? And when was that, pray tell?"

"That day when we were talking about birds and monoplanes. You know, comparing them." Now why had he brought that up? It was two months ago.

But she remembered. "You mean what you said about birds not having propellers? I thought you raised a very good point. I didn't feel 'put down.' Was that your intention?"

She was looking at him rather penetratingly and he was flustered.

"No, no. I just thought, afterwards, that you might have gotten that impression."

"Don't be silly. I said you raised a good point. I really hadn't thought the matter through."

"No!" he confessed. "I *meant* to put you down, and I'm sorry."

Her lips curved in a semismile. "Because I'm a woman."

"Because you're a woman and because I think you're going to be a better flier than the rest of us put together. And I'm going to be the worst, if I make it at all."

He hadn't intended to play on her sympathy, yet what else did he have to appeal to her with?

"Now you're putting yourself down, William. Let's make a fresh start. I want you to forget I'm a woman. We're all in this adventure together, we're all equal. I'm not surprised if you had some bias toward me at first. I've encountered that all my life. Claude Grahame-White insists that women are physically and emotionally incapable of learning to fly as well as men can. My own editor was doubtful about it and I think even André was too in the beginning. So you see, you really have nothing to apologize for."

She was getting it all wrong. He was saying it all wrong.

"It *wasn't* because you're a woman." How could he explain it? "I've wanted to do nothing but learn to fly an aeroplane ever since I saw Wilbur Wright at the Hudson-Fulton Celebration. It means everything to me. I just assumed that for you it was . . . well, just something different to do. A lark."

"I'm serious too, William. I believe aviation is going to change the world. For me it was seeing Johnny Moisant fly at Belmont Park and the encouragement he gave me when I talked to him. It devastated me when he was killed. Oh, maybe part of it is to prove that Grahame-White and the others are wrong and unfair in their opinion of women. But I'm doing it for myself, nobody else. I want to be the first licensed female aviator in this country, but whether I succeed in that or not I want to fly. I don't know if I will make a career of it, it's a bit early to be thinking of that."

"But I'm so far behind everyone." He hadn't intended to say that either. He was making a perfect ass of himself.

"Stop being so hard on yourself, William. I told you that some of the best aviators have been the slowest to learn. But you're not slow at all. You're doing fine."

"Is someone picking you up? I'm still available anytime you need a ride."

Her manner underwent a subtle change. She frowned. "Yes. Thank you. See you next time." She started toward the back of the hangar.

He called after her. "Harriet . . . Friends?"

She turned around briefly. She looked at him for a second, and the frown softened.

"Of course. We always have been, William."

Then she was gone inside her dressing room.

Why hadn't he been able to tell her? He was glad he hadn't; it would really have "spoiled things," spoiled their "fresh start." But sometime he would have to tell her of his feelings for her, if only to unburden himself of them, if only to have her reject them outright and end this agony once and for all.

Still . . . she had taken the trouble to look up the Langley article. That must mean something.

Forget she was a woman? Would to God he could.

9

WILLY SET HIS alarm clock as usual for four A.M. on Tuesday, the first of August. At the previous lesson André Houpert had announced that on that day (the constant bugaboo of weather permitting) both Harriet Quinlan and Ferdinand DeMurias would take their licensing tests. André told Harriet he would arrange to have representatives of the Aero Club pick her up at the Garden City Hotel before first light.

That was how momentous the occasion was considered to be, not only for Harriet and André and the Hempstead Plains Aviation Company but for the Aero Club of America itself, which had never before been called upon to evaluate the aviating capabilities of a female.

He shut off the alarm after one ring and jumped out of bed and raised the blind. Brooklyn was enveloped in thick fog. He could hardly see the streetlight in front of the house. But summer fogs always lifted when the sun came out. This fog had to lift.

He dressed and went downstairs quietly and left a hasty note on the kitchen table for his parents. They knew it was a lesson day but if his mother woke up and saw the fog and found him gone she would worry. So he scribbled that the weather looked good, hoping it would be good by the time they got up. He had no thoughts of taking a lesson on this day, however. Today was Harriet's day.

He went outside to the dark hulk of the car parked at the curb and removed the old horse blanket covering the hood and fired up the engine and started along the deserted street. No traffic at all, no need to worry about cops. He could not have exceeded the limit if he tried. The fog seemed even thicker when he left the lighted cobblestone streets behind and entered farm country. At one point he had to go so slowly he was almost dead in the road. The electric headlights were useless in this kind of soup, reflecting back blindingly from the solid wall of white into which he pushed. He considered turning them off; he could probably see better without them. But another car or some sleepy farmer driving a wagon to market might come along, and without his lights they might not see him until too late.

It was five-thirty by the time he found the road to the aerodrome. Two other cars were already parked behind the office. He could make out that building but not the hangars. The flying field itself was lost in nothingness.

Harriet and André and two men he had never seen before were sitting in the office. Ferdinand DeMurias, whose tests were scheduled after Harriet's, had not arrived, nor had any of the other students.

Harriet looked up in surprise when he entered. "*William*. I never expected to see you here so early today, with this fog."

He had been afraid she might not appreciate his appearance at this, the crucial, culminating, most important moment in her flying career, but her smile was sincere. She was not just being polite because of the others there.

I came for you, he wanted to say. He tried to say it with his eyes but she had looked away.

She introduced the two men, who stood up and shook his hand. "Mr. Campbell-Wood and Baron D'Orcy are representatives of the Aero Club of America. Mr. Campbell-Wood is the secretary. They are here to supervise the tests."

Then to them, "I can't tell you how gracious you gentlemen are for coming out so early on such a dismal morning, and for providing transportation for me from the hotel—for the second day in a row!"

Then to Willy again, "We've been here since a little after four. We just couldn't wait at the hotel any longer."

"We must still wait," André said.

Willy gave Harriet a puzzled look. "You were here yesterday?"

Her mouth curled up. "Yes. André called me on Monday and said the weather was so good there was no reason not to take the tests that evening. The weather *was* good . . . but I wasn't. I failed."

"Not at all," said Campbell-Wood. "You fulfilled every requirement perfectly except for the precision landings. I'm entirely confident you will have no trouble doing that today."

"I forgot to shut the engine off in time and rolled right past the target," Harriet said. "Too bad aeroplanes don't have brakes."

"You were only a few feet off, Miss Quinlan," D'Orcy said. "It's really only a technicality."

Willy could hardly believe that the star of the class had failed her licensing tests. But in his heart he was glad she had. If she hadn't failed she wouldn't be here now and he would have missed it entirely. He smiled at her encouragingly and took a seat in one of the chairs.

They waited. Campbell-Wood and D'Orcy sat with their eyes closed, dozing, or trying to doze. André went in and out, checking the fog and looking for the sun. Harriet, dressed in her flying costume, sat alertly, looking straight ahead. If she was nervous it didn't show. Willy poured a cup of coffee and sipped it slowly.

They waited. It was getting perceptibly brighter outside. At six Hardy appeared and assured them that the fog would undoubtedly soon lift. No more than another half-hour, he said.

At six-thirty the fog was almost entirely gone. The day was improving by the minute. They went outside. André walked into the field to measure the wind. It was a formality only, for the anemometer's cups were stationary. Hardy and another mechanic carried two poles topped with pieces of red cloth into the field and erected them, one at the near end, the other at the specified five hundred meters distance from the first. Their pennants hung limply. Campbell-Wood and D'Orcy placed a large triangular piece of white canvas, weighted at the corners, in the middle of the field between the posts. Then each of them stationed himself at one of the flags. All was in readiness.

The international licensing rules required that the aviator (or aviatrix) ascend, make five circuits of the field in the form of figure eights around the posts without touching the ground, and then land with the engine stopped within fifty meters, or about a hundred and sixty-five feet, of the canvas patch. She then had to take off again and repeat the same procedure. Finally, on a third flight, she was to attain an altitude of no less than fifty meters.

The rest of the class had drifted in by this time and a few spectators were gathering in the viewing stand. Alfred Moisant and a number of men Willy did not know arrived. There were also several reporters. They walked into the hangar without invitation and tried to talk to Harriet but André made them stand to one side. Willy wondered if the reporters had been there yesterday as well. Probably. It was a newsworthy occasion.

He helped push the fifty-horsepower Moisant monoplane — No. 1, the one Harriet always used — onto the apron and face it downfield in line with the nearer post. With no wind it did not matter in which direction Harriet took off. She climbed in and André gave her last-minute encouragement and told her he would stand near the first flag and wave a handkerchief to signal her when she had completed five figure eights. Hardy flipped the propeller and Willy and his fellow students and another mechanic held onto the shaking craft as the Gnôme wound up to its maximum revolutions. Harriet raised and dropped her hand and they let go.

She was in the air within yards and banking left around the first post at a height of some seventy-five feet, then banking the other way to round the second course marker. In two minutes she was heading back and banking again around the first post to begin the second circuit, André waving her on as she passed over him. If she could do it four more times, Willy thought, and then another five . . .

But there was no "if" about it; she had already done it the day before, hadn't she? Not to mention countless times in practice. It was the landing that was the crucial thing.

≈ ≈

As the plane diminished again in the distance, Willy was suddenly conscious of a phenomenon (if that was what it was) that he had experienced a million times before in everyday life but whose significance (if it had any) had never struck him before:

Inside that structure moving through the air was a human being, an infinitely complex organism, that he had stood beside only moments before. The top of her head had come up to his chin. She was a certain, measurable size. She occupied a certain, measurable space. All the infinitely complex, interrelated parts of her that made up the whole organism—the cells in her hair, the corpuscles in her blood—had a certain, measurable dimension and occupied a certain, measurable space. Yet now her head was little more than a dot and the huge machine itself reduced to the size of a bird. All her complexity and all her dimensions had been reduced to a dot he could blot out with his thumb. From his perspective Harriet was nearly as small as the smallest organism one could see with the naked eye. If she were to keep going away from him she would eventually become invisible, become "smaller," in relation to his perspective, than the smallest organism that could be detected under a microscope. Yet all her complexity in all its various dimensions would remain the same "size" in relation to herself.

If he had a telescope or binoculars he could enlarge her. Wouldn't that be the same as enlarging something under a microscope? If the atom was the smallest possible particle of matter, with presumably a certain, measurable dimension, what "size" at this moment was one of the trillions of atoms that made up Harriet's being, if he had an instrument powerful enough to measure it? What "size" were the cells of her hair, the corpuscles in her blood, the neurons in her brain? If she kept going forever she would become infinitely small, from his perspective, ceasing to have any existence as far as he was concerned. She would be even "smaller" than the unseen atoms in his thumb. How could anything be smaller than the smallest particle of matter? Yet in relation to him and his perspective, she would be smaller than an atom, all the while continuing to exist in all her infinite complexity in relation to herself.

And it struck him that from Harriet's perspective, it was he who had diminished, yet in relation to himself he was still the same.

All this passed through his mind in a moment. He laughed to himself. It was silly. The same "phenomenon" happened when someone walked away from you on the street. Yet for a moment it had stunned him with its profundity.

Harriet had completed the last of the first series of eights and was coming down for her first precision landing. She cut the engine off just before her wheels touched and rolled toward the canvas target. From where Willy stood it looked like she nearly rolled right on top of it. She couldn't possibly have failed this time!

He glanced at his watch. It was six fifty-one. It had taken her only nine minutes to cover the course of some fifteen miles.

André ran up to the monoplane as Harriet climbed out to stretch her legs and let the engine cool. Willy stayed where he was. She had to do it all over again, plus the altitude test. He would congratulate her later.

The plane was rolled back to its starting point. A little after seven Harriet was back in the air, executing the figures as perfectly and effortlessly as before. Her landing was not as close to the target this time, but still well within the requirement. Again the men on the field rushed to the plane.

At quarter to eight Harriet took off once more for the final time, for her altitude test, which was as nothing compared to the other tests. She made a circle above the field at more than the required fifty meters, a barograph in the cockpit recording her altitude. Six minutes later it was all over. There was no question she had qualified. Brilliantly. The previous day's "technical" failure had been wiped out entirely.

This time everyone present rushed up to the plane. Harriet stood beside it, smiling, laughing, her face shining from the oil, accepting the hands offered to her. Matilde Moisant, who did not have a jealous bone in her body, gave her a hug.

"Well, I guess I get that license," Harriet said to the two Aero Club officials.

"I guess you do!" Campbell-Wood said.

Was anyone else there aware that she had come back from infinity?

In the hangar André produced two large bottles of champagne and paper cups to toast the occasion. Everyone was talking excitedly, everyone discussing with whoever was nearest each turn and maneuver Harriet had made.

"Do you think you may have set a record for accuracy with your first landing, Miss Quinlan?" one of the reporters asked.

Harriet looked at André.

"Certainly with a monoplane," he said. "To my knowledge the record for accuracy is one foot, six and one-half inches, set by the Englishman Tom Sopwith in his biplane. Unfortunately, it is not an internationally recognized category. But that is not important. Miss Quinlan has become not only the first American woman to qualify for an aviation pilot's license under the difficult new Nineteen-ten rules of the Fédération Aéronautique Internationale but the first woman in the *world* to do so in a monoplane. The only other woman who has qualified as yet is Madame Driancourt of France, who performed her tests in a Caudron biplane."

This of course called for another round of congratulations and a reraising of cups and a topping off of all within André's reach.

"How high were you, Miss Quinlan? During the altitude test?"

Harriet looked to André again.

"Miss Quinlan's barograph registered two hundred and twenty feet," he said.

That was no record of any kind but the reporters recorded it anyway.

"What was it like up there, Miss Quinlan? What did you think about?"

Harriet was still excited and rather unfocused. She had cleaned most of the oil from her face but there were two semicircular smudges under her eyes from the goggles.

She laughed. "Mostly about my engine, hoping it would keep perking along."

Then she became thoughtful. "As for what it is like . . . there's such a clearness about everything in the air. The ruts in the road—I saw a dog running across the road—the chimneytops of houses, almost the individual blades of grass. I saw all of you down below, the domes of Garden City to the west, a glimpse of the ocean on the south, Long Island Sound on the north. Everything is so easily seen from the air that I am not surprised by the recent statement that the aeroplane can make a submarine distinguishable in any harbor and will seriously impair its usefulness as a weapon of warfare."

The reporters scribbled in their notebooks.

"What are your plans now, Miss Quinlan?"

"Well, the first thing I want to do is write everything down, record my sensations and impressions while they're still fresh in my mind, for an article in Leslie's Weekly. I get so many letters from readers wanting to know what it's like to fly."

She was already writing, Willy thought.

"But what are your long-range plans?"

"Well, I'm thinking of doing some exhibition flying at one or two county fairs this summer and maybe some competition flying at the second international meet on Long Island that will be held at the Nassau Boulevard aerodrome at the end of September."

"Hèléne Dutrieu, who won the Coupe Femina in France, is coming for that meet," a reporter said. "Do you intend to compete with her?"

"Well, if she's willing, I am too. I certainly hope to meet her. But as for my long-range plans, Alfred J. Moisant is reconstituting the Moisant International Aviators, the touring group his brother, the late John B. Moisant, started."

She nodded to Moisant, who stood beaming at his school's prize pupil even more proudly than on the day he had introduced her to the class.

"I understand Roland Garros from France and other well-known fliers will be rejoining it," Harriet said. "Mr. Moisant has kindly invited me to participate also, along with his sister Matilde, who will shortly qualify for her license."

The reporters directed their eyes momentarily to the shyly smiling Matilde. She would be the second licensed female pilot in America. But second was, well, only second.

"There is going to be an exhibition in Mexico City in December in connection with the inauguration of President Madero to which the Moisant fliers have been invited," Harriet continued. "I don't know. That is another possibility. I still have my responsibilities at Leslie's Weekly."

Not only did Harriet move in a social world Willy had no part of, she was poised to enter another world—professional flying—that still seemed as far out of his reach as it had the day he had run the trainer into the hole.

"You must stay with aviation," he heard himself say.

She saw him then, really saw him for the first time since (could it only be two hours ago?) he had stumbled in from the fog and she had looked up in surprise and, he had thought, gladness. She nodded again, her lips compressed.

"Yes," she said to everyone in general. "I mentioned the letters I receive. Most of them are from young girls asking my advice on learning to fly and what kind of opportunities there are for women in aviation. If I can contribute nothing else, I hope to wake up the people of this country to the potentialities of the aeroplane. It is far more than just a sport. We're so far behind. France is investing millions of francs and even Spain is spending more than our government. In France schoolchildren contribute their centimes to buy aeroplanes for the army."

The reporters continued scribbling. She went on:

"In this country flying is still considered to be only a spectator sport, a novelty. But as I have heard Mr. Moisant say, we have the finest human material for great pilots that can be found anywhere in the world. We have the factories to make aeroplanes and motors. There is no reason why in a few years we could not see aeroplanes making regular flights between distant cities, perhaps as far as fifty or sixty miles apart, delivering passengers and packages and mail — and with women flying them as well as men. In France an aeroplane recently flew a short distance with twelve passengers! Of course, that was only a stunt but it is an indication of what will soon be possible."

Reporters never seemed to get enough answers to enough questions, but eventually when Harriet began repeating herself and André and the officials left to begin DeMurias's trials, the group gradually moved outside. Only a couple of reporters stayed to watch. The next flier was merely a male.

Ferdinand also qualified easily and also received hearty congratulations, but no toasting with champagne for none was left. When his tests were over the mechanics retrieved the canvas patch and began removing the marker poles. Then Harriet and André and the two Aero Club officials left to return to the Garden City Hotel for a celebration brunch.

Willy had the opportunity only to go up to Harriet and shake her hand and tell her how wonderfully she had done.

"Thank you, William," she said, almost absently. Then, with the merest nod, but from which he read volumes: "It'll soon be your turn." An instant later she was surrounded again.

He waited until the jam in the parking lot was eased, barely able to endure the pain that racked him, though he savored every bittersweet second of it. He would not be seeing Harriet again, unless by chance she came out to practice sometime when he was taking a lesson. And if she didn't . . .

He drove home, wondering how the world could seem so dreary on so grand and glorious a day.

10

T HE DAY CAME when at last Willy was to go up into the air in true flight. No longer merely to skim the earth in short kangaroo hops in a straight line but to go up *into* the air and turn around in it. It was inevitable. The only way he could have avoided it would have been to quit the course outright, as he had once almost done. But though he was still unsure of his competence as a pilot, the idea of giving it all up after coming this far was unthinkable.

(It was the day every student longs for, Harriet had written in her second article on "How A Woman Learns to Fly"—except, she had added, for those who have had an accident that tested their nerves too much. Did she have him in mind when she wrote that? Did she ever have him in mind at all, for that matter?)

What he was supposed to do today was almost as crucial as what he would eventually be required to do for his license. Even more crucial, really, for if he could take off and turn around and land without mishap, then the rest—figure eights and precision landings—would be only a matter of routine practice.

It was early September. All the members of the inaugural class of the Moisant Flying School—H. Quinlan, F. DeMurias, S. Jerwan, H. Kantner and M. Moisant—had won their licenses in August. A new class of hopeful students was starting.

The day could not have been more favorable. The morning sky was blue and cloudless when Willy arrived at the aerodrome. Whatever was to happen today, he would not be able to put any blame on the weather.

André knew how important this day was for Willy and had everything in readiness. The new students could wait. Monoplane No. 1, the same one used by Harriet in her licensing tests, had already been rolled out of the hangar and pointed toward the east end of the field, the direction they always took off in because they always took off in a calm.

This day however there was a gentle breeze coming from the west. André measured it. Between two and four miles an hour. Not enough to worry about, not enough to make it necessary for Willy to go all the way to the other end of the field for his takeoff. The breeze behind him would make his eastward takeoff a trifle longer but would aid him in his landing westward.

He explained what he had in mind. "After you ascend, *Weelee*, make a left turn and come back along the north side of the field. When you reach the 'angars turn left again all the way around and proceed along the south side of the field to the far end once more. Then make a final left turn for your landing. Do you understand?"

Willy gulped. Holy blue, André! Harriet's first flight and those of all the others had involved only one turn; they had all been told to come down immediately after making a one-eighty at the end of the field. Was André pushing him too fast again? But he merely nodded, telling himself that if he could manage one turn there was no reason he could not manage three.

When he came out of the hangar in his coveralls and helmet his mind was in suspension, vacant of thought. Yet he was intensely alert to everything going on around him: the final checking over of the plane by the mechanics . . . the new students watching him . . . André's last-minute words to him (more of encouragement now than of instruction, which itself was encouraging) . . . the slight give of the shock absorbers as he stepped onto a longeron and grasped the mast to climb into the cockpit . . . the firmness of the seat against his back and bottom . . . the easy motion of the control column and rudder yoke as he moved them to verify their operation . . . Then the roar of the Gnôme and blast of wind from the propeller striking his face and the acrid, familiar smell of castor oil.

At Willy's signal the mechanics let go. *So much power.* In just a few seconds he was going fast enough to raise the tail. So far so good; he was heading straight for the flag at the end of the field on which his eyes were fixed. Keep it straight. Build your speed. He pulled back gently on the wheel. He was in the air and rising.

How easily the aeroplane balanced; just a little correction with the warp was all that was necessary. It was almost as if he were controlling the machine by thought alone. In a few more seconds Willy was at his assigned height of between fifty and seventy-five feet, and in the next minute before he had to make his first turn he became conscious of—and marveled at—a sensation he had been too nervous and preoccupied to be aware of during his low-level kangarooing runs. It was a sensation he would experience each time he left the ground and would always love:

The craft *wanted* to fly. Its only *purpose* was to fly. This ungainly-on-the-ground contrivance of wood and metal and cloth, this geometrical arrangement of struts and wires and curved planes, could not *help* but fly. He could feel the air, the thin, insubstantial, invisible air, embracing the wings, buoying him, lifting him up.

Yes—the *buoyancy*. That was what he hadn't felt before. This was what it was like to fly.

Had Harriet felt it too?

He couldn't see the flag when he reached the end of the field. That was good; it must be directly below him. He eased the wheel forward a degree as he passed over the perimeter, increasing his speed for the turn—and all at once was lost.

He was amazed that he should be lost. Reason told him the aerodrome was just behind him but everything looked strange. He saw a road—but what road? He was in the air over Long Island—but where over Long Island? How could anybody possibly fly across country?

He moved the column and rudder bar to begin the left turn that would swing him around in a half-circle to face him back toward the aerodrome. The aeroplane, assisted by the engine torque, felt its head and banked steeply of its own accord. The left wing dipped toward the ground at what seemed to him a dangerous degree. He immediately leveled the wings and, using mostly rudder, made a skittering, fluttering turn. He was over the Meadowbrook golf course, well beyond the boundary of the aerodrome, by the time he was all the way around and straightened out and heading back. But he had made the turn.

He skirted the north edge of the field, keeping the plane at no more than seventy-five feet. As he neared the hangars he glanced down past the trailing edge of the left wing and saw the small figures of André and the mechanics and the new students and people in the grandstand looking up at him.

The disorientation he had experienced a moment before was gone. He laughed at himself. How could he have thought he was lost? Why, there alongside him on the left was the aerodrome, off to his right Old Country Road, ahead of him in the near distance the "domes" of Garden City Harriet had mentioned (although the only structure he could see that might be called a "dome" was the cupola of the Garden City Hotel), and on either side of Garden City the villages of Hempstead and Mineola.

He banked over Clinton Road, just as he had seen Earle Ovington do on that afternoon in May that now seemed almost a lifetime ago. Hardly as expertly as Earle had of course, but a little more confidently this time. He flew east along the southern boundary of the field, as André had directed him to do. Then the last turn, to the west again. Still sloppy, but he was lined up with the getaway.

The landing was joy unalloyed. Even more delightful than the lifting sensation during the takeoff was the floating of the aeroplane when he blipped the engine off as he crossed the gully. This was buoyancy too, but a different kind, a sinking rather than a rising buoyancy. The air seemed reluctant to release its embrace. With the engine silent momentarily, he could hear the wires sing as he swept down toward the turf. A few seconds before the front wheels would have met the ground he pulled back on the column—no, too soon, he was stalling too high, the machine was starting to drop. He pushed the column forward again quickly, recovering gliding speed. *Now* . . . all the way back on the wheel. Full stall. He dropped, but only a foot or two, and on the front wheels and tailskid simultaneously, bouncing once.

The machine was no longer a thing of the air. The earth took jealous repossession of it, the grass whispering as it clutched at the wheels and skid, slowing him. It was a near-perfect landing, as perfect as he could have wished.

He taxied back to the hangar and cut the engine. He sat in the inert contrivance, contented, savoring the wonder of it. (Had Harriet felt this exuberance?) *He had flown.* Not only had he flown but he had done so as well as if not better than any of the others had on their first turning flight. He removed the helmet and wiped the castor oil off the goggles and off his mouth and cheeks with a rag from his pocket.

André, ever the encourager, was full of praise as he helped Willy climb out of the cockpit.

"Excellent, *Weelee*. A most excellent landing. Your turns must become better but you have passed the great hurdle. Now we shall really begin to fly."

As the mechanics pushed the machine back to the starting point he and André followed. Having praised him enough, André now discussed his deficiencies.

"Your turns were adequate for the purpose but you have now to begin to learn how to bank them better. That is the only way to turn efficiently in the air. Or on the ground as well. Even on the ground the turns of a running track are banked. When you have reposed yourself I want you to go up again and practice circles over the field, to the right as well as to the left, and a little higher this time. Do not be alarmed when everything tilts crazily. As long as you keep your speed nothing will happen. Of course, only if you make gentle banks, not steep ones. I also want you to learn to accomplish both ascending and descending turns."

Willy had not expected André would have him fly again this lesson and despite his sterling performance and André's obvious satisfaction he felt a return of the apprehension that had been below the surface of every waking thought since the moment in the hangar, three months before, when it first struck him that sometime or other he was going to have to take an aeroplane up in the air alone.

Yes, he had taken off, turned around three times and landed. But that was only the barest beginning of learning to fly. Now André was telling him to go up again—higher—and do figure eights. Should they push it that far, that fast? Even Harriet hadn't done that much in one day.

But André knew what he was about; he wouldn't ask him to do more than he thought he could handle. ("You must believe that we know more about flying than you do," he had once lectured the class.) It was really a great compliment to Willy. He had crossed over into, or had at least approached close to, that all-essential confidence in oneself and one's machine that Harriet had talked about. He had passed the great hurdle.

He clapped André affectionately on the shoulder. "Let us strike while the iron is hot, *mon vieux*."

"*Mais oui*," said André, laughing. "Or as we say in France, *en l'air*."

Willy spent a cigarette's worth of time walking back and forth in front of the row of hangars to stretch his limbs, then climbed back into the cockpit again. God, how he loved the feel of the bucket seat cradling him, the smooth wooden wheel in his hand, the rudder bar against his feet, the noise and odor and vibration as the engine whirled—and then the buoyancy as he took off again.

It was amazing. One minute all you were doing was rolling along on the ground in what was for all intents and purposes merely a strangely configured motorcar, confined to the two dimensions of length and breadth. You could drive down the street in it, pause at intersections, turn corners, stop completely and get out if you wanted to. But then, the next minute, speed gathered, with a slight pull on the wheel you entered the third dimension of height—and everything changed. The instant your wheels left the ground a wholly different and complex new set of circumstances came into play. You were now in intimate partnership with the air, the medium that at once sustained you and resisted you, and gravity, scarcely considered on the ground, became your constant nemesis.

How could the simple addition of a third dimension make such a difference? All of his reading about aeroplanes, all of his imagining about flying, all of André's teaching—none of it had fully prepared him for the astonishing reality of it.

He was still far from being at home in the air, though, far from being at one with the machine. He worried constantly that something would go wrong, that the engine would quit, that he would overstrain the wings. He flew cautiously, tensely. He forced himself to relax the grip of his fingers on the wheel and the rigidity of his legs on the rudder yoke.

He allowed the plane to climb to nearly two hundred feet while he completed one circuit of the field, practicing a climbing turn, then leveled off and banked left to begin a descending turn. He was impressed by how little movement of column and rudder was needed to begin a bank or stop it. He watched the edges of the wings but could detect no flexing in them. The aeroplane responded to the slightest, indiscernible change of wing curvature.

He dared let his eyes wander around the horizon. Harriet had said how clear and vivid everything had been, how much she had noticed from the air even during her preoccupation with making figure eights for the test. On his first flight he had seen hardly anything; all his concentration had been on controlling the machine. Now he began to appreciate the true beauty and wonder of flight. The roads and fields and houses of Nassau County were laid out to his view. He saw vehicles crawling along the road to Garden City that he had driven on with Harriet, the town itself like a toy model with a miniature Long Island Railroad train approaching it from the west. Even at his low altitude he could see Long Island Sound to the north, the hazy blue line of the Atlantic to the south, as Harriet had.

He began a third circuit, still banking only to the left, and decided it was time to do a figure eight to practice right-hand turning. He held the leftward bank until he was straightened out and facing north. He crossed the aerodrome, then started his first one-hundred-eighty-degree turn to the right. For the first time he looked down at the ground from the right side of the cockpit. He saw one of the new students inching the trainer uncertainly across the field in a grasscutting run and grinned. That had been him, not so long ago.

It did seem more natural to turn left, as Harriet had said. It was not too difficult to turn to the right, though; all it required was firmness on the rudder. But he knew it was sloppy, mostly all rudder, hardly any warp. He would need a lot more practice turning right.

With the growing heat of the sun he felt the air becoming rougher. In place of the gentle buoyancy of the first moment of rising, now twice experienced, there was a pounding. The air fought the machine that forced its way through it, challenged it, played with it, jarring it upward one second and dropping it down the next. It was like riding a boat crosswave in choppy water.

If it had been like this on his first flight that morning he would have panicked and crashed. If André had known the air would become this unstable on his second flight he would never have allowed him to make it.

He straightened out again. He probably ought to land before it got worse. He had been in the air nearly half an hour, three times as long as his first flight. A line of dark clouds was moving in from the west. A summer squall. It was unusual for a storm to build up so early in the day. But he was not panicked. He was getting to know the air and its rising and falling currents and, more importantly, to understand that the aeroplane knew them better than he. He tried to let the plane fly itself. If it jumped upward, slamming him down in the seat, there was no need for harsh correction with engine speed or wheel. The machine knew what it was doing. And if in the next instant it dropped out from under him, it was only momentarily. In another instant the air was smooth again. The air was not really fighting him, it was just being itself.

How could he seriously have entertained the thought of quitting? How could anyone not want to fly, and once having flown ever want to do anything else?

It was because of Harriet that he knew this joy. If it hadn't been for her he would have quit, and never have known what he was missing. God, he loved her. He loved this machine. He loved the dour, laconic Wrights, who had made it all possible. He loved the world. *Everything.*

He did one last figure eight, then banked again to the east and flew widely parallel to the south side of the aerodrome above Stewart Avenue and the Curtiss factory, still reveling in his newly discovered companionship with the air. Now one last turn, the best one that day, beginning as he passed over the gully, to point him west for the landing approach. But by the time he completed the turn, maintaining altitude, he was surprised to find he was far from the field, though straight with the getaway. The breeze he had started out in had become a wind that had blown him nearly a mile from the aerodrome while he was concentrating on the turn. If nothing else, the whipping field flag in the distance would have told him about the wind when he had soared by it, if he had been paying attention. Now the sudden slowing of the ground passing beneath him as he faced into the wind unmistakably confirmed its strength.

Wetness stung his face. He thought it was oil, then to his astonishment realized it was water. The squall line had moved in even as he had been flying along the southern boundary of the aerodrome before his final turn. The sky was black just beyond the hangars and gray all around him, and the air suddenly chilly with the sun gone behind clouds that had materialized out of nowhere.

Now he did know fear again. He was flying straight toward that ominous blackness. Would he be able to beat it? Why the hell hadn't he landed sooner? Why hadn't he watched the sky?

The field was clear. The trainer had been put back in the hangar — something else that should have alerted him — and André and the students and mechanics were clustered in a group on the apron watching him, and maybe praying for him.

But he had plenty of height. He pointed the nose down a few degrees to increase his speed. Remembering André's caution about oiling up the plugs be blipped the ignition off and on every second or so. Between blasts from the engine he again heard the wind whistling past the wires and rushing over the wings, even heard the raindrops drumming against the wing fabric.

He was too high! He depressed the nose further and to his astonishment gained even more altitude. For a moment he began to think he would have to go around again. But it was too late to do that; the storm was already enveloping the aerodrome.

He blipped the engine off and tried raising the nose and found that, paradoxically, this caused him to lose height. It must have something to do with the increased drag of the monoplane when the nose was high, he guessed. God, there was still so much he didn't know about flying.

He had underestimated the resistance of the wind. He was down to fifty feet before he became aware that the field did not seem to be getting any closer. *All at once he was too low! He wasn't going to make it! He was heading straight for the gully!*

Instinctively, he let the engine run full speed and pushed on the column to maintain level flight. The field came toward him oh so slowly, spreading and merging with the horizon. Finally — thank God — he was over the boundary. And now he was afraid he was coming in too rapidly! The aerodrome hangars loomed ahead. He blipped the ignition off. Twenty feet above the ground he eased the nose up slightly. Yet even with the engine off the plane wanted to stay in the air. He lowered the nose again and at ten feet cut the ignition once more, met the ground evenly on the front wheels, pulled the column all the way back, hit the ground on all three points — and was in the air again!

Immediately he pushed the column forward, and this time when the mains touched the ground he kept them there by leaving the tail high and restoring the spark. Gradually, as he slowed, the tail settled to the ground — even with the wheel in full forward position and the power full on! He was amazed. He had discovered something about landing in a high wind, but he did not quite understand what it was he had discovered.

All that mattered was that he was on the ground, and safe. Triumphantly, infinitely relieved, he taxied at nearly full power toward the hangars against gusts of wind that tried to lift him into the air again.

André and Hardy and two other mechanics had already been running into the field when he was making his landing approach. When they reached him Willy cut the engine for the last time and the mechanics grabbed the wings and tail and put their weight on them as they pushed the plane the rest of the way to the hangar—as the rain came pouring down.

André looked at Willy with tense alarm on his face. "*Mon dieu!*" he shouted as he trotted along beside the cockpit, his hands gripping its edge. "The wind is up nearly to thirty kilometers! Did you know?"

"I thought it was getting a bit rough," Willy said matter-of-factly, grinning stupidly.

André shook his head. "You are the best student yet! Never have I seen anyone fly in such a wind! How did you know to land on the front wheels the way you did, and with the power on?"

Willy couldn't answer. He didn't know how he had known. Instinct? Maybe he was a born aviator after all!

The wind was almost more frightening now that he was back on the ground than it had been in the air. But he had conquered the wind. In his triumph he was hardly conscious of the fact that he was getting drenched.

"Today you have jumped ahead by weeks," André said to him with great seriousness inside the hangar, where he finally climbed out of the cockpit. "A dozen more flights, perhaps even less, to perfect your turns and landing on the spot and you will be ready for the licensing tests. Yes, that is all you will need, I am sure."

He gripped Willy's arm and looked at him closely.

"What do you think?"

Willy was lightheaded, rubber-legged. He watched the water dripping from the aeroplane make puddles on the concrete floor.

"If you think so, André." Then: "I think so—*yes!*"

"*Bon.* With you I am going to do something I have never

done with any student. I want you to come every day this week and next to practice." He reflected a second, then laughed. "If there are no more storms, that is! But in no more then ten days' time you will take the tests. I will arrange it."

Will was surprised to see that a few dedicated aeroplane-watchers were still in the stand, some of them holding soggy newspapers over their heads. They applauded Willy as he and André dashed toward the office building and as the hangar doors were being rolled closed behind them. He grinned and waved at the people, pitying them.

He was still in the air.

New York City

1

WILLY REYNOLDS spent a lot of time during the dwindling days of summer thinking about Harriet Quinlan and about flying, the two of which had long since conjoined in his mind as a single subject of contemplation. Flying was Harriet Quinlan; Harriet Quinlan was flying. He could not think about the one without thinking about the other.

He continued to follow her from the distance of a reader of *Leslie's Illustrated Weekly*, reading all her reviews, one or two articles on new developments in aviation, the final article in her series, titled "How I Won My Aviator's License." She lived and worked in a milieu he knew nothing about and had no possibility of entering. Her wide circle of friends obviously included many well-known actors and actresses and others associated with the theater, as well as fellow journalists. There had always been at least one group of acquaintances and admirers at the aerodrome when she was practicing for her license.

He had used to watch as the men in these parties, all of them more dashing and debonair than he, would talk to Harriet in a free and easy manner, and had wondered if any of them was more than merely a friend to her.

He consulted her picture on his dresser daily. Had any man (or how many men?) ever enfolded that graceful form, kissed

those lovely lips, that perfect face? Had any man (or men) ever
. . . made complete love to her?

He did not know whether he hoped she was still virginal or
not. But it was some consolation to think that had he only been
a few years older and established in life there might have been a
chance with her. Some consolation, at the last, to believe that it
was not any fault or deficiency in himself that he could do anything about.

She had said it was the summer doldrums, nothing much
going on in the theater. Yet she had continued to write reviews of
plays all summer and now the new season was beginning. She
had forgotten her offhand promise to get tickets sometime, had
not really meant it, had just been acting big sisterly toward an
unsure boy who was still wet behind the ears. She had permitted
him to approach her only as close as she wanted him to, and no
closer. As close, he wondered, as she had ever permitted any other
man? Any "boy," certainly.

When Willy took his licensing tests in mid-September, when
he finally realized what had seemed to him to have been a life-
long dream although it was only a two-years' dream, it was almost like an anticlimax. Bolstered by André's confidence in him,
and with his skills honed to a fine edge by dint of the unprec-
edented daily practice André had decreed for him, he passed the
Aero Club's examination with ease.

His parents came out to the aerodrome to watch him, fearful
at first, then marveling, then proud. That evening they all went
out for a celebration dinner.

John and Ellen Reynolds, thankful that their son was still
alive and whole, hoped he would now be over his obsession with
flying. They knew nothing about his other obsession.

School had started again, his junior year. He went through a
desultory first week of it, his mind elsewhere. On Friday he decided to cut his afternoon classes and went to a public telephone
and called *Leslie's Weekly*. Miss Quinlan was not there, he was
informed, but was expected back within the hour. He passed

some time in the library, made a stab at studying, gave it up and went outside and paced around the campus. Then on a sudden impulse he caught an omnibus to midtown Manhattan.

At the Leslie-Judge Building he checked the directory for the editorial offices of *Leslie's Weekly* and then took the elevator. A girl was sitting behind a desk in a small reception area. He gave her his name and said he was there to see Harriet Quinlan. The girl said she would buzz her. "A Mr. William Reynolds to see you, Miss Quinlan," she spoke into the headset. A second later, "You can go right in, Mr. Reynolds, through that door." She smiled at him, thinking he was someone of importance.

Almost the entire floor housing the editorial staff of *Leslie's* was one huge room filled with desks and tables and cabinets amid the supporting pillars. There was a humming of numerous electric fans on the desks or cabinets stirring the humid, late-summer air. Dozens of people were busily at work. Many of them were young ladies, who looked up at Willy interestingly as he threaded his way. Several glass-enclosed offices, evidently those of the officers or editors of the firm, lined one outer wall. Harriet however did not have a separate office. He located her sitting at a large desk in a corner near an open window, although two file cabinets in front of the desk and a table piled with newspapers and magazines on one side afforded her a measure of isolation. She got up when she saw him and came toward him. She was wearing an ankle-length navy blue skirt and, like most of the other women in the office, a snowy white, long-sleeved shirt-waist.

"William," she said, offering her hand. "This is a surprise. How nice to see you."

She led him to a straight chair next to her desk and sat down again in her own swivel chair. There was a typewriter on the desk, directly in front of her, with a sheet of paper in it, and wire baskets full of letters or memos or copy, and more stacks of newspapers and back issues of *Leslie's* and other magazines.

"Forgive this clutter, William, but I was in the throes of something."

"I shouldn't have popped in like this," he said. "I just happened to be in this part of town and I thought— I won't stay. I just wanted to say hello." He sat down tentatively on the edge of the chair.

"Not at all. I'm glad you did. I could use a break. I won't finish this piece today anyway."

He swept his eyes around the room. "I didn't realize you were such a large operation."

Harriet beamed at him with sparkling, pleased eyes.

"Everyone is always surprised. And this is just the editorial department, William, just the tip of the iceberg you might say. We have lots more people working in the circulation and subscription departments on other floors. Forty girls do nothing but handle subscriptions. The mailroom—we receive hundreds of letters every day. And this is only our headquarters. We have sales representatives and subscription offices in, oh, fifty other cities. We have subscribers all over the world. All told we employ about two thousand people and we print well over three-hundred thousand copies every week. This is not even to mention Judge, the humor magazine, which is an entirely separate operation."

"I'm flabbergasted," he said. And he was.

She looked at him for a moment. "Well, aren't you going to tell me your good news? I heard you passed your tests. How wonderful. Congratulations."

He was surprised again. How had she heard? Had she run into someone from the school or—impossible thought—had she made a point of inquiring about him? He was afraid to ask.

Yes, he had passed, somehow, he said. He hadn't come anywhere near her performance, he added, but it had satisfied the Aero Club.

"There you go minimizing yourself again, William. It doesn't become you. I'm sure you did extremely well. You had to. They don't just hand out those licenses to anyone."

He resolved not to minimize himself again.

"Speaking of which . . ." Harriet lifted a large purse from the floor next to her and pulled out what looked like a small leather billfold or wallet and handed it to him. "I carry this with me all the time. You should be getting yours in a few days."

He opened the wallet. On a card inside, below the names of the Fédération Aéronautique Internationale and Aero Club of America, he read:

"The above-named club, recognized by the Fédération Aéronautique Internationale as a governing authority of the United States of America, certifies that Harriet Quinlan, having fulfilled all the conditions required by the Fédération Aéronautique Internationale, is hereby licensed as an aviator."

The number penned on the card indicated that she was the thirty-seventh American to win the coveted license.

Printed on the other side was a sentence in English, French, German, Russian, Italian and Spanish:

"The civil, naval and military authorities, including the police, are respectfully requested to aid and assist the holder of this certificate."

He closed the wallet and gave it back to her. "It's really something, isn't it? Ferdinand DeMurias must be number thirty-eight then. I wonder what my number will be."

"It shouldn't be too much higher. It depends on how many students at other schools qualified this month. The numbers are climbing fast though. Matilde's is forty-four, and she got her license only two weeks after me—on the thirteenth of the month, appropriately enough."

"Have you decided about going on tour with the Moisant International Aviators?"

"Oh yes. We'll be appearing at a number of places out West and then wind up the tour in Mexico in December, 'Tilde and I, and André of course and Hardy. President Madero's inauguration is going to be a very historic event in Mexico. I'm quite excited about it."

"I imagine you are. Have you been doing any flying since you got your license?"

"Oh, didn't you hear? I made a moonlight flight over Staten Island during the Richmond County Fair on Labor Day." She laughed happily. "Got paid fifteen-hundred dollars for it."

He and his parents had been visiting relatives in Connecticut on Labor Day and he had missed that.

"You flew at night?"

She nodded. "Of course there was a brilliant moon out and lots of lights on the field. I was tempted to fly across the harbor to Manhattan and back but I didn't have the nerve, although I did fly over the Narrows. I was only up seven minutes but when I landed, my mother—she was watching me—said if I hadn't come down when I did she was going to go up and get me!"

He didn't know what to say to her. She had not only flown at night but had already earned back double the cost of her lessons.

"That's amazing, Harriet," was all he managed.

"Then of course there's the meet at Nassau Boulevard starting the twenty-third of October. I'll be flying at that, and so will Matilde. And Hèléne Dutrieu is supposed to be there."

"I'll certainly come out and watch you," he said, with a solemn promise to himself. They exchanged nods and smiles.

"Well now, what about you, William? You're back studying hard at NYU, I suppose?"

He started to answer, but before they could begin to pursue that subject an interruption detoured them onto one of an entirely different nature.

A boy with an armful of magazines he was delivering around the office came up to Harriet's desk and handed one to her.

"Thank you, Tommy." Then to Willy: "Hot off the press. Friday is the day we print. Excuse me a minute. There's something I always check first."

He supposed she was looking for her latest article. She turned to a page and scanned it quickly, shaking her head.

"Look at this, William." She held up the opened magazine to him and he leaned forward to see.

It was an article titled, "The Girl That Wanted Ermine." He recognized it as one in a series *Leslie's* was publishing under the general title of "The Girl That Goes Wrong," ostensibly an exposé of the white-slave traffic by a Mr. Kauffman. He had read a few of the articles and found them all to be generally the same, and generally uninteresting.

"We get the magazine at home," he said. "Why do they always say, 'The Girl *That*'? It sounds so awkward. It should be 'The Girl *Who*', shouldn't it?"

"I don't know. You'll have to ask the copy editor."

She threw the magazine down on the desk and scowled at Willy fiercely. "What I'd like to know is why we're running them at all. Every Friday when Tommy brings me my copy the first thing I do is turn to 'The Girl That Goes Wrong' page to see what new indignity this man has foisted on my sex. It makes me so angry I have to suppress the urge to go and pull the issue from the presses and rip out the article and trample it on the floor!"

He was startled by her vehemence and sat back in the chair. She continued to glare at him.

"These articles purport to be about white slavery, which heaven knows is a real enough problem in society. But—"

She picked up the magazine and scanned the article again. "'The Girl That Wanted Ermine,'" she said in a mocking tone. "This is typical." She threw the magazine down again.

"All they are—and probably phony at that—are stories about girls who trade their virtue for gifts from men. I wouldn't mind having ermine myself. Actually, I've always wanted a sable stole, which is the same thing. But I have certainly never considered doing anything wrong or immoral to get it."

She swept her hand around in the air. "Look at this office. There are maybe two hundred single girls who work for Leslie's. They're not overpaid. Many of them have families to support. I know some who are supporting aging parents, as I am myself, with a lot of doctors' bills. But none of them is tempted to compromise herself for furs or jewelry or a dinner in an expensive restaurant. There are thousands like them in every city. Hardworking, virtuous girls. Why doesn't he write about *them*? Or about *real* white slavery."

Harriet herself had written an article about real white slavery two months before, which he had of course read: "How White Slaves are Shackled." It was about immigrant girls being shanghaied off the boat and forced into prostitution and how the authorities looked the other way and ignored evidence of the traffic gathered by investigators and refused to close down the bawdy-houses.

Until he read the article he had never thought about the girl at the Hudson-Fulton Celebration being a "white slave." She hadn't been an immigrant, and they hadn't gone to a bawdyhouse. At least the shabby hotel hadn't been his idea of a bawdyhouse.

He was about to mention this article when there was another interruption, this one serving to keep them on the same subject.

A man approached Harriet's desk. He glanced at Willy curiously. Harriet introduced them.

"This is John Sleicher, the editor and publisher of Leslie's," she said. "William Reynolds." Willy got up and shook hands.

"William is, or was, a fellow student of mine at the flying school. He's just received his license also."

Sleicher seemed impressed. "You don't say? Congratulations, Mr. Reynolds. No doubt you've read Harriet's series of articles?"

Willy said yes indeed he had.

"I was just filling William's ears with my complaints about the Kauffman series," Harriet said. "I'm afraid I've been boring him to death. As I've bored *you*."

"That's just what I want to speak to you about," said Sleicher. "Excuse me a second, Mr. Reynolds. I've been thinking, Harriet, if you feel so strongly why don't you write a rebuttal to him? Something like 'The Girl That Does *Not* Go Wrong.' I'd like to run it in next week's issue. Do you think you could—"

"It's already written in my head, Mr. Sleicher," Harriet said eagerly. "You'll have it on your desk by tomorrow noon at the latest."

"Monday will be fine, Harriet. Don't rush it. You don't have to come in tomorrow. Unless you want to."

The employees of *Leslie's Weekly* apparently were required, as in most business offices, to work at least half a day on Saturday. But Harriet obviously enjoyed a degree of independence not accorded those who did not have the distinction and prestige of their own byline.

Willy stood self-consciously by the chair, feeling like an intruder. He was glad when the man said, "It was a pleasure meeting you, Mr. Reynolds," and started away, and was dismayed when Harriet said, "Oh—Mr. Sleicher. William made a complaint to me about something we ran in the magazine."

Oh God, she still remembered that.

Sleicher turned and fixed his gaze on Willy. "Is that so? What was it about?"

Willy gave Harriet an appealing look. "It was an article we ran a couple months ago about Professor Langley's experiments," she said. "William thought it cast doubt on the Wright brothers' claim as inventors of the aeroplane. That was your complaint, wasn't it, William?"

"How's that?" Sleicher said to him. "I can't say we like to hear complaints but we do welcome all comments. Did you think the article was inaccurate?"

Willy tried to explain what it was he had found objectionable. "It seemed to imply that it was just bad luck that Langley's machine didn't fly before the Wrights'," he said apologetically.

"Well, wasn't it?" Sleicher challenged.

"I don't think so. I mean, the Wrights found that the calculations Langley used, and everyone else had used, were simply all wrong. Tables of air pressure, wing trussing arrangements . . ." He tailed off lamely. "His machine was simply incapable of flying."

"But there's no way of proving that now, is there? The Smithsonian Institution says that Langley's machine was the first aeroplane capable of carrying a man. His models certainly flew well. The poor man was hounded to death by ridicule. In any case, the Wrights have received their just dues, in spite of themselves. It's too bad they had to be so secretive about their experiments for so many years."

It was true that the Wrights hadn't invited publicity, but they had flown at Dayton, Ohio, in full view of anyone who wanted to watch. The fact was that no newspaper—or magazine—had bothered to send reporters to investigate the reports. They had missed the scoop of the century. But Willy did not want to argue with the editor and publisher of *Leslie's Weekly*. He said nothing, and Sleicher, considering the conversation ended, nodded to him and Harriet and left.

"The Chief—that's what we call him—is really a very nice man," Harriet said. "He's quite democratic. His door is always open to anyone, even the office boy."

Willy was still standing up. "Well, I'd better be going." Then, as if it had only just occurred to him: "Uh, you remember you promised"—he deliberately used that word—"something about our going . . . about your getting tickets to the theater sometime. Did you mean it?"

"Oh." Harriet frowned and didn't answer for a moment.

"Yes, I remember. Well of course I meant it. I don't make promises frivolously, William. I don't know when it could be, though. I'd like to get you a complimentary ticket, and I'd like it to be for something I think you'd enjoy. The season's just opening and they don't hand out a lot of tickets for new plays. But I should be able to wrangle something. Here, write down your telephone number. I'll call you." She tore a page off a pad of paper and handed it to him.

He wrote down his number and added his name for insurance and handed it back to her. He had imposed on her long enough. She obviously wanted to get back to whatever she had been typing.

"Well, I'd better be going," he repeated.

"I'm so glad you stopped by, William."

"Well . . . goodbye then. Until you call . . ."

He threaded his way through the maze of desks again to the elevator and rode it down to the main floor, his mind absorbed with renewed speculation about Harriet.

She had not been pleased to have been reminded about her promise. Yet she could easily have put him off, have gotten out of it entirely, simply by saying it was impossible, no tickets were available. Why hadn't she? He could hardly believe she'd promised to call him.

Stop minimizing yourself, Willy. Confidence. Confidence.

2

To Willy's disbelieving wonderment, Harriet called two days later, on Sunday afternoon. His mother answered the phone.

"Miss Quinlan?" she said questioningly as she handed Willy the earpiece. The telephone was on the opened desk lid of the secretary in the hall. He waited until she went into the kitchen.

Harriet spoke rapidly and to the point: "Hello, William, we're in luck. I can get you in to see a new play opening tomorrow evening at the Empire. It's supposed to be a very entertaining comedy. I was going to go with someone else but they just called and said they won't be able to make it. I know it's short notice but would you be free?"

Would he be free? He had never felt freer in his life—nor more enchained by her.

"Why . . . yes. Yes, certainly."

"The Empire is at Fortieth and Broadway. You know how to get there? They'll be holding the tickets at the box office in both our names until eight o'clock, so try to get there a little before that. I'll try too, but if you get there first you can pick them up. The play is supposed to start at eight-twenty but they never do. That's one of my constant complaints but"—she laughed softly—"it doesn't seem to do much good. I'll meet you in the lobby."

She asked him if he understood everything and he assured her that he did.

"All right," she said. "See you tomorrow evening. Oh—just in case something comes up and you can't make it I'd better give you my office number. Do you have a pencil? It's Madison Square six-six-three-two. And the number of the Hotel Victoria is Madison Square one-six-nine-oh."

He already knew both numbers; he'd looked them up in the

telephone book months before. She was either being very officious (did he know how to get to Fortieth and Broadway!) or was
very anxious that there be no slip-up in their arrangement. He
was glad in either case. Her giving him her numbers, as public as
they were, was almost like confiding an intimacy to him.

"Okay," he said, pretending to write them down. "I've got
them."

"Well . . . see you tomorrow evening then," she repeated.
"Goodbye."

They were going to sit together. From what she had said in
her office he had thought she meant she would try to get him a
single complimentary ticket, maybe in the back of the balcony.
But wonder of wonders, not only was he going to attend the theater as the guest of one of New York's most prominent (and without challenge its most beautiful) dramatic critics, who was now
even more of a celebrity as an aviatrix, he was going to accompany her. He was not just going to be her guest but her *escort*.

It was purely by accident of course. The ticket had been intended for someone else. (Helen Vanderbilt?) Yet when that someone else couldn't go Harriet had immediately thought of him.
Him, not one of any number of other people she might have
asked. She'd said *we're* in luck, not *you're* in luck.

He began analyzing. She had called so soon, so unexpectedly. Was she just being thoughtful, considerate? Or was she
merely discharging as quickly as she could the obligation he had
imposed upon her?

Wait a minute. She said the tickets would be held in both
their names. She'd expected him to go with her even before she
called! Did that mean there wasn't someone else, that she really
wanted to go out with him?

The very idea was laughable. She was simply a gracious,
friendly person, and it meant absolutely nothing at all that she
had favored him and not another of her friends with the fortu-
itously available ticket.

Yet . . . she had thought of *him*, not someone else.

"What was all that about?" his mother asked with transparent casualness.

He told her.

"Harriet Quinlan invited you to the theater with her? Why would she do that?"

"She just wants to expose me to the cultural side of life," he laughed. "I told her one time that I'd never seen a Broadway play."

"She must be quite a bit older than you, William. Older women sometimes . . . She's very glamorous and famous. I hope you don't—"

She didn't finish, and he didn't tell her that it was much too late to warn him not to be ensnared by a glamorous and famous older woman.

He was at the Empire at seven-forty-five. He asked for the tickets at the box office—there was no charge—and then stood to one side of the lobby, a little distance from the doors, which were open to allow the pleasantly warm September evening air outside to circulate. There were a dozen or so other earlycomers there, in pairs or small groups, chattering away. A few of the men were dressed in evening clothes. He wondered if this was the expected attire on opening nights. Harriet hadn't said anything about his needing a tux. Other people came in as he waited and he was glad to see that most of the men were in ordinary business suits like himself.

By eight o'clock the lobby was fairly crowded and noisy. Only a few people had gone to their seats. Then Harriet appeared, and his was not the only head to turn toward her. There were appreciative glances from some of the men near the street doors, appraising ones from their female companions.

She was dressed in a hat and gown Willy would have been unable to describe for the fashion pages except that the hat, of satiny material, was small compared to most hats one saw on women and was kind of coiled like a turban—a toque, he thought they called it—and the gown was deep blue. Over the gown she wore a short white brocaded jacket that nipped in at her waist and flared over her hips, and on her hands she wore white lace gloves. The jacket was unbuttoned, falling open to show several long strands of pearls around her neck, complementing the single pearl at each ear. She carried a small, sparkly purse in her hand. Everything about her was very tasteful and fashionable.

She saw him and smiled and waved, and as she walked up to him Willy was pleasedly conscious that he was now the object of appraising glances from nearby men.

"The tickets were there, William?" He showed them to her. "Good. Why don't we take our seats now before someone I know sees me and I get involved in a conversation. As I said, these things never start on time but somebody has to set an example."

Their seats were among the best in the house, in the middle of the orchestra section a few rows from the stage. He helped Harriet take off her jacket and arrange it over the back of her chair.

"I specifically requested center row seats," she said as she removed her hat and placed it in her lap. "The other evening at the Liberty Theater I was on the aisle—I really don't need an aisle seat because unlike the critics for the morning newspapers I don't have to rush out at the end to write my review. Anyway, I was on the aisle and was obliged to get up, clutching my bag and glasses and hat and everything, no less than five times between each act so that a number of gentlemen could file out individually for a smoke. And then get up again when they returned at different times. That's another of my pet peeves. I don't see why men who can't forgo indulging in the habit for a couple of hours don't purchase aisle seats. Or else the management should make it plain that the purchase of a ticket doesn't entitle a person to make a nuisance of himself to others.

"But I forgot. You have the habit too, don't you?"

He might not have thought too much about disturbing people to go out to the lobby for a cigarette between curtains, but never for a moment would he have considered leaving Harriet and depriving himself of even a minute of her company, or miss the frequent opportunities he took to study her profile when her head was turned away from him. He was not even able to read the playbill the usher had handed to him with any comprehension, so conscious was he of her presence beside him.

"You're quite right," he said. "At least they could all leave and return together."

She laughed. "That would help. But that's really the least of my complaints. Some people are really quite boorish, talking, laughing inappropriately, spoiling the play for everyone else. Sometimes I think the management is afraid to crack down because some of these people, who should have better manners, are socially prominent. That's a poor excuse. But they won't do anything until enough other patrons complain."

Willy was amazed. He would have thought that anyone attending the theater, the "legitimate" theater anyway, would be on his best behavior. Maybe not a bunch of rowdy college boys, but certainly socially prominent people. He was really pretty naive about things.

Harriet was quite talkative. "Another thing that annoys me is the use of claques of paid applauders. So far it seems mostly confined to the Metropolitan Opera, but I've been to plays where the actors were called out for eight or nine curtain calls when they didn't deserve one. I hope this is one European custom we don't import."

He had nothing to offer, so he nodded sympathetically and made a pretense of trying to read the program again. He registered that the play was called "A Single Man" and that it starred John Drew and Mary Boland.

He registered little more even during the performance, which, contrary to Harriet's warning, started only a few minutes late. The plot revolved around Drew's attempts, as a middle-aged bachelor, to emulate the happiness of his married friends by finding a wife. He focuses on a young and effervescent and athletic girl, who leads him a merry chase for most of the three acts, until at the end he realizes (as the audience had known from the beginning) that he was in love all along with his faithful secretary, played by Miss Boland.

It was quite clean—no "hells" or "damns." Something Harriet could recommend that "one can take his wife or daughter to."

Harriet took her opera glasses out of her purse and looked through them occasionally, and at one point handed them to him. They were so close to the stage, however, that glasses weren't necessary.

During the first intermission a number of people got up to go into the lobby but there was no undue disruption or loud talking. It seemed to be a very well-mannered crowd. He remarked on that to Harriet.

"I'm glad," she said. "I wanted your first experience to be a pleasurable one. Are you enjoying the play? Everyone is quite good, don't you think? Especially Caroll McComas, the actress playing the young girl. She's cute without being silly. This is her first dramatic role, she's been in musical comedies. If she keeps it up she'll set quite a pace for other ingénues, like Marie Doro or Billie Burke."

He was later to read almost those same words in Harriet's review of the play for *Leslie's*. As she had done in the hangar after her licensing tests, she was writing even as she engaged in conversation.

She fingered the glasses in her lap. "You're sure you don't want to go out for a cigarette? I don't mind." He shook his head.

"Well, we'll just sit here then. It would be nice, though, if they served glaces or mineral water or some refreshment during the intermissions, like they do in London. I mean, bringing them down the aisles. They started doing that at the New Theater last spring."

"Maybe we could go somewhere and get something later?" he ventured.

"Well . . . I don't know. I was thinking of taking you backstage after the performance to meet the players."

"Really?"

"I want to make this evening a complete introduction to the theater for you, William."

The stage manager knew Harriet of course and they were readily admitted backstage, where stagehands were busily occupied with manipulating ropes and moving backdrops and furniture and props, preparing for the next day's opening act scene. In Harriet's company Willy was introduced to a realm he had not known existed.

The actors and actresses, still in their stage clothes, were all in a large room in the upper part of the theater, toasting each other with champagne, exuberant with the certainty that they were involved in a "hit." Everyone seemed to know Harriet and she seemed to know everyone else. She introduced him to the leading man and lady and a few others. By virtue of being in her company and, as she told everyone, a fellow aviator and former student at the Moisant Flying School, he found himself immediately enveloped in a cloud of friendly intimacy that was as unexpected as it was, he felt, a bit overdone. But then these were actors, always "projecting," on or off the stage, even as Harriet, a writer, was always writing, whether she was at her typewriter or away from it.

Everyone was admiring of his accomplishment, but after he answered a few questions one or two people asked him about his flying experiences they quickly turned back to the subject of greatest interest to them, and that was the play and Harriet's reaction to it. They were of course pleased when she said she would give it a rave. Of more immediate concern, however, were the opinions of the newspaper critics, especially those on the morning papers whose reviews were even now being composed.

Someone had given Willy a glass of champagne and he stood sipping it self-consciously in a corner of the room. Harriet was still busy talking with the leading man and lady. A young girl came up to him smiling, also holding a glass.

"What was your name again?" she asked. "I couldn't hear."

"Willy Reynolds." Harriet had introduced him as "William."

"I'm Caroll McComas's understudy. My name's Carole too, but with an 'e' and only one 'l'. Carole Cunningham." She offered her hand.

Something about the way she smiled up at him reminded him of the girl at the Hudson-Fulton Celebration and the thought embarrassed him. She was about the same size as that girl, but much prettier, with blue eyes, not brown, and vivid blonde hair instead of the dishwater variety. She had too much makeup on, but of course that was for the stage.

"Have you met everyone, Willy? Did you meet Mr. Frohman, the producer?"

Yes he had, he said. He supposed he had.

"You're with Miss <u>Q</u>uinlan? Something about you two taking flying lessons together?"

"Yes, we did. That is, we started together but she—" He was going to say that Harriet had qualified for her license long before he had but checked himself. No more minimizing, remember?

"She must be a remarkable woman," Carole said. "But so is anybody who can fly an aeroplane. I've always wanted to go up in one. Do you think you could take me up sometime, Willy?" She smiled at him coquettishly.

"That would be a little difficult," he laughed. "All the planes we fly only have one seat."

"Oh. That's too bad." She sounded genuinely disappointed.

The corners of her mouth were turned down in a way that, except when she smiled, gave her pretty face a kind of sad, pensive look. Her mouth might be awfully nice to kiss, he thought.

"What about you, Carole? What do you do during performances—just wait backstage?"

She laughed and looked into his eyes again. "That's about it. Waiting for my big break."

Her eyes dropped and she looked toward a group of people nearby, then added, almost to herself, "I should say *we* wait. Elliot Raymond and I. He's John Drew's understudy."

Carole was so easy to talk to and so full of questions about aeroplanes and flying that he began to forget his feeling of being out of place in this group. He asked her more about herself. She was from some small town in Pennsylvania he had never heard of and this was her first job in the theater, though she had never yet actually appeared on stage.

Just then, however, someone announced in a loud voice that

they were going to continue the party at Delmonico's while await-ing the all-important first reviews.

Harriet suddenly seemed to remember him and beckoned to him with a gloved hand. He excused himself from Carole and was only a little disappointed when Harriet said she wasn't going to the restaurant. Tomorrow was a working day.

"But you could go if you want to, William. I wouldn't mind at all." She darted a glance toward the girl he had been talking with. "I see you've met someone."

He told her he wouldn't think of it. Much as he might have enjoyed prolonging his evening with all these charming and at-tractive people, he knew that he really did not belong. He was glad when they left and he had Harriet all to himself again.

They stood outside under the darkened marquee. The theater crowd had long since dispersed. The night was still warm and Harriet wore her jacket unbuttoned as she had when he had first seen her that evening.

"I'll get a cab," he said.

"I think I'll walk home, William. It's such a nice evening."

"All the way to Twenty-seventh Street?"

"It's not all that far, straight down Broadway. I've walked much farther many times. I like to walk."

"All right," he said eagerly. It would give him that much longer with her. He offered his arm.

"Oh you don't have to accompany me, William. It's late and you have to go all the way to Brooklyn. It's really all right."

"Nonsense. What kind of gentleman would I be if I let you go home alone?"

"You're a very nice young gentleman and it really isn't necessary. But if you insist."

She slipped her hand through his arm, thrilling him, and the thirteen blocks to her hotel seemed too few, he was in such a daze. They walked, saying nothing for a long while.

At Herald Square a police wagon roared by with its bell clanging.

"New York never sleeps, does it?" Harriet said.

"I guess not. Brooklyn is much quieter." What a dumb response.

"You're very quiet yourself, William. I hope you didn't find the evening too tedious." Her tone was mischievous.

"Are you kidding? It was wonderful. I enjoyed it tremendously. I'll—I'll never forget it. I hate to see it end."

She gave his arm a tiny squeeze, thrilling him again.

God, don't let it ever end. Don't let us ever get there.

But all too soon they were crossing Twenty-eighth Street—Tin Pan Alley—and he thought of asking her jokingly if the pianos every bothered her. But that would have been even dumber. In another minute they were standing outside the Hotel Victoria.

She withdrew her hand. "I wish I could ask you up, William, but it's late and I live alone and, well . . ."

"Of course," he said. The thought had never entered his head that she might ask him up.

"Maybe another time," she said.

"Another theater—?" He hesitated to say "date." "Another play? You've really made an aficionado of me tonight."

"Well, I don't think I would be able to get you a ticket for an opening night again, although there are at least eighty legitimate theaters in this city, with new plays opening all the time. But later in the season, when their attendance drops, I'm sure I could get a ticket for you for any number of plays. Maybe two tickets, if you have a friend you'd like to take sometime. Some young lady . . ? You must know a lot of girls. Who was that one you were talking with tonight? I didn't get a chance to meet her."

He was mildly puzzled. She'd had a very good chance, but she had motioned him away from the girl. Carole probably would have liked to have met her.

"Carole Cunningham, the ingénue's understudy. As a matter of fact, I did make a date with her."

He hadn't really. He'd simply mentioned the possibility of taking her to the Nassau Boulevard meet and Carole had told him where he could reach her on the telephone. The girl had dropped entirely out of his mind when they left the theater.

A change came over Harriet's face. He could see it happen clearly in the streetlight.

"Oh—you *are* a fast worker, aren't you? Well, I'm sure you could learn a lot about the theater from her."

She was actually incensed. It was in her face and in her intonation, and he was all the more puzzled.

"I didn't make a date. I don't know why I said that. I merely said something about going to the Nassau Boulevard meet because she seemed to be interested in aeroplanes. She's never seen one fly and I— Look, I'd much rather go out with you again, Harriet."

"Those weren't free tickets tonight, William. I usually attend second night performances—most of the reviewers for weekly or monthly publications do. There weren't any free seats available and I had a hard time getting the ones I did."

What was she saying? That she had paid for the tickets herself? She had been that eager to give him an "introduction to the theater"? There hadn't been anybody else she had asked first?

Or—the wild idea came to him again—was it actually possible that she had simply wanted to go out with him?

"I want to see you again, Harriet. Whether it's the theater or for dinner or . . . "

But she had become suddenly distant, unreachable.

"No. I don't think that would be a very good idea. After all, I'm—" She paused. "No, you really should go out with someone closer to your own age."

He was in confusion. During their walk, when Harriet was clinging to his arm, he had planned to kiss her, at least once, on the lips, before they parted. But now he knew that if he tried to, out here on the street, she would turn her head and it would only be a brushing peck on the cheek, a meaningless gesture like the kisses the actors and actresses at the theater so freely exchanged with each other. He wanted more than that.

She said, pleasantly but abruptly, "Good night, William. I'm glad you enjoyed yourself. Have fun with Carole."

And before he could do or say anything she had turned and gone through the door of the hotel and it had closed behind her.

3

WILLY WAS MORE perplexed—and vexed—by Harriet than ever. Yes, it was his own doing again. She had graciously invited him to escort her to the theater, even paying for the tickets herself—and he had been so much of an ass as to give her the idea that he had made a play for another girl the very same evening.

But it was ridiculous. It was she who had broached the possibility of getting more tickets, not for them again but for him and a friend, maybe "some young lady." It was she who had brought up the subject of Carole Cunningham. Why should she be offended when she thought he'd asked the girl for a date?

She had acted for all the world as if she were jealous!

That was even more ridiculous, yet it was in the back of his mind when he called Harriet at *Leslie's Weekly* the next day to try to make some kind of amends. By the time he hung up—or rather, she hung up—she had thoroughly disabused him of the notion.

She seemed pleased at first to hear from him. At least there was no hint of displeasure in her cheery, "Hello, William. Did you get home all right?"

"Oh sure. I—I just wanted to tell you again how much I enjoyed last night." He paused, waiting to see where she might lead the conversation.

"I'm glad."

"Well . . ." The ball was back in his court. He decided not to apologize about Carole.

"I meant what I said about wanting to see you again, Harriet."

Now she paused. Then, very softly, "I know you did. And I told you that it wouldn't be a very good idea."

He ignored that. "Not necessarily to go to a play but maybe for dinner or to a museum or something. Coney Island, maybe? No, that's closed now, isn't it?" He laughed nervously. "I mean, a regular date."

There—he had used the word. "On me this time." He waited again.

"Listen, William," she began, speaking so low that he could hardly hear her. "I'm really quite busy right now. I'm sorry if I may have given you the wrong impression about my paying for the tickets. I shouldn't have told you that and I realized later that you might have thought— But all I had in mind was that it would be nice for you to have the experience of attending an opening night. Nothing more than that."

Then, as if to assuage his feelings, she laughed gently and said, "Think of it as a present from me for your winning your license."

He wished he could see her face. "Harriet, don't you know I'm nuts about you? I think about you all the time. Why isn't it a good idea? Is it because you're six years older than I am? Six years isn't all that much. Is there someone else?"

"I really am busy, William. I have to hang up now. I'm expecting another call."

"When would be a good time to call you?"

He could hear the exasperated exhaling of her breath in the receiver.

"I don't want you to call me again, William. Please don't make me be rude about it. I really am glad you had a nice time last night. Let's just leave it at that, shall we? I must hang up now. Goodbye."

"Harriet, wait—" But the line was dead.

He was in a dejected mood for the rest of that day, until he began to rationalize away his dejection.

He had tried his best and there was nothing more he could

do about Harriet Quinlan. If she hadn't made it plain before that she did not welcome his personal advances, she had made it abundantly clear now. For a second time she had put him in his place, and he wasn't going to step out of it again. He had been stupid to kid himself that the beautiful and accomplished and famous Harriet Quinlan could have the slightest romantic interest in him. Even if she weren't beautiful and accomplished and famous, it was preposterous to have imagined that a mature 27-year-old woman could want anything to do with a 20-year-old postadolescent college student. "Sophomoric" was the word for him all right, although he was now a junior and would enter his majority in another month.

Now it was his turn to be angry with *her*, for being beautiful and accomplished and famous, and absolutely unattainable by the likes of him.

So the hell with Harriet Quinlan. She was not the only beautiful woman in the world. New York was full of them, and much younger than she.

Carole Cunningham was beautiful. Well, not like Harriet, but highly attractive, and more attractive in a fresh and natural way than he had remembered when he saw her for the first time without her heavy stage makeup. Her eyes were clear blue and the bridge of her strong nose had a little bump in it that he found as fascinating as her downturning mouth, and eventually adorable.

She lived at a hotel for single women on Lexington Avenue, she'd told him. He called the number from home Thursday afternoon. She wasn't there but he left a message. An hour later she had called him back and they had arranged to meet at a restaurant near the Empire Theater at six on Friday.

Carole Cunningham wasn't unattainable.

She was a lighthearted, very open person, easy to talk to and comfortable to be with, not at all affected or "theatrical." No slack trencherman himself, he smiled with pleasure at the relish with which she tackled her dinner, as if it were the first good meal she'd had in a long time. She couldn't eat like this every day or she wouldn't be so petite. He listened as between mouthfuls she answered the questions he plied her with.

She was 19. She had acted in plays in high school and that was when the Broadway bug had bitten her—like a lot of other girls, she added with a kind of rueful shrug. But she was unbelievably lucky, getting the understudy part so soon after coming to New York, and in a play produced by Charles Frohman, the country's leading producer. It really wasn't much but it was a start and would be a good credit to have. And who knew? Caroll McComas might catch a cold someday.

He liked the way she laughed. "If you ever do get a chance to go on," he said, "be sure to let me know. I'll tell Harriet Quinlan to give you a review."

He was trading on his acquaintance—that was all it amounted to—with Harriet and disliked himself for doing so. But why not? He would never see Harriet again. And Carole was impressed.

"Do you now her that well?" she said eagerly. "But then you must, both of you taking flying lessons together. I'd heard of her of course but I'd never seen her in person before. She's very attractive, I think one of the most attractive women I've ever seen."

Matilde Moisant had said much the same thing. Was he really never going to see Harriet again? He tried not to think about it.

"She ought to be on stage herself," Carole said. "But I'm glad she isn't. There's already enough competition!"

She laughed again, then looked at him soberly. "Are you . . . seeing her? I mean besides flying together. Are you in love with her?"

The last question threw him for a second. He had never met a girl who talked so directly.

"We've never flown together. All the school machines are only single place. As for . . . She's a little bit out of my league, don't you think? Maybe not as a flier but—"

"Did you happen to meet Elliot Raymond the other night?" Carole said suddenly.

"He's John Drew's understudy, or did I tell you that? I think he's even more handsome than John Drew. Maybe John Drew and Caroll McComas will both come down with a cold some evening and Elliot and I can go on together."

This time she didn't laugh. An almost wistful look came into her eyes and her mouth turned down even more than usual.

At her urging, he told her about his experiences as a student aviator, especially the accident, trying to make it sound hilarious to Carole. (It almost was now, in retrospect.) He magnified his initial clumsiness and fright, until he became conscious that he was really bragging in a kind of backhanded way. Carole knew that he had eventually won his license so he couldn't have been all that inept.

Then he found himself talking about Harriet, how she had outshone everyone else, how she had encouraged him, how she was going on tour with the Moisant International Aviators—and realized that this also was a kind of bragging, a bragging by association.

"It must be so exciting, up in the air," Carole said. "Oh I really wish you could take me flying, Willy. Willy-Nilly."

She fluttered her eyelashes at him, and then positively shocked him by starting to rub her foot against his leg under the table.

He pretended to ignore what she was doing, while liking it very much.

"So do I," he said. "I'm hoping to buy my own machine someday, I don't know when. I'll make sure it's a two-place. But there's that meet at Nassau Boulevard I told you about, the last week in October. Lots of famous aviators'll be there. We could go see that. Would you like to do that?"

"Oh I'd love it. I really would."

By the time they had dessert, Carole consuming a large piece of chocolate pie as enthusiastically as she had demolished her steak, it was after seven and she had to get to the theater. In a few minutes they were at the stage door and he had made another date.

He began seeing a lot of Carole over the coming days. He took her out to dinner again, and afterwards she got him in backstage where they watched the play (with Carol McComas and John Drew unfortunately both in fine fettle) and he was introduced to cast members he hadn't met before, including Elliot Raymond, who was indeed handsome, but not all that handsome, he thought. He flushed with the feeling that Carole was showing him off to everyone.

He started meeting her at the stage door after the play and they would go and have cocktails at a bar Carole knew where they permitted women. The first time they went there he was shocked by her again when she produced a package of Laurens, a new brand of cigarettes that was currently being advertised, and waited for him to light one for her.

Well, why not? he thought. If it was all right for men, why not for women? He had never been able to understand the moral objections to smoking. Harriet of course did not "have the habit."

A girl who smoked cigarettes was a girl who would do anything, the moralists said. The thought excited him.

The very first night, after they had watched the play backstage, he had escorted Carole home to her hotel and kissed her good night without doubt or hesitation, and did so again, more fervently each time, on other nights. No male visitors were allowed in the residents' rooms, and none in the parlor after nine o'clock, so he began visiting her there in the daytime after his afternoon classes, where they sat on a divan and talked a lot and, when no one was around, necked a little. Several evenings they had an early supper and he took her dancing at a place in the Village where they had a good ragtime band.

If you laka me lak I laka you . . . under the bamboo tree . . .

One warm afternoon he took her for a ride in a hansom cab through Central Park, holding her and kissing her at every opportunity.

Another afternoon he took her to the Columbia burlesque house on Forty-fourth Street, where she seemed to get a kick out of the crude ribaldry of the comics. He could not imagine escorting Harriet to such a place, to look at all those girls in their form-clinging tights, wiggling their derrières at the audience.

He liked Carole, exceedingly. She was a delight. She could mimic dialects and accents perfectly. The first time he grabbed her for a kiss in the residence hotel parlor she had pretended innocence.

"Sure and ya wouldn't be th' kind o' gintlemin who'd be tryin' t' take idvantage of a young colleen now, would ya? Willy-Nilly. Stage-door Willy."

Then, whispering against his ear, breathing heavily: "*Zut alors!* Ze gentleman know what ze lady like."

"I love you!" he blurted after one tongue-touching kiss, and he wondered if he did.

She took his hands from her waist and held them in hers and gazed into his eyes.

"Tell me, Willy-Nilly. Who do you think about when you kiss me?"

"What?"

Her mouth curved in a strange sweet little smile and she squeezed his hands.

"It's all right, Willy. It doesn't matter."

So enchanted was he with Carole that he was able to think about Harriet quite dispassionately. He didn't even consider going out to the Nassau Boulevard aerodrome on a weekday during the meet but instead deliberately took Carole with him on the last day, a Sunday, when he knew Harriet would not be there.

There was a good crowd, despite an attempt by a prominent Long Island churchman to get a court injunction against flying on the Sabbath. From a distance they'd seen Hèléne Dutrieu, whom the press had tried to build up as a rival to Harriet, though as far as he knew the two of them hadn't competed. She looked as cute as Harriet in her flying costume. Matilde Moisant had set a woman's altitude record of twenty-five hundred feet earlier in the week. People said Teddy Roosevelt was supposed to be there this day but they hadn't seen him. They watched Earle Ovington make a demonstration flight. The day before, on Saturday, he had delivered the first mail by air, to Mineola, all of three miles away.

But otherwise the meet, the one day he saw of it, was a bit of a disappointment to Willy. There was little really exciting flying because many of the pilots who had competed earlier in the week had left. Carole, though, enjoyed herself and seemed interested as he pointed out aviators he knew and described the different aeroplanes.

His mother eventually asked him about the uncertain hours he was keeping, going out in the evening and not coming back until after midnight, the odd hours during the day as well. She never knew anymore when he would be home for supper, if at all.

He told her about Carole, briefly mentioning that she was an actress he had met through Harriet Quinlan and emphasizing that she was only 19, fresh from the country, more or less alone in the big city. He went on at great length about what a nice girl she was and how much he liked her.

Ellen Reynolds was both relieved and concerned anew. She was relieved that her son had gotten over his infatuation or whatever it had been with the Quinlan woman; he had taken her picture off his dresser, although he still kept it in the drawer for some reason. But now he was all wrapped up in a girl from the stage and (she did not say it of course) she had heard about the kind of lives theater people led.

But her William would not let himself become involved with a girl who was . . . *fast*, and she was even surer of that when he suggested inviting Carole for dinner some Sunday. In fact, why not the coming Sunday, he suggested.

"I think she'd really enjoy a home-cooked meal. And I've been promising for weeks to take her out to the aerodrome. We could go there afterwards."

He drove into Manhattan and picked Carole up at her hotel shortly before noon. She was waiting inside the door and came out as soon as he pulled up to the curb, looking sweet and wholesome, as he knew she would. He grinned in self-satisfaction when she took in the Chalmers with appreciative eyes and remarked about what a nice automobile it was. Her folks didn't own a car, she said.

He went a little out of their way to drive them over the Brooklyn Bridge. "It's really something, isn't it?" he said, sweeping his arm around grandiosely, as if the magnificent span had been constructed just for his convenience, to enable him to impress a girl.

After he parked in front of the house and they were walking up to the door he said, "Uh, I don't think it would be wise for you to smoke in my parents' presence, Carole."

She gave him an arch, amused look.

"Only if you offer me one. I didn't bring any with me. Really, Willy. Just how dumb do you think I am?"

The dinner went well. The Reynoldses had forgone church so Ellen would have time to prepare the meal. John greeted them at the door and Ellen emerged from the kitchen. His mother conveyed just a touch of put-uponness in her manner toward Carole at first, Willy felt, merely saying a polite "How do you do?" and then bustling back into the kitchen, declining over her shoulder Carole's offer to help in bringing the dishes to the table. But once they were all seated and eating his mother began to warm up.

She watched as Carole dug into her serving of leg of lamb and braised potatoes and gravy and vegetables with zest, quite properly and ladylike to be sure, doing nothing that would have offended an authority on etiquette, but nevertheless digging in. The girl ate as though she hadn't eaten for days, she thought. She was pleased that William had invited her.

So was John Reynolds. "I'm glad to see you're not one of those modern girls, Carole, who pick at their food and eat like birds and starve themselves to keep thin."

"How do you do it?" Ellen asked. "I mean, keep your figure?"

Carole looked at her plate in embarrassment. It wouldn't do to admit that she did starve herself, involuntarily, most of the time.

"Acting takes a lot of energy," Willy said, trying to rescue her.

"And you're young of course," Ellen said. "That makes all the difference."

After dinner, while his mother and father did the dishes, his mother again declining (with warm thanks this time) Carole's offer to help, Willy and Carole sat on the sofa in the parlor. He picked up the copy of *Leslie's* that carried Harriet's first article on her flying lessons and started to show it to Carole before he realized it was the one that had printed the formal portrait.

"Someone has cut something out," Carole said.

"Oh, that was just—" He was going to say it was just a good picture of an aeroplane, but he hadn't cut out the caption and Carole was reading it: "Miss Harriet Quinlan . . ."

She gave him a look.

He closed the magazine. "If we're going to the aerodrome we ought to leave now. It gets dark early these days and it looks like it might rain, but we can still go just for the ride."

4

Halfway there the clouds let go their burden, the rain suddenly coming down so hard and blindingly that Willy had to pull over to the side of the road to wait it out. He kept the engine running to burn away any moisture that might get under the hood and he and Carole huddled close together in the middle of the seat with the horse blanket around them to shield them from the rain slanting in. He'd put the top up before they left Brooklyn but the side curtains were not much use in this kind of deluge.

"I don't think anybody'll be flying this afternoon," he said, listening to the heavy drops pound against the canvas over their heads and watching the water stream down the windshield. "I'm sorry."

"I don't care, Willy. I'm having fun. Did I do all right?"

"Hmm? Oh, yes. I think they were quite taken with you."

"I'm glad. Your parents are very nice. Especially your father. Not many husbands help their wives do the dishes."

His father always had, and Willy had never thought it unusual. He did have great parents.

The rain stopped as abruptly as it had descended. In a few minutes the sun was out again, even brighter than it had been before. He wiped the steam off the inside of the windshield and resumed driving, going slowly through the puddles on the road. When they reached the field, the sky, cleansed by the passing squall, was crystal clear except for a line of dark clouds moving off to the north.

The storm had also cleared the aerodrome of spectators, as well as anybody who might have been flying. The place looked deserted. He led Carole around to the first hangar. The side door was unlocked but no one was inside.

"Gosh," Carole said when she saw the school machines. "Look at the planes. I didn't know they were so big close up. Which one did you fly?"

He pointed at No. 1. "That's the one I took my test in."

"Did Harriet Quinlan fly that one too?"

"Uh-huh. We all did, at one time or another. There are more planes in the other hangars."

"Oh I want to see you fly, Willy. Can you take one of them up?"

He hadn't planned on flying; he'd only wanted to show Carole the aeroplanes, and possibly watch someone else fly. But now he was suddenly eager. He had been up only once since getting his license the month before, in an Anzani-powered Moisant André had rented to him. With the rain gone it was a beautiful afternoon for flying, very warm for late October and windless, one of those Indian summer days the New York area was blessed with at least once each fall.

"I don't know," he said. "Let's see if we can find somebody. There must be someone around."

They found two of the mechanics Willy knew working on an

engine in the next hangar. One of them was a new man named Felix. He was another French import.

"*Bonjour*, Felix. Are you holding down the fort all alone today?"

Felix bowed politely to Carole. *Oui*, he said. With Messieurs 'Oupert and 'Ardy away on the tour and classes suspended, there was little activity at the field these days.

"I'd like to rent a plane for a short hop," Willy said.

"I am just about to lock the doors and leave."

The mechanic pursed his lips dubiously. Monsieur Reynolds wished to display for the mademoiselle. *Mais naturellement*. She was most pretty.

"Let me see how the ground looks," he said, and his breath nearly knocked Willy over. The man had been drinking, and not just a little.

The two mechanics slid open the doors of the hangar that had been closed against the storm, and Felix walked—weaved, rather—a little way out into the field.

"The grass is wet of course," he said when he came back, "but the ground is firm. The wind is calm. The Anzani again, Monsieur Reynolds? You have flown it before, no?"

Willy grinned at Carole. "Looks like you're going to get your wish. Just let me get into some flying togs. I'll bring a chair you can sit on in front of the hangar."

"Oh I don't want to sit down, Willy. I'm too excited."

The monoplane had been rolled out onto the apron in front of the third hangar when he returned from the locker room. Carole nodded approvingly at him. "You look like a real aviator, Willy."

He didn't. He was just wearing ordinary coveralls. The only thing "aeronautical" about him was the helmet and goggles. But he grinned with pleasure at her remark.

"We'll see. I hope I can remember how the thing works. Don't expect any tricks."

He wanted to show off for Carole but he was mostly indulging himself. It would not really be very exciting for her, waiting on the ground while he had his fun in the air. He decided he would only do a few turns over the field and maybe a low pass or two over the hangars for Carole's benefit.

Unlike the training planes with their Gnôme rotaries, this machine was fitted with a conventional fifty-horsepower, six-cylinder Anzani engine — actually two twenty-five-horsepower, three-cylinder engines mounted front to back and operating a common crankshaft. Anzanis made even more racket than the Gnômes and were notorious consumers of oil, even though the oil wasn't mixed with the gasoline. But on the plus side, because of the stationary cylinders, they developed far less of the torque that had been his bane during training.

This was his second time in the plane and he took off routinely. It was a quick climber and easy to handle.

He made two passes over the line of hangars at fifty feet, then circled around for a landing and taxied back. Carole was running up to the plane even before the engine had stopped.

"That was beautiful, Willy." She looked at him with renewed admiration as he climbed out.

"Too bad I can't take you up," he said, meaning it. "I've never seen it like this. It's like a fairyland."

He tried to describe it to her. The squall had left behind a ragged low-lying mist. Fifty feet up the air was clear as a bell, but around the branches of trees and the roofs of houses and across the fields tendrils of white clung like strands of soft cotton.

"Let me sit in it, Willy."

"Well, I don't see how . . . "

But she had already taken off her hat and placed it and her purse on the wing and was trying to climb up on the fuselage, oblivious of the length of legs she revealed as she hitched up her long dress, and of the two mechanics watching as she did so. Willy boosted her over the side and into the cockpit, then crouched on the frame behind her and reached around her shoulders and explained the controls and how to work them, as André had done so many times with him, but unlike André, making much delightful contact with her cheek and hair and hands.

"Oh take me up in it, Willy! *Please.*"

"I wish I could, sweetie, I really do, but I could hardly fly with you sitting in my lap. Though that would be very nice."

She giggled. "Couldn't I hang on behind you somehow? I mean, couldn't you make some kind of seat for me? It's all open back there. There's room." She looked at him appealingly.

He laughed. "Silly goose. There are all kinds of bracing wires in the way, and even if there was something to sit on your feet would hang out the bottom or get tangled with the rudder wires."

"Then let's see if there's room for me on your lap. *Please,* Willy."

He was more than willing to try. "Okay, but just to sit, not to fly or anything."

Carole stood up and with a great deal of difficulty, and more delightful body contact, he managed to get into the seat behind her. There was barely enough room for her to sit crosswise on his lap, her bottom on his left thigh and her legs tucked between his two spread legs, her dress hiked up almost to her waist.

"Satisfied?" he said.

Her head moved up and down against his cheek. But she wasn't satisfied.

"Couldn't we—what do you call it? Taxi around the field a little?"

"Hardly," he said.

But actually there was no reason why they couldn't. The Anzani had a throttle, so he wouldn't have to try to reach around Carole constantly to blip the ignition off and on as he would have with a rotary, and since they wouldn't get anywhere near flying speed he would only have to work the rudder bar. And it was so nice having Carole on his lap, even if his left leg was starting to get numb.

"Felix," he called. "Miss Cunningham and I would like to drive across the field and back."

The Frenchman, who had been watching the proceedings in the cockpit with amusement, and a bit of envy, threw his shoulders back in exaggerated astonishment.

"*Monsieur* . . ."

"We'll just taxi aross the field and back," Willy repeated. "I'll take the entire responsibility. If anything happens to the machine you know I'm good for it."

"It is not the machine, Monsieur Reynolds. "It could be dangerous for you and the mademoiselle." His accent made the word sound almost like the French *dangereux*.

Despite his better judgment, still shaking his head, but for the young man and his lady, Felix directed the other mechanic to hold the tail while he went to the front of the monoplane. He put his hands on the propeller.

"Only across the field and back," he said. "Your promise."

Willy nodded. "Switch on."

Felix pulled down on the propeller and the still-warm Anzani caught with a roar. Carole's hat and purse, which everyone had forgotten, blew off the wing and the hat went sailing.

Willy began moving across the field, slowly at first, then just fast enough to lift the tailskid to save it wear and tear. He could easily have let the plane rise off the ground—there was plenty of power to lift the two of them—but he throttled back and turned around at the far end and started taxiing along the perimeter to return to the hangar.

Carole shouted into his ear: "*Let's go up, Willy!*"

He idled the engine and let the plane roll to a stop. "We can't. I promised Felix I would just— Anyway, it's impossible with you on my lap."

"Why not? I'm not afraid."

"Because—look." He moved the column back. "I can't fly if I can't control the plane, and when I pull on the wheel it jams right into your . . ."

"What is the wheel for, Willy? It doesn't seem to turn."

For the first time Willy wondered himself. The wheel was fixed and had no real function other than as something to hold onto. Blériot, he recalled, had once been a manufacturer of acetylene headlights. The wheel was really a carry-over from automobile design, just as the first automobiles had been literally "horseless carriages." All you needed was the stick part of the control column. You really didn't need the wheel. All you needed was stick and rudder.

"I'll make myself small," Carole said.

And somehow she did just that. Somehow she made her already compact person even more compact, snuggling against his chest. She tucked her hair down underneath his chin.

"Please, Willy-Nilly. Silly Willy."

She was either very naive or very brave, or as reckless as he felt at that moment. "Silly Willy" was right.

It had been all he could do to keep the plane from taking off when they were taxiing fast. With Carole sitting on his lap its center of gravity was not changed; it was the same as it would be if there were just one heavy pilot. And the air had been as smooth as he had ever known it, not a bump in it when he had circled the field. There would never be a better opportunity to show Carole what flying was like.

"Shift over to my other leg," he said. "This one's numb."

She did so, shrinking herself down again.

"See that thing that looks like a bell at the bottom of the column and those wires attached to it? Whatever you do, keep your feet away from them. Understand?"

She moved her head up and down. The wash from the propeller was blowing her hair in his face.

"Here, put my helmet on. It'll protect you from the wind."

Her head was smaller than his but with her mass of hair tucked inside the helmet fit her snugly. He fastened the strap under her chin and helped her adjust the goggles.

"All set?"

She was.

He took a deep breath. He didn't know how he was going to explain this to Felix. André would probably ban him from the field when he found out. But then Felix wasn't going to tell; the man had been imbibing and was feeling frolicsome himself.

What the hell.

He turned onto the getaway and opened the throttle. He let

the plane build up speed, and then the ground was dropping away from them and the landscape was widening around them. He flew with his left hand on the wheel and his right hand on the throttle, reaching around Carole. The wind beat at his unprotected eyes, but fortunately there was no oil spray from the Anzani engine as there would have been with a Gnôme.

He would just do a couple circles. But as they banked around and started back over the field the plane wanted to climb. He let it. The air was absolutely smooth. It was like skimming a sheet of glass. It would be a shame to waste it.

They passed over the hangars and Clinton Road. He would go over Garden City and maybe as far as the Nassau Boulevard aerodrome, then come back. It wouldn't start getting dark for at least another hour, especially with the sky so clear.

Much of the ground mist he had seen before had evaporated, but cottony fingers of white still clung to low places. It was still a fairyland.

A few lights were already visible in the triplet towns of Hempstead and Garden City and Mineola as they passed over them, still climbing, though the sky overhead seemed as bright as it was when they'd taken off. The sun was well above a band of clouds low on the western horizon. In the far distance the towers of lower Manhattan came into view; they were already that high and it was that spectacularly clear.

He had always wanted to fly over New York. What a sight it would be to see Manhattan from an aeroplane, especially at this time of day when its millions of lights would be coming on. But it was too risky with Carole with him. He decided they would fly as far as Jamaica and then turn around.

They were at three thousand feet and still climbing. The engine was performing perfectly. Carole was peering over the side of the cockpit. She was not afraid.

He tapped her shoulder and yelled against the earflap of the helmet: *"Try to straddle my legs."*

He moved his legs as close together as he could and still keep his feet on the rudder bar. She struggled to pull up her dress and managed to get her legs over his knees. Her knees were jammed against a fuselage cross member on either side.

He took her hands and placed them on the wheel and guided her through the movements of the column; first left, then right, dipping each wing in turn, raising and lowering the nose and then leveling them out again, performing an aerial ballet. She moved her head in understanding.

With his hands still on hers he moved the column back to resume their climb, then removed his hands entirely.

"You're flying!" he shouted.

Her dress was as high as it could get. He put his hands on her waist, then allowed them to rest on the bare thighs exposed above her stockings. The skin felt cool. Either she was so intent on holding the wheel that she didn't notice or she didn't care. What a girl.

If only it could have been Harriet with him.

Because of their constant climb they were not traveling as fast as they would have in level flight. By the time they were over Queens the sun was edging into the bank of clouds on the horizon, turning them all pink and golden. Yet the sky behind them in the east was still bright. The city was so near. Maybe they could make one pass over it and then head back home in a long, straight, descending line. It would only be about twenty miles back to the field. With their speed increased by gravity they could hit eighty miles an hour and make it in plenty of time to land in daylight.

The altimeter read a little over seven thousand feet. He had never been this high before. How much you could see: Manhasset Bay and Little Neck Bay on the right, their shorelines looking like the edges of a lace tablecloth; then Flushing Bay and Rikers Island Channel, where Long Island Sound merged into the East River. He took over the wheel from Carole and leveled the plane. At this altitude they could glide to a landing almost anywhere.

They passed over the East River just above Fifty-ninth Street, the Queensboro Bridge he and Harriet had driven over off to their left. The river was a mere thin dark ribbon, except where the wakes of boats glinted, the bridge itself winking with the lights of cars driving over it. They could plainly see the grid pattern of the streets of upper Manhattan, like narrow pencil lines, splashed by light from streetlamps. It was a vast miniature city, a child's huge playset.

He banked over Central Park and pointed them toward downtown and the tall office buildings in the financial district. The peak of the Metropolitan tower was lit up, and beyond it to the south the upper stories of the Singer Building glowed in the rays of the lowering sun, as did the nearby Woolworth Building that would be the world's tallest skyscraper when it was finished.

Was it only two years since he had seen Wilbur Wright make his historic flight from Governors Island? He was more than sixty times as high as Wright had flown. What advances aviation had made in a mere two years!

The moon was a slender crescent, bright silver. But you could see its entire orb, the unlighted portion darker than the sky around it. He pointed at it and felt Carole's head move against his cheek. He kissed the back of her neck under the helmet in his gladness that she had talked him into taking her up.

Far below them two rivers of lights from moving vehicles— Broadway and Seventh Avenue—were converging on a point. He followed them and then banked steeply to the left, locking one wingtip on the bright glow where the rivers met.

"Times Square!" he shouted.

He was ebullient. The greatest city in the world was spread out below them, from the Battery to the Bronx, and they were the masters of it. God, how could anyone not want to fly? How could anyone want to do anything else but fly?

As they turned a half-circle he picked out Madison Square and the Flatiron Building at one end and the Leslie-Judge Building on the other—how tiny they looked!—and traced along Twenty-seventh Street to Harriet's hotel, looking even tinier.

Look up, darling. I'm right above you.

But she'd gone on the tour with the Moisant International Aviators and wasn't there and they were much too high for anyone to see them anyway. All those millions of people down below were completely unaware that two crazy fools were soaring nearly a mile and a half above them.

They were still pivoting over Times Square. It was so absolutely smooth that when he lifted his hand from the wheel for a moment the plane held its bank without varying. *This was flying*! It was so perfectly smooth that were it not for the air rushing past he would have thought they were suspended immobile in space and that it was the sparkling city that was wheeling around beneath them.

It was time to go back. Reluctantly, he reversed the bank and turned east, and saw with alarm that darkness that crept over the surface of Long Island. It was going to be a close thing.

He nosed down and started to apply full throttle when—

The engine stopped. Completely. Absolutely. Even though the wires screamed in the wind it was like a sudden dreadful silence.

"Oh thank you, Willy," Carole said. "That's much better."

My God, she was so naive she thought he had done it on purpose. This brave little girl trusted him so much—and he was going to kill her, kill them both.

5

HIS IMMEDIATE thought was that they were out of gas. But the tank had been full when he'd gone up by himself, for maybe fifteen minutes. It held enough for at least two hours of flying and he and Carole had been up for less than one. Even with her added weight they couldn't have used up all the gas. And the propeller was still turning from the force of their forward movement. That meant that the engine wasn't seized up for lack of oil.

It was a gravity-feed tank. He switched the ignition off and on, off and on. If there was any gas left the engine should catch. It didn't. He tried again, and finally switched off. Either there was a clog in the line or something more serious was wrong. Whatever it was it was something he couldn't possibly do anything about in the air.

Carole still seemed to be enjoying herself. "Are we going to glide back to the field?" she said calmly.

They almost could—if they had more altitude and he could see the ground to know where he was. But there were other aerodromes on Long Island, closer to Manhattan. There was the Belmont Racetrack, where Harriet had met John Moisant the year before and made her decision to learn to fly. *If he could locate it.* But although there were dark areas that might be parks or fields there were too many houses in Queens and Brooklyn. It was too big a risk to try to find Belmont Park or anyplace else to land on that side of the East River.

Central Park. Sheep Meadow was big enough to land on—in the daylight. But it wasn't daylight and there would be people strolling. Tall buildings all around anyway. Central Park was out of the question too.

By the time Willy had dismissed all these alternatives they had already lost several hundred feet, still heading toward the East River and Queens. He looked behind them. There was light on the higher ground in New Jersey to the north and west, beyond the Palisades. That area looked within reach.

"Try not to move, Carole. Don't talk to me. Everything's all right but we have to find somewhere to land."

He spoke as matter-of-factly as he could, only a little louder than a normal voice over the rushing of the wind. But Carole was not so naive that she didn't know that everything was not all right. She shrank herself again.

He banked around toward the dark line of cliffs on the far side of the Hudson, trying to establish the most efficient glide angle, one that would squeeze the most distance out of their precious, diminishing altitude.

Lincoln Beachey had volplaned from ten thousand feet with a dead engine. But he had deliberately used up all his gas to set an altitude record, and his field had been below him all the time.

For the next few minutes Willy held the monoplane in a steady descent, entirely oblivious now to the shining city passing beneath the wings. He had to resist the temptation to raise the nose to slow them to just above stalling speed, for he knew that would be the worst thing to do.

Altitude is like money in the back, pilots said. Speed is cash on hand. The one was instantly convertible into the other. Altitude was also translatable into distance.

But without power they had no way to deposit more money in the bank by climbing. What they had in the bank was all they had, and if he didn't convert it into cash at just the right rate, if he slowed their speed in an attempt to conserve the money in the bank, he would waste both their cash and their reserve because they would drop more than they moved forward and would lose more altitude than they gained in distance.

He used the windmilling propeller as his gauge, knowing almost instinctively how fast it should turn. If its revolutions slowed and the disk the blades described became visible, he was pulling the nose up too much. If the blades blurred to transparency and the singing of the wires rose in pitch, he was letting the nose dip too low.

But God how slowly, how agonizingly slowly the Palisades approached. The propeller was his gauge, but it was also acting as a brake. He looked over Carole's head at the altimeter. They were down to four thousand feet and not yet to the Hudson. *What was he doing?* The Palisades were much too far. He banked sharply left, aimed at the New Jersey docks lining the river across from Manhattan. There were open areas to the west, around the glinting Hackensack River. Of course—the Hackensack Meadowlands!

At last the wide Hudson was below them. But they just seemed to be hanging there. Were they running into a wind? There were boats on the water but he couldn't see any smoke or waves to tell him about the wind. Nor could he any longer see the Hackensack River. He nosed down, spending cash.

He breathed a little easier when they crossed the New Jersey shoreline and were gliding over Union City. The terrain beyond sloped down and for a moment he could see the Hackensack again, until they lost more altitude and the river disappeared into the flattening horizon. They had less than a thousand feet remaining in the bank, sinking fast.

He steered away from the lights of settled areas and headed toward a large area of darkness. There must be fields, otherwise why would they call it the Meadowlands? But the darkness could also be woods.

Time was up, no more money left. He banked toward what he hoped was a meadow, into what he hoped was the wind, if there was a wind.

Yes—it was a meadow. Or at least an open space with no houses or buildings on it that he could see.

They were too low now for the altimeter to be of any use. He could no longer read it anyway, it was so dark, and it didn't matter because they didn't have enough height to turn again. They were committed, to whatever lay ahead. He couldn't see the propeller either. Now the song of the wires had to be his gauge for speed.

A line of trees bordering a barely visible road suddenly loomed ahead of them. He yanked the column back—the plane barely cleared the tallest trees—then pushed the column forward just before the point of stall to cash in the last few pennies of height that were left.

"Hold on! Hold on to the sides of the cockpit!"

He wrapped his right arm around Carole's waist. There was a *whishing* sound that was not from the wires. They were skimming over tall grass and rushes. He held the wheel all the way back with his free hand, squeezing it against poor Carole.

He could hear, and feel, the reeds clutching at the undercarriage, rasping against the underside of the wings. The tailskid made contact, then the wheels. They were on the ground, bumping, rumbling, slowing. They were going to make it!

But then he felt them run into a hummock and their forward momentum was still great enough that they climbed up it—and then nosed steeply down. The propeller dug into the ground and, almost leisurely, the fuselage lifted straight up, paused, then toppled over heavily onto its back and one wingtip.

As they turned upside down he let go of the wheel and grabbed at the cockpit coaming but his hands slipped. He hit the ground on his shoulders. Fortunately the drop was only a few feet.

Carole must have been hanging onto the wheel. Her legs dangled out of the cockpit above him.

"Willy . . . I can't hold on!"

"All right, let go—I've got you."

She tumbled down on his chest and he clutched her to him. She had not even screamed.

They lay like that for a moment, she on top of him with her face against his and his arms tight around her.

"Are you all right, honey?"

Carole started laughing. "This isn't the way you usually land, is it, Willy?"

He burst into laughter too, in relief and joy, now that they were on the ground and safe. They shook against each other in their laughter, and that made them laugh the harder. What a pair of fools they were.

No—he was the fool, and she the trusting ingénue. They were safe, but they had no right to be. He had had no right to get them into this situation in the first place.

He wondered how badly wrecked the plane was. The propeller was undoubtedly cracked but that would be the least of it. The rudder had to be smashed, the fabric of the wings certainly torn, if there was not worse damage. How was he going to get the thing back to Long Island, and what was he going to say to Felix, and later to André? He would be banished from the field for sure. And what was he going to say to his father when the bill came in?

God—his parents. Felix. He had to get to a telephone.

They had passed over a road, but where it led he had no idea. Felix would probably be long gone from the aerodrome. As for his parents . . .

He stopped thinking about it. Carole was kissing his cheek, making murmuring sounds. He unfastened the helmet and flung it aside and lost his fingers in her hair. He rolled her over on her back and kissed her hard on the mouth as he fumbled with the buttons of her blouse, seeking her breasts. She kissed him back as hard.

A long time later they lay quietly in the soft grass beneath the cockpit. He reached for the coveralls he had frantically ripped off and draped them over Carole and curled up close beside her.

His worries returned, and now he had a new one. What if Carole . . ? He was not ready to be a father.

"This has been the most memorable day of my life, Willy," she whispered. "You certainly know how to give a girl a thrill. In more ways than one!"

He didn't say anything for a moment. When he did it was in short sentences, with hesitations between them.

"We'll get married, darling. I promise. I'll make it right. During Christmas break. That would be best. We'll get an apart—"

"Oh Willy. Do you really think you have to make 'an honest woman' out of me? Do you think I've never . . ? You *are* a Silly Willy."

He didn't know what to think. He didn't know how you could tell if a girl had "never." But it didn't matter whether she had or not. It was up to him to do the right thing.

"I love you, Carole. I want to marry you."

"No you don't. On both counts. You've very fond of me, as I'm fond of you, tremendously fond of you. We've had such fun together. But we're both—" She didn't complete the sentence.

"Anyway you can't get married, Willy. You still have two more years of school."

"I'll go into business with my father. He's always counted on that. I'll go to night school to finish my degree."

She sat up. "I'd like one of your cigarettes now, Willy."

He found the pack in his jacket and gave one to her and put one in his own mouth. He lit a match and held it to the end of her cigarette—and immediately snatched the cigarette away and crushed both it and the match against the ground.

"Christ! The gas tank!"

Gasoline was dripping out of the filler cap of the upside-down tank a few feet away from them. He had smelled it before but had forgotten about it when they had started making love.

That would really do it—not only to wreck the plane but burn it up completely, if not them along with it.

"We'd better try to find some civilization," he said. "Get to a telephone."

"Do you have any idea where we are?"

"I'm not sure. I think the area's called Secaucus. I saw a road just before we landed. There must be a farmhouse somewhere."

"It's so dark. We could wander around for hours. Why don't we wait until morning? I'm very comfortable here. What time is it anyway?"

He risked a match to look at his watch.

"It's not even seven o'clock yet. Won't the people at your hotel be concerned? They're pretty strict about girls staying out all night, aren't they?"

"I'll make up something. An emergency. I had to stay with a sick friend in Brooklyn. The storm blew down the telephone lines. Don't worry about it."

Carole was right. There was no point in wandering around in the darkness. Although it was early evening it seemed like the middle of the night. Even if they found a house the people might not have a phone.

"Let's move out under the wing," he said. "I think it'll be safe to smoke there."

He crawled to the end of the one wing that was sticking up in the air, its broad shape blanking out the stars, and flattened the grass to make a bed for them. They sat there smoking, their heads rubbing against the upperside of the wing, which was now the underside.

He watched the end of Carole's cigarette flare bright orange when she drew on it. Each puff made enough glow that he could distinguish her features. Otherwise her face was in almost complete darkness.

He crooned: "If you laka me lak I laka you . . . under the aeroplane wing . . ." She giggled.

"So what will it be? A Christmas wedding?"

"Sweetheart, I told you you don't have to marry me. I'm just starting out on my career, and you haven't even begun yours. It would be a mistake for both of us."

"Your name's too long to fit on a marquee."

She laughed softly. "They'll just have to give me a bigger one then, won't they?"

"You could have your career. I wouldn't stand in your way. I'd be proud, I really would."

"What'll I do with this?"

She held the shortened cigarette up between her thumb and forefinger. He took it from her and snuffed both their butts against the earth under the grass, making sure the coals were out.

"Don't you love me, Carole?"

"As much as you love me, Willy."

"Well then."

"Dearest, you know what I mean. What is love? We've *made* love, and now you feel you have to 'do the right thing.' My first proposal! But 'the right thing' would really be the wrong thing, don't you see? You don't have to marry me. You really don't. Aren't you relieved? It's getting chilly. Put your arms around me. Don't talk. Don't think about anything. Just—"

She opened her lips to his.

"Waltz me around again, Willy. My impetuous Willy."

If it wasn't love, it was still something extraordinarily wonderful. His better judgment, if not his morals, told him they shouldn't be doing this, but his heart brimmed with tenderness for this brave little girl, and his own desire overwhelmed him again. He kissed and touched and caressed her. He had never known anyone like her.

She gave herself to him again, willingly, eagerly, wanting nothing from him but the exquisite joy he could give her, that they could give each other. There were on another planet, on the moon they'd almost been able to touch above Manhattan. No one else existed. Nothing else mattered . . .

But afterwards he pressed her again.

"Why won't you marry me, Carole? This day has been so wonderful. We belong together."

"*Oh . . . Willy.*"

She asked for another cigarette and he watched the glow against her face again, and waited.

"Willy," she said. "Why would you marry me when you're in love with another woman?"

"What are you talking about, you little nitwit?"

"I saw the way you kept looking at her that night at the theater, when we met. Even while you were talking to me. It was quite obvious. And I saw the way she looked at you. And at me—there were daggers in her eyes when she saw you talking with me. Don't tell me you didn't know. The way you always bring up her name. This afternoon—my God, was it only this afternoon?—you'd cut out her picture. But it's all right. I'm in love with someone else too."

He knew who it was, and he was jealous. No, more than jealous. Affronted.

"Then why the hell—why the hell did you let me—?"

"I didn't *let* you do anything, Willy. But if you want a reason, because you're a hell of a good-looking guy, because you're a hell of a nice guy, and because the hell I wanted to. Oh for Christ's sake, Willy. Don't be so . . . *conventional.*"

She could sense the confusion in him. She snuggled against him and rubbed his arm. "Ah Willy, poor Willy. Why don't you go after her?"

"Why don't you go after *him*?"

"I have. And he's in love with me too. But he's married."

"Oh—I imagine that puts rather a damper on things, doesn't

it?" he said sarcastically. "What makes you think I'd have any chance with—" they hadn't used any names—"with her?"

"Have you tried, Willy? Really tried?"

"She's out of my reach. Out of my class. She's also somewhat older than me, you know."

He was two years older than Carole, yet he felt much less worldly-wise, much less experienced than she. He buried his face against her neck, seeking something. Solace . . .

"Let's not talk about them anymore," Carole said. "We've still got a whole night together. Let's forget about everything else. Make me forget everything else. Just hold me. All night. *Please . . .*"

6

WHEN WILLY awoke in the stark and disenchanting light of morning and crawled out from under the wing, he saw that the trees they had barely cleared were only yards away. It was then that he fully realized how close they had come to disaster, and began to appreciate the full extent of their luck—and his foolhardiness.

He looked over the aeroplane, afraid of what he might find. It wasn't as bad as it might have been; in fact, much better than by all rights it should have been. The propeller was ruined, as he had known it would be, one blade of it buried in the soft ground. But the horizontal stabilizer and even the rudder, cushioned by the reeds when they overturned, seemed to be intact. Likewise the wings, except for large rents in the fabric. A small branch was caught where two bracing wires on the underside of the fuselage crossed—*it had been that close!* But he could see no cracks in any of the fuselage members or the undercarriage struts sticking up in the air. The wheels were still in place on the axle. The nose had taken a hard thump when they overturned though. There might be damage to the engine or its mounting that he couldn't see.

His movement through the rushes wakened Carole. She sat up and bumped her head against the wing and slithered out from under it and stood up. She was a mess, as he was sure he was too. Her hair hung in tangles, strands of grass clinging to it and to her rumpled clothing. She brushed some of it off.

"Do you have a pocket comb, Willy?"

That made him laugh. He handed her his comb and watched as she tried to restore some semblance of presentability to herself.

"So this is how a girl looks in the morning, eh?"

She stuck her tongue out at him saucily and pulled the comb through her hair with hard strokes.

"Can the plane be fixed?" she asked.

"Yes, I'm pretty sure. But not here. It'll have to be dismantled and carried out."

He couldn't see the road but knew it was just behind the trees. Even so it would be a job getting the wreck to the road and all the way back to the aerodrome. He didn't want to think about what that might cost, much less what the repairs might amount to.

"Well," he said, "we may as well see if we can find out where the heck we are. Are you all right, honey? We may have to do some walking."

Carole said, "Uh-huh." He picked up his coveralls and folded the helmet and goggles inside them. He led the way toward the trees, following the path the plane had mashed through the reeds. The ground was wet and spongy, almost marshlike. They had apparently spent the night on the only dry spot in the entire field. By the time they reached the road, a narrow, rutted dirt road, their shoes were full of water and they had pieces of vegetation clinging to them again. The both looked more ragamuffinly than before.

They had been even luckier that he had thought. If the wheels had bogged down when they first touched the ground the plane would have somersaulted violently and they surely would have been killed or badly injured. You couldn't see the plane from the road. Their bodies would have lain there for who could have known how long.

Judging by the sun the road ran more or less north and south. He didn't know which direction to take and chose one at random. Their luck continued to hold. They had walked only a short distance when a farmer driving a horse and cart came along going in the other direction and, more luck, going all the way to Weehawken with a load of late-season produce destined for the Manhattan market, they learned.

The man eyed both of them suspiciously when Willy hailed him and explained how they came to be there. He had heard some tall tales in his life, but an *aeroplane*. He looked at their rumpled, dirty clothes and nodded knowingly. They had been in the grass all right.

He had a mind to take the horsewhip to the pair of them, and then thought better of it; the young fellow looked mighty fit. And the story he told was just outlandish enough that it might be true. It was none of his business anyway. He brusquely told them they could ride on the back of the wagon if they wanted to.

There was just enough room for them to sit with their legs dangling over the end of the cart. Willy put the coverall bundle behind his head and leaned back against bushel baskets of beans and other vegetables. He put his arm around Carole and she rested her head against his shoulder. They didn't talk. They had said just about everything the night before.

In Weehawken Willy suggested they have breakfast somewhere but Carole wanted to get back to town, so he saw her onto a ferry to Manhattan.

"I'll call you as soon as I can," he said. "Later today."

The people at a shack on the pier were good enough to let him use the telephone. He placed a call to Brooklyn. His parents were too relieved to learn that he and Carole were safe to press him for all the details. (The elaborate lies and explanations and apologies would come later.) They had stayed up all night, his mother said. His father hadn't gone to work that morning. They'd called the aerodrome yesterday evening—no answer—and first thing in the morning, but the people there had no idea what had happened to them and feared for the worst. They were just on the point of calling the police and hospitals.

He reassured them as best he could that everything was fine and asked his father to call the aerodrome again and tell Felix what had happened and what would be needed and that he would wait for him in Weekawken. He found a little restaurant and got something to eat, and then waited out the long hours at the pier until Felix and the other mechanic who had been at the aerodrome the day before arrived in the afternoon on the ferry with a flatbed truck designed to transport aeroplanes. Felix had also brought Carole's hat and purse.

When they finally located the right field, Felix looked at the swath the plane had cut through the grass just beyond the line of trees and shook his head. But when he examined the wreck and saw that it could be repaired he no longer looked at Willy with the sad, silent reproach he had at the pier and during the ride to the scene.

It was not as bad as he had feared. Save for the damage Willy had noted the machine had come through remarkably unscathed.

"A good landing. But any landing one can walk away from is a good landing, eh, monsieur? And the young lady also was unharmed? *Vraiment*, that was most lucky."

They were collaborators now. Felix knew he would be in serious trouble if André and Hardy found out that he had allowed Willy to take a girl up in the aeroplane. He could have the machine repaired before they returned from the tour and no one would be the wiser, except that there would be the matter of the bill. So it was agreed that Felix would say that the accident had happened at the aerodrome, with Willy alone in the machine. Willy would not mention about the drinking and Felix would see that the other man kept his mouth shut.

It was a laborious process: first righting the fuselage, then detaching all the wires and removing the wings, then slogging the parts out of the field and securing them on the truck. It took all their strength to manage the fuselage alone. By the time they were finished the spot where Willy and Carole had spent the night had been totally obliterated by the general trampling down of the grass and reeds.

He looked back as they were leaving and wondered: had it really happened? He was conscious only that something magical he and Carole had shared was over with. All evidence of it erased. Flattened. Never to be recaptured. It was just an ordinary scrubby field.

Willy went his own way when they arrived on the Manhattan shore. He was later informed that a cracked magneto had been the cause. Again, not his fault. Yet again, entirely his fault.

He dropped off Carole's hat and purse at the Empire (the stage manager knew him well by this time and too many questions might be asked if he took her things to her hotel) and hurried on home. By the time he was able to call Carole she had left for the theater. He left the message that he would call the next day.

There was a terrible row with his parents, after they saw that he truly was safe and unhurt. He had never seen them so angry, especially his mother. She was so angry she couldn't even cry.

How dared he put them through what he had? How could he have been so foolish and so reckless as to take Carole up in an aeroplane and endanger both their lives, not to mention people on the ground? And to fly over New York City! What had he been thinking of? They had been distraught with worry. *How could he?*

He let their anger run its course, and when he could he told them that he and Carole had found a farmhouse where they'd spent the night — in separate rooms, he emphasized. There hadn't been a telephone or he certainly would have called. He'd stayed up all night himself, worrying about them worrying about him. No, there was hardly any damage to the aeroplane. It was probably already back at Hempstead Plains.

It was the only time in his life he had ever told a direct lie to his parents, but it would have broken their hearts to know the truth. So he had looked them straight in the eye and lied, the lie made convincing because of his own conviction that what he and Carole had done was not that terribly wrong.

෨ ෮

Two years before, following his encounter with the girl at the Hudson-Fulton Celebration, he had spent anxious weeks dreading the appearance of a sign that she had given him a "souvenir" to remember her by. Now he was to wait anxiously for word of a different kind of consequence.

When he had started to make love to Carole the second time, and she to him, when they had given themselves to each other with renewed passion, he hadn't cared. If she got pregnant that would definitely settle the question of marriage. And he had wanted to marry her, at that moment. So why shouldn't they enjoy each other, a young man and a young woman, who cared deeply for each other? If society or the system of the universe required a reckoning, a price to pay, he would willingly pay it.

But now, back in the quotidian, back in the unmagical routine of his life, he cursed himself for jeopardizing both their futures.

He called Carole daily for the next few days, but she was either not at the hotel or was just leaving and said she had no time to talk. When they did talk finally she sounded lighthearted, the same as she always had. Yet she didn't suggest they see each other, and neither did he. To the question uppermost in his mind every waking minute she answered simply, "I'll let you know, Willy. As soon as I know."

He didn't call her again. "Soon" was three weeks later.

He'd told Carole that the best time to call him was in the late afternoon when he was home from school and his father still at work and his mother preparing supper in the kitchen. There was an added measure of privacy in the fact that the telephone was in the front hall. He waited near the phone every afternoon, and when it rang he was right there.

"You can stop worrying, Willy. Everything's back to normal."

His mother appeared and he waved her off, pointing to himself. He waited until she was out of hearing.

"You're sure?"

"Of course. I wouldn't lie to you."

"No, I know you wouldn't. I just mean—you're positive?"

She laughed. "No, actually negative. Honest, it's all right. Aren't you relieved?"

He almost said he wasn't. For a few seconds he felt a profound disappointment. He took a deep breath and sat down at the secretary. He didn't know what to feel. Yes, he was relieved—immensely so. Unburdened of a tremendous weight. *Free.* Yet it didn't seem right, it wasn't natural somehow, that the only consequence of their intense lovemaking should be this sense of gladness he now felt in the knowledge that it was finished between them. It wasn't right that it should just end like this.

"I have to see you, Carole."

"I don't know about that."

"Please, dearest. We can't just— We ought to see each other again." He didn't need to say for the last time.

Carole was the same as before, yet almost like a stranger to him. Even prettier than he had thought her before, sitting across the restaurant table from him, so charmingly girlish in a pinafore and a sailor hat perched on top of her upswept blonde hair. He was conscious that he was losing something very precious, even if it was not his to lose.

As they ate they talked about everything but what they knew they had to talk about, until it was almost too late and she had to get to the theater.

"Don't you love me at all?" he appealed.

"It's interesting you should put it just that way, Willy. 'At all'? Yes, I love you 'at all'."

"We had such good times together. We belong together."

"We did have a lot of fun, didn't we?"

"The most wonderful fun of my life. It could still be wonderful."

She inclined her head and looked away, then back again.

"Dearest Willy. Why do you think you have to put yourself through this? You don't owe me anything. I'll always remember—I'll *cherish*—the times we had together. Truly I will."

He waited. She was so much wiser than he.

She smiled at him tenderly. "We're just two people who happened to meet and enjoy each other for a short while because . . . because we were both lonely. Because . . . I don't know. But you're in love with Harriet Quinlan and I'm—"

"I'm not! I don't give a damn about her!"

"Yes you do, Willy. But it doesn't matter because I've been in love with Elliot since the first time I met him. Sometimes, I think—I know it sounds silly—but even before I met him. And he's in love with me. Unfortunately, he's married, which is a problem you don't have with Harriet Quinlan. But that's going to change. He's leaving his wife. 'A Single Man' will be ending its run soon. Ethel Barrymore is coming in a new play, her annual appearance at the Empire. Elliot's got an offer of a leading part in another play opening in New Haven—and I'm going with him!"

Again there was that feeling of relief, yet tinged with jealously and injured pride. And a gnawing sense of loss.

"They why . . ?" he asked again.

"Why did I make love with you? Because you're sweet, handsome, a good dancer, fun. Because we both wanted to. Shall I go on? Because Elliot and I tried to break it off and I thought for a while that maybe I would fall in love with you, that if we *made* love . . ."

He knew then that he didn't really love her. He was thinking only of himself.

"You'll be throwing your life away, Carole," he said flatly. "Is he worth it?" All at once he was the avuncular, disinterested adviser. "Is he going to divorce her? It's not easy in this state, you know. What if he can't get a divorce? You could be letting yourself in for a lot of heartache."

"No more than you if you try to go after Harriet Quinlan. And I think you should, Willy. What is the purpose of living other than to try for what you want in life? If you and I were to continue seeing each other, if we eventually married, could we be happy? Or would there always be some . . . some unresolved memory of other people we might have made a life with?"

She looked at him searchingly. He didn't know the answer.

"At least this guy is in love with you, you say. What makes you think I would have any chance with Harriet Quinlan? She moves in a whole different world. She's way out of my class." Then, realizing the possible implication that Carole was of a less desirable class, he added quickly, "She's not half the woman you are anyway."

"Aha, if only that were true. Don't underrate yourself, Willy. And don't forget you and she have in common an interest in flying, which seems to be very important to her. How many of the men she knows are aviators?"

"She's six years older than me."

Carole didn't seem very surprised at that. "Well, I assumed she was older. So what? Six years is nothing. Elliot is ten years older than me. Did you ever think that maybe that's what's stopping her too—her age? If you love her, go after her, and devil take the hindmost!"

She laughed gaily and pushed her chair back from the table.

"I'm glad you're in love with her, Willy. Otherwise I couldn't bear the thought that I'm hurting you, and I have enough guilts as it is. Come on, let's get out of here. Walk me over to the theater."

He held her hand as they walked without speaking along the short block of Fortieth Street between Seventh Avenue and Broadway. He was savoring the sadness-gladness of their last minutes together, and knew she was too.

They stopped at the narrow alley leading to the side entrance of the Empire and he held both her hands.

"Well, Willy-Nilly. Here we are."

She smiled up at him, searching his face. "Ah, don't look so sad, darlin'. Sure'n it's after breakin' my heart, y'are."

He pulled her to him and kissed her softly on her lips and hugged her briefly.

"I do love you, you know."

"Yes. I understand."

She squeezed his hands and then started edging into the alley, facing him as she moved.

"Carole . . . Weren't you the least bit afraid? In the aeroplane?"

She shook her head, still moving away. "Oh, a little bit, at the end. I knew something was wrong. But I knew you were a good pilot and would get us down all right."

She turned and went up the steps to the stagedoor landing and turned again.

"Look for my name up in the lights, Willy," she called. "I'll be looking for you—up there."

She pointed at the sky, and then waved goodbye.

He blew her a last kiss. He never saw her or heard of her again.

7

H E LUXURIATED in a kind of delicious, self-pitying agony for a while, for a few days, wounded pride mixed with relief mixed with regret, remembering Carole.

He knew he would never know another girl quite like her, so genuine and down to earth, and wondered why it was that he couldn't have fallen truly in love with her—and knew it was fortunate he hadn't; there was somebody else for her. It was only by chance that their different paths had briefly crossed. If he had tried to follow her, or bend her to his path, she would eventually have had to hurt him, and he had no right to make her do that. But he would never forget her.

It was hard to believe that their whirlwind affair had lasted just a little more than a month. God, he wished the best for her.

Yet Harriet had hurt him—*was* hurting him. What right had he to make *her* do that, however unknowingly, however unintendedly on her part? Thoughts of Harriet, which he had almost managed to submerge when he was with Carole, came back in full force, and he welcomed them. She was like a low-grade fever in his blood, a dull and constant ache in his soul, but an ache made bearable now by a sliver of hope.

Carole had merely been guessing about Harriet, maybe trying to make their parting less painful. Still, Carole had a way of seeing into people. Wasn't there a chance, more than a remote one, that the matter of their ages was a barrier that Harriet thought too much to be surmounted, that that explained why she could seem to be so obviously interested in him yet push him away at the same time, why she had always permitted him to approach just so close to her but no closer?

Had he tried to go after Harriet Quinlan? Carole had asked. Really tried?

He concentrated on his studies. He even dated a few girls, but all of them suffered by comparison to Carole, let alone to Harriet Quinlan. He even took a girl to the theater one time with the wild thought that he might see Harriet there, knowing that he wouldn't. She was somewhere out West on the tour and besides had already reviewed the play when it had opened in the fall.

He went though the motions of his life until near the end of December. He called *Leslie's Weekly* and was informed that Miss Quinlan was not expected back until the day after Christmas. He gave her that day, a Tuesday, then called her office again, and when she answered identified himself stupidly.

"Well, how silly can we be? Of course I remember you, William. How have you been? Have you been doing any flying?"

Her voice on the phone was warm, familiar, welcoming. Their evening at the theater had been just the other night. The next day's embarassing telephone conversation had never happened.

His heart lifted. He had been fully prepared for aloofness, if not coolness, if not outright frigidity, on her part.

"Yes, a little," he answered cautiously. He didn't know whether to tell her about the flight with Carole or not, but if he did it certainly wouldn't be now.

"I'm going to be in Manhattan this afternoon, Harriet." (He wasn't; school was out until after New Year's.) "I was wondering if I might drop in and see you for a minute. I want to wish you a merry Christmas and happy New Year in person."

There was just the barest pause. "Why, that would be very nice, William. But I'm working on something for the magazine. I'm always glad for an excuse to put off writing but I have to finish this today."

"We have a lot to catch up on," he urged. "I want to hear all about your Mexican adventure. How did it go?"

"Oh, very well. We, uh—" There was a longer pause. He could tell she was thinking and he gave her the time.

"Listen," she said. "I'm going to be busy at the office every day this week and probably Saturday too. I've got a stack of things to do on my desk. Could you . . . could you possibly come over to the city sometime next Sunday? To my hotel?"

Possibly? He almost kissed the mouthpiece of the telephone.

He replied with a calculated measure of hesitance. "Why, yes, I don't see why not. What would be a good time?"

"Well, my parents and I usually go to a restaurant after church—St. Thomas's Episcopal on Fifth Avenue. We only eat one big meal on Sundays and we like to do it leisurely. Umm, would, say, around three o'clock be convenient for you?"

He assured her it would.

"Fine. Oh—there probably won't be anybody at the desk downstairs, the manager lives in the back. Just come on up. I'll be expecting you." She gave him the suite number.

"All right," he said, and with a cheery "See you Sunday afternoon" rang off before she changed her mind, and as if the sooner he started counting the minutes the faster the hours until Sunday afternoon would pass.

He had plenty of time to wonder what it all meant, if anything. God, Harriet was doing it to him again, all over again. Why had she invited him to her home when she could have given him a few minutes in her office and been done with him? Why had she made a point of letting him know she was a communicant of one of the most fashionable churches in the city? To impress him? She must know there was no need to do that.

He spent so much time wondering and anticipating that it was late Saturday afternoon when it occurred to him that he ought to take a gift of some kind with him. He rushed out of the house and got to Hegeman's drugstore on Fulton Street just before it closed. He had no idea what to buy. Candy, maybe. But there was a display of cosmetics on a counter and a young salesgirl behind it. She gave him an inviting glance.

"I'm looking for something for a lady," he said. "Sort of a token gift."

The girl smiled at him. "Perfume is always nice. How much did you want to spend?"

She held up a small bottle. "This is a new scent called Parfum Rose d'Or." (She pronounced it "duh-or.") "Only fifty-eight cents for a half-ounce bottle, or you can get a two-ounce bottle for only ninety-nine cents." She pointed to another tiny flask. "Then there's Cherie. Only seventy-nine cents, and you can't tell it from the French perfume it's copied from."

Those were a little too "token," he thought.

"Don't you have something more . . ?"

"Expensive? Sure. We have Mary Garden at four dollars, all the way up to Cyclamen for nine-ninety. Our more expensive perfumes all come in cut-glass bottles and include attractive satin-lined jewel cases covered with real leather. You wouldn't even need to wrap them."

He hesitated. He didn't want to be cheap; neither did he want to embarrass Harriet with something ostentatious.

The girl was a good salesman. "Here's a new one I like. Idylle." She uncapped the vial and transferred some of the liquid from her fingertips to her wrist and held it out to him. "Isn't that nice? It's seven-seventy, including the case."

He liked the name and liked the price and it did smell good. He said he'd take it.

"Lucky lady," the girl said.

But when he got home he wondered if he should have bought something so personal. Women were particular about their perfumes. A scent that was good for one woman another woman simply couldn't wear, his mother had once said. Well, it was the thought that counted.

Sunday was overcast and cold, hardly any people on the streets. He got off the subway at Herald Square at two o'clock and spent the next hour walking around the block between Broadway and Sixth Avenue and Twenty-seventh and Twenty-eighth Streets.

He saw the Hotel Victoria for the first time in daylight. It was a small building for a hotel, only five stories, brownish brick, with bay windows on every floor on the Broadway side and a decorative limestone cornice around the edges of the flat roof.

At a quarter to three, thoroughly chilled, he stood on the sidewalk in front of the hotel, checking and rechecking his watch. At precisely three he entered the lobby and was surprised by its dimness and narrowness. There was a counter to one side, in front of a bank of pigeonholes on the wall, presumably for holding mail and not keys since this was a residence hotel. Against the opposite wall were two overstuffed chairs with a small and sparsely decorated Christmas tree between them, and at the far end a stairway. No elevator. It was not a luxury hotel.

Harriet opened the door two seconds after his knock. "William. How nice to see you again." She held her hand out to him. "Please come in and get warm. You look cold."

He hung his hat and coat and muffler on one of the pegs of a mirrored stand near the door. Harriet chattered as she led him into a small sitting room overlooking Broadway.

"I'm so glad you called, William. It was good of you to come over today. My mother is resting but she wants to meet you later. I've told her all about you. Please sit down and make yourself at home. If you'll excuse me for just a few minutes I'm afraid I'm working on another article I want to finish."

"Oh, I'm sorry."

"Not at all. I'm almost done. Just take me a minute."

What he was really sorry about was that her mother was there. "Is your father also . . ?

"No," she said over her shoulder. "He'll be picking Mother up later."

She sat down behind a large table with graceful curving legs placed at right angles to the bay window so that what light there was flooded it. Like the desk at her office the table had a typewriter perched on it, but was relatively uncluttered except for her typing paper and a few sheets of yellow, ruled tablet paper which evidently were her notes. There was a small lamp on one side of the typewriter and a miniature Christmas tree on the other side.

"It's about the floating gardens of Xochimilco, outside Mexico City," she said. "Actually a kind of bread-and-butter piece for Leslie's since they gave me time off to go on the tour. I did another one for them about Christmas customs in Mexico."

She began reading what she had typed on the paper in the machine.

He sat a few feet from her in an upholstered chair without arms and looked around the room. There was a matching chair, a short sofa with a low table in front of it, a bricabrac cabinet against one wall, a floor lamp and other pieces and a few pictures on the wall. The ceiling was stamped metal, enameled white. The tubing that had once been used for gas illumination was still in place on the wall, now containing electric wiring. At one side was a closed door, evidently the bedroom where her mother was resting.

The whole place seemed quite small. He would have thought New York's most glamorous drama critic would have more commodious accommodations. Yet he felt comfortable in this room. There was a sense of quietness, of serenity, despite the rumble of automobiles and streetcars passing in the street below, an occasional horn sounding, the clacking of Harriet's machine when she began typing.

He felt comfortable with her. She was in profile to him. Her slim figure sat erectly in the chair, inclined a bit toward the table. Light diffusing through the window curtains made a halo around her hair and threw into soft relief the curves of her forehead and nose and chin, and lips that were compressed in concentration.

Such perfect symmetry, he thought. (Not fearful, recalling a line from Blake.) Perfect. Serene. How delicate and vulnerable looking her throat above the high-necked lace collar of her dress. She occasionally lifted one hand from the keys to touch lightly the hollow with her fingertips, just above the collar, as she composed a line in her head before typing it out. He could not see her arms because of the long sleeves of her dress that ended in ruffles at her wrists — indeed had never seen her bare arms — but knew they must be as perfect and symmetrical as the rest of her. Her graceful bosom lifted and fell with her breathing.

How breathtakingly lovely she was. How exquisitely feminine. He drank her in boldly. He could have sat in this room, looking at this woman, for the rest of his life.

She glanced at him and he did not drop his gaze. Her bold dark eyebrows arched ever so slightly. She looked at him steadily for a moment, directly into his eyes, then back to the paper. He forced his own eyes to look away. Another moment and he would have thrown himself at her feet.

"William," she said suddenly. "Did I ever give you one of my cards?" She reached inside a drawer under the tabletop.

He thought she meant a business card, but when she handed it to him it was much larger than a business card. It was a color lithograph of her in her purple flying costume posed in front of Monoplane No.1 with the Moisant school hangars in the background. It had apparently been painted from the silhouetted photograph that had accompanied her first flying-lesson article. The artist's name and "Compliments of Miss Harriet Quinlan" were printed at the bottom.

"It's very nice," he said. "Striking, really."

"Just a little promotional souvenir I pass out to people."

He carefully slipped the card inside his jacket. It would not replace the picture of Harriet in his dresser drawer, but he would treasure it even more.

He'd completely forgotten the perfume. He got up hastily and went to retrieve the package from the pocket of his overcoat.

"I want to give you something too . . . Harriet." His lips formed another word that he did not speak: *"darling."*

He placed the package on the table and sat down to watch her reaction.

"Oh William, that wasn't necessary." She opened the little box and exclaimed, "Coty's Idylle! Now how did you know? I've been wanting to try this fragrance."

She uncapped the bottle and dabbed a little on her wrist and passed it under her nose, then extended her wrist toward him, just like the girl at the store had. "What do you think?"

He took a longer sniff than necessary, holding her fingers in his.

"It fits you. I hope. I wasn't sure."

"Thank you so much, William. This is so thoughtful."

She replaced the bottle in its box and set it next to the type-writer. She concluded her typing with a final burst and announced that that was good enough for now, she would polish it up later that evening.

"I'll go see if Mother's up. It's almost coffee time. Would you like a cup? Then we can talk. Or you could have tea. I'll ring one of the servants. There is actually a larger staff in this hotel than there are residents. But most of them are immigrant girls. They're not paid very much." She carried the perfume with her.

"Coffee would be fine," he said.

Mrs. Quinlan was shorter than her daughter, he saw when she entered the room. She had a thick, formless figure, wore a shawl over her shoulders. She returned his greeting somewhat vaguely when Harriet introduced him. Her name was Ursula.

There was a knock on the door and Harriet went to answer it. She returned with a young girl in starched maid's uniform carrying the coffee service, which the girl placed on the table in front of the sofa.

"Thank you, Bridget," Harriet said.

"You're quite welcome, mum. If you need anything else, just call."

Harriet and her mother sat on the sofa and he on his chair drawn up to the small table and Harriet poured for them.

Looking at the two women side by side he could see nothing of the daughter's beauty in the mother. She was a quite elderly woman, in her sixties at least. She must have had Harriet rather late in life. He gathered that there was another daughter, evidently living in California. The two women discussed Harriet's having stopped in San Francisco during the tour, where she was interviewed by *Overland Monthly,* and a name—Kitty—was mentioned but not identified to him, although Mrs. Quinlan referred to her as "your sister." He wondered where the father could be, on a Sunday afternoon. Was Harriet really supporting both parents, as she'd said that day in her office? It was a rather strange family.

"Tell me about Mexico," he said.

"It was quite something, William. Especially Mexico City. It's over seven thousand feet above sea level, you know, and the air is very thin and dry. You're nearly a mile and a half high before you even take off! Even though my propeller made the same number of revolutions it does at sea level there seemed to be a lack of power, because of the altitude. James McCurdy and Charles Willard weren't able to get their Curtiss biplanes off the ground at all."

She recited the names of a few of the other fliers who had been on the tour: The French flier Roland Garros and Captain Patrick Hamilton and George Dyott, the latter two with Anzani-powered Deperdussin monoplanes. Captain Hamilton had survived a bad crash in Mexico City. His machine had turned a somersault a few hundred feet up—he must have run into some rarified air, Harriet thought—and when it reached the ground had pinioned him under the chassis. The plane was a complete wreck but by some miracle he wasn't injured.

"Oh—and Matilde Moisant had a bad crash during a landing in Guadalajara. She did a complete flip-flop and was pinned underneath too like Captain Hamilton but she also wasn't injured in the least, beyond the nervous shock. Did the papers report it?"

He shook his head, both in answer to her question and in

wonderment. Mrs. Quinlan had apparently not heard about the accidents either.

"You didn't tell me about Matilde, Hattie." It was the first time he had heard Harriet called by that nickname.

"She wasn't hurt at all, Mother. Really."

"And you had no problems," he stated. "You were always the best. Your daughter's making quite a name for herself in aviation, Mrs. Quinlan."

"Yes," the mother said dubiously, and then immediately to Harriet: "Don't you really think you've done enough, Hattie? This new idea of yours . . . "

She stopped and glanced at Willy, then at Harriet again, as if she had brought up something he might not know about, or wasn't supposed to know about.

"Mother," Harriet said. "There is nothing inherently dangerous about flying. William will tell you that, and haven't I proved it? You know I never go up in dangerous conditions or without checking every wire and screw in my machine. It's only twenty miles. I've flown much farther than that many times. There's really not all that much difference between flying over land and over water."

Willy was intensely curious, but Harriet did not elaborate on the subject, whatever it was, and Mrs. Quinlan only said, "Just so you make sure and keep on being careful. Promise me that."

He looked at his watch. It was going on five. Late enough to take his leave, as he probably ought to, and too early to say what he said next. But it was the only thing he could think to say to prevent his having to leave, and he did not expect anything to come of it.

"I was wondering," he said to Harriet. "I'd like very much to take you and your mother out to a restaurant. I know it's a little early but—"

Oh, why, that was very kind of him, Harriet said. But they'd had their big dinner after church. Her father would be coming along to take her mother home. There was the article she wanted to finish.

To his surprise Mrs. Quinlan said, "Why don't you and Mr. Reynolds go, Hattie? You can finish your article at the office tomorrow. You shouldn't have to work on Sunday. There's not that much hurry about it, is there? I'll wait here until Father comes for me."

And to his infinite pleasure Harriet was easily persuaded.

Well . . . if you're sure you don't mind, Mother." She looked at Willy. "I'm not hungry but perhaps we could have a dessert or some refreshment. There's a Child's down the street. You could have a regular meal there too, William, if you want to."

Oh no, he said. He'd had his big meal at noon too, at home. But a dessert sounded good.

"Well then," she said, getting up. "If you really don't mind, Mother. Just let me get my things, William, and then . . . "

And then he would be with her for perhaps another hour, alone with her. And sometime during that hour, he vowed, he would finally tell her what was in his heart.

8

THERE WERE not more than ten or twelve people in Child's, most of them sitting at long tables extending out from a marble-faced interior wall. There were also a few small round wire-legged tables, so small they could comfortably accommodate only two persons. Willy picked one next to a streetside window that was ringed with tinsel and whose glass was opaque with condensation from the warm air inside the restaurant, hiding the outside world.

He helped Harriet out of her coat and hung both their coats on pegs that were in a row on the wall near the door. She kept her fur muff with her. Then he sat down across from her. The other customers were making enough sounds to create a homey atmosphere but not enough to impede quiet conversation.

When a waitress appeared Harriet said she didn't want anything from the menu or the cafeteria and thought she'd just have
a chocolate soda. Willy ordered the same. It was like a high school
date after the nickelodeon, so much better than sitting stiffly and
inhibitedly in some more formal restaurant, and with her mother
along.

Harriet had not only welcomed his coming to her home; she
had not wanted him to leave. She had wanted to come here with
him. His spirit was as effervescent as the soda water in his glass
when the waitress brought it.

Harriet was bubbly too. She removed her suede gloves and
pulled something out of her overblouse. "How do you like my
new lucky charm, William? I got it in Mexico." She held it up so
he could see.

He reached across the tiny table and fingered it. It was an
Indian head, carved of onyx or some kind of mottled stone, suspended by a silver chain around her neck, with two strands of
chain hanging down from the bottom of the head.

"It's an Aztec charm," she said. "Isn't it ugly? But very ancient. I was told it's two thousand years old."

He hoped she hadn't paid a lot for it. The Aztecs weren't
around two thousand years ago. Yet it could be several hundred
years old, if it was genuine. It was ugly all right.

"Very unusual," he said. "But I hardly think you need any
lucky charm."

She laughed softly, looking admiringly at the piece. "You
never know." She tucked it back inside her blouse.

He watched her as she moved the ice cream around with a
long spoon and then took a sip with the straw. "Umm, this is
good," she said. "You don't usually think of an ice cream soda on
a cold day like this."

"Ice cream actually warms you up later, once it gets inside."

He sipped a little from his own glass. He wanted to make it
last. He intended to tell her what was in his heart, before this day
was over, but not just yet.

She asked him about his college studies.

"So you did decide to continue with business administration," she said. "I think you were wise to. Whether or not you go into aviation eventually any kind of degree is always valuable. You're so young. You're just beginning your life. You have all kinds of choices."

More slow sipping, glances and smiles over the straws.

"Have you seen anyone from the flying school lately, William? Did you hear what happened to Matilde Moisant? Not the accident. She was arrested in Nassau County for flying on Sunday! Can you imagine?"

"She was?"

Alfred Moisant had been entertaining a guest from France one Sunday, Harriet said, and the man had not believed it when he was told that Matilde was a licensed pilot. To prove it they had gone to the aerodrome and Matilde did a demonstration flight. On the way back from the field they had been chased down by a policeman. It seemed that some good citizens on Long Island had been complaining about people flying on Sunday. More "aeronuts" again.

It was a very funny story as Harriet told it, describing the chase scene and altercation with the arresting officer—Alfred Moisant had apparently become very belligerent when he found out why they were stopped—and they both laughed. The upshot was that the policeman took Matilde before a magistrate or sheriff or whatever he was, but when she told him she hadn't been flying for pay, just for pleasure, the judge said that if people could drive automobiles on Sunday he didn't see any reason why they couldn't fly aeroplanes on Sunday.

"Sounds sensible," Willy said.

"Of course. I personally choose not to fly on the Sabbath, but I certainly don't demand that everyone else conform to my beliefs."

They exchanged smiles again, resumed sipping. A moment later, though, Harriet studied her soda with a serious expression.

"Have you been seeing, what was her name, that girl from the theater, Carole Cunningham?"

She asked the question casually, uncuriously, and looked to one side at some people at one of the long tables. But it must mean something that she remembered Carole's name, he thought.

He spoke to his own glass. "We went out a few times. She's pretty involved with . . . with her career."

"I just wondered."

Out of loyalty to Carole he felt compelled to say more. "She's quite a girl. She's as brave as you are."

He decided to tell Harriet about the flight over New York and its unforeseen conclusion, trying to make it a humorous story too. Her eyes widened as he spoke. He revised the lie he had told his parents and said that a farmer had driven them into Weekawken that evening.

"Oh my," Harriet said. "You were so fortunate, William. You actually flew over the city? I don't think I would ever do that, especially at night. You see, I told you you had the makings of an expert flier. But it really was quite reckless of you, taking a passenger up in a one-seater. How in the world did you do it?"

Her eyes were still wide as she looked at him and he wondered if she was trying to picture how the two of them had managed to squeeze into the cockpit, and let her assume that Carole had been wearing pantaloons.

"What happened to the aeroplane? You say it wasn't badly damaged?"

"I'm actually thinking about buying it. I've heard from Alfred Moisant and he says they'll credit me the cost of the repairs. I think they want to get rid of it. But it's still a lot of money. I don't know."

That reminded him. "What is this idea of yours your mother mentioned?" He was not only curious but it was another subject to talk about to continue delay telling her what he intended to tell her.

"Can you keep a secret, William? No one knows about it except A. Leo Stevens. You've heard of him, the balloonist? Or former balloonist. He's my manager and publicist now. He's been

quite active in fostering interest in aviation among young people.
He awarded a cup to the builder of the best model aeroplane
in a contest last January. And my parents know, of course, but
no one else at this time. Promise me you won't tell anyone."

He promised.

Harriet looked around the room, as if the other customers
might be overhearing, and then spoke in almost a whisper.

"I just don't want this to get out prematurely in case someone might try to beat me to it. The idea suddenly came to me
while I was in Mexico. I intend to be the first woman to fly across
the English Channel!"

"*Really?*" he whispered back. "You mean it? You're serious?
When?"

She made a series of eager little nods and then continued
speaking in a confidential tone.

"Not until this spring. Sometime in early April, I hope. Leo
and I have booked passage to England on the Hamburg-Ameri-
can liner Amerika for March seventh. I want to go to London to
talk to the editor of the Daily Mirror about getting their backing
for an exclusive, then to Paris to see Louis Blériot. I've written to
him about ordering one of his latest seventy-horsepower two-seater
models, but when I get over there I hope to talk him into lend-
ing me a fifty-horsepower plane, one similar to the Moisant ver-
sions we're used to, for the flight."

"You really *are* serious," he said. "So do you intend to cross
from France to England, the same way he did?"

"No, I don't think so. Those Dover cliffs are pretty formi-
dable. It will probably be the other way, from Dover to Calais.
I'll have the plane shipped across from France after I've tried it
out."

They had just been talking about his idiotic flight over New
York and his inconsequential college studies and the possibility
that he might eventually find some kind of career in aviation, or
otherwise someday make something of himself. And here she
was planning an exploit that only a few male aviators since Blériot
had dared that would make headlines around the world and make

her even more famous than she already was. And put her even further beyond him than she already was. She had even hired a manager and publicist to help promote her career.

He was speechless, as much from sudden misery for himself as in admiration for her. In adoration *of* her.

"So that's my little secret, William. Wish me luck?"

"Oh—I do. Yes, of course I do."

Harriet finished her soda but seemed in no hurry to leave the place. She smiled at him, glanced around the room, smiled at him again. She was waiting for him to say something. But how could he possibly say what he wanted to say now?

"So . . ," finally, backing in to it, still speaking little above a whisper, "I take it marriage is not in your plans?"

Her closed lips turned up wryly. She leaned back from the table, playing with the edge of the marble tabletop with the fingers of both hands.

"I'm too independent a person. What man would ever put up with me? We'd both have to be crazy." She shook her head, dismissing the subject.

"You must have all kinds of suitors. You're so . . . beautiful, Harriet. Haven't you ever been in love? Don't you want children someday? Hasn't there ever been any man you . . ?"

"Are you going to make me tell you all my secrets, William?" Her gray-green eyes seemed to turn a deeper hue.

She looked away. "I've known a lot of attractive men. I was very attracted to Johnny Moisant. Of course, he was married. I know I fell in love with his aeroplane anyway."

She made a little laugh, but her expression was serious as she leaned toward him again.

"As a college student minoring in English you should know what Sir Francis Bacon said about marriage, William. 'The man who hath a wife and children hath given hostages to fortune, for they are impediments to great enterprises.' Or something like that. If that's true of a man, how much more true is it of a woman? But I really don't think it's true of a man. Many great men—*most* great men—have had wives and children and they have not been an impediment to their enterprises. Quite the contrary. But how many famous women have had husbands and children? I can't think of any. A man is free to go out and pursue his career whether he's married or not, but a woman is expected to stay home and keep house and care for the children. *Humph*, I doubt if Leslie's Weekly would have considered hiring me if I had been married. I certainly wouldn't be flying if I were married and had children."

"There's Madame Curie."

"That's one, and she works in the same profession her husband did. Go on, name some others. Queen Elizabeth never married, she just played off her suitors against each other. The Brontë sisters. Jane Austin. Mary Ann Evans, who wrote under the name George Eliot. And that Frenchwoman who used the pen name George Sand, I can never remember her real name."

"Amandine Aurore—uh, something-something," he said.

"Yes, and the fact that they found it necessary to use male pseudonyms tells us something too, doesn't it? All these women either never married or were independent of their husbands. And they could be only because they were novelists. That was about the only career open to women in their day, other maybe than the stage, which is something else entirely. But would they have accomplished as much, or done anything at all, if they'd had husbands and children to look after?"

"Well, what you said about Madame Curie. You could marry another writer. Or an aviator." (He wanted to say: *like me*.) "Someone in your own field. Have a joint career."

"Listen, William. Do you know that in most states in this supposedly enlightened twentieth century a wife is not even entitled to her own earnings, they belong to her husband. In some states a woman and her children are still considered the 'property' of the husband."

"But the law doesn't *require* that," he objected. "I mean, that the husband has to control everything. What does it matter what the law says if two people base their marriage on equality? My parents' marriage is that way."

"William, even if the kind of marriage you're talking about were possible, even if this theoretical husband were agreeable to both of us having careers, what would happen if he decided he wanted children? That's assuming I could—"

She broke off abruptly and seemed slightly flustered for a second, and he wondered why.

Then, recovering: "What I'm simply saying is that it's one thing to be a wife and mother and still be able to work in a laboratory with your husband like Madame Curie or write novels at home. It's another thing to be gallivanting all over the country in an aeroplane. No, William, I'm afraid marriage is quite out of the question for me."

What about a lover then? he asked himself. "George Sand" was supposed to have had many of them; Chopin was only the most notorious. "George Eliot" had some kind of scandalous "relationship" with a married man. What about sexual desire? Didn't women have physical needs? Hadn't this infinitely desirable woman ever known—didn't she *want* to know—what it was like to experience the ultimate expression of love between a man and a woman? He had never known, not really, even with Carole. He'd only known fornication.

"I'm very much in love with you, Harriet. I've been crazy in love with you since the first instant I saw you."

God, how clichéd that sounded, that last sentence.

"Well, no, not from the first. I hated you at first. No—that's not true either. I resented you, for being beautiful and a celebrity and . . . older than me. For being a better flier than me. Even when I started falling in love with you I tried to keep resenting you. But it didn't work."

He was making a mess of it, and his heart began sinking.

Harriet was absently, nervously running her fingers along the rim of the table again, smoothing an invisible tablecloth. She became aware of it and placed her hands in her lap on top of her muff.

"I know," she said gently. "I mean . . . I know you've had a crush on me and that you probably *think* you're in love with me.

You think I'm beautiful and glamorous and all that and I can't tell you how flattered I am that you do. But when you called the other day I hoped you'd gotten over your illusions about me by this time and that we could just be friends. Apparently you haven't, and now I'm only hurting you. But believe me I would hurt you much, much more if I let you go on thinking that we could ever be more than just friends."

He played the only card he had.

"You wanted to see me today too, Harriet. Not just as a friend. You didn't have to invite me to your apartment. That evening at the theater, you didn't invite me just—" He hunched his shoulders. "Just as a friend."

He bored into her eyes.

"Do six years really make all that much difference to you?"

A strange, solemn look came on her face. She didn't answer for a moment, and then, not answering, breaking her eyes from his, said evenly, "You've got your whole life ahead of you, William. You're a very handsome young man, and you'll become more and more handsome as you grow older. A year from now you won't even remember me. You'll fall in and out of love many times before you find the right girl. Yes you will!"

No he wouldn't! his soul cried out. He had been in love before, or thought he had. This was different. There had never been, never would be, anyone else. It was not just another "crush."

"This has been such a lovely afternoon, but I really think we shouldn't see each other again, William."

He felt a muscle in his cheek start twitching and he rubbed it to try to stop it. He lifted his soda glass stupidly. It was empty. He put it back down.

He was desperate. "Say—I just thought of something. I could join your team! You'll need a crew in Europe, won't you?"

"Yes, but we plan on hiring local people in Dover. It would be totally out of the question. You have school."

"Why not?" he persisted. "I've learned a lot about mechanics. You wouldn't even have to pay me. I have my own funds. I can pay my own way to Europe. I'll quit school. Just let me—"

He stopped, before he started sounding like a child begging for a trinket.

"I hope you're joking, William. You wouldn't really try to follow me to Europe, would you? If you care about yourself, let alone about me, you wouldn't do anything like that."

"Yes. I would. *Because* I care about you."

"William," Harriet said firmly. "If you were foolish enough to do that, and if I were thoughtless enough to allow you to, I would feel even guiltier about you than I do now. You wouldn't want that, would you?"

"Why in the world should you feel guilty about me, Harriet? What possible reason . . ?"

"Yes . . ," she said thoughtfully. "I think you just might do something like that. I think you do have a reckless or impulsive streak in you I didn't appreciate before. Anybody who would fly at night over New York City . . . "

She frowned. "I'm sorry I told you about my plans."

Then the frown changed subtly into something else. She breathed deeply once or twice.

"So, to nip that idea right in the bud, I see I'm going to have to tell you another secret after all. Actually, I should have told you long before this."

She glanced at the other people nearby as she had before. They were all eating or talking among themselves. Even so, she spoke so softly that he had to lean forward to hear her.

"There's a very good reason why we mustn't see each other again, William, the best reason in the world. I'm not just six years older than you. It's . . . rather more than that."

She began moving her head up and down, looking at him steadily with her lips compressed.

He waited, but she merely kept nodding at him, as if she expected him to agree that she had given sufficient answer to his question.

"Well *what*?" he said finally in exasperation. "Seven years? Eight?"

"More than that, William. I was born in San Francisco in Eighteen-seventy-five. That makes me—"

The numbers leaped into his mind. That would make her 36. Not 27. Not six years older—*fifteen*. And it would be *sixteen* in five more months.

He laughed nervously. What kind of game was she playing with him?

"That's the silliest thing I ever heard. Everybody knows—"

"It's true, William. I'll be thirty-seven next May. Please forgive me for not telling you before. I should have told you that time you called me at my office, after we'd been to the theater. I don't know why I didn't. It wasn't fair to you, knowing how you felt about me, or thought you felt. But I never intended . . . "

She tilted her head and pouted her lips placatingly.

"Are you very shocked? You really never guessed? But don't you know it's a woman's prerogative to fib about her age? I'm sure half the actresses I know on the stage are much older than they pretend to be. But now you understand why we can never be anything more than friends. And why you must not even consider the idea of going with me to Europe."

He was not so much shocked as nonplused. "I don't believe you! Why are you making this up? If you don't want anything to do with me why don't you just say it straight out? Why don't you just say so?"

He tried to keep his voice down, but the words came out loudly enough to cause a few people to look their way curiously.

Harriet reached across and touched his hand. "Dear William. Don't be hurt because I didn't tell you before. You'll always be my special friend. Believe me, whatever pain you're feeling now, and I can see you're in pain and that hurts me too, will pass. You're so young. It's really for the best if we don't see each other again. But I am so very, very flattered."

She withdrew her hand and slid her chair back from the table. "I should be getting home."

Still stunned and confused, moving automatically, he left money for their sodas and helped Harriet with her coat and then put his own on and followed her out the door. In the street she withdrew one hand from her muff and slipped her arm through his, sweetening his pain even as, unintentionally, she magnified it. He clasped her gloved hand under his arm with his free hand, and she returned his squeeze and pressed against his side.

Out in the cold air his bewilderment suddenly vanished. He felt elated, lightheaded, possessed of a confidence, a potency, he had felt only once before in his life, the day he had conquered the wind at the aerodrome and discovered he was meant to fly.

Harriet had known how he felt about her all along, he exulted. She had known it all along. And she *cared*. And it *was* the six years that mattered to her after all. Those silly six years mattered so much to her that she had manufactured a ridiculous story magnifying their age difference to sixteen years.

He almost laughed out loud. That was her mistake. If she had been clever she would have said nine or ten. But maybe she thought that wouldn't be enough, that he would have said what's a few more years. And he probably would have. But she'd only confirmed what Carole had guessed and what he had hoped: it *was* the six years' difference in their ages that was stopping her.

Oh what a strange, silly little girl she was.

When they reached her hotel and went inside—oh God, the lobby was still deserted. He gripped both her hands tightly and looked down at her in the pale light from a chandelier in the ceiling.

"This isn't the last of it, Miss Harriet Quinlan. Beautiful Harriet Quinlan. You're going to fly the English Channel and become the most famous woman in the world and I'm going to be there when you do and you'll come home in triumph and you'll marry me and I'll be your slave and—"

Oh Christ, shut up, Willy.

He drew her to him and kissed her at last. Full on the lips, firmly, without timorousness. God, the sweetness of her lips, cool from the outside air; the feel of her in his arms, in his arms at last, even bundled up as they both were. He felt faint. He nestled his face in her hair and against her neck—*"I love you, I love you"*—and slid his cheek against her cheek and started to kiss her lips again, and this time she turned her head away and pulled free.

"William, don't. Please. We can't do this."

There was a look of pleading on her face. "Don't you under-stand? We mustn't see each other again. Promise you won't try to. Promise you won't leave school and follow me to Europe. Promise you won't do anything so terribly foolish."

He moved his head from side to side, slowly and deliberately.

No, he would not make that promise.

"Tell me you don't love me," he demanded. "Tell me you don't love me and that will be the end of it. You can't, can you?"

She gave him a searching look, shaking her own head gently, then turned and started toward the stairs, and when she reached them turned again and called gaily:

"Happy New Year, William. See you at my ticker tape pa-rade! Maybe. If they have one for me."

He went home in a glorious daze. He had told her. And she had known it all along, from the beginning. How stupid he had been. *And she cared.* He knew with all the certainty of his own being that she cared for him, far, far more than as just a friend. She *wanted* him to love her, despite everything she said, telling him he mustn't, telling him that crazy, ridiculous lie about her age.

And most wondrous thing of all, most wondrous thing of all—that meant she wanted to love *him* too.

Oh God. *God, God, God.*

9

L IFE WAS AN aeroplane ride. You soared through the air one moment, light and lifted as a feather dancing on the wind; the next—your wings were broken off. Such was Willy's plunge from ecstasy to utter destruction.

It was a long fall, however, extending over many days.

Harriet would not talk to him. Oh, she did speak to him, granting him a few minutes when he called her at her office on Tuesday, the day after New Year's. And she was kind again at first. It was so nice, she said (pleasantly, not yet coldly), that they had been able to have the afternoon together and catch up. But when he reiterated his love for her and told her of his need to see her he could sense the change in her, like something palpable in the ensuing silence.

Finally: "I thought we'd settled this, William. Didn't you hear anything I said to you?"

"The only thing I didn't hear you say is that you don't love me. I know you do. Tell me you don't."

"I care about you very much, William. I said you were my special friend. I wouldn't have told you what I did if I didn't care about you."

"And I said I didn't believe you. You yourself said that your employment record with Leslie's Weekly shows you're twenty-seven. Why did you think you had to make up that crazy thing about being thirty-six? Prove it to me."

He could hear her breathing. She must have been holding the speaker very close to her mouth.

"What am I supposed to do, for heaven's sake—show you my baptismal certificate? I'm sure I don't even know where it is. Anyway, I don't have to prove anything to you, William. I revealed something to you very few other people know about me. That in itself should be proof that I care about your best interests. It's very flattering that you're finding it so hard to believe, but if you won't believe me, I can't help that. Look—I have to go, I haven't got time to talk on the phone."

"Let me see you after work today then. We can go somewhere. We need to talk."

"No! There's nothing to talk about! Please don't make this difficult, William. I'd hoped we could continue being friends, but now it is clear to me that I cannot allow you to see me again under any circumstances, nor do I wish to see you. I forbid you to call me again."

"Do you love me or don't you? That's all I'm asking you to say."

She took a deep, exasperated intake of breath. Then, in a low, toneless voice:

"You're forcing me to be cruel, William. I'm sorry about that, I really am. I resent being placed in such a position, but apparently it's the only way. I thought we'd settled this but I see now that you refuse to listen to a single thing I say. All right, I don't know how I can put it more plainly. There cannot ever be anything between us, there simply cannot be. *I am almost sixteen years older than you!* Why can't you accept that? Just—just go on living your life and let me live mine."

He was reduced to outright begging. "Please let me see you just once more."

"Goodbye, William."

She hung up.

He tried again the next morning, and she broke the connection before he barely got out, "Harriet, I—." He tried once more in the afternoon, but another feminine voice answered Harriet's extension, a secretary she must have asked to screen her calls, to screen out one William Reynolds. For when he identified himself he was told Miss Quinlan was not available and it was not known when she would be available. He wasn't asked to leave his number so Miss Quinlan could return the call. He could tell that the answerer was embarrassed.

He thought of using a false name, just to get Harriet on the line, but what would be the use? It would only irritate her the more and she would just hang up on him again.

Damn it, he shouldn't have called her in the first place. They couldn't talk on the phone. He should have gone to her office. She would have had to talk to him there, face to face, or at least have agreed to meet him somewhere later just to get him to leave the office.

He could still go. But what if she told the receptionist she was too busy to see him? What if he went in anyway? That would be embarrassing for everyone, especially for Harriet in front of her fellow workers.

He thought about waiting outside the Leslie-Judge Building some afternoon and accosting her as she left, but what little pride and good judgment he still had concerning Harriet told him that would not be a good idea either. No, better to wait and let things cool for a few days, hard as that would be to do. Give her some time to think.

What was it with her?

He was forcing her to be cruel, she said. But how could she *be* cruel? They had been so close, so intimate, that hour they'd spent in Child's. How could she be so warm, so gay with him, so *confiding* in him—and turn around and squash him like a bug?

God—what if she really were 36? And what if she had told him in the very beginning, that day at the aerodrome when he had made his bumbling attempt to ask her for a date? Would he have believed her then? And if he had, would he have fallen in love with her anyway, or would he have laughed at himself for being so mistaken and shrugged it all off and simply have admired her for the attractive woman she was and concentrated on learning to fly? Or what if she had told him that evening after the theater? Would he have decided then to fall *out* of love with her?

It had taken him weeks to reconcile himself to Harriet's being six years his senior. The possibility that it could be ten years more than that was simply too much to absorb. It required too great a readjustment of everything he had ever thought about her, too radical a reassessment of his own convictions about himself.

Yet (he forced himself to consider the unthinkable) it *would* explain something that had always puzzled him: how she could have gone to finishing school in France and still have been a journalist in San Francisco in 1902 at the tender age of 18. But if she had already been 27 . . .

(But that would only create another mystery: what had she done during those thirteen "lost" years between 18 and 31, which was how old she must have been when she was hired by *Leslie's* in 1906? Had she been married and divorced, or widowed?)

It could also explain the way she had behaved toward him

when they were learning to fly at Hempstead Plains—showing interest in him, then repelling him when he tried to become too personal. And at the theater—acting jealous of Carole, then withdrawing from him when he asked to see her again. It would all make sense, if she really were so much older.

But she had known he was falling for her. Why wouldn't she have set him straight about her age right at the start and saved him a lot of useless speculation, not to mention heartache? Why would she let him and everyone else believe she was so much younger? Because she could get away with it, and because lots of other women did it? Surely Harriet couldn't be that vain.

No, she could not be 36, he eventually convinced himself. *She simply could not be.*

She said she cared about him and his "best interests." How much difference was there between caring *about* someone and caring *for* someone? And the biggest question of all: why couldn't she say she didn't love him?

Was she afraid he might be an "impediment" to her career? It was possible that that might be the explanation; she'd brought the subject up in Child's. But if she would only let him talk to her he could convince her he wouldn't be a hindrance to her, he'd be an ally.

He nearly drove himself crazy with his thoughts, until another one struck him and he knew what the explanation really was: it was *his* age, not hers, and his being still in college. Harriet must simply think it would be wrong of her to encourage his feelings toward her.

She hadn't said—she *wouldn't* say—that she didn't return those feelings. If she didn't return them, if she didn't care for him, deeply, more than just as a friend, he would have known. He wasn't totally obtuse.

She simply thought it was wrong because he was so young. That was what she'd meant about feeling guilty about him.

Carole hadn't wanted to feel guilty about him either. How could women be so kind and gentle and sensitive—and *cruel*?

His life had been so uncomplicated and straightforward before he had met Harriet Quinlan. There were thousands of beautiful women in New York, more beautiful—and younger—than she. Millions in America. Millions more in the world. Why in God's name must there be for him only one?

He thought about writing her a letter, a long, literary letter, the way lovers used to do. À *la belle dame sans merci*. A letter would give him the leisure to express his feelings at length and in depth. He would quote some appropriate lines from the early English lyricists, keep it light and entertaining. But when he prowled through his freshman English lit textbook he found mostly lamentations over unrequited love. He composed the letter over and over in his head, wittily, cleverly, fervently. But when he started to write it down such a feeling of inadequacy possessed him that he tore the paper up. When she saw it was from him would she have even read it?

Quit, quit for shame! This will not move
  This cannot take her.
If of herself she will not love,
  Nothing can make her:
The devil take her!

In the end he decided to send her merely a note, no return name and address on the envelope so that she would not immediately throw it away without opening it, and brief enough that she could not but help read it at a glance. Just a couple of sentences: "Dearest Harriet—Wishing you every success in April. My heart will be with you, then and always. William."

It made him feel a little better, for a while. He had reminded her of his existence. For a while he even entertained the hope that she might reply, if only with a thank-you note. But as the days and weeks passed he wondered if she had even received it and sank into a despondency he thought must kill him eventually.

Shall I, wasting in despair,
Die, because a woman's fair?

It was not easy to will oneself to die. Pride goeth before destruction, but from rejection pride ariseth anew, he coined.

Again he resolved to try to put all thoughts of Harriet Quinlan out of his mind, at least for the time being. He would wait until April. Things might be different when she returned from Europe. They *would* be different then. He tried to lose himself in his studies. He stopped reading *Leslie's Weekly*.

In mid-February he came down with a fever that laid him low for two weeks. They had to call the doctor, who took his temperature and wrote a prescription and told him to stay in bed. The doctor could not tell with his thermometer and stethoscope, but it was nothing Willy wouldn't have shaken off in a few days had his spirit not been so weakened.

Ellen Reynolds knew that something more deep-seated and incurable than a winter cold had infected her William. He had been moody and depressed since New Year's. Ever since that Sunday when he had gone to visit that Quinlan woman.

The day he got out of bed he sat in a chair in the parlor, bundled up with a blanket, and she brought him a cup of hot lemon. She sat down on the sofa and waited while he took a few sips and set the cup on the table.

"Is it Carole?" she said, knowing it wasn't Carole, almost wishing it was.

The illness had left Willy in a pleasant languor. It was so peaceful in this room, in the home of his childhood and boyhood, the pale afternoon sun slanting through the curtains, only the ticking of the mantle clock to be heard. As peaceful as it had been at Harriet's.

"I love her," he said, and for the moment before he spoke again she hoped it was Carole after all.

"She's . . . " He grasped after his original belief. "She's six years older than me."

Ellen didn't know whether to be relieved or dismayed anew. Six years was a rather big difference on the woman's side, but certainly not unheard of. Why couldn't it be ten years? If it were that many years she would have been able to reason her son out of this awful infatuation.

She sighed. "I wish you had never taken flying lessons."

She looked down at her hands. "It's really not her age though . . . is it? It's how she feels about you. If she doesn't return your feelings, you have to accept that, William."

He pulled the blanket from around him and tossed it aside, along with the languor, and went and knelt with his head in his mother's lap. She stroked his hair as he wept in one brief, wracking burst. Her heart swelled for him. Poor William. Poor, poor William. He was so handsome, he could have any girl he wanted. Why did it have to be this woman?

He swiped at his face with his hands and sat beside her. He was ashamed of himself, but immensely glad he had purged himself. Now he could talk, logically, unemotionally, and he needed to talk.

"Sometimes I'm sure Harriet cares for me, Mother. Other times I wonder if she feels anything at all. At first I told myself it's the difference in our ages. I thought, if only I . . . I don't know. I've never known what to do. She's warm and cold, warm and cold. She asked me to visit her, then she told me she didn't want to see me anymore."

Ellen Reynolds sighed again. "Oh, I don't know why women do this to men. She has no right to toy with your affections this way."

"It isn't her, it's me. I forced myself on her."

No, that wasn't true—not until after Harriet had encouraged him. She had approached him first. But yes, it was true. She hadn't "approached" him; she had just been friendly to a fellow student, nothing more. No, no, it was more than that. If it wasn't more than that, if it was just disinterested friendliness on her part he would have known, he wouldn't be spending his life going over and over and over it, analyzing every word she ever spoke to him, every look she ever gave him.

"I don't believe that, William," his mother said. "You couldn't have forced yourself on her if she didn't let you."

In one simple sentence she had touched the heart of his confusion, he thought.

"I tell myself it's because I'm just a college student that she doesn't want to get involved with me, that she thinks it's wrong. Then I wonder if she wants anything to do with any man, because her career is so important to her. I'm pretty sure there's no other man. I almost wish there was."

This confirmed something that Ellen Reynolds had suspected about the woman from the first. Harriet Quinlan belonged to a modern generation of young women, more and more of whom, she'd read, were abjuring the roles of wife and mother to seek "personal fulfillment." Maybe all this suffragette agitation had something to do with it. But what kind of fulfillment they thought they would find in spinsterhood, she couldn't fathom.

She patted her son's hand. "I think that may very well be the case, dear," she said soothingly. "Harriet Quinlan has her career and that's all she wants right now. I'm sure she has worked very hard to get where she is, so young. Maybe in a few years when she gets older she'll discover that that isn't enough. But either you're going to have to wait until she does realize there's more to life than a career or go on with your own life, try to find someone else."

His mother didn't realize how much better she was making him feel, Willy thought. She actually seemed to have dismissed Harriet's age as the real obstacle. It never had been, only in his thinking, and in Harriet's.

He wanted to tell her what Harriet had tried to make him believe, that she was actually 36. He needed to talk about that too, to reason out with someone else why she would have said it. But he'd already reasoned it out. What good would it do to put more doubts in his mother's mind than she already had?

He turned to her and took her hands in his.

"Do you know what that amazing girl is going to do, Mother? She's planning to fly across the English Channel in April! She'll be the first woman in the world to do it."

It had really been nothing more than a wild, spontaneous idea before, something he'd seized on in an attempt to break through to Harriet. Now he made an instant, irrevocable decision. Go after her, Carole had said. What good is living if you don't go after what you want from life?

"I intend to be there when she does."

"Europe? *No, William, no.*"

Ellen Reynolds held her son's hands tight and shook them as she spoke. "Don't be foolish. Don't even consider it. What about school? You've already missed two weeks. You only have another year. What if she wouldn't want you there?"

"I'm twenty-one, Mother. I can do whatever I want."

"Not as long as you live under this roof. We've always let you do anything you wanted to do. But not this. I absolutely *forbid* you to do this. I will not stand by and watch you throw your future away on a woman who doesn't want you."

"Then I'll leave. I have my trust fund, or most of it."

"Yes, and if your grandmother could have foreseen what it might be squandered on she would never have left it to you. It was supposed to put you through graduate school, give you a start in life, not spent on flying lessons and aeroplanes. Not for—"

She sighed again. "What would we tell your father?"

He brought her hands to his face and placed them on his cheeks. She was already relenting, already conspiring with him.

"We'll tell him I need some time to think, to get away from school for a while. I'm not sure I want to go on with business administration. I'd still like to be able to do something in aviation. If I were graduated I would probably want to go to Europe. People do that. Your education isn't complete unless you make a tour of Europe. I'll just be doing it ahead of time. We have a break coming up over Easter. So what if I lose an extra week or two, I can make it up. And when I come back, whatever I decide about a major or about flying, I promise I'll go back to school."

He put his arms around her and patted her back. "I *have* to, Mother, don't you see? I love her so much, so very much. She's my very life. I know she cares for me too. I *know* she does."

He kissed her cheek and held her away from him and laughed with joy.

"Look at me. See how happy I am? I'm happier at this moment than I've been in—I don't know how long. Just the thought of being with her."

Ellen couldn't see. Her eyes were closed, tears coming from them. She fumbled for the handkerchief in the cuff of her sleeve and daubed at her cheeks. Then she looked at him, her head shaking. So terribly young he was, so much ardor. If only it were focused on someone worthy of it, someone who could return it.

"I'm so afraid for you, dearest. What if she *doesn't* love you? What if she really doesn't?"

"Then I'll know, Mother, for once and all. And that will be the end of it. I promise. That will be the end of it."

He tried at first to get passage on the *Amerika* but by then it was much too late; it was fully booked and had been for weeks. He was thankful it was. It would have been excruciatingly awkward and embarrassing for Harriet, and probably for her manager as well. It would be bad enough when she found out that he had had the outrageous nerve to trail her clear across the Atlantic and intrude himself in the most important undertaking of her life, her great enterprise. But this way, crossing separately, he would at least have the element of surprise in his favor, surprise that would not have been poisoned by a week of awkwardness and embarrassment on the same ship.

And after all, there was no law to say he could not use his midsemester break to visit Europe.

As it was, it was only through constant haunting of the steamship ticket offices and a last-minute cancellation that he was able to secure a second-class cabin on the *Campania* departing for Liverpool near the end of March and sail in Harriet's wake three weeks after her.

Hardelot

1

I T WAS NOT until Willy got off the London-Dover train at the Priory Station in Dover on a dreary Thursday morning that he was forced to confront the fact that he had absolutely no idea what he intended to do. For weeks he had been able to think of nothing but that he must get to England and to Dover. He had thrown over everything: school, his parents' hopes for him, possibly his entire future, as he mother feared. And all he had to go on was Harriet's whispered secret that it was from Dover that she intended to embark on her channel flight, sometime in early April. It was already the eleventh of the month.

He followed slowly behind the group of fellow passengers from the train. They all seemed to know where they wanted to go or had people meeting them.

There was a policeman standing outside the station.

"Excuse me, but I wonder if you could tell me what would be the likeliest hotel a party of Americans might be staying at? I'm looking for some people."

The bobby touched the brim of his helmet. "I couldn't say, sir. It could be any of several." He looked at Willy curiously.

"Is there one especially convenient to the aerodrome? They intend to do some flying." It was safe to say that. It wouldn't give away Harriet's plan.

"The aerodrome at Whitfield, sir? That's only a few miles from here." He nodded toward the higher terrain to the north.

"They recently constructed two new hangars there. But almost any hotel in Dover would be about as convenient to it as any other, I would think. Or the field at Swingate, for that matter, beyond the Castle." He pointed at the ancient Roman lighthouse and the complex of structures situated around it on a bluff to the east looming over the small city.

"But if they are to do flying, I would say to try the Lord Warden Hotel first. That seems to be a headquarters for aviators. When Blériot and Latham were competing to be the first to fly across the channel a Marconi wireless station was maintained on the roof. Yes, I would say to try the Lord Warden, sir."

"Is it far?"

"It's down by the inner harbor. Just follow York Street there to Snargate Street and the Viaduct." He looked at Willy's large suitcase. "Perhaps too far to walk with that, though. There should be another cab along shortly. Just tell the driver where you want to go, sir."

"I think I'd better telephone first." Willy thanked the helpful bobby, who touched his helmet again, and headed for a red-painted booth with a gold crown on top of it near the station doors. He asked the operator to ring the Lord Warden Hotel.

"Yes—hello," he said to the answering voice. "Do you by any chance have a guest named Harriet Quinlan?"

He waited while the man checked. No, sorry, there was no guest by that name.

He groaned. Now what? He would have to start calling every hotel in town and now someone else was waiting to use the phone. What if Harriet wasn't at any of them? What if something had happened to make her change her plans and she had given up the idea of a channel flight and had gone back to America? Or possibly never left America at all?

"Uh, is there a Mr. Leo Stevens? Or A. Leo Stevens? I'm looking for him and another American, a young woman. They may have checked in some days ago."

"Just a moment, sir."

He waited again. Then the voice said, "Yes, we have a Mrs. and Mrs. A. Leo Stevens. Mr. Stevens has also reserved rooms for a Miss Craig, a Miss Vanderbilt and a Mrs. Griffith. Ah, just a moment, sir."

Willy heard him talking to someone. Then, "Are you there? Yes, Miss Craig will be coming in later from Paris. Mrs. Stevens, I believe, is in London with Mrs. Griffith and Miss Vanderbilt. But Mr. Stevens is at the hotel." A pause. "Yes, his key is here. He is either out or possibly is in the dining room. Do you wish to have him paged or leave a message for him?"

"Miss Craig." That could only be Harriet.

"You say Miss Craig is in Paris?"

"Just a moment, please. Let me check the reservation. Yes. Miss Craig won't be arriving until next week."

"I would like to reserve a room for myself, if I may, beginning Monday the fifteenth, for an indefinite stay."

He could be in Paris that afternoon. He would have the rest of the day and all of Friday, Saturday and Sunday to try to find Harriet. That should be more than enough time.

Another wait, while his heart paused. It was the off-season; they couldn't be booked up.

"We shall certainly have a room for you on the fifteenth, sir. Easter week holiday will be over. In what name, please?"

It was but a short cab ride to the ferry dock and only an hour's wait for the next cross-channel steamer, but it seemed forever to Willy in his impatience. So too the hours consumed by the crossing and going through the *douane* at Calais and changing his money and the wait for the train to Paris and then the final leg through the countryside of northern France, which he observed uncuriously through the window. He saw the spires of a cathedral in the distance and idly wondered which one it was and how old it was.

He was in France, the center of Western art and culture, at least in the eyes of French-adoring Americans, and now the world's center of aviation, and all of that meant nothing to him. He was in Europe for the first and possibly the only time in his life, and he was seeing nothing, wanted to see nothing. Most people would be thrilled by the idea of voyaging to Europe on an ocean liner, but all he had thought about was how long it was taking. He was squandering not only his money and his future but an opportunity most people could only dream of. He might as well have been on the Long Island Railroad.

Why was he going to Paris? he asked the passing countryside. Why hadn't he just stayed in Dover and waited for Harriet? He should simply have gone to the Lord Warden and found Leo Stevens and introduced himself as a flying school classmate of Harriet's who happened to be taking a kind of sabbatical in England and had decided to see if he could be of any service to her.

Why yes, he would have told the surprised manager, Harriet had told him all about her proposed channel flight. The fact that he knew Harriet well enough for her to have revealed her secret plan to him would have impressed and disarmed Stevens. By the time Harriet arrived she would have found him already well integrated into her plan.

The man at the hotel might have been misinformed. Harriet might already be on her way to Dover. He might waste the whole weekend looking for her in France.

Paris at last, the beauties and attractions of which he also had neither eyes nor time for, even were he not self-imprisoned in the Gare du Nord because of his feverish pursuit. It was late in the afternoon but still time enough to find a phone and make himself understood to an operator and put a call through to the Blériot factory in Levallois.

Thank God for modern transportation and communication. Thank God someone was there to answer. Thank God for his high school French.

He almost used the name "Miss Craig." But Harriet would have had no need to disguise herself when she saw Blériot.

"'Arriet Quinlan?" the woman who answered the telephone repeated pleasantly. "*Une moment.*"

Oh God she was there! He hadn't really expected—he wasn't prepared. What was he possibly going to say to her when she came on the line? But then:

"À *regret*, monsieur. Mademoiselle Quinlan is departed this afternoon for Monsieur Blériot's aerodrome at 'Ardelot. Monsieur Blériot is here, however. Do you wish to speak with him?"

Another chance of a lifetime. He resumed breathing.

"*Non . . . merci. Òu est Hardelot?*"

It was a small fishing village on the coast below Boulogne. Another train ride, his third that day, to Boulogne. (Was it possible that only that morning he had been in London?) Then a final trip of an hour and a half on a crowded ramshackle tramcar to Hardelot. He had to stand all the way. It was dark and cold and windy when they reached the town.

"Where finds itself the hotel?" he asked the conductor, who was standing on the platform.

The man pointed to a large dark building in the distance at the end of the street. But it was *fermé*, he was informed. Closed. Open only in the summer. Try one of the cafés, monsieur. They have rooms.

He entered the first one he came to. Yes, they took lodgers but unfortunately they were *complet*, full up. The Easter holiday, monsieur.

Was there by any chance a young American woman staying there?

Non, monsieur. Rien des Américains.

Hefting his suitcase again he went on down the street to another café, the only other one he could see, and entered it . . .

. . . And there she was, seated at a table, half-turned away from him, a pen in one hand as she concentrated on something she had written in a notebook, in the act of lifting a glass of wine with her other hand to take a sip.

He could not believe he had found her so easily. And now that he had, he belatedly acknowledged to himself the utter rashness of what he had done, of what he was going to do. For weeks he had been living in an imaginary future. In the space of a second he was jolted back into the stark here and now.

His knees felt weak. He closed his eyes momentarily, took a deep breath, and approached her.

"Miss Craig, I believe?"

She almost dropped the glass. Her mouth fell open in a mute gasp and her hand flew up to it.

"*Oh my God! William!*"

He set the suitcase on the floor and sat down in the chair opposite her.

"I was beginning to think I'd never catch up with you."

He looked at her, drinking in her astonished face. Her mouth was still partly open.

"You didn't— *Tell me you did not do this.*"

"Are you terribly angry?"

She took a deep breath herself and let it out audibly through her nostrils, her lips set tight now.

"Am I *angry*? I'm so angry I could—I don't know what!"

She tossed her head irritatedly and looked around at the other people in the café, just as she had that day in Child's, but this time as if afraid their speaking in English was drawing attention. There was no irritation or anger in her voice, however, only soft pleading.

"You didn't leave school, did you? You did exactly what I begged you not to do. You're a very foolish young man. You're throwing your life away, you know. I'm not worth it."

He smiled wryly. "I was dying—I was *dead*—back home in Brooklyn," he said. "Now I'm alive again."

Harriet made a little sound of exasperation and shook her head again.

A waitress came up to the table and asked Willy if he wished to be served.

"Have you eaten?" he asked Harriet.

"Yes, but you go ahead, if you're hungry. I'll lecture you while you eat."

He was hungry; he'd only had a sandwich on the ferry for lunch. He ordered soup and *rosbif avec pommes frites* and a small bottle of wine, and then asked the girl if they might have a room available. She thought they did. She would check.

"Or maybe you'd prefer I went . . ?" he said to Harriet.

"Back to America. Yes. But I doubt if there's another tram to Boulogne at this hour. If they have a room you'd better take it. It's probably the only one left in town. Another café I went to was full up. Easter week, you know. They seem to make a big thing of it over here. Hardelot is becoming quite a popular resort. Louis Blériot has a seaside home here and the Duke of Argyle, the former governor-general of Canada, has a summer cottage."

That probably explained the crowded tramcar, though why anyone would come to Hardelot for holiday in early April he didn't know. It was blowing a gale outside. Maybe it was pleasant in season.

"How on earth did you find me here, William?" The flat tone of her words suggested she didn't really want to know.

"It's been quite an odyssey."

He smiled broadly, beginning to feel rather pleased with himself. He told her how he had managed to book passage on the *Campania*, the telephone calls he had made in Dover and Paris to trace her. It seemed to him now that the whole journey had taken no time at all.

She was still shaking her head at him but the movement was gentle, more in disbelief than displeasure, he thought.

"What am I going to do with you, you foolish, foolish boy? I guess I should have tried to find my baptism certificate after all, but I never imagined you could be so wrongheaded."

He merely maintained his smug smile. He would play along with her for now.

"And willful," he said.

"Yes. And stubborn and obstinate and headstrong and every other synonym. Do your parents know I'm the reason you're over here? Your mother must think I— No, don't answer. I don't want to know."

The waitress returned with a little girl in tow who was timidly clutching a postcard in her hand.

There was one room left, she said to Willy in French, then to Harriet in intelligible English: "She would like your autograph, mademoiselle."

"My autograph? Whatever for?"

"We 'ave 'eard you are to fly La Manche. In ze aeroplane."

"La Manche?"

"Ze channel, mademoiselle."

Harriet took the card and signed her name and beamed at the little girl and squeezed her hand. The child was thrilled.

"Someone at the Blériot hangar must have been talking," she said to Willy. "Quite innocently, I'm sure. But so much for keeping secrets."

"You're already famous in France."

For some reason that statement seemed to break the ice. Harriet began speaking in a stream of words. She had been waiting all afternoon for the wind to die down so that she could try out the aeroplane she was borrowing from Blériot. He had a hangar nearby. But it seemed to be getting worse, didn't it? All she had done was look at the machine. If she couldn't test it tomorrow she would have to have it shipped to Dover and hope she would be able to make a trial flight there. People from the London *Daily Mirror* and the Graumont Cinematograph Company would be arriving in Dover the first of the week. But the plane was essentially identical to the ones they had flown on Long Island, so maybe it would be all right.

She paused and took another deep breath. "In any case," she said resignedly, "I am not going to be the first woman to cross the channel by air."

"What?"

"Gustav Hamel took a girl across as a passenger a few days ago. Some woman named Eleanor Trehawke-Davies."

He had heard of Hamel, of course, an English aviator, one of the first men after Blériot to conquer the channel.

"Well, if she was only a passenger that doesn't change anything, does it?" he said. "You will still be the first woman to fly herself across, won't you?"

"Yes, but it takes something away from it. It upset me very much when I heard, especially since he did it just after I confided my own plans to him. I felt betrayed. Leo Stevens and I met him in London. He offered his services as an adviser for the flight. In fact he was quite insistent about it. I just cannot understand why he did it, taking that woman across. He knows how important this is to me. He's supposed to meet me in Dover."

"Are you going to let him now? I mean, advise you?"

"Gustav is a very proficient aviator and knows the channel better than anyone. I need all the help I can get."

"I want to help you too. I told you I wanted to join your team."

"Yes," she said coolly. "It would seem you have." Then, not quite so coolly, "You're a very unusual young man, William. I've never met anyone quite like you. Nothing I say seems to get through to you. I simply do not know what I'm going to do with you."

"Did you get my note?"

"Yes. I tore it up!"

"I don't think so."

When the waitress brought his meal and he began eating Harriet did not lecture him or say anything at all. She did not look at him. Her silence could mean either that she was reconciled to his being there or she was thinking of how she was going to rid herself of him. But for the moment she seemed to have accepted him. He was almost able to enjoy the food.

Fortunately several other people came up to the table asking for the autograph of *l'aviatrice Américaine* and he could at least observe Harriet's smile and the lively pleasure in her eyes, even if he was not the cause or the object of them.

He had done the impossible, the insane, the stupidest thing he could ever have conceived doing for love of a woman. And she did not hate him for it. Not too much.

2

I N THE END he had to force down the last of the meal. His appetite was displaced by a queasiness in his stomach, but not from the food, for the beef was fresh and lean and the potatoes not excessively greasy. The doubts and uncertainty that had seized him momentarily when he had entered the café and seen Harriet at the table churned inside him again.

She sat calmly, her pen poised once more above her writing tablet. Having apparently gotten over the shock of his appearance, she seemed almost unaware or unconcerned that he was there.

Well, how had he expected her to react? That she would be overcome by this proof of his love for her? That she would be full of admiration at his daring and ingenuity in trailing her halfway across the world? That his recklessness, his "throwing away" his life for love of her, would finally compel her to admit that she loved him too?

He had hoped for all that in his waking dreams during the voyage over. In his fantasies she had thrown herself in his arms, confessing and exclaiming her love. In his soberer moments he did not know what to expect and was afraid to think about it. For weeks he had thought only of finding her and had closed his mind to the possible consequences.

He wiped his mouth with the napkin and looked at her. She was writing in the notebook.

"What is that?"

"Just some notes. An article for Leslie's."

"Always scribble, scribble, scribble, eh, Mr. Gibbon?" He tried to laugh.

"What?"

"Nothing. Is it about the flight?"

"No. It's about what it's like to travel on a modern ocean liner. I interviewed the chief steward of the Amerika on the way over. It amazed me all the food they serve you—continuously. You could do nothing but eat if you wanted to. Even in third class and steerage. They had no less than six separate kitchens, including a kosher one, plus two for the crew! I don't know how they do it when they charge only thirty dollars for steerage and only thirty-eight-fifty for third class. First class or cabin of course can go up as high as eight hundred dollars, but also as little as a hundred and fifty, and second class for only about two-thirds of that. Where could you get such luxurious room and board for a week, not to mention your transportation, for that little money? I could get used to that kind of comfort very easily."

She was talking more at him than to him, but at least she was talking.

"Yes, it is amazing. It was the same on the Campania. I guess there must be a lot of competition among the different lines."

She closed the notebook and put it and her pen in her purse. She still wasn't looking at him.

"So . . . what have you been doing in Europe all this time, Harriet?" She must have arrived in the middle of March, two weeks before he even left New York. She couldn't have spent all that time negotiating with the *Mirror* in London or with Blériot in Paris. "Much sightseeing?"

"Some."

There was a little wine left in the bottle. He offered to share it with her.

"No, thanks. I've had two glasses. That's enough for me. I'm going up to my room, such as it is. I want to go out to the Blériot hangar first thing tomorrow—if this weather lets up. You'd better get to bed early too if you want to go with me. You must be exhausted. From your odyssey."

His eyebrows lifted. He was accepted. Perhaps grudgingly, unwillingly, unjoyfully. But accepted. She had said it so matter-of-factly. He had completely misread her mood. Yet it wasn't the first time.

"Of course I do. I do want to. You don't mind . . ?"

"I've just about given up minding when it comes to you, William. Or being surprised. I do really appreciate your wanting to help me. It's possible you may have your uses."

Her voice was light and she smiled at him then for the first time, and the apprehension that had been inside him ever since he'd left New York began to subside.

Harriet got up, said good night, and headed toward the stairs past the concierge's counter. He waited a decent interval, aware that the other people in the room were watching him curiously. Another American. He drained the last of the wine in his glass and then inquired of the concierge the location of his room and went up the stairs. It was on the second floor, at the end of a narrow hall. There was a third floor, apparently reserved for the concierge and his family. No numbers on the doors. Judging from the sounds of voices coming from the first two rooms he passed they were occupied by vacationing French families. He deposited his suitcase in the last room and then tapped softly on the door of the silent room next to it.

Harriet opened the door a few inches. She was in a dressing gown under a robe, which she held closed in front of her with one hand. Her hair was down, outlined by the yellowish light cast by a table lamp in the room behind her. He had never seen her hair this way. It was longer than he had thought.

"I wanted to ask you before you went to bed," he said. "You forgot to tell me what time you're getting up."

"Four o'clock," she whispered. "Do you want me to wake you?"

"I have a little alarm clock. I'll set it."

"All right. Good night." She started to close the door.

"Harriet . . . Can't we talk a little more? We've hardly said anything all evening. That is, I haven't. I want to explain . . . "

"I'd ask you in, William, but I do need some rest. The trip from Paris was very tiring. I'm not dressed. There's only one chair."

He glanced past her at the Spartan room. Besides a straight-backed chair on which she had placed her overcoat and hat there was only a large old bureau, much too large for the room, with a wash basin and towel and a lamp on top of it and a very discolored mirror on the wall above it. And a narrow bed, the coverlet of which had been turned down. Her opened valise and an umbrella were on the floor. It was the same as his room.

"One of us could sit on the bed," he said.

"William. Really. The French may be very broadminded but they're as fond of gossip as anyone. As you've seen, everyone seems to know who I am. There's an English family living nearby, they had me over for tea this afternoon. You wouldn't want them to hear that I entertained a man in my room, would you? And in my nightclothes?"

Her voice was controlled and flat, schoolmarmish. But there was a certain tremor in it that did not escape him.

"Who's to know? There's no one here." He extended his hand to the dark, empty hallway.

He pushed against the door. She made a sound of irritation but did not resist his push. He stepped inside the room. But when he started to close the door she did resist, holding the door halfway open.

"William, if you want to be on my team you're going to have to promise you'll be a good boy. I cannot have this."

"Boy" again. He was one once, but not anymore. He boldly slipped his arms around her waist and pulled her against him and buried his face in her neck. He removed her hand from the door and closed it.

"I do love you so much, Harriet. I truly do. Don't you believe that? Haven't I proven that to you?"

She let him hold her that way for a moment, then pushed against him and stepped back.

"You've proven that you have impossibly romantic notions about me that you've let take over your judgment. I want you to go to your room now."

"Not until . . ."

He pulled her to him. She pushed against his chest with her hands, but not hard enough to break his embrace. She turned her face away from his but he turned it back with his fingers under her chin and kissed her, long and gently. He felt her lips move slightly against his.

He looked down at her.

"I want to marry you, darling. Oh not right away. I know it's not possible for you to consider it now. Just tell me there's a chance that someday we might marry. That if you marry anyone it will be me. That's all I ask. I know you care for me. Tell me you don't. Not on the telephone where you can't see me but right here and now, looking into my eyes. Tell me you never want to see me again. Tell me you feel nothing for me, and I'll leave Hardelot tomorrow and that will be the last of me. *Tell me.*"

She broke from his arms then and moved a few paces away and turned her back to him.

"All right. If that's what you want to hear. I'll never marry anyone. You or anyone else."

"Tell me you don't love me. Tell me you hate me. Tell me you can't stand the sight of me. Say it looking at me."

She didn't answer.

"You can't do it, can you?"

He put his hands on her waist again from behind, began moving them upward. She pried them away.

"*I hate you.*" But the smallness of her voice told him other-wise.

He laughed happily. "In only two or three years I'll be out of college and be established in something. We'll—"

She spun around suddenly, her robe flying open. He could see the form of her breasts through the thin fabric of her night-gown, the protruding nubs at their tips.

"*Don't talk like an idiot!* In three years I'll be in my forties! And you still only in your mid twenties!"

The words were an urgent whisper, lest the sound go beyond the room. She realized she was exposing herself and quickly folded the robe around her and looped its belt.

"I am *too old* for you, William. I am going to be thirty-seven next month! Even if I loved you, which . . . which I don't . . . and wanted to marry you, which I definitely do not, I am too old for you. Why can't you accept that?"

"Because everyone knows you're twenty-seven," he stated. "Or are you telling me you lied to your employer, you've lied to everyone who knows you, you've—"

"Yes, I've lied!" she said, her voice momentarily rising. Then, whispering. "I lied in my application to Leslie's because I was afraid they would prefer someone younger and I felt that my true age shouldn't have anything to do with my qualifications. After that I had to keep up the pretense and eventually almost started believing it myself. Fortunately, I've been able to get away with it because I still have a youthful appearance. But that won't last forever."

Talk about *his* stubbornness, he thought. She wasn't going to give it up. But her words and the direct look she gave him were very convincing. A smug grin that had been on his face faded. He didn't want to think about it.

"Just let me be with you, Harriet," he said weakly. "That's all I ask."

With an *"Oh—you!"* and a toss of her head she turned her back to him again.

"What am I going to do with you? What can I do to make you believe me?"

There was nothing else to do but to put his arms around her again. He pressed himself against her tightly. She made no attempt to break away.

He moved her to the bed and sat down on the edge and pulled her down beside him and covered her mouth with his. Her lips were soft and yielding. Her neck, which he kissed next. She seemed surprisingly small and fragile in his arms. She was trembling. He undid the belt of her robe and slipped his hand inside and moved it up to just below her breasts.

She ran her hands over her face nervously, as if trying to wipe away his kisses.

"This is so unfair . . . you're coming here like this."

He thought she meant his coming to her room. He remembered the shabby room the girl had taken him to in New York and he felt unworthy. But this was different. He loved this girl.

"Please don't think that, Harriet. I had no ulterior motive. I wouldn't . . . you know. Even if you wanted me to, though God knows I want you to want me to. But I know we mustn't until we're married, when it will be right."

"You had no right following me to Europe. That was unfair."

He put his mouth against her ear, tracing its delicate convolutions with his lips.

"Why? How was that unfair? Can't you even yet believe I truly love you? I know you can't think of anything but the channel flight and if I thought my presence would . . . I would never do anything to interfere or hinder you or upset you. Please tell me you're not upset."

"You upset me a long time ago, William."

His heart lifted. It was the most wonderful thing she could have said short of an outright admission of love for him. It was the most wonderful moment in his life. Not even in his fantasies had he thought that if he found her he might actually be holding her in his arms like this. In a bedroom. On a bed.

"God, I do love you so," he whispered into her ear.

"*William . . .*"

"Tell me how I upset you, darling. What do you mean that I upset you long ago? How? When?"

When she made no answer, forgetting everything he had just said, he eased her down onto her back and opened her robe and took both breasts in his hands, feeling them lift and fall with her rapid, shallow breathing. He buried his face in the valley he created.

"*Oh God, William . . .*"

He released one breast and, kissing the swell of the other one above the neck of her gown, moved his hand slowly down across her stomach. Then . . . lower . . . under the hem of the gown . . .

This was unfair.

He folded her robe around her and sat up. The ancient bed creaked with his movement. If he had gone on anyone in the next room could have heard everything.

"I'm sorry, darling. I just couldn't help—"

Harriet lay with her eyes closed, one hand over them, palm up, moving her head from side to side like a sleeper disturbed by a bad dream. Gradually her quick, tremulous breathing slowed. After a few moments she got up off the bed and stood at the bureau, looking in the mirror. She pulled at the two ends of the belt, tightening it, then cupped her face between her hands, then ran them down her sides and dropped her arms. He could see her reflection in the mirror, but the light was so dim and the mirror so clouded that he couldn't read her expression.

"Harriet . . . I'm sorry."

Seemingly having recovered herself, she turned to face him.

"It was my fault. I should never have let you in. Thank you for being enough of a gentleman not to—not to have . . . But nothing like this must ever, ever happen again. I simply cannot allow it."

She went to the door and placed her hand on the lever. She spoke calmly.

"William, if I let you go to Dover with me and help with the flight—I don't know how I will explain this to Leo and Mrs. Stevens. I certainly cannot have them know you followed me to Hardelot. Helen Vanderbilt is there too, and another good friend of mine, Linda Griffith."

"Linda Griffith? Is she related to that movie producer you mentioned you'd written screenplays for?"

"David Wark Griffith. Yes, his wife. Or I should say, his estranged wife. Unfortunately, they've separated. But there are going to be a lot of other people as well, reporters and photographers from the Mirror. But if I let you come with me, you must promise you won't—"

"Embarrass you? Compromise you? Of course I won't. I would never, *never*. I'll be the epitome of circumspection and propriety. We'll tell them some story. We're fellow fliers, aren't we? Old friends. They won't think anything of it."

"And that will be the end of it. When you hear I've made it to Calais—*if* I make it—you'll go back home. Or go see Europe, as long as you've come this far. As soon as you hear. You won't wait for me in England."

"If you promise you'll see me in New York. You won't hang up on me."

"I hope by then you'll have come to your senses. But all right, we've both promised." She opened the door.

He got up and stood at the doorway. She avoided his eyes. He resisted the impulse to take her in his arms once more and only squeezed her hands. He had pushed his good fortune, his fantastically unbelievable good fortune, far enough. Almost too far.

"Sleep well, my dearest darling. I'll see you bright and early tomorrow. We'll talk about everything then."

She closed the door soundlessly. He heard the key turn in the lock.

He slept well himself, after an initial period of restless tossing and turning in both the frustration and the comfort of knowing that only a few inches of wood and plaster separated him from her, that beyond the wall only a few feet from where he lay chastely in his bed she lay chastely in hers.

He must have been more exhausted than he realized. When the alarm rang he fumbled for it and shut it off. Just a few more minutes . . . It was after eight o'clock when he fully awoke. Shivering in the cold, he used the chamber pot and splashed icy water from a basin on his face and body—there was no soap— and quickly toweled himself dry and put on everything but his shirt and tie and jacket. He probably could have gotten a pot of hot water from the concierge but he couldn't wait. He shaved haphazardly with cold water only and then finished dressing.

There was no response when he knocked on Harriet's door. He tried the lever and found it was unlocked. The room was empty. Her valise was gone. Surely she would not have broken their agreement. He hurried downstairs.

She was sitting at the same table as before, her valise beside her with her overcoat draped over it and the umbrella propped against it. This time she was sipping coffee, and not writing. She saw the anxiety on his face.

"I thought I'd let you sleep," she said. "When I got up it was pouring outside so I went back to bed myself. The concierge says it could very well go on like this for days."

In his profound relief that she was there, only then did he become conscious of the fact that sheets of rain were driving down on the gray, deserted street outside and that a gusting wind was rattling the windows of the café.

"There's no point in staying in Hardelot," Harriet said. "I've called the Blériot hangar—fortunately someone there speaks English—and told them to crate the plane and ship it over to Dover immediately. Let's have some breakfast and then start for Dover ourselves."

Ashamed that he could have thought Harriet had abandoned him, suddenly hungry again, he sat down at the table. He was so grateful to her that it didn't occur to him to question why, if she had been educated in France, she would say it was fortunate that someone at the Blériot hangar spoke English. Or indeed why, the night before, she hadn't known that *La Manche* was what the French called the English Channel.

Dover

1

A. LEO STEVENS was a trim and energetic man, as befitted a balloonist, or former balloonist, in his mid thirties. Harriet had telegraphed him from Boulogne advising him of the time of her arrival in Dover and he was sitting in the lobby of the Lord Warden reading a newspaper and smoking a cigar when Harriet and Willy walked in on the afternoon of Friday the twelfth of April. He dropped the cigar in an ashtray and got up from his chair when he saw them. There was a quick raising and lowering of his eyebrows when Harriet introduced Willy to him and they shook hands.

Harriet did some hasty, breathless explaining. She and William had been fellow students of André Houpert on Long Island, she told Leo. William was touring England and had just arrived in Dover and—would you believe such a coincidence?—they had encountered each other as they were both entering the hotel. She pretended to ask Willy some questions about his itinerary, putting perhaps a little too much marvel in her voice.

Willy didn't know if Stevens credited the "coincidence," but fortunately the man had more important matters on his mind.

"How did it go in France? Were you able to—?" He caught himself and looked from Harriet to Willy and back to her.

"Uh, does Mr. Reynolds . . ?"

Harriet was quick on her feet. "Yes, I've told William about the flight. He's graciously offered to be of assistance in any way he can. As I said, we were fellow students of André's."

They would have had to have done a lot of fast talking on their way into the hotel, but Stevens seemed to accept that.

"Were you able to try out the plane, Harriet?"

Shaking her head, she described the atrocious weather in Hardelot, and Willy made some sympathetic sounds, as if it was news to him. There had been nothing for it but to instruct the Blériot people to pack up the machine and ship it to Dover, Harriet said. It should be arriving tomorrow, she hoped.

She had also telegraphed the *Mirror* during the stop in Boulogne. Had any of their representatives arrived?

Leo was still holding the newspaper in his hand. He folded it and placed it on the chair he had vacated.

"They're waiting in London for a call from me, but I told them you couldn't possibly fly until next week. I think you really ought to test the machine out before you make the flight, Harriet. If it gets here early enough tomorrow we may have time to assemble it and you can try it then. If not, it will have to be on Monday. The day after tomorrow is Sunday of course."

Willy thought he detected a trace of irony in Leo's last words. If so, he sympathized with Leo. If there was anything that irritated him about Harriet, it was her staunch aversion to flying on Sundays.

There was a little confusion at the desk when they checked in. Mr. Reynolds's reservation was for the following Monday, the clerk said officiously. They were full up for the Easter holiday, he was afraid. He sounded like the same stuffy person Willy had spoken with before.

"Surely you must have a room," Harriet said. It was a statement, not a question. "With this weather you must have had some cancellations or early departures. Mr. Reynolds is a member of my party."

This also irritated Willy. She was taking control again, acting as the guide and shepherd of the naive college student, as she had the night at the theater. Actually, she had started acting that way in Calais.

The clerk riffled through his list and, after making them wait in uncertainty the proper length of time, managed to find an available room. In fact, it was on the same floor as Harriet's and the Stevenses' rooms, although, as he found out, well separated from Harriet's this time, at the other end of the corridor.

It was still the middle of the afternoon but Harriet said she was tired and wanted to take a nap.

"Gustav Hamel is here," Leo said. "I'll tell him you've arrived. Let's plan on the four of us having dinner together." To Willy: "My wife is here also, but she went to London yesterday with Helen Vanderbilt and Linda Griffith to do some sightseeing and shopping. I expect her back tomorrow evening."

Willy pretended this was more news to him. "I look forward to meeting her, Leo."

In his room Willy lay down on the bed and thought about the day's trip from Hardelot. It had been wonderful despite the weather. Because of the weather, really. In the beginning anyway. They had huddled together against the rain under Harriet's umbrella as they waited for the tram, and on the tram it was as if they were in their own little world. Unlike the day before, there were only a few other travelers and he had sat very close to her on the narrow, uncomfortable wicker seat and held her hand, for a while, until it became awkward and she drew it away. He didn't try to talk to her; talking would have destroyed the intimacy he felt.

He was content just to be sitting beside her, feeling her body next to his, remembering the night before, looking at her profile every other second to confirm and refresh the image of her in his mind.

On the ferry at Calais they had stood on the deck watching the restless gray water as they pulled away and he had put his arm around Harriet. He wanted the trip never to end.

That was the last of the intimacy. Harriet removed his arm and spoke sternly. "We must decide what we're going to say when we get to Dover, William. No one must ever have the slightest suspicion that we spent the night together in Hardelot, inadvertent as it was."

For a second he had thought she was going to say "innocent." It was and it wasn't.

She then suggested the story they later told Leo, and he had agreed it was probably the best they could come up with. Coincidences did happen.

The cold soon drove them inside the cabin among the other passengers. As they progressed across the channel Harriet became more and more self-absorbed, sitting silently, staring straight ahead or at the salt-streaked windows through which nothing could be seen. The nearer they came to Dover, the nearer came the time of her flight and—he could sense it happening—the further she withdrew from him, in her mind, if not in physical proximity. (A "channel change," he thought sardonically. Was that the same as a sea change?) The only mitigation, and he dwelled on it, was that she had acquiesced in their subterfuge when she might well have repented her promise and ordered him to leave her when they reached Dover, and if she had there would have been nothing he could have done about it.

Less hurriedly than he had that morning in Hardelot, Willy washed and shaved properly (at least this time there was a bathroom and soap and hot water) and put on fresh clothes and at seven-thirty went down to the lobby.

Leo Stevens was sitting in the same chair as before, but now in the company of another man. It was Gustav Hamel. Willy recognized him from pictures he had seen in aviation magazines. Hamel shook his hand vigorously when Leo introduced them as fellow fliers. He was surprised at how young Hamel looked in person; he could not have been more than a few years older than himself and already a famous aviator.

"Sit down, Willy," Leo invited. "Harriet will be joining us shortly. Gustav and I were just having a discussion about the future of lighter-than-air craft. He's been trying to tell me there isn't any future."

"For observation in wartime, possibly," said Hamel in a clipped educated Englishman's accent that sounded supercilious to Willy.

"And sport. But not for commercial purposes, despite the money the Germans are putting into Count von Zeppelin's dirigibles."

"How can you say that, Gustav? The zeppelins have been carrying out regular passenger service for at least two years. I fully expect one of them to cross the Atlantic in not too many years. And if there ever were another European war, think of a fleet of those things carrying tons of bombs soaring well above the reach of guns or any present-day aeroplane. They could devastate any city at will."

"Present-day aeroplanes—precisely," said Hamel. "Aeroplanes are being improved all the time. In the next war—and there will be another war, take my word for it—zeppelins will be sitting ducks for fast chase planes. What do you think, Willy?"

Willy was flattered that the famous Hamel should ask his opinion. He looked apologetically at the balloonist. "I'm afraid I tend to agree with Mr. Hamel, Leo."

"Gustav," said Hamel.

"Gustav." He nodded at Hamel, and then back to Leo. "I can see dirigibles carrying passengers and cargo on long flights, even across the Atlantic. But for any other purpose an aeroplane can fly rings around them."

"I'd be willing to wager," said Hamel, speaking with authority, "that the first flight across the Atlantic will not be in a dirigible but in an aeroplane, and well before any of us are old men. Even you, Leo."

He pointed his cigar at Leo, grinning. "Not with today's single-engine craft of course. It wouldn't be able to carry enough fuel and there would be no backup if the engine failed. But a large bimotor, at an average speed of, say, one hundred miles an hour, it would take only a day to fly from London to New York on a great circle route. Or perhaps the other way first, from New York to London, because of the prevailing winds. But in any case it will be done."

Leo began arguing that even a two-engine plane would be unable to stay in the air that long. It would need to carry so much fuel that it would require a huge airframe and huge engines to lift it, which in turn would increase the amount of fuel necessary to keep the engines going, which would increase the size of the plane needed to hold the fuel and the engines to power it, and so on in a vicious circle. There would be no capacity left for crew or cargo. And this was wholly to ignore the problem of navigating over two thousand miles of open ocean.

Hamel laughed. "You underestimate the pace of aeronautical progress, Leo. I recall that at least one noted scientist — I forget his name — 'proved' that an aeroplane would never be able to lift its own weight and that of a pilot. And that was just before — "

"Simon Newcomb," Willy interrupted.

Hamel nodded. "The name isn't important. But it was just before the Wrights flew. In fact, I may be underestimating, myself. Jules Vedrines exceeded one hundred miles an hour at Pau in February, in a Deperdussin. With an efficient and reliable engine, I am even willing to wager that a single-engine monoplane will cross the Atlantic, and do it within the next five years."

This time Willy disagreed with Hamel but he said nothing. It struck him that it was a bit ridiculous for them to be sitting there talking about a flight across two thousand miles of Atlantic Ocean when the immediate concern of all of them was Harriet's flight across a mere twenty-one or twenty-two miles of English Channel.

Leo must have had the same thought. He said to Gustav, "And you're the one who thinks Harriet should give up her idea of flying the channel as too difficult or dangerous."

Hamel was defensive. "She's been flying for less than a year. Actually, only eight months, what? She's never used a compass before. And you tell me she wasn't able to try out the Blériot."

"It's similar to what she's used to. That's right, isn't it, Willy? I'm sure it won't give her any problem. She'll be able to see France as soon as she takes off."

"The weather over the channel is so unpredictable," said

Hamel. "It can change quite quickly. It's chancy enough even in good weather and in a machine you're familiar with."

"And she's a woman."

"Not at all. Her sex has nothing to do with it. But however competent a pilot Harriet may be, if she ran into fog and got off course just a few degrees she could end up in the North Sea. Her being a woman has nothing to do with it."

At that moment the subject of the conversation appeared and the three men rose to greet her. Harriet was dressed in an elegant but simple gown, the more elegant because of its unfussiness. It seemed too fresh to have been stowed in a suitcase and transported across an ocean, Willy thought. Maybe she'd purchased it in London or Paris.

He watched as Hamel kissed Harriet's extended hand in the continental manner and was surprised, after what she had said about him in Hardelot, at the apparently genuine warmth of her words to him.

"Hello, Gustav. How nice to see you again. Thank you so much for coming." She scarcely glanced at Willy.

To his added surprise, during the meal the conversation, which he listened to without contributing much of anything, touched on everything but the upcoming channel flight: the menu, English cuisine (if it could be called that) versus French, the quality of the wine, Dover, French trains, the weather, etcetera, etcetera. He noticed how Hamel, and most of the other people in the Lord Warden's ornate dining room, ate with their forks in their left hands and their knives in their right, so much more sensible than the American way. For some reason it pleased him that neither Harriet nor Leo affected the European style.

They eventually talked about aeroplanes and flying, when dessert was being served, with Hamel dominating the conversation, and Willy was surprised for a third time when Harriet said: "William had quite an experience a few months ago. He was in a Moisant monoplane with a young lady passenger even though it was a single-seater and they were right above New York City when the engine stopped."

Both Leo and Gustav exclaimed and Harriet smiled at Willy across the table, almost slyly, he thought. It was the first time she had looked at him, much less smiled at him, since she had joined them in the lobby. Indeed, since the moment she had introduced him to Leo that afternoon he had been getting the strong message from her that the only reason she intended to acknowledge him at all was to keep up the pretense of their "accidental" meeting.

Hamel looked at him with sudden interest and for a moment was at a loss for words. Willy realized then that Hamel had more or less dismissed him as dilettante. Was Harriet trying to take some wind out of Hamel's sails?

"Really?" Hamel said. "What happened. How high were you?"

Willy briefly recounted the experience, or most of it.

"You were lucky," Hamel said, nodding. "No, I take that back. You had to be very skillful. Remarkably skillful. It's happened to me, engine failure, but fortunately I've never had to glide as far as you did with a dead engine, and certainly not at night over a big city. And certainly not with a woman on my lap!"

Willy glanced at Harriet and wondered again if she was trying to visualize him and Carole in the same cockpit. She blinked and dropped her eyes and the smile faded.

"But there's no feeling, is there," Hamel said, "like that when you're sailing along as nicely as can be and you suddenly have no power."

Leo said, "To borrow from Doctor Johnson, it must concentrate the mind powerfully, I imagine. That's one thing balloonists don't have to worry about."

"It was really quite pleasant," Willy said. "If it hadn't been for the panic!" He laughed self-consciously. "I mean, it was so quiet. Except for the wind of course. It was the first time I ever felt what it must be like to be a bird."

"I just hope I never find out what it's like," Harriet said. "Not that way."

Hamel seemed subdued and his manner toward Willy was now interested and respectful. "That's really quite remarkable," he repeated.

He looked at Harriet and then at Willy again, as if, Willy thought, he was beginning to question whether there might be some connection between the two of them besides their having been fellow flying students. Willy felt smug.

"Well, on this happy note," Harriet said, "If you will all permit me I'd like to retire to my room. I hate to leave such pleasant company but I know you men would like to talk."

She stood up and as the men began to rise also said, "Don't get up. Enjoy your after-dinner cigars." To Leo: "I want to go out to the aerodrome tomorrow morning to see the ground. Not too early. Perhaps we could drive there around nine or nine-thirty? I'll have breakfast in my room."

"I'll go with you," Hamel said.

Leo said that would be fine. He would arrange to have a motorcar waiting for them at nine-thirty at the latest but he had better stay at the hotel and check with the docks periodically for the hoped-for arrival of the Blériot.

Leo and Gustav both lit fresh cigars, luxuriantly blowing clouds of blue smoke into the air. Willy had a modest cigarette. Nothing had been said about his going to the aerodrome. Evidently it was simply assumed he would. He began to feel comfortable for the first time since arriving in Dover and meeting Leo and Gustav. They had accepted him into their company, unreservedly, unlike Harriet. He even began to feel pleasantly fuzzyheaded as they polished off the bottle of wine the waiter left on the table and ordered liqueurs.

Hamel asked him a few questions about the Houpert school and aviation activities on Long Island and he answered absent-mindedly. He was thinking of how Harriet had looked when she had appeared in the lobby, her bright eyes at the table during dinner, though only once directed at him; thinking about Hardelot again, the journey to Calais, standing beside her at the rail on the ferry . . .

And wondering why she had seemed so pleased to see Gustav Hamel.

2

WILLY DECIDED that the best way he could be of service to Harriet and to the furtherance of her great enterprise was to accompany Leo to the waterfront to help oversee the unloading of the Blériot and its transport to the aerodrome at Whitfield.

Word of the machine's arrival had been sent to the hotel shortly before noon. Harriet and Gustav had not returned, so Leo left a message for them and he and Willy started walking the short distance to the channel ferry docks.

"I really didn't expect the plane to get here this soon," Willy said eagerly. "Harriet and I only left Hardelot yester—"

Oh Christ. Where was his brain?

Leo stopped abruptly and his head snapped around. "Eh? You were in Hardelot with Harriet? I thought—"

Willy attempted to cover his gaffe. He started to say that it was in Hardelot that he and Harriet had happened to encounter each other and that for appearances' sake they had agreed to say it was in Dover. But he immediately realized that pretense piled upon pretense would only make Leo read more into his relationship with Harriet than there actually was. There was no "relationship." Not yet. Not the kind he wanted.

"Yes," he admitted. "But it was all my doing. Believe me, there's nothing between Harriet and me, Leo. Nothing has ever happened between us."

He didn't want to say that. He said it for Leo's benefit, and for Harriet's, but saying it made it seem somehow . . . official, a conclusive fact. There *was* something between them, wasn't there? Something *had* happened, almost.

He felt a sudden need to unburden himself to the older man.

"I'm in love with her, Leo," he said huskily. "I've been in love with her ever since I met her at the flying school. But I'm afraid that so far it's been pretty much one-sided, on my part."

He decided to tell Leo the whole story, briefly relating how he had fallen for Harriet at Hempstead Plains, of her warm-and-cold behavior, how against her wishes he had followed her to England and to Dover, then to Paris and Hardelot. He felt like he was talking to his mother again, spilling out his heart.

Leo listened, nodding; then in politeness, or probably embarrassment, looked away from Willy's glistening eyes.

He patted Willy's arm. "I had no idea it was anything like that. I'm sure my wife would have, though. Women are much more perceptive about these things than we mere men. I'm sorry if it's all one-sided. You must feel terrible."

"You won't say anything about this to anyone, to Mrs. Stevens?" Willy said. "I wouldn't want anyone to think that . . . that Harriet . . . that we . . ."

"No, of course not, of course not." He patted Willy's arm again and resumed walking.

"Leo?" he started. "Do you—?"

There was still the gnawing possibility that Harriet might really be almost 37; she had been so adamant about it. As her manager and associate, Leo would surely know. Willy deliberately chose his words to give Leo an opening.

"Do you think it might be because she's—she's so much older than me?

Leo paused again. "Well, I don't know. I suppose that could be a factor. How old are *you*, Willy?"

Willy told him.

"And Harriet's going to be, I believe, twenty-eight next month," Leo said. "She's not all that much older than you. No, I wouldn't think that should necessarily have anything to do with it—not that I suppose that makes you feel any better. But Harriet is very intent on making her name in aviation. Maybe the time isn't right. Or maybe you're just going to have to face the fact that she simply doesn't feel the same way about you."

Willy felt wonderfully better, for a heartbeat, before Leo's last words plunged him back into uncertainty. If it wasn't the age difference, and if it wasn't her career plans, all that was left was that Harriet really didn't feel the same way about him. But why couldn't she just say so and put him out of his misery? Why would she persist in that story about being sixteen years older?

Unless . . . unless she had also lied to Leo.

The huge crate had already been lifted off the deck of the ferry by a crane and lowered onto a waiting flatbed lorry, where it sat in a cold drizzle that had begun falling. The paperwork took more time than the unloading. After Leo completed that business with the customs people they followed the truck in a taxi-cab to the field in Whitfield on the heights above Dover, about three miles back from the channel.

Willy's services proved to be redundant. There were more than enough mechanics at the aerodrome to unload and assemble the plane, all of them eager to be part of the American aviatrix's great enterprise—for which they were being paid of course. And in any case Hamel soon arrived and proceeded to take over direction of the operation.

He and Harriet had gone to see the famous castle after lunch, he said to Leo. He'd just dropped her back at the hotel, where they found Leo's message.

Willy thought Hamel's services were also redundant, as the resident mechanics seemed to know quite well what they were about.

The crate was broken open on the truck and the parts carried into a hangar where the doors were shut against the blustery weather outside. There the monoplane quickly took shape. It took less than two hours, for the engine, fuselage, undercarriage and rudder had been shipped in one whole assembly so that all that was required was to attach the wings and horizontal stabilizers and connect their bracing wires and control cables. This required precise and careful rigging, however. When it was completed, Hamel sat in the cockpit and checked to see that all the controls were as they should be. He indicated his satisfaction to Leo and Willy.

"She's ready," he said.

Satisfied as he was, Gustav had a glum expression on his good-looking face and Willy knew why. He would have liked to have tried the plane out, but the weather was too marginal even for him, even if it had been his machine. Willy wondered if it ever stopped blowing and raining in the vicinity of the English Channel.

Hamel had driven to the field in the car Leo had hired and the three of them rode back in it to the hotel after agreeing that there was nothing more to be accomplished at the field. Willy sat in the back, not speaking.

Although Leo had told the *Mirror* that Harriet would not make her channel attempt that weekend, several people from the newspaper had come down from London anyway and were milling about in the lobby. Hamel was recognized and the reporters gathered around him and Leo and began peppering them with questions. They had been waiting to see Miss Quinlan — "Miss Craig," that was — but she seemed to be sequestered in her room.

Unnoticed, Willy got his key and went up to his own room where he threw himself on the bed. He had something sent up for dinner that evening. No one inquired after him. He was redundant.

Sunday would have been a perfect day for flying across the English Channel. The weather was totally different from what it had been in Hardelot, or in Dover just the day before: the sun bright and warm, the wind moderate. The sky was so clear that Harriet's party, now increased to seven with the return of Mrs. Stevens and Helen Vanderbilt and Mrs. Griffith from London, could with just a little straining make out the French coast dimly outlined against the distant horizon.

Whether the two other women had also come across on the *Amerika* or had traveled separately, Willy didn't know. But they were all at the table for breakfast in the dining room Sunday morning, when hunger had overcome his self-disgust for his stupidity in blurting out about Hardelot to Leo, and for his weakness in crying on the man's shoulder to boot, and he had been unable to stay with himself in his room any longer.

Harriet greeted him pleasantly enough. (The pretense had to be maintained.) "We were wondering why you were, William. You didn't come down for dinner last night. You remember Helen Vanderbilt of course. And this is Linda Griffith."

He shook hands with Helen, returning her "How nice to see you again," and with Mrs. Griffith, a pretty woman who greeted him warmly while giving him a frankly appraising look.

Harriet had evidently told Helen the same story she had told Leo, for Helen said, "What a coincidence your being in England just at this time. *And in Dover.*"

"Yes, isn't it?" He glanced at Leo but the man was wearing a poker face. He introduced Willy to his wife, a pleasant, plumpish woman. Would she see through his and Harriet's masquerade? Willy wondered. Would the other women?

There was an empty chair next to Gustav. He sat down on it and was thankful that a babble of conversation among the others allowed him to sink into silent obscurity. He felt out of place and like an intruder in the company of these older people, and suddenly acutely conscious of how foolish it was to think that he could win a place in Harriet's life, let alone in her heart.

For all Harriet's obsession with secrecy, everyone in Dover had apparently heard the rumor that a woman was going to attempt to fly the channel. Certainly every guest at the Lord Warden had (although there was some confusion about who "Miss Craig" really was). Or if they hadn't heard, they could not very well have been unaware of the fact that London newspaper people were at the hotel for some reason. Indeed, a few of the reporters sharing a nearby table were even now coming up to the attractive young woman with notepads in hand. After Harriet politely fended off the reporters, one or two guests ventured to approach her, holding menus or cards like the little girl in Hardelot, to ask for her autograph.

Harriet gave everyone at the table a resigned look as she signed her real name to the first request. The secret was out. But it had never really been much of a secret.

When they went to the aerodrome that afternoon—Hamel driving, with Harriet between him and Leo and with Willy and the three other women squeezed into the back seat, and trailed by two automobiles carrying the news people—they found a small crowd gathered along the wooden fence at the edge of the field.

Which one is she? Is she going to fly today? Something was going on. Why else would reporters and photographers and men with motion-picture cameras be there? (People from the Graumont newsreel company, either unaware of Harriet's rule of not flying on Sunday or disbelieving of it, had also arrived from London.)

The Blériot was rolled out of the hangar and Harriet bent her rule far enough to allow herself to inspect the cockpit, as well as she could standing on tiptoe on a stool. Wearing a dress, not her flying costume, she would of course have scandalized the spectators if she had actually climbed into the machine.

Hamel, unrestricted either by gender or by Sabbatarian sensitivities—or by shyness—did climb into the cockpit. Willy hoisted himself up on the fuselage frame on one side as Gustav discussed the features of the controls with Harriet standing at the other side. There were no important differences from the Moisant version she was used to.

There was one addition to this aeroplane, however: a long, tubular airbag inside the fuselage, extending from behind the cockpit nearly to the tail. It was intended to keep the plane from sinking if it came down on water. Blériot himself had used a similar flotation bag on his history-making flight nearly three years before. Better than a strapped-on canoe, Willy thought, remembering Wilbur Wright's flight up the Hudson, now also going on three years past.

"Let's give it a try!" Hamel announced enthusiastically. He looked back over his shoulder. "If you would be so good, Willy, to help hold her down." He signaled to the waiting mechanics. The motion-picture photographers positioned their tripods and began cranking their cameras.

Harriet moved some distance away from the plane and stood by herself. At last having a useful purpose, Willy grabbed hold of an upper longeron midway between cockpit and tail and two of the mechanics gripped the frame just forward of the small rudder. Two more held onto the wheels, while a fourth man spun the propeller. The fifty-horsepower Gnôme exploded into life immediately.

Hamel raised his hand again and dropped it and they let go. The monoplane leaped forward and was tail up and off the ground within thirty feet.

Harriet was watching the takeoff intently. Willy walked over and stood beside her.

"He *is* good, isn't he?" she said, almost to herself.

She turned her head then and smiled and put her hand on his sleeve. She looked at him penetratingly, her eyes making small, quick darting movements from side to side.

Willy was transported. *Those eyes of hers*, Matilde had said. They had never looked so steadily and deeply into his, never so probingly. He felt his very soul dissolving and being drawn out by them—drawn *into* them—, all the doubt and misery that had gnawed at him for the past two days evaporating.

She must love me. She must. She couldn't look at me this way if she didn't.

"Why don't you go?" he urged. "You'll never have a better chance."

The spell was broken. Harriet shifted her gaze toward the castle that could clearly be seen three miles away and at the faint streak that was France, another twenty-two miles beyond. She shook her head and took her hand away.

Willy had to admit that Hamel knew how to fly. He ascended surely in a wide, graceful, curving climb that took him to several hundred feet by the time he had turned one-hundred-eighty degrees and passed over them. He leveled off, executed two fig-

ure eights over the field and then, to the delight of the spectators, banked in a descending glide over the hangars and brought
the monoplane down to a featherlike three-point landing. It was
ten minutes of perfection.

"A good machine," he said when he climbed out. "I think
the engine could stand a trifle more tuning, however."

When the people along the fence saw the aeroplane being
rolled back into the hangar and realized there was to be no more
flying—and none by a woman—they began dispersing. Nor was
there any point in the rest of them staying at the field much
longer.

On the way back to the hotel they took a detour to the memorial on the grassy hillside where Louis Blériot had ended his
historic flight on July 25, 1909. This was a full-size replica in
concrete of his monoplane in plan view, lying flat on the ground.
They all remarked on how appropriate it was.

"It's hard to believe it was less than three years ago that he
landed here," Harriet said to Leo.

"They're already talking about instituting regular aeroplane
passenger service between Dover and Calais," Hamel interjected.
"I understand a company is being formed for that purpose." He
winked at Leo. "Talk about aeronautical progress."

As they drifted away individually to return to the car, Willy
came up beside Harriet and placed his hand familiarly on the
small of her back and leaned his face close to hers. "Maybe they'll
do something like this for you in Calais."

She whirled away from him. *"Don't ever do that again!"*

The words hit him like a snarl.

He dropped behind in renewed confusion. That one moment on the field had apparently meant nothing. They were back
where they had been.

As if deliberately mocking any mortal who dared invade their
realm, the gods of the ether were back to their usual antics on
Monday. Having taunted Harriet with ideal flying weather on
Sunday, they now presented her and her party with another bleak,
chilly, gusty day.

A little after five A.M., in complete darkness, and despite the unpromising outlook, the seven of them again motored up to the aerodrome, this time with only one car carrying the moving-picture people following them. The *Mirror* reporters were taking a tug out into the channel to witness Harriet's takeoff over the cliffs. Another group from the newspaper had ferried across to Calais the evening before and was waiting there to witness and record her landing.

The plane was as ready as it would ever be. Harriet was dressed in her flying togs, under a long sealskin coat. Now if only the weather would cooperate. It was not to be. All day, except for a luncheon break back at the hotel, they hovered around the aeroplane in the hangar or sat in the automobile or stood on the field watching the sky, hoping for an opening in the overcast and a glimpse of the sun or a drop in the wind. But the wind not only continued strong; it blew occasionally in dangerous gusts that could have overturned the Blériot before it got off the ground. To add to the bleakness of their spirits and their physical discomfort, splashes of cold rain came down periodically.

Harriet was the calmest and most patient of them all, thoughWilly knew she must be teeming inside with frustration.

"I keep thinking of those reporters on the tug," she said at one point. "It must be very choppy out there."

Most of the time she spent in quiet conversation with the other women in the aerodrome office or did a little writing in her notebook. She maintained her disengagement from Willy, physically as much as possible, in attitude constantly.

He tried to tell himself it was because she didn't want anyone to suspect that he was there by any chance other than accident. But her withdrawal from him was now even more pronounced than it had been since landing in Dover, more than was necessary to maintain the pretense. She seemed to be making up for the one brief moment of warmth and closeness she had granted him the day before.

Slowly the long hours passed and they endured them until the latest possible hour the flight could have been made had come and gone. Long after the movie people had given up they wearily returned to the hotel, telling each other that surely the weather would break tomorrow.

Harriet's party encountered a strange air of subdued excitement inside the Lord Warden. The lobby was crowded with people buzzing among themselves over something. A number of them were reading copies of newspapers that had been delivered from London.

Leo asked a passing bellboy what was going on.

"'Aven't you 'eard, sir? The Titanic went down. Ran into a 'niceberg, she did."

They were stunned. Gustav borrowed a copy of the *Mirror* and held it up as they all looked at it. The news was sketchy. All that was known at this time was that shortly before midnight on Sunday, April 14, 1912, the White Star liner *Titanic*, the world's most modern and luxurious ocean liner, had struck an iceberg off Newfoundland on its maiden voyage and sunk. Many hundreds were believed lost.

"How terrible," Harriet said. "How could it have happened? The Titanic was supposed to be unsinkable, wasn't it?"

She looked pale. She said she wanted to go to her room to rest and would have supper there. She asked Leo to leave a wake-up call for her for three-thirty on Monday.

A minute after Harriet left, Helen said to Leo, "This news has shaken her terribly."

"Yes," said Hamel. "I think I'd better go see how she is. I want to talk to her some more about the plane, take her mind off this." He handed the newspaper to Leo.

"That might be a good idea," Leo agreed, to Willy's annoyance. He was already annoyed by the way Hamel had taken charge of things, by his paternalistic, almost condescending, attitude toward Harriet. He was annoyed with himself for liking the man in spite of that.

3

L IKE THE CLOUDS outside, a pall cast by the *Titanic* catastrophe hovered over the Lord Warden. The gloomy atmosphere one sensed in lobby and lounge and dining room was also due in part to the fact that many guests had departed with the ending of their Easter holiday. Those who remained spoke to each other in hushed voices, as if they felt they had no right to enjoy themselves when, according to the latest reports, more than eight hundred souls had perished in the icy Atlantic.

Partly for appearances but mostly because he did not want to eat alone in his room, Willy shared a table with Leo and his wife and Helen Vanderbilt and Mrs. Griffith. Both Harriet and Gustav must have decided to use the room service because neither of them appeared.

They were served quickly, for most of the other tables were unoccupied. Everyone seemed subdued for they talked very little, and that little was, recurringly, about the beastly weather.

"All this waiting has taken a lot out of Harriet, I think." Helen said. "I hope she's able to get a good night's rest."

"She'll be all right," said Leo. "If it's at all flyable tomorrow the waiting will be over. She's determined to go."

And if she goes, thought Willy, more than the waiting will be over for him. He hoped it wouldn't be flyable, then for her sake hoped it would. No, for his sake too. To go back to resume dying in Brooklyn could not be more painful than to prolong the dying in Dover.

Later, after the ladies retired to get a good night's sleep themselves, he and Leo had their cigar and cigarette over cordials again.

Leo surprised him when he said, "You know, I'm just as glad Harriet didn't fly yesterday. The story would never have made the newspapers—not the way it would deserve to. As it is, the Titanic is going to crowd out everything else for days, maybe even weeks. I'm thinking it might be wise if she postponed the attempt until next month. The weather will be better then too."

This possible consequence of the disaster had not occurred to Willy. He knew Leo was not being heartless, but he was Harriet's manager and publicist. It couldn't help but be a severe disappointment to him that the most ambitious exploit of Harriet's career was threatened to be eclipsed by the most spectacular tragedy of modern times.

"Do you think she's thinking the same thing, Leo? I mean, the news angle. Do you think she might postpone the flight?"

"I'm sure she is, and probably hating herself for thinking it when hundreds of people, possibly thousands, have just lost their lives. But no, she won't postpone it. She's the most determined woman I've ever met."

"And the most enigmatic I've ever known," Willy added softly.

Leo looked at him closely. "You've got your own problems, haven't you?"

"What?"

"I've noticed how she's been treating you. Even if you hadn't told me what you did, I would have wondered what reason there was for her to act so standoffish toward you, an old friend, the way she has. My wife remarked about it too—though rest assured I didn't say anything to her, about your following Harriet to Hardelot and all that. But since you did tell me, I've seen the way you look at her."

Willy was taken aback. "Does it show that much?"

Leo nodded.

"Is there any hope for me, Leo?"

Leo cocked his head and shrugged. "Harriet is not only a very determined and independent-minded woman but this flight is the most important step in her career so far. If I were to give you my advice, I would tell you to pack up and go back home right now. But you wouldn't take it, so all I can say, Willy, is try not to fall in love with Harriet too deeply. The plain fact of the matter is she's not for you. Nor, I think, if it's any consolation to you, for any man."

Try not to fall in love too deeply. How does one do that, Leo, especially after it's already happened?

Willy almost wished that Leo was right, for that would mean that Gustav Hamel, who he was beginning to believe had something more than purely professional interest in Harriet and her channel flight, had no chance with her either.

Leo said he hadn't told his wife anything. But Leo really knew nothing about "Hardelot and all that"—how close he had come to . . . how he and Harriet had almost . . .

Leo interrupted his thoughts with another concern.

"Do you know anything about an English aviator named D. Leslie Allen?" he asked. Willy shook his head. "I saw an item in one of the papers today. He intends to fly across the Irish Channel tomorrow, from London to Dublin."

"How far is that?"

"I have no idea, Willy, but much farther than from Dover to Calais. I don't think it's ever been done before. It'll be a new record."

So even if the *Titanic* did not push Harriet out of the news, an even more ambitious aviation exploit might. Everything seemed to be conspiring against her. Would they arrive at the aerodrome tomorrow and find that some intrepid Frenchwoman had just flown across the channel and landed at Dover?

They sat in silence for a while. To cheer them both up, Willy changed the subject. "I wonder who Lord Warden was," he said.

"Oh, it wasn't any particular person," Leo said. "I wondered that myself until I asked about it. It seems that in olden times the lord warden was sort of the king's guardian over the ports. No doubt Dover has seen a number of lords warden over the years."

"Interesting," Willy said. He had learned something. His trip to Europe hadn't been a complete waste of time.

Leo had another cordial but Willy ordered wine for himself; it took too long to get drunk on liqueurs. They sat and talked a while longer, Willy telling Leo more about himself and about the flying class at Hempstead Plains. He forgot the bumbling of his first attempts to control an aeroplane, how close he had come to giving it up, the agony of falling in love with Harriet and realizing the hopelessness of it. He had been happy then, despite it all, and knew he would never know such contentment again.

"So what are you going to do when you get back to the States, Willy? Go back to the university? Can you make it up?"

"I don't know, Leo. I really don't know what I'm going to do."

Willy stayed behind when Leo went to his room and ordered a full bottle of wine and proceeded to empty it, and to ruminate.

He should have made love to Harriet that night. He could have, she wouldn't have stopped him. But he hadn't. He had let go the golden chance to bind her to him forever through the act of love. Out of respect for her, out of obeisance to the hypocritical morality of society.

No, it wasn't that. It was because of all the instances of her inexplicable behavior toward him, inviting him, repelling him. *Damn her.* Even alone in a bedroom with her, he hadn't known what to do, or what she really wanted him to do.

Every time they had ever been alone together—at the theater, at Child's, even that time in the hangar at Hempstead Plains—he had felt a closeness between them, verging on intimacy. And in her room in Hardelot—for God's sake!—every intimacy short of the ultimate one. But when others were around, she became cool and aloof. Today, at the aerodrome, she had wrapped him around her finger again, only to firmly put him back in his place at the Blériot memorial.

How could she turn it on and off like that?

Damn her. He should have *taken* her in Hardelot and let the devil worry about the consequences. Now it was too late.

He thought again about Hamel, so close to his own age, and look at what he'd already achieved in aviation. Hamel would not have thrown aside his career and crossed an ocean to be with a woman. He should never have left America. He should be there right now, flying at Hempstead Plains.

All he had ever wanted to do was fly. Why did she have to come along and intrude herself in that dream? He wouldn't have quit, not for good; he would have come back on his own eventually, without her encouragement. Why did she have to exist to complicate his life, to derail all his plans?

As he drank, a terrible and unjust anger against Harriet Quinlan began to grow and fester and seethe in Willy Reynolds.

Eventually, when the wine was gone, he wandered up to his room. He had just opened the door when he heard another door opening down the hall. He turned and saw Gustav Hamel emerging from Harriet's room, his back to Willy. He couldn't see Harriet, only her extended arm. Hamel was holding her hand. He bent and kissed it.

Willy closed his door quickly and leaned back against it inside his room, his chest heaving, a pounding ache inside it. Had Hamel been with her all this time? It was after nine.

He leaned against the door, agonizing. *That bastard. That bastard.*

But it couldn't be. Hamel was a gentleman. Even if he wasn't a gentleman, he wouldn't stoop so low as to try to—to take advantage. And if he did try, Harriet would have quickly put him in his proper place.

Or was her carefully correct politeness to Hamel, her seeming deference to his greater experience as a flier, another sham?

In Hardelot she'd said she felt "betrayed" because Hamel had flown a woman across the channel. It was much too strong a word to use if that was all there was to it. Had her admiration of him the day before been only for his flying?

Hamel had gone up to her room after they had returned from Whitfield, right after she had, supposedly to talk to her about the flight. Neither of them had come down for dinner. They could have been together for hours.

He was in a turmoil of jealousy.

The hall was empty. He walked down it, staggering a little because of the alcohol he had consumed, and knocked lightly on Harriet's door. He waited, then knocked again, harder. She opened it partway. She was in the robe and nightgown he had seen her in in Hardelot. She had to have been in them when Hamel was there. She wouldn't have had time to change her clothes in the minute since he had left.

"William? What is it?" she whispered. "I was just going to bed. You should be in bed too. You know how early we have to get up."

Her voice was controlled and schoolmarmish again, and with no tremor in it this time.

"I have to talk to you. Why have you been so cold to me? Don't you know what you're doing to me?" He put his foot against the door to keep her from closing it.

A look of irritation crossed her face. "I told you I was just about to go to bed. Oh all right. I don't want anyone to see."

He stepped inside. "That didn't seem to concern you about Hamel," he said acidly. "I saw him. Was he here all this time, since we came back from Whitfield? It's been hours. Was he here last night as well?"

She looked at him archly, visibly angry now. But she spoke softly, and the very softness of her voice underlined her anger.

"Please keep your voice down. Do you want everyone in the hotel to hear you? Do you intend to disgrace me totally?"

"*Disgrace* you? Why would it be so terrible if people knew we were more than casual friends, that we meant something to each other?"

"I've had to walk a very fine line here in Dover because of you, William. Society has names for women who consort with younger men."

"*Consort?*" he exploded again, quietly. "Is that all you've been doing, *consorting* with me? I asked you about Hamel. I want to know what he was doing here. What is going on between you two?"

Harriet's face darkened. "I'll ignore your insinuation, William, but I don't know if I can ever forgive it. I wouldn't have thought you capable of thinking such a thing about me — or of

Gustav. You have gravely wronged him too. I hope it's only because you've obviously had too much to drink. But it offends me
very much. In any case you have no right whatsoever to interro-
gate me about anything."

They were shouting at each other in whispers.

"*I have every right in the world!* You know how I feel about
you. For the past three days you've been killing me with your
coldness. I thought, in Hardelot, that we . . . well, at least had
come to some kind of understanding. About the future. But ever
since then I've felt like you've merely been tolerating my being
here, when you even as much as acknowledged it. You told me
Hamel had betrayed you. Why have you let him take over the
way he has? What was he doing here?"

"If you must know, he merely came to see how I was a few
minutes ago. He's really quite concerned about my safety. Would
you believe—" She made a nervous, giggling sound. "He actually suggested that he fly the plane disguised in my clothes and
that I meet him at some deserted field in France and change
places with him. He was quite serious. I laughed politely and
thanked him. Can you imagine such a preposterous thing,even
if he could fit into my clothes? As if everybody at the aerodrome
wouldn't see?"

It was too preposterous for Harriet to have invented it. Hamel
must be as crazy as he was. If not crazy in love with Harriet, then
just plain crazy.

"I do value his experience and advice though," Harriet said.
"Gustav's been very helpful to me and I'm grateful to him for
that."

"And by way of payment you—"

He had been stricken by her coldness the past two days, but
he had not really seen coldness in her eyes—not like this, not
focussed directly at him. Always, when she was talking with the
others, or even with the reporters and autograph-seekers, always
there was only warmth and brightness. And at worst, with him,
but for that one moment when they were standing on the field at
Whitfield, nothing at all. Her eyes devastated him—far more
than the hand that struck his face and rocked his head back.

Harriet gasped. "Oh—I'm so sorry, William. I didn't mean to do that."

He tried to take her in his arms but she wouldn't let him. He could do no more than grip her hands helplessly.

"No, no, I deserved it. I know nothing happened with Hamel. Please forgive me, darling. I'm just so desperately in love with you I can't think straight."

She pulled her hands free of his and backed away.

"Then go, William. For God's sake, if you love me, if you care at all about me, go back home and start living your own life and forget me and let me live mine like I asked you to before. I should have made you go from Hardelot. That was my mistake and it will always be on my conscience. But I have told you and told you there simply cannot be anything between us. Why couldn't you have accepted that?

"I'll never accept it! I know you care for me. What are you talking about, your conscience? There's no reason—"

"You know the reason, William. One reason among many, but the very best reason. The same reason there could not possibly be anything between Gustav and me."

"God, Harriet, why are you trying to keep up that lie about being thirty-seven next month?"

She stamped a slippered foot on the carpet and put her fists on her hips defiantly.

"*I am not lying!*"

He laughed mockingly. "You're saying you lied to your employer, you've been lying to everyone, all your friends, even Leo. Why should I believe you're not lying now?"

"Because it *is* the truth, William! Won't you believe me at last? You're the only one who knows. No one else does, not even Helen or Linda. And yes, not even Leo, since it's clear from what you just said that you took it upon yourself to discuss my age with him."

He stood there for a long moment, staring at her, searching her wide, unshielded eyes. And felt his heart shatter.

She wasn't lying. The truth was in those eyes, the truth a part of him had known all along, as far back as the day he had driven her into the city and had wondered how she had crammed so much into so few years.

The sarcastic words erupted from him: "How about your mother? Does she know?"

He turned away from the pained look on her face and started pacing before her, moving his hands and arms up and down uselessly, unaware that he was doing do, aware of nothing except the ravening bitterness inside him.

"All right," he said finally, evenly. "I believe you. Why in God's name didn't you tell me from the beginning? Why did you let me think that—?"

"Oh—that is so unfair of you! You know I told you. At Christmastime. I can't help it if you—if you are nothing but a stupid schoolboy. I never asked you to fall in love with me. I never wanted your—your puppy love. And that's all it is, really, isn't it?"

She could not have cut him down more effectively.

"Puppy love? *Puppy love?*"

"You see. I told you I would only hurt you."

He wanted to wring her neck. He actually moved to seize her, to do something. He clutched at her robe.

"I don't care, darling. It doesn't matter. All that matters is that I love you. I still want to marry you."

She wrenched her robe from his grasp and backed toward the door.

"Marry *me*! What makes you think I would ever consider marrying *you*? I said I wished you would go home in Hardelot. Now I'm ordering you to. I want you to leave for America tomorrow."

"You don't mean that!"

"I mean precisely that. I said you could stay for the flight, but you broke our agreement. Leo knows about our being together in Hardelot. Oh, he hasn't said anything directly but I can tell from little things he's said that he knows, and there is only one way he could know."

"It was a slip! I didn't mean to. But he understands that nothing—"

"Leo is a good and virtuous man, William. Whatever he knows or understands, you've compromised me in his eyes. I can't forgive that. I would be greatly surprised if Helen and Linda didn't also suspect something, though they have been gracious enough to keep any such suspicions to themselves. I want you to leave for home tomorrow. I don't want you to come to the aerodrome."

"In Hardelot I asked you to say you hated me, that you never wanted to see me again. You couldn't say it, not really. Sweet Jesus, Harriet, you let me start to make love to you! What kind of woman are you?"

"Hate is a very strong emotion, William. I have no strong emotions about you. I don't hate you. I'm merely coming to dislike you. Oh, I was flattered. I even admired your impetuosity in following me to France. I thought it was very gallant of you. That was as foolish of me as it was of you. But now the only emotion you arouse in me is embarrassment, if one can call that an emotion. Please don't embarrass me, or yourself, any longer."

Hatred he could have accepted and learned to live with. But mere dislike . . . embarrassment . . . puppy love . . . He felt like the stupid schoolboy she said he was and, when all was said and done, what he always had been.

But all was not quite said and done. And like a stupid, helpless, lovesick schoolboy he dropped to his knees before her and gripped her robe again and buried his face against it.

"Please, Harriet, please don't do this. You don't have to. I love you so much. It doesn't matter about your age, we'll work something out. Just let me stay. I promise I won't do anything again to embarrass you. Please don't send me away like this."

She was trembling, close to tears.

"Oh God, look at you. Have you no pride at all? Not a shred? You disgust me. There's an emotion for you. You don't embarrass me—*you disgust me*! Must I slap you again? If you do not leave this instant I'll—I'll—"

Disgusted with himself, at his self-humiliation, he slowly got to his feet. He had abased himself before her, and he surged with anger at her for reducing him to that. He fought against the quaver in his voice. His throat was constricted.

"I think I'm beginning to understand you at last, Harriet. It's not me, it's all men, isn't it? You're afraid to let any man get close to you. You're thirty-seven years old and you've been a nun all your life. You've never had a man make love to you, have you? I almost wish Hamel had. Then at least I would know you were a real woman."

All of a sudden she was beating her fists against his chest.

"Damn you damn you damn you! I hate you I hate you!"

She glared at him, then whirled, sobbing into her open hands.

"Oh why did you have to come into my life? Just leave. Just leave."

She ran into the bathroom and slammed the door.

He had played it out with her, from start to finish. He had gone the whole bitter distance. It was over at last. At dawn the next morning, but when he was certain that everyone had left for the aerodrome, with his mind absolutely dead, Willy took the first train he could to London, and there booked the earliest available passage on a steamer from Liverpool to New York.

A hundred miles off Newfoundland, not far from where the *Titanic* had met her end, they encountered a fearful storm. He stood near the bow, refusing to hold the handrail, balancing himself while the great ship plunged and wallowed and listed and shuddered as it drove against foamy mountains of water. He stood there, the stinging spray pummeling him, defying the sea as he had defied the sky before.

Until an anxious steward made his way along the rail and seized his arm and pulled him back and made him go inside.

Boston

1

ELLEN REYNOLDS had begun saving copies of the *Times* and *Tribune* and *Eagle* for William when the *Titanic* went down. The first chance he got on the day he arrived home he carried the pile of newspapers up to his room and paged through them, but not for the details of the disaster.

He would answer the question in his mother's eyes later. She already knew the answer; it was in his own eyes. But he owed her more than that. He would tell her, later. Some of it. Enough of it. There was no need for her to know that Harriet Quinlan was only five years younger than herself.

He tried the *Times* first; it had always given a lot of coverage to Harriet. The earliest issue in which a report about her channel crossing could have appeared would be Wednesday, April 17.

As he expected, page after page was still full of stories about the tragedy of three days before: eyewitness accounts by the survivors, happily numbering more than fifteen hundred; biographies of some of the well-known people who had perished with the ship, they and those who had shared their fate sadly numbering some eight hundred.

But not everything was about the *Titanic* and on page eighteen he found what he was looking for: Harriet Quinlan, the noted aviatrix, had taken off from Dover on the sixteenth of April and successfully completed a flight across the English Channel. Although she had missed her goal of Calais by some thirty miles and come down on the beach at Hardelot, below Boulogne, she had attained her goal of becoming the first woman to fly the English Channel alone.

The sixteenth. Tuesday. The day after all possible hope of a future that included Harriet had been smashed for good and all. (Or rather, his eight months' delusion that there had ever really been any hope.) Even as he had been waiting for the train in Dover that morning she had already landed in France, although he did not know this until he reached London and read about it in the *Mirror,* which of course prominently played the story.

He checked the *Tribune* of the same date. There was but a single paragraph about Harriet, buried in the middle of a column. He didn't bother looking in the *Eagle.*

Three days after the *Titanic* disaster that story had still overshadowed everything else in the New York papers, and probably every other newspaper in the country, as Leo Stevens had feared. But at least Harriet's accomplishment had received some recognition and he was happy for her. The *Times's* story ran for a full column and a half. But it should have been on the front page.

There had been no tickertape parade.

It wasn't until the May 16 issue of *Leslie's Weekly* was delivered that he read Harriet's personal account.

"An American Girl's Daring Exploit." Under that heading: "The First Woman Pilot to Cross the English Channel in an Aeroplane Tells the Story of Her Adventure." An editor's note described Harriet Quinlan as "the foremost aviatrice in the world" and stated that "her simple and modest narrative will be read with intense interest."

It was by one reader. Willy read the article over and over, searching between the lines for hidden meanings.

In the opening paragraphs Harriet related how the idea for the channel flight had occurred to her in Mexico, how she had arranged for the loan of a Blériot in Paris, described the frustrating weather in Hardelot, the little girl who asked for her autograph, the English people who invited her for tea, the decision to have the plane shipped to Dover without having tested it.

Then the flight itself:

"It was five-thirty A.M. when my machine got off the ground. The preliminaries were brief. Hearty handshakes were quickly given, the motor began to make its twelve hundred revolutions a minute, and I put up my hand to give the signal of release. Then I was off. The noise of the motor drowned the shouts and cheers of friends below. In a moment I was in the air, climbing steadily in a long circle. I was up fifteen hundred feet within thirty seconds. From this high point of vantage my eyes lit at once on Dover Castle. It was half hidden in a fog bank. I felt that trouble was coming, but I made directly for the flagstaff of the castle, as I had promised the waiting *Mirror* photographers and motion-picture men I would do.

"In an instant I was beyond the cliffs and over the channel. Far beneath me I saw the *Mirror's* tug, with its stream of black smoke. It was trying to keep ahead of me, but I passed it in a jiffy. Then the thickening fog obscured my view. Calais was out of sight. I could not see ahead of me at all nor could I see the water below. There was only one thing for me to do and that was to keep my eyes on the compass.

"My hands were covered with long, Scotch woolen gloves, which gave me good protection from the cold and fog; but the machine was wet and my face was so covered with dampness that I had to push my goggles up on my forehead. I could not see through them. I was traveling at over a mile a minute. The distance straight across from Dover to Calais is only twenty-two miles, and I knew that land must be in sight if I could only get below the fog and see it. I dropped from an altitude of about two thousand feet until I was half that height. The sunlight struck upon my face and my eyes lit upon the white and sandy shores of France. I felt happy, but I could not find Calais. Being unfamiliar with the coastline, I could not locate myself. I determined to reconnoiter and came down to a height of five hundred feet and traversed the shore.

"Meanwhile the wind had risen and the currents were coming in billowy gusts. I flew a short distance inland to locate myself or find a good place on which to alight. It was all tilled land below me, and rather than tear up the farmers' fields I decided to drop down on the hard and sandy beach. I did so at once, making an easy landing. Then I jumped from my machine and was alone upon the shore. But it was only for a few moments. A crowd of fishermen — men, women and children each carrying a pail of sand worms — came rushing from all directions toward me. They were chattering in French, of which I comprehended sufficient to discover that they knew I had crossed the channel. These humble fisherfolk knew what had happened. They were congratulating themselves that the first woman to cross in an aeroplane had landed on their fishing beach."

Harriet's account continued for another column, but that was the essential story. Only two photographs accompanied the article — one a larger reproduction of another formal portrait of Harriet that had appeared in the magazine before, the other a snapshot of her Blériot as an unrecognizable speck high above Dover Castle.

What an adventure that must have been. What a coup for her. But was it only by accident that she had landed at Hardelot? Why hadn't she simply turned north and followed the coast to Calais? Why did she say she had comprehended "sufficient" of French? When had she written the article? No doubt she had worked on it during the voyage back to America, probably arriving in New York not long after he had. Even now she was in the city, was even this minute at her desk at *Leslie's Weekly*.

He knew there would be no overt reference to himself. Harriet spoke of her "party" which had shared the frustration of waiting out the weather in Dover, but mentioned no names except those of Leo Stevens and Gustav Hamel — "whose courtesy and consideration I shall always remember."

(What else would she always remember? Or had she been able to forget it?)

Yet despite what had happened the night before her flight he was pained that she did not make at least some passing reference to an "American friend," a fellow flying student from Long Island who had also shared her frustration—not in Hardelot, of course, but in Dover. Did she despise him so much that she could not have given him some small, subtle message to tell him she had at least some small thought of him? It was as if he hadn't been there at all.

Well, thank God for that. Thank God for her strength. If anything had happened to her because of me, because of anything I'd said or done . . .

In the eight months since Willy had earned his license Hempstead Plains had transformed itself into the premier center of aviation in America. New hangars seemed to spring up by the week, both on his own field and on the surrounding ones, housing the machines of the Sloane and Beatty and Heinrich Brothers flying schools as well as of numerous private aeroplane owners and experimenters, among the latter a young Sicilian immigrant named Guiseppe Bellanca.

The sky was starting to get crowded over Long Island.

Willy had broken his promise to Harriet. Now he broke the one he had made to his parents. Over their unavailing protests he did not attempt to make up his missed classes or express any intention of returning to school in the fall.

Ellen Reynolds grieved for her son. He had aged years in one month, not in appearance but in demeanor. He was not the same young man who had gone to Europe with such high hope. There was a hardness about his eyes. It was as though, having had his heart broken by a woman, he was determined to let no one ever touch it again. Before she had feared William was throwing his life away to be with Harriet Quinlan. Now he seemed bent on throwing it away because he could not be with her.

Willy purchased the Moisant monoplane he had crash-landed in the Hackensack Meadowlands (they gave him credit for the repairs as they had said they would), nearly depleting his trust fund and beginning the process of depleting the rest of it in hangar fees and fuel costs as he threw himself into flying.

Daily, whatever the weather, he went to the aerodrome. When no one else flew, Willy Reynolds did. As the owner of his own plane he needed leave from no one to fly whenever he wanted to, and he wanted to every day. Unless fog shrouded the field or the wind blew a veritable gale, Willy was in the air. He quickly gained a reputation as a daredevil, both at Hempstead Plains and at other fields on Long Island he dropped in on. Student pilots, grounded as they were more often than not because it was too windy for them, gaped at him when he climbed out of his plane after what was now to him a routine practice flight. The spectators applauded him and girls asked for his autograph—and made suggestions that they might like more than that from him. But his mind was only on flying.

Had it only been a year since he had been terrified at the thought of taking one of the training planes off the ground?

André, frowning, approached him one day after he landed in a downpour driven by a high wind that soaked the mechanics rushing to the machine and gave them all they could do to move it back into the hangar without its being blown end over end. It was like the day of his first turning flight, but now he thought nothing of it. He was used to the wind.

"M'sieur *Weelee*. If you wish to kill yourself, there are easier ways to do it. If you have no regard for yourself, think of us who would have to pick up your remains. I ask you to think of the example you are setting for my students. I tell them the wind is too strong to fly—and they cannot hear because of the noise of your engine and all heads turn to watch you venture into weather no sane man would consider. Just why is it you wish to die so young?"

Willy put his arm around his old mentor's shoulders. He had no wish to die. Neither, though, had he any overwhelming desire to reach old age.

How could he explain it to André, cautious, concerned André? That having learned to fly, in the first decade out of all the thousands of decades of human history in which an ordinary person was able to learn to fly, he wanted to explore this wonderful new magic, this new dimension, to its uttermost limits. To see how high, how fast, how far a man could take his machine. How vertical a bank, how quick a turn, how steep a climb or sharp a dive. To become one with his machine and with the air. To challenge the wind and ride it. To chase the shifting, insubstantial clouds.

Or if to die, to do it in the most soul-satisfying manner ever given to a man.

"You're right, André," he said. "I didn't realize I was setting a bad example. I didn't intend to."

"I had thought of asking you to become an instructor," said the Frenchman. "But now I wonder. It is essential to have confidence, but there is also such a thing as overconfidence. You have become reckless. Are you trying to be another Lincoln Beachey?"

Willy had never thought of himself as reckless. Daring perhaps, but never reckless. He never went up in conditions he didn't think he could handle, never asked his machine to do anything he did not think it capable of. There is such a thing as overcautiousness too, André, he thought. But he didn't attempt to argue with the man who was now more his friend than teacher.

"Thank you, André, *mon ami*. That's the highest compliment you could have given me, to consider me as an instructor. Thank you, but I wouldn't take such a position even if you offered it to me. And I won't be setting a bad example any longer. I think I'm ready now, for other things."

The Third Harvard-Boston Aviation Meet, scheduled to begin Sunday the thirtieth of June at Squantum Field, promised to be one of the most important events of the 1912 aviation season. The country's most prominent aviators were entered to compete for nineteen thousand dollars in prize money, including Lincoln Beachey, Charles K. Hamilton, Glenn L. Martin, Phillips W. Page, Paul W. Peck, Arch Freeman, J.F. Terrill and Farnum Fish, the latter at 15 reputedly the youngest aviator in the world.

And the world's most celebrated aviatrix, Harriet Quinlan, along with two potential rivals of her sex, Blanche Stuart Scott and a fledgling named Ruth Law.

The two-hundred-mile flight from Hempstead Plains to Squantum Field on the edge of Dorchester Bay near Quincy was by far the longest Willy had ever undertaken. The safest route, which André recommended when Willy told him his intention, would have been to fly due north from Hempstead Plains to cross Long Island Sound where it was only about five miles wide, then bear northeast over Connecticut and refuel halfway in the vicinity of Norwich.

But a moderate southwesterly wind was blowing when he took off Saturday morning, and when he got into the air and saw nothing but clear skies on every horizon he decided to attempt the more direct and challenging route, flying northeast from the start, over the waters of the sound much of the way but high enough that he could glide to the Connecticut shore in the event of engine failure.

He reached Squantum without incident in a little over four hours, including a refueling stop at a field outside Providence. With only a slightly larger tank he was sure he could have gone the whole distance without stopping, especially with the wind behind him all the way.

It was not any kind of speed or distance or endurance record, although a few years before it might have been. But it was a good warm-up for an attempt at a prize in one of those categories at the meet, and he was impressed with himself. He had been over water longer than Harriet. But he'd had land in sight all the time only a few miles away and on a sunny day; she had flown blind across the channel in fog and numbing cold.

The getaway at Squantum (or "runway," as some pilots were starting to call it) was nearly half a mile long and a hundred and fifty feet wide, paved with oiled and rolled gravel. On one side was a row of wooden hangars, and a short distance from them the meet headquarters building. On the opposite side was a huge grandstand Willy was later told could hold ten thousand spectators, and behind it an autopark capacious enough for five thousand cars and carriages.

All the hangar space was reserved for "name" aviators and their crews, so he had to park his plane in the open next to those of several other solitary unknowns like himself. He walked over to the headquarters house to register—and into confusion. A dozen aviators were milling about, arguing noisily among themselves and with two men who apparently were officials of the meet.

Lincoln Beachey stood apart from the others. Willy could have picked him out even if he hadn't seen the aviator's picture many times in aviation magazines. He was a cocky fellow of 25 who, like the Wright brothers, flew in business suit, high collar and tie. (Like the surviving brother, Orville, that was. Wilbur had died in the spring of typhoid fever, worn down, it was said, by the strain of constant patent litigation.) The suit Beachey wore today was pinstriped blue serge. On his head was a large cap in clashing plaid.

A year before he would scarcely have dared speak to the man. Now he went up to him and asked him what was going on.

Beachey gave him a twisted grin. "That's what we'd all like to know, kiddo. Willard"—he inclined his head toward the larger of the two officials—"says the Aero Club has withdrawn its sanction for this affair."

William A. P. Willard was the meet manager and the father of the famous Charles F. Willard, who had retired from flying as too dangerous. The elder Willard was not a flier.

"It has?" Willy said. "What does that mean?"

"No prize money, kiddo," was the laconic reply. "Maybe no money at all. But the people will be coming to see blood. We can't disappoint them."

Willy didn't think he liked Beachey. He was a little too cynical. Maybe he had been flying too long, taken too many risks for the delight of the crowds. What was this condescending "kiddo" stuff anyway? There was only four years' difference between their ages.

"But we have contracts," he started to say, but at that moment Willard raised his hands for silence.

"Gentlemen, please. I ask for your patience. We have given the Aero Club of America assurance that all the prize money will be forthcoming from the backers and we have tried, and are continuing to try, to satisfy them as to our financial responsibility. But we are not going to turn over the business conduct of this meet to them. Whether or not they lift their constructive prohibition, this meet will go on as scheduled on Monday."

"What if they don't lift it?" someone said. "Without the Aero Club's sanction you can't have any competition for prizes. If you do, we could lose our licenses."

"The Aero Club has never done anything but make rules," another voice said sarcastically. "They've never even been able to hold a successful meet in their home town of New York."

"But we *can* conduct exhibitionary flying," Willard answered. "And we will. If nothing else, you will be paid for that. Your contracts will be honored to that extent. I'm sorry but that is all I can say at this time."

This was received with much grumbling. Willard left the office, followed by several aviators who continued to argue with him. Willy still did not quite understand what the problem was and did not really much care. All that mattered to him was that there would be flying of some kind.

There was a copy of the *Boston Daily Globe* on the floor. He picked it up. The front page was dominated by the Democratic presidential nominating convention in Baltimore, deadlocked between Woodrow Wilson of Virginia and Champ Clark of Missouri for ballot after ballot. But on page three was a large half-page advertisement under the headline "AVIATION MEET."

"Fifteen aviators, including two women, will make daily flights . . . First appearance in New England of Miss Quinlan and Miss Blanche Stuart Scott . . . Special trains from South Station or electrics to Neponset Bridge and special boats to field . . . Stand seats 25¢, 50¢ and $1.00. Automobile $1.00 . . . Music daily by Teel's band of forty pieces."

Superimposed on tiny caricatures of their bodies were photographs of the faces of Freeman, Hamilton, Martin, Terrill, Scott,

Beachey and Quinlan, with the last three prominently displayed in the center.

He carefully tore out the ad and folded it and stuffed it in his pocket.

It occurred to him that he had to find out how to get into Boston and get a hotel room there. The meet was to last all week. He went back outside and started walking to his plane to retrieve the travel bag he'd left wedged under the seat.

A monoplane with shimmering wings was just coming in for a graceful landing. He watched as it taxied up to the row of planes that could not be accommodated in the hangars and came to a stop. Two figures climbed out.

One was that of a man. The other, smaller figure, the pilot's, was that of a woman in a purple costume.

2

SEVERAL MEN were pushing Harriet's plane toward a hangar. One of them was Hardy. Willy hadn't seen him since before he'd gone along on the tour the previous fall with the Moisant International Aviators. According to André, Harriet had engaged him as her personal *mechanicién* after her return from Europe. He waved to Hardy and the Frenchman lifted one hand from the fuselage and waved back.

Harriet was standing where she had gotten out of the cockpit, chatting with her passenger. The two shook hands and the man headed for the headquarters building. Harriet began walking toward the row of hangars, following in the wake of her plane. Without plan or thought, his legs suddenly taking command of his body, Willy hurried across the field and placed himself in her path. She stopped a few feet from him.

Willy looked at the face he had not seen for nearly three months. But that night in Dover it had not been Harriet's face; it had been that of an angry, distraught woman, a stranger. Now it was her face again. It was shining, not entirely from oil spray.

Harriet removed her helmet and smoothed her rumpled hair. She looked at him, her lips partly open, almost verging on a smile.

"I heard you were going to be here," she said matter-of-factly.

"And I you."

In the days following his decision to enter the meet, and especially during the flight up from Long Island, he had wondered what his feelings would be, or if he would have any at all, when he encountered Harriet at Squantum. Now he found himself looking at the familiar face quite dispassionately, looking at it the way one looked at any thing of beauty, with simple appreciation. And he told himself that he was glad that he could do so, that he was happy to have this proof that he truly was cured of longing for her. Cured *by* her.

He nodded toward the Blériot that was now being positioned inside the hangar. "Beautiful craft," he said, matching her matter-of-factness. "How do you like it? I'm told it's rather tricky."

"It hasn't given me any trouble, since I've gotten used to it. It almost got away from me the first time I took off in it, it's so powerful. I nearly went straight up. You just have to be careful about the ballasting in the rear seat."

"Where have you been flying? I haven't seen you at Hempstead." He knew very well where she had been flying, but there was no reason he could not be decent to her.

"Mostly at Nassau Boulevard. I haven't been doing very much though. The plane only arrived a few weeks ago. Oh, could I tell you a story about what I had to go through to get it past customs."

"I know. I read your article."

Earlier that month *Leslie's Weekly*, which Willy had resumed reading—dispassionately—after he had emerged from his private hell, had published Harriet's article on "New Things in the Aviation World" in which she described her experience with the U.S. Customs House in New York when her new seventy-horsepower, two-seater Blériot had been delivered from France.

"Did they really list it as a 'polo pony'?"

"Can you believe it? There actually is no category for a flying machine so the customs people classified it as a pony, even though they admitted themselves that it was ridiculous. It certainly is another indication of our government's lack of interest in aeroplaning. We're so far behind other countries it would be funny if it weren't so serious."

Thanks to all the newspaper publicity there already were numerous spectators in the stands and along the fences, though the meet would not begin officially until Monday. Some people were walking among the parked aeroplanes on the field itself. There were no police to stop them. Willy hoped there would be better security once the meet got under way.

These people had seen Harriet's plane land and when they realized that it was the famous aviatrix they had stared. Now they flocked toward her.

Harriet also saw the approaching group. "Are you staying in Boston?" she said urgently. "Leo has rooms for us at the Tourraine. He's renting a car and will be picking me up here. Why don't you wait?"

He was taken completely by surprise. He had wondered too how she might react when she saw him again and was not at all prepared for this unaffected friendliness on her part. A minute before, he had fully expected her to brush right past him. Now he almost wished she had.

"No," he said. "I was just about to go into the city. I have to get a room myself."

"Then maybe you could meet us later at the Tourraine? Say about eight? Will you? We can all have dinner together and talk."

"No," he said again, firmly. "I don't think—"

But he had no time to elaborate a refusal, for the first of the celebrity-seekers had reached Harriet and were gathering around her.

He was turned away from the first two hotels he inquired at. A lot of people were in town for the aero meet, the clerks at both said.

He had better luck on the third try, at a small establishment a few cuts above the seedy, and correspondingly cheap. The place was within walking distance of the Tourraine, on the opposite side of the Commons.

He lay down in his room and tried to rest, disgusted with himself that he was unable to. How many times had he lain on a bed thinking about Harriet Quinlan? How many hours and days of his life spent in fruitless speculation about her?

In frustration he got up and started pacing around the room, glancing out the window at the people on the Commons.

Anyone hearing the words they had exchanged at the field would have thought them just old acquaintances renewing their acquaintanceship. Well, it was more than he had thought they would ever be again, more than he cared or wanted that they would ever be again.

It angered—it *insulted*—him that she should have been so friendly. It was as if the terrible scene in Dover had never taken place. Or as if Harriet had merely shrugged it off, put it behind her. No wonder he had found no hidden "message" for him in her account of her channel flight in *Leslie's Weekly*.

He was angry at himself for having been pleasant to her, for having let himself even speak to her in the first place, for having been glad she had been able to put what had happened that last night out of her mind and make the flight across the channel the next day. What had happened that night was not something one merely shrugged off. The things they had said to each other had wounded too deeply for that, at least for him.

Even afterward, during the dreary voyage back across the Atlantic when he had nothing to do but think, before he was fully able to accept the fact that he had only been living in a fantasy world regarding Harriet Quinlan, there had been the recurring thought that the depth of her outrage might have been telling him something wholly different from what her words did: that she could not have been so angry and hurtful toward him, and seemingly hurt by him, if, deep down, he was not vitally important to her.

Even after he had arrived home, he had wondered, for the first few days, if she might call him or send him a note, if only to let him know she was back.

But nothing. Nothing at all. And now this hint of importuning in her invitation to have dinner with her and Leo at the Tourraine. What did she think he was made of? Did she really expect him to agree? If so, she was sadly mistaken. He would find a bar to kill the evening in, and maybe—why not?—a girl to spend the night with.

For something to do, he opened his bag and began hanging up his clothes on the one broken hangar the room provided. He had brought a good suit and tie.

All right. All right. He would go to the Tourraine, but only because of Leo. He would continue to be pleasant and polite to Harriet Quinlan. But he would go only to see Leo. He liked the man and wanted to see him again, and why should he let the presence of Harriet Quinlan stand in the way of that?

Damn her. She was still in his blood. He wasn't cured of her, he'd only been in remission. Tonight he would purge Harriet Quinlan out of his system once and for all.

The lobby of the Tourraine was filled with people when Willy entered it shortly before eight. He looked around, but neither Leo nor Harriet was among them. He waited a few minutes, wondering if he was supposed to go directly to the dining room or, more sensible yet, whether he should simply leave and spare himself from having to test his resolve to be pleasant to Harriet. He was almost on the point of doing the latter when he saw Leo coming toward him.

"Hello, Willy," Leo said, smiling broadly and gripping his hand. "How are you? Good to see you again. Harriet said you might be having dinner with us. I just called her room and she'll be right down."

Willy had expected some degree of astonishment on the manager's part when they met. Although Leo surely didn't know about the scene that had been played out in Harriet's hotel room in Dover, he must have guessed that she had been the cause of his disappearance the day of her channel flight. But if Leo was surprised by his reappearance now—and at Harriet's invitation—he was too diplomatic to show it.

"And how are you yourself, Leo?" Willy asked. "And Mrs. Stevens? Did she come to Boston with you?"

"Top drawer, thank you, both of us," Leo replied. "No, she decided to stay in New York this time. So, do you intend to do some competition flying at Squantum, Willy?"

"I intend to try. I've been practicing a lot at Hempstead Plains since I got back from Europe."

"Yes, I've heard about that. Well, I hope you're able to compete. You know about the problem they're having with the Aero Club, don't you? Oh—here's Harriet now."

Harriet was, as usual, quite fashionably dressed and the object of admiring glances from nearby men as she crossed the lobby toward them. For a moment Willy imagined he was back in the lobby of the Empire Theater, and the recollection made him distinctly uncomfortable.

"Hello, William," she said to Willy brightly. "I'm so glad you decided to come."

This made him even more uncomfortable, and only for Leo's sake he returned her "Hello" but said nothing more.

He was still ill at ease after they were seated at a table against one wall of the restaurant and had placed their orders. Fortunately an orchestra was playing rather loudly and Leo was there and he did not have to force himself to engage in small talk with Harriet.

Instead, over entrées they discussed the crisis the meet had unexpectedly been confronted with. As far as Leo had been able to learn, the Aero Club's prohibition was still in effect. Unless that situation changed very quickly, he said, there could be no competition flying.

"Do you think there's any chance they can persuade the club to change its position, Leo?" Harriet asked.

"There's always a chance. Willard has been making a lot of

phone calls to New York trying to do just that. But in any case you'll be able to make the flight with him. As a purely demonstration flight, it won't fall under the prohibition. I specifically cleared that with the Aero Club."

"I'm thinking of William and all the other aviators who've come here to compete," Harriet said. "Some of them shipped their planes from as far away as Chicago."

Willy said, "I don't care, there'll be other meets. But I heard talk that the club has threatened to suspend the licenses of any aviators who fly in competition. Would they do that, Leo? Because of a squabble over some ridiculous financial technicality? After all, if we pilots are willing to take a chance we won't collect any prize money, that's our lookout, isn't it? What legal authority does the Aero Club have anyway? You don't need their permission to fly. As far as I know, Blanche Stuart Scott has never bothered to get her license, and Ruth Law has just started working on hers."

"Whether they have licenses or not doesn't enter into it in their cases," Leo answered, "because they'll only be doing demonstration flying too. But competition flying comes under the international rules, and you should know as well as I do, Willy, that no promoter who wants to keep in the good graces of the Aero Club will violate those rules either by hiring uncertified pilots or, in the present instance, by failing to satisfy the prize money requirements. Legally, of course, the club can't prevent them from holding the meet, so the only leverage it has over them is through you pilots. In fact, the club might do more than suspend your licenses—it could revoke them entirely, and I wouldn't blame them. You can't have aviators going around thumbing their noses at the body that makes the rules that are supposed to govern aviation in this country, a body the aviators themselves have set up. If the club turned a blind eye this time it would happen again, and if it happened often enough it could foreseeably bring about federal regulation, and nobody wants the bureaucrats in Washington who know nothing about aeroplanes meddling in."

"Amen to that," Harriet said.

Willy now had a clearer idea of the problem and the conversation lulled after that as they finished eating. It still seemed to him, however, that the Aero Club was engaged in a lot of officious nitpicking and that the whole thing was a purely manufactured crisis.

To his renewed uneasiness Leo declined dessert to the waiter and asked them to excuse him, saying he was going to go to his room to read before going to bed. He put some bills on the table.

"This should cover the dinner and the tip, if you don't mind taking care of the check, Willy. I trust I'll see you at the field sometime tomorrow. Harriet and I will be going out around noon."

Willy started to protest about the money and Leo dismissed it with a wave of his hand as he left. The waiter began clearing the table.

"I don't think I want any dessert either," Harriet said. "But you go ahead."

Willy shook his head. "I'd better be leaving, myself. I plan to go to Squantum early in the morning."

"Won't you stay a few minutes for coffee?"

Again there was that same curious note of importuning he had detected at the field that afternoon.

He was half-risen from his chair. He sat back down.

"Just two coffees, please," he said to the waiter.

3

HARRIET WAS staring down at the table somewhat vaguely, absently fingering the ugly amulet she still wore. Willy had avoided looking directly at her the entire evening. But now he peered at her, running his eyes over her face, scrutinizing it, hoping to discover some signs that her age was beginning to show:

wrinkles around the eyes that were not from smiling, an incipi-
ent crepiness in the skin of the cheeks, a certain softening of the
chinline. But it was the same face, still beautiful, still girlish looking.

He didn't know what to say to her. Had she flown up from
New York? he asked casually. When he'd seen her land he'd
thought she might have.

She looked up. Oh no, she said. They'd had the plane shipped
to Quincy by train. That was just a test flight she'd made with
Harry Willard, the younger son of the meet manager.

"But I'm going to fly back, after the meet. I have a contract
with the Post Office to deliver the first mail by air from Boston to
New York." Her voice was bubbly, the way it had been that afternoon in Child's.

"Do you?" he stated, keeping his own voice level. "How many
more firsts can you possibly chalk up?"

"Well, for one thing I've agreed to take a girl up next week,
Gertrude Stephenson, a reporter with the Boston Herald Post. It
will be the first time a woman has flown as a passenger in a plane
piloted by a woman."

"That should just about deplete the list of firsts!"

She laughed lightly. "Just about, I guess. But before that, on
Monday, I intend to try to beat Grahame-White's time to Boston
Light and back that he set during the first Harvard-Boston meet
in Nineteen-ten. I'll be taking Mr. Willard senior as my passenger. He thinks it'll be good publicity for the meet."

"Is that the demonstration flight Leo mentioned?"

"Yes."

"That's farther than across the channel."

She nodded. "About thirty miles, round trip."

"I flew up from Hempstead. The direct route, over the sound
most of the way. André advised me not to, but it was such a fine
day I had to see if I could."

Now Harriet's eyes widened the way they had that afternoon
in Child's when he had told her about his flight over New York.

"Did you really? Didn't I tell you you were going to be a

great aviator, William? We've both come a long way, haven't we? I know you've been making quite a name for yourself at Hempstead Plains. I would have taken the easier route myself, over land. I'm like a cat. I don't like cold water."

"You flew the channel."

"Only twenty miles."

"Twenty-two. And in fog."

She lifted the Aztec head. "He brought me luck."

"Luck is made, it doesn't just happen. Like Matilde Moisant with her number thirteen. If you weren't a skillful pilot in the first place no lucky charm or lucky number would have helped you. That English pilot, Allen, who was going to fly to Dublin the same day you flew the channel, I read in London that he disappeared over the Irish Sea."

"Yes. Very tragic."

Harriet's expression turned pensive.

"Flying really is a dangerous business. My mother keeps telling me I've done enough and now I'm beginning to think maybe she's right. Matilde has quit flying. She's had at least three bad crashes, you know. Her plane caught fire in one of them in Texas and she was almost burned to death. I'm thinking maybe after I fulfill the Post Office contract I should quit too, before . . . I still want to write books someday. It's time I buckled down to it."

"I can't imagine you giving up flying," he said.

"I don't know, William. Aviation is advancing so fast. So many other women, younger women, are moving into it. With newer and better planes they're going to do things in coming years that will make my little hop across the channel look like, well, hardly anything at all. Nobody will remember it. They probably won't even remember me."

He was surprised to hear that kind of talk from her. "Don't be silly, Harriet. You were the first. Nothing any other woman will ever do will change that. Of course you'll be remembered."

"Well, I certainly hope so," she said, putting on a brighter face.

That exhausted all the small talk he could think of. He looked around for the waiter. Had the fellow forgotten about them?

"So . . ," after a minute, with distinct coolness in his voice, "how do you know what I've been doing at Hempstead? I'm sure you didn't make a point of inquiring about me."

"I didn't have to, William. You're the talk of the Long Island aviation community. And I'm in touch with André Houpert frequently of course."

"I see. Well, that saved you the trouble of finding out if my telephone number was still in service."

He was sorry he'd said that. Not because it made Harriet's face fall but because the one thing he did not want to do was give her the slightest impression that it mattered to him that she had not gotten in touch with him. Only that it did *not* matter.

She nodded again, with her lips pursed. "You've changed, William. I saw that right away at the field this afternoon. I can also see you're still quite angry with me. Well, I don't—"

"Not at all," he pretended. "Why should I be angry with you?"

"As I started to say, I don't blame you. We—I—said some rather unpleasant things . . . the last time. I'm glad Leo left after dinner because it gives me the opportunity to apologize for my behavior in Dover. I truly didn't want to hurt you but when I saw that you still refused to accept the fact that I'm sixteen years older than you, and then when you said you did believe me but that it didn't matter to you, there seemed to be only one way to make you come to your senses—by telling you that . . . well, that I disliked you and wanted nothing more to do with you. I simply could not let you throw your life away because of me. But you know I could never hate you, don't you, William?"

She had brought him to his senses all right. There was no point in pretending that she hadn't hurt him, nor any point in telling her there were some hurts no apology could mend. He almost asked her why, if she had wanted to apologize, she hadn't done it in New York after she'd returned from Europe.

But he said nothing and looked away.

"You've really changed, William. You're more—I don't know. More self-assured, self-possessed. *Manly.* Flying has done that for you."

That and other things, he thought. He was conscious that she was looking at him intently. He met her eyes directly for the first time that evening.

"You do forgive me for Dover, William? You do understand why I had to say the things I did?"

He shifted uncomfortably in his chair. "Please, Harriet. There's nothing to forgive."

"No, of course you don't understand—there's no way you could. I owe you more than an apology, William, I owe you an explanation. Not just for Dover but for . . . other times. There are certain things about me I have never told you. Not just about my age—that's really the least of it. Secret things only one other person in the world knows, my sister. But only if you know will you be able to understand why—"

But then the waiter came with their coffees and Willy was hardly aware of tasting it when he lifted his cup to his lips. He was recalling another scene from the past: of him eating a meal in a café in a fishing village in France, and Harriet sitting opposite him.

But that was the only similarity to the present. Something about her had changed as well. That evening in Hardelot she had been preoccupied with herself and her journal and her channel plans. Now there was a definite openness, a receptiveness, in her manner toward him. She thought him manly, no longer a boy. Was it possible that, having realized her all-consuming ambitions to be the first American aviatrix and the first woman to fly across the English Channel, was it possible that she could now permit herself to consider something deeper than just friendship with him?

He shook his head to rid it of the thought. How quickly and easily she was disarming him. And confusing him again. How close he was to letting himself be placed in her thrall all over again. The fact of their ages hadn't changed—she had reminded him of that in so many words. So what could she possibly tell him about herself that he didn't already know? And what possible difference could it make about anything?

Before Harriet could resume speaking, she was interrupted again, this time not be a shy little girl as in Hardelot but by a rude woman.

"You're Harriet Quinlan, aren't you?" the woman gushed. "I've been such an admirer of yours for years. Would you please give me your autograph?" She thrust a menu and a pen at Harriet.

Harriet smiled politely and complied with the request and the woman gushed some more before she finally left.

"I can see we're not going to be able to talk here, William, even though I asked Leo to reserve an inconspicuous table. People have been watching me ever since we came in and I have a feeling that others beside that woman are trying to work up the nerve to approach me, and now that they've seen me sign one autograph . . . It's too noisy here anyway."

"Maybe we could find a quiet corner in the lounge?"

Damn it. He was letting his emotions take over again. Hadn't they already been talking, or at least sitting there, for nearly an hour, and an hour or more with Leo before that?

He was relieved when she said, "No, I'd be just as recognized there."

"Well, it will have to be at Squantum tomorrow then. It'll be Sunday and you won't be flying and I'm sure all I'll be doing is a lot of waiting around. The competitions don't start until Monday."

"It would be just as difficult there. You saw all those people this afternoon. There'll be reporters too. No, I'd rather do it this evening while we have the chance. What I want to tell you is something that can't be said in a public place. It must be in absolute privacy."

It was time to end this, time to purge himself of her once and for all. He slid his chair back from the table.

"I really don't think we have anything to say to each other that we haven't already, Harriet," he said evenly. "I accept your apology and I apologize myself for everything I ever said and did, or thought. You're thirty-seven and I'm twenty-one and we can never be anything but friends. So, as you once asked me to do, let's just leave it at that, shall we?"

Harriet smiled sadly. "Well . . . at least you have finally accepted the truth about my age. And you're finally over me, I hope. But you're still very angry with me, the way you're scowling. I don't want you to hate me, William. I want you to understand why I am the way I am. There are things about my background. As I said, secret things . . . "

She was looking at him intently again, yet almost shyly, he thought.

"Would you . . . would you think it terrible of me if we went to my room? Just to talk of course. It would only take a few minutes."

Willy was startled, and speechless for a second. He had no idea what Harriet felt she had to tell him, and why she couldn't tell him just as well where they were. She was breathing deeply, her bosom rising and falling. He knew what idea had immediately leaped involuntarily into his own mind and he was thoroughly exasperated with himself.

"I don't think that would be very wise," he said firmly. "Someone might see us. A hotel like this probably has a house detective. Let's let it wait until tomorrow, Harriet."

It would be even more unwise for another reason. The infection was still there, flaring up as strong as ever. Why was she doing this to him again, and why was he letting her? Did she really think she could invite him up to her room and—just talk? And about what, for God's sake?

He stood up. "I'd better be going. I told you I want to go out to Squantum early."

She sighed, almost in resignation, then lifted her purse off the floor next to her chair where she had placed it and got up. He followed her out of the restaurant.

In the lobby she turned to him and spoke softly. "You mustn't hate me, William. You think you have reason to, but it's only because you don't know what it is I still want to tell you. Will I see you at Squantum tomorrow?"

"I don't suppose we can very well avoid it, can we?"

It was the meanest thing he could think of to say.

ϖ ∾

He was pleased with himself as he walked across the Commons to his own hotel, breathing deeply of the warm summer's night air. He had shown Harriet Quinlan that she no longer had any power over him. She had tempted him—for whatever inexplicable reason only she could know—and he had put her in *her* place for a change. He had passed the test.

Once in his room, however, tossing and turning in bed, he knew that he had done no such thing. She had won again, without even having to try, without even knowing she had won, or even knowing that she was a party to the self-imposed contest in his mind. It was no use pretending, no use trying to fight it. It was insane, it was hopeless, but he still loved her, despite her age, despite Dover, despite everything. Or was it hopeless? Oh God, she must feel something for him that was as close to loving him as she would allow herself to feel. Else why that hurt look in her eyes when he said those last harsh words?

Why had she wanted him to come to her room? She'd almost implored him to. Surely not just to talk. They could have done that in the restaurant.

He got out of bed and lit a cigarette and paced up and down the small room, blowing smoke at the walls.

What if she did love him? It would be worse than it was now. It would be hopeless for *both* of them. She would still be 37. They would both have to be completely crazy.

He finished the cigarette and got back into bed and tried to think about the flight from Long Island and about the coming week at Squantum. But one intruding, and eventually comforting, thought kept coming back and coming back:

He would see Harriet again tomorrow.

4

SQUANTUM FIELD was still rife with conflicting rumors concerning the status of the meet, Willy found, after he checked his plane first thing to make sure it was where he had left it and no one had tampered with it and then began talking with some of the other pilots. All that was known was that the meet was still apparently without official sanction but that Willard insisted nevertheless that all competitions would be held as scheduled.

On the way he had bought a copy of the Sunday *Globe* and scanned it on the streetcar to the Atlantic terminus near the field, mostly to try to occupy his mind with uncertainties other than those he'd gone to bed with and found still there on wakening.

A short item headed "Aero Meet Will Go On" gave the Aero Club of America's side of the controversy. The club had no choice but to withhold its sanction, according to Winthrop D. Southworth, the assistant secretary. To protect the fliers, the international rules required a financial deposit equal to the amount of the prizes, and the promoters of the meet had failed to post a sufficient surety with the club. There was, however, no prohibition against purely exhibition flying.

Willy read the article with detachment. He had come to Squantum to compete in as many of the speed or altitude or distance contests as he could, but he didn't delude himself that he offered any serious challenge to the likes of Lincoln Beachey or any of the other experienced fliers with his underpowered Moisant.

With or without competition flying, all kinds of aerial displays and stunts were planned for the coming week. There would be aerobatics and "bomb-dropping" contests with sacks of flour. Red Sox catcher John Murray would try to catch baseballs dropped from an aeroplane. In dull moments the band would entertain the throng with popular and patriotic selections.

But this day before the official beginning of the meet was more or less unstructured and he was restless on the ground. Several aeroplanes were in the air, cutting capers over the field and the stands or executing touch-and-go landings.

He decided to take his plane up for a view of Boston and the surrounding area. The day before he had been too anxious to land and register to do any aerial sightseeing. It might be a good idea to pick out some landmarks just in case he flew in one of the cross-country competitions. It might also help clear his mind.

The wind was moderate but the air was choppy at a thousand feet. He climbed another thousand and another and another, circling above the field, and found it smoother.

What a marvelous view. He could see for miles in every direction. To the north, almost within reach, Boston Harbor and the city itself between the crooked Charles and Mystic Rivers, its toylike buildings like mere bumps on a relief map. To the west, other towns he didn't know the names of. Far to the southeast, the flattened hook of Cape Cod on the horizon. Plymouth, where the Pilgrims had landed, was somewhere in the curve of the coast north of the cape. Pointing east to the Atlantic, a string of islands, at the end of which was Boston Light. Below him, Dorchester Bay and the Squantum peninsula and the tiny field and the nearby town of Quincy, and another thousand feet above him ranks of billowy cumulus.

He didn't want to come down. He was tempted to try to outsoar the clouds. How beautiful was the world, how strange and wonderful was life. This was what he'd always dreamed of— to be flying like this. If only he could stay up forever, all his problems would be solved.

Harriet and Leo were in her hangar when he went to it a little after noon. Hardy and another man were making some adjustment underneath the Blériot.

"Were you up, William?" Harriet said. "How was it?"

"A little rough down low, but otherwise a great day for flying," he replied casually.

In her Sunday finery she looked even younger and fresher than she had the previous evening, and he wished he could be angry with her again because she did. She smiled at him brightly, as she had the evening before, but today with a funny, strange kind of sadness or distance in her eyes, he thought.

"Hardy's replacing a turnbuckle on one of the warping cables," Leo said to him. Then to Harriet, "The plane ought to be tested again before you fly with Willard tomorrow."

"Would you like to try it out, William?" Harriet said.

He certainly would. He was curious to see what it was like to fly a two-seater, and a plane with such a powerful engine.

"Will you be my passenger?"

She shook her head, as he knew she would. It was Sunday and she had promised her mother. She was not dressed for flying anyway.

"Take Hardy up," Leo suggested.

Hardy and the other man—Willy saw he was just a kid in his teens—had crawled out from under the plane. "Eh? Ah no, m'sieur," Hardy said to Leo. "But this young man has never been in an aeroplane."

The youth looked at them eagerly. He was probably a local boy helping out around the hangars in hopes of earning an aeroplane ride, Willy guessed. Big, though, and heavy enough that they wouldn't need any additional ballast in the rear seat.

Hardy got the assistance of two other mechanics and they pushed the plane out onto the getaway.

"I won't be long," Willy said to Harriet.

"Be careful." Then, teasing him, "It's an expensive machine."

He laughed and fell in love with her all over again and gave her a quick, impulsive peck on the cheek. He wanted to do more but there were other people in the hangar.

"What is that perfume you're wearing . . . Hattie?" he whispered, teasing her, exposing all his wounds.

"Don't you know?" she whispered back, healing them.

❧ ❦

He climbed into the front seat and the boy climbed into the rear. Hardy went to the propeller and the two other mechanics positioned themselves on either side of the rear fuselage. Leo held onto a longeron next to the boy and cautioned him: "Sit well back in the seat at all times. Do not under any circumstances move around or lean forward or you could upset the balance."

Starting straight ahead, the youth nodded his head up and down and gripped the edges of the cockpit tightly on both sides. Willy turned and looked at him. They had neglected to give him a helmet and goggles. Wait till he felt the wind.

He took off carefully, feeling out the torque of the seventy-horsepower rotary, and climbed to five hundred feet over the bay, then leveled off. If anything, conditions were better than before, hardly any roughness. The machine was fast; his poor Moisant would have been left far behind. But now that they were flying level he sensed something about Harriet's plane that he did not like. He had trimmed his own plane so that it virtually flew itself; the Blériot had to be controlled every second. He did not feel at all at ease in it. He was so intent on handling the machine that he was oblivious to the wonderful view that had enthralled him earlier.

He did two circles over the field, the Blériot behaving well in the banks. But just as he was preparing to bring them back down, blipping off the ignition and lowering the nose to maintain their speed, he suddenly found himself losing control. The descent angle abruptly steepened and he immediately pulled back on the wheel with both hands—*yet the nose did not respond!* Even with power restored the tail kept rising and the nose kept dropping until he was looking straight down at the Neponset River and they were diving toward it with terrifying speed, the wires singing at a pitch he had never heard before and the wings shuddering.

For a split second—*eternity*—he felt centrifugal force lifting him off his seat. Natural instinct told him to pull the control column back more—*pull out of the dive*—but it was already back as far as it would go! In that split second, in unthinking desperation, he jammed the wheel all the way forward, simultaneously kicking hard left rudder and wrenching the column into full left warp. The plane turned completely over and instantly was rightside up and gliding innocently—but in the opposite direction as before and two hundred feet below where they had been! If they had been any lower when he started the descent there would not have been enough height to recover from the dive.

The boy was ashen-faced when they landed.

"What did you do up there? Why didn't you warn me for Christ's sake? If I hadn't been hanging on and my legs hooked under the seat I would have fallen out!"

Willy, certain that his own face must be white, started to apologize. "It wasn't me. I don't know what happened." Then, laughing crazily in his relief, "Nothing happened. I just wanted to see how fast we could get down."

"Yeh. Well, thanks for the ride, mister."

The boy jumped out of the cockpit and hurried away on wobbly legs.

There goes one kid who will never go up in an aeroplane again, Willy thought. If it had been my first flight, I wouldn't either.

He saw Leo and Hardy approaching. He was so unnerved that he couldn't move to leave the cockpit. His sweaty hands inside his gloves were still clamped on the wheel. They felt almost paralyzed.

"What happened up there?" Leo said anxiously. "I hope you did that intentionally."

Stiffly, his whole body shaking, Willy got out of the plane. "You saw it? I don't know, Leo. There's something that isn't right about this machine. I don't know what happened but all of a sudden I had no control whatsoever. It started to dive. It nearly threw both of us out. If I hadn't done a flip-over it would have."

Hardy gave him a baleful look and began checking the wings for signs of stress damage. He thinks I did it, Willy thought, and is probably thanking his lucky stars he didn't go up with me.

"Did that kid do anything?" Leo said. "I mean, lean forward or shift around or anything?"

Willy shook his head. "I don't think so. Every time I looked back he was sitting very still, hanging on for dear life."

Leo was also shaking his head. "I agree with you that there's something not quite right about this plane. The French army has grounded all monoplanes because they've had so many accidents. I heard even Blériot has warned about this model. I think it's the tail. Look, here, at the horizontal stabilizer."

Willy had examined the machine before he took it up but now he saw something that hadn't registered with him as particularly important. The stabilizer had about the same deep camber as the wings—it was actually like a small, third wing in itself—but now he noticed that its angle of attack was more acute than that of the wings.

"See how it's angled up?" Leo said. "That's why this plane can't be flown without a passenger or the equivalent weight in ballast."

He saw what Leo meant. The stabilizer was placed at such an angle that it exerted a constant lifting force in flight, a force that was neutralized by the weight in the rear cockpit. If that weight moved in a forward direction or the delicate balance was somehow altered—by a rising current of air under the tail or too abrupt a pitch down or whatever he had encountered up there—the stabilizer would keep lifting the tail until . . .

"Are you sure he didn't shift forward?" Leo said.

"I don't know. Maybe he did. I just thank God we were both holding on. Maybe it *was* me. Maybe I nosed it down steeper than I thought."

"The machine is in perfect condition," Hardy said, and the look he gave Willy was even more reproachful.

Leo shook his head again. "I don't know why all you pilots don't use belts or straps. I've tried to tell Harriet she ought to strap herself in."

Hardly anybody used belts. The only pilots Willy knew who did were Lincoln Beachey and Glenn Martin and others who flew pusher biplanes. But then they not only perched out in the open at the front end of their machines with no structure around them but Beachey did things with his Curtiss no one else did, or was crazy enough to try.

"You don't think the machine is inherently dangerous, do you, Leo?"

"If I thought it was inherently dangerous I wouldn't let Harriet go up in it. She just has to be careful about the balance. She knows that and she's never said she noticed any problem. As long as the weight in the rear is installed so that it can't shift, or she doesn't carry a passenger who jumps around, nothing can happen."

Leo seemed to have reassured himself. "The French accidents have mostly been with inexperienced trainees. I think probably you just ran into some kind of freak updraft or downdraft that momentarily upset the balance just as you were descending."

Willy was not quite convinced. If he hadn't just flown the plane himself none of this business about the stabilizer would have occurred to him. But he *had* flown it, and what had happened to the plane—and had almost happened to him—could just as easily happen to Harriet.

Still, Harriet had flown the Blériot at least several times, both with and without a passenger, and was well acquainted with its characteristics. She'd obviously had no problem when she'd taken Harry Willard up on Saturday. As long as she was careful she was as safe in it as she would be in any other aeroplane. After all, she was an experienced flier. It must have been a freak occurrence up there.

Yet . . . the air had been smooth, and he hadn't done anything with the controls that he hadn't done a thousand times in his own plane.

Leo began walking toward the hangar where Harriet was waiting. Willy touched his arm and he stopped.

"Did Harriet say anything to you, Leo? About us?"

"When? Yesterday? Just that her bad penny had turned up again." Leo grinned at him.

"I mean today."

"No. Should she have said something?"

It suddenly disturbed Willy to realize that Leo really was ignorant of Harriet's actual age. It might be one thing for her to disguise the fact to her employer and even to people who were her friends, though that was hard enough to understand. But that she would maintain the masquerade with the person who was such a close and important associate in her flying career seemed inexplicable.

He was on the point of telling Leo the truth then and there, not for Leo's benefit (there would be no benefit for Leo that he could see) but for his own, for he desperately wanted the older man's advice. But Leo might not believe it either, and he knew what the advice would be if Leo did believe it.

"I'm still in love with her," he said. "I thought it was over, but . . ."

What was the point? Leo couldn't help him, except to look at him sympathetically.

"Well, frankly, Willy, I have to admit I was a bit floored when Harriet said she'd talked to you yesterday and invited you to have dinner with us. I mean, after what you told me about you and her, how it was all one-sided, and the way you left Dover without a word to anyone. We all wondered where you were. Harriet said she thought you'd been called home suddenly, an illness in the family or something, but that was pretty transparent to me. I thought, well, either Willy's taken my advice or she's sent the boy packing herself."

He peered at Willy. "It *was* that, wasn't it?"

"She explained why she did it, Leo. Last night in the restaurant, after you left. For my own good, she said. Because she's older." (*Ah, Leo, if only I could tell you how much older.*) "So that must mean she cares for me too, don't you think?"

"I'm sure I wouldn't know, Willy. I long ago stopped trying to figure out women. But the course of true love ne'er did run smooth, did it? Life is short. If you think you and Harriet could be happy together, the only thing you can do is try to convince her of that. And if you can't, well then you're just finally going to have to give it up as a bad job. But I'm more than Harriet's business manager, I consider myself her friend. My only concern is that you don't do anything that—well, I would hate to see her reputation tarnished in any way."

"I would never do anything to hurt her!" Willy exclaimed. "I—I would give my life for her, Leo."

Leo looked at him steadily. "I know you would, Willy."

Neither of them said anything to Harriet about the Blériot when they rejoined her in the hangar. For one thing, they had only been guessing that its tricky lifting tail had had something to do with the near-catastrophe. For another, Harriet hadn't witnessed it—she must have been distracted at the moment by one of the omnipresent reporters roaming all over the place and it had happened in a flash—for she merely asked Willy how he liked the plane.

"Very nice," he said. "A little touchy though."

"Yes, it is."

He was about to say more. But why alarm her unnecessarily? She knew the plane better than he did. It was just one of those freak occurrences.

As Harriet had said, there was no chance for them to talk at the field, certainly not in the hangar. There were other reporters who wanted to interview her, prominent Boston citizens who wanted to meet her.

Only enough chance, in a minute when no one was commanding her attention, for her to say hurriedly: "Leo and I are having dinner with some people this evening. I'll make some excuse to get away early, before ten at the latest. Will you meet me at the hotel? Not in the restaurant. In my room. Only to talk. It's important to me."

But not enough chance for him to protest that there must be some public place where they could meet and still talk privately before she had whispered her room number to him and then was out of hearing.

5

H E WAS THE only passenger in the elevator. The operator, a wizened little pasty-faced man, thanked him when he told him the floor as if Willy were doing him a favor. "How are you tonight, sir? Are you enjoying your stay in Boston?"

Two very good questions, Willy thought. "Yes, thank you," he replied politely, automatically.

When they reached the floor, he waited until the elevator gates had closed, then, making sure no one was in the hallway, tapped on Harriet's door. When she opened it he saw she was fully dressed in the gown she had apparently worn that evening. Even though she had again emphasized "only to talk," he had not known what he expected . . . or hoped.

Coming up on the elevator, his honest intention was only to talk too. Rather, to listen to what she felt was so urgent to tell him. But when the door opened and he saw her beautiful face looking up at him, all his resolutions and all rationality abandoned him, all his carefully nurtured bitterness was as if it had never been, and he slipped inside and immediately embraced her.

The lobby at her hotel in New York . . . her room in Hardelot . . . Dover . . . now Boston . . . It seemed his only purpose in life was to hold Harriet in his arms inside a doorway. She was sixteen years old than he was and he didn't care. It didn't matter. Nothing mattered but that he still loved her. And wanted her.

And she wanted him, he knew, though she breathed protestingly against his shoulder, "William, stop it! This isn't why I asked you here."

"I think it is."

He covered her mouth with his and felt her lips open to his for a second before she turned her head away.

"*No!* We can't do this. It's wrong. Completely wrong."

If she had resisted him convincingly, fought him, pushed him away, he might have stopped. But she merely stood there, trembling like some small captured creature in his hands.

"I love you, Harriet."

Now he made bold to explore the body he had lusted after even as he had worshipped the spirit that glorified it. Laughing, trembling himself, he caressed her, from hair to face to neck to shoulder to breast to waist to hips, dropping down onto his knees again—not in helplessness and humiliation this time but in adoration—, molding his face against her thighs through her gown. Then he rose to his feet and, taking her in his arms again, began undoing the buttons down her back.

She was his for the taking. His mind reeled with the certainty of it. All he had to do was lead her to the bed. It was Hardelot all over again, but this time he knew what to do, what she wanted him to do.

"You do love me too, don't you, Harriet? You have from the very first, haven't you?"

She shook her head, her eyes half-closed, moisture glistening in them.

"Say it," he demanded softly. "Say it."

Her voice was tiny and husky, pleading. "No. That isn't what I have to tell you. You still don't understand. You don't know—"

"*Say it!*"

She sighed, and it was a surrendering sound.

"All right. I'm not going to fight you any longer. I can't fight you any longer. Yes—I love you. You know I do."

Then suddenly, struggling inside his arms. "Oh God, what am I saying? I must be out of my mind! We can't— I haven't the right— *This is so wrong.*"

He stopped her words with a fingertip on her lips, and then traced it along the curve of one cheek. He held her away from him, his hands squeezing her narrow waist.

"It's *not* wrong. It's the rightest thing in the world. I love you, so very, very much. We love each *other*. We're going to be married."

He moved them to the bed and turned off the lamp on the nightstand, leaving only a dim light penetrating the window blind from the street below. He resumed undressing her, laughing again as he fumbled inexpertly with her corset. So many clothes women wore.

Then she stood before him naked in all her loveliness, though in the dimness it was only with his hands and lips that he could know the loveliness. God, how perfectly formed she was, how soft and warm and vulnerable. He pulled the covers back with one hand, the other holding her against him, and lowered her down onto the bed and then stripped away his own clothes. He lay beside her, pressing his demand against her thigh, and took her hand and placed it on it, and began running his own hands and mouth over her body. For long moments he kissed and caressed her—over, under, around an *in* every sweet new discovered part of her, as she gasped and moaned and writhed . . .

Thank God she had never promised her mother she would not make love on a Sunday.

Harriet had put on a nightgown and robe and was sitting in a chair to one side of the bed. He leaned over on one elbow and looked at her. She had left the light on in the bathroom and partially closed the door, but enough illumination entered the room that he could see her face. It was shadowed, from within as well as from without.

She was crying quietly.

They should still have been lying close together in the bed, in each other's arms, savoring and sharing the afterglow of lovemaking. There was no afterglow, only a faint regret, a feeling almost of shame, in his heart, seeing her cry. But he could not have been that clumsy and selfish a lover.

Something was still wrong. Something was missing. It wasn't like it had been with Carole. Carole had made love *with* him— and *to* him—eagerly, abandonedly, meeting him kiss for kiss, caress for caress, thrust for thrust. Harriet had been passive and inert, almost as if she were in another world, the way she had been on her bed in Hardelot.

He sat up and swung onto the edge of the bed and reached down and fished for the pack of cigarettes and matches in his jacket. Their clothes were all in a mixed-up heap on the floor where he had thrown them, so impatiently, jubilantly thrown them. He slipped on his drawers, to match her modesty.

He drew on the cigarette. "Harriet. What is it?"

Daubing at her eyes with a handkerchief, her voice toneless, "I suppose we shall have to be married now, shan't we? That's what people would say if they knew. Except that we can't be married." She made a pathetic little laugh.

He had never seen or heard weakness in her before. He wondered if he should go to her.

"I should never have asked you to come here, William. I knew this would happen. A virile young man like you."

"For God's sake, Harriet, we did nothing wrong. We love each other. You wanted it to happen too. Is the thought of marriage to me so dreadful?"

"It would be the worst mistake you could possibly make, William. It's not just my age, though heaven knows that should be enough, more than enough. It's— You really know nothing about me. I'm not the person you think I am."

Something in her face and in her words made him apprehensive. He tried to joke. "You mean you're not really Harriet Quinlan the famous aviatrix? Or someone else writes your articles for Leslie's? I forgive you."

He waited while she got up and went to the dresser and got a fresh handkerchief and blew her nose delicately. She sat down again, no longer crying.

"You're not already married, are you, Harriet? You don't have a husband hidden somewhere?"

"No, no, nothing like that. Although I once was engaged. It's— Let me start at the beginning."

He waited again while she seemed to be gathering resolve.

"I'm not from California, not originally. My family moved there later. You see, I even lied about my birthplace. I was born on a farm near Coldwater, Michigan. But it *was* in Eighteen-seventy-five, as I told you at Christmastime."

"Yes."

She continued, speaking rapidly: "We were very poor. My father had no real trade, except farming, which he wasn't very successful at. He was a cook in the Union army during the Civil War. When I was about four we moved to California. My parents ran a grocery store for a while in a little town called Arroyo Grande, until that failed. Then we moved to San Francisco, to a house on Van Ness Avenue. There our fortunes improved a little, mostly thanks to my mother. She made herbal medicines my father sold out of a wagon. When she wasn't doing that she sewed bags for a prune-packing factory."

"There's nothing shameful about that, Harriet." He was relieved. "Is that your terrible secret, that your family was poor? Is that what you thought was so important to tell me? Do you think I'm some kind of snob?"

"I've only begun, William. Please let me go on. My mother became very ambitious for us as we grew up, my sister and me. We were both very pretty. She wanted us to break into society. So she concocted stories about tutors and foreign educations and early on we learned how to 'put on airs,' as they say. I really have no education beyond common school."

He was even more relieved. That explained Harriet's poor knowledge of French when she was supposed to have gone to finishing school in France, the way she had of trying to impress people with little bits of unasked-for information about herself, both true and phony—finishing school, the fashionable church she went to, the well-known people she knew. As if, unconsciously, she had to keep reassuring herself that she had risen above her humble origins.

"You've never spoken about your sister. 'Kittie,' is it? Is she older or younger?"

"Five years older. She still lives in California, she has her own life. Anyway—"

"You said you were engaged to someone once."

"Yes, I was coming to that. He was the scion of one of the city's wealthy families. I was very young, barely twenty, and he was thirty. Isn't it funny? I didn't want to marry a man ten years old than me—and here I am, sixteen years older than you."

"Why didn't you marry him? Didn't you love him?"

"I thought I did, or was supposed to. But when we became engaged, he seemed to think it gave him the right to—"

She stopped again and clasped her hands in her lap and stared down at them. wringing them nervously. Then, so low he had to strain to hear, "One afternoon . . . we were alone in the house . . . my parents were away and we were alone and . . . and he . . .

"He *violated* me! In my parents' house!"

She started crying again.

"Oh, Harriet . . ," was all he could manage at first. He felt— he didn't know what. A faint disgust. But disgust of what, or with whom?

Then, weakly, "I'm so sorry. And I just did the same thing, didn't I? I forced myself on you. I guess that makes me no better than he was." He wondered again if he should go to her.

"*No, no, no!* You mustn't say that. Don't you *dare* compare yourself to him. It's not the same with you, not the same at all."

"What happened then? Did you bring charges?"

"For what purpose? It would have devastated my parents and the scandal would have ruined my family's name. I just wanted out of it."

His relief was complete. He did go to her then and took her hands in his and smiled down at her. "I'm glad you told me all this, Harriet. I understand everything now. But it was a long time ago. It has nothing to do with us now."

"No, you *don't* understand, William. You haven't heard everything yet. There's more. The real reason you can't marry me."

"Good Lord, Harriet. How much more can there be?"

He needed another cigarette. He went to the nightstand where he had placed the packet and lit one and drew on it deeply.

She watched him. "I wish you wouldn't smoke so much, dear. I don't care what the medical profession says, it can't be good for you."

A sardonic laugh escaped him. "Do you realize what you just did, Harriet? You nagged me. Only a little nag, but it's a start. We might as well be married."

"When you hear the last of it, you won't want to marry me. I'm not just soiled goods."

"*Don't talk like that, damn it!*" he exploded. "I hate that kind of talk. Sweet merciful Christ, what kind of man do you think I am? What more is there? I don't want to hear any more."

"I'm almost done."

He waited again, and when she spoke her voice was stronger and the words came quickly.

"This man, this fine, upstanding gentleman from a good family, was a frequenter of the crib women in a notorious area of San Francisco called the Barbary Coast. It was a hotbed of crime and prostitution and every other social evil. I guess it still is. He gave me a serious disease. It didn't appear until much later, after I had broken off the engagement. The doctor said he would have to . . . remove part of me. *Inside.* As a 'precaution,' he said. He cured me, but it meant I could never have children."

He groaned. "*Oh . . . Harriet . . .*"

"I begged him not to tell my parents. I knew my father would kill the man if he knew the truth. So he said it was a cyst or something that he was afraid might become cancerous. My sister was the only one who knew. I don't know what I would have done if I hadn't had her to confide in. When I recovered from the operation my parents managed some money, and Kittie had been working and saved some, enough to send us both to Europe. We spent some time in France, so that much about me is partly true. When we came back I decided to go into journalism and, well, I've told you about that."

He furiously stubbed out the cigarette and compulsively lit another one. He sat on the bed in stunned silence.

For the past year, every time he had turned around Harriet had been older than he had thought she was. And every time, he had talked himself into accepting it, pretending it didn't matter.

But this!

"Is that when you started lying about your age? When did you start doing that?"

"Not at first. It was when I wrote to Leslie's Weekly about a job. I was afraid they would think I was too old, so I gave my birth year as Eighteen-eighty-four. I don't know why I didn't say Eighteen-eighty-five and have taken an even ten years off my age. I guess I thought that would be a little too much. Eventually I almost came to believe it myself, along with everything else my mother made up. My biography is going to be in the Nineteen-twelve edition of Who's Who in America and I told them the same lies. But I never really thought of it as lying until you—"

"Why didn't you tell me all this right at the first, Harriet?" he said, and even as the words came out of his mouth he realized how stupid and unfair they were.

Hello my name is Harriet and I'm sixteen years older than you and I was raped and can never have children so please don't fall in love with me.

And would it really have made any difference if he had known from the first? He didn't know. He hadn't *chosen* to fall in love with her, had he? It had just happened.

His question didn't deserve any answer but she answered it.

"I almost told you, in Hardelot. I wanted to, I should have, but I couldn't. I couldn't bring back all that . . . sordidness. So I tried to use reason with you. Then, in Dover, I thought if I—if I hurt you deeply and sent you away . . . I didn't think you could ever forgive me for that. Then yesterday when I landed and saw you on the field I was so happy."

She took a deep breath and exhaled it in a long sigh.

"But now you know everything. *Everything*. It makes a difference, doesn't it? All the difference in the world."

"*No! No!* It doesn't make any difference. You're the same person I fell in love with, aren't you? I still want to marry you."

His own words startled him. Someone else was using his voice, and the words rang false. She *wasn't* the same person. It *did* make a difference. All the difference in the world.

"You're being very gallant, dearest, even though you do know

now that it's absolutely out of the question. You're a young, handsome, virile man. I can't be the kind of wife you want, the kind you deserve. I'm not a—a complete woman. You'll want children someday."

He stared down at the floor, taking puff after puff from the cigarette.

"I'm fully old enough to be your mother, William."

"We don't have to marry," the someone else blurted. "We could just be lovers."

"Don't talk foolishness. Something like that couldn't be kept secret, it would be a tremendous scandal, we'd both be disgraced. I'd lose my job, and probably be banned from flying as well. We've already taken a great risk. If the management of this hotel knew what happened in this room we'd both be thrown out on the street, if they didn't have us arrested."

"I refuse to let the world cheapen what we did!" he exploded again.

But she was right, of course. If it came to that, the man in the elevator would remember him. He should have taken the stairs.

Damn the management. Damn society and its hypocrisy that dirtied everything beautiful. Damn to everlasting hell the son of a bitch who had destroyed his dream even before he'd met Harriet and dreamed the dream.

"Other people do it," the alien voice persisted for some reason. "The people you know in the theater. Didn't Grahame-White have what they politely call a 'liaison' with that actress, Pauline Chase? Kings and dukes and rich people get away with it all the time and everybody admires them."

"We're hardly of their class, William. It would absolutely kill my parents. I couldn't do that to them."

"Well then, we will just have to be married, won't we? As for children, there's always adoption. We could do that."

"William, won't you *please* be reasonable at last? I am too *old* for you! Time is out of joint for both of us, don't you see? I don't know if I would have wanted children in any case. How could you ever take me home to meet your parents? They'd call me a cradle-robber. They'd disown you."

"They wouldn't have to know your age," he said, and wondered why he was arguing the point. "No one has to know. No one *would* know. Everyone thinks you're twenty-eight. And you always said I was very mature for my age."

"Stop torturing us both this way, William. Oh, if it were only six years and there wasn't this—this other thing, it might be possible, though even then people would talk. After all, you're still in college, or you were, and I've been with Leslie's for almost eight years. But sixteen years is simply too great a difference. *Sixteen years.*"

"You've always been concerned about what people thought about you, haven't you?"

"We have to live in this society, William."

He put out the cigarette and stared again at the floor, conscious that she was trying to see his face.

"You think I'm beautiful, dearest, and perhaps I am. But in a few years . . . physical beauty is the most ephemeral thing in the world."

He raised his head to her. "You'll always look young. You'll always be beautiful."

"No I won't. In a few years the wrinkles will start coming. I'll turn fat and ugly."

"We could have ten good years together. Maybe fifteen. Even twenty. We could be a team. 'Quinlan and Reynolds, the Flying Fools.'" But his laugh was hollow.

"You *are* a fool. In twenty years you'll only be four years older than I am now. I'll be an old woman. I'll be an albatross around your neck. You'll wish you'd never laid eyes on me."

His entire world had crashed. He wished to God she had never made her confession.

Yet she was still beautiful, wasn't she? Still young looking, even as she sat anguishing in the chair. She was still the same person he had fallen in love with, wasn't she? His desire had been so *strong* when he had come to her room. Now he didn't know what he felt. He felt nothing. She *wasn't* the same person. She never could be the same person again.

He got up abruptly and started dressing. He carefully placed her clothing on the bed.

"We'll talk about this tomorrow. I'd better go."

He finished tying his tie hastily and put on his jacket and went to the door. He stood there lifting his cap up and down in his hands.

"I have to go," he said.

She got up from the chair.

"Come here," he said.

She came to him and he held her and buried his face in her hair. And now it was she pressing herself against him, and for a moment he felt desire reburgeoning. But it was only carnal desire.

He released his embrace. "Just give me some time to think, Harriet. To absorb all this."

But how could he possibly absorb it? In a million years how could he absorb it?

She smiled up at him timidly. The tears had left faint streaks on her face.

"You do hate me now, don't you?"

"Of course not. Of course not. *Never*."

But he did not kiss her goodbye.

As soon as he was on the street he wanted to go back to her. And the next day, and every day for the rest of his life, he would damn himself that he didn't go back.

6

HE SPENT another fretful night in his hotel room, unable to sleep. At five A.M. he gave it up and got dressed.

Squantum Field was already bustling with activity when he arrived a little before six, both inside and outside the hangars, as pilots and mechanics worked over their planes, revved engines, made the inevitable adjustments. Two planes were already cutting figures high above. One was a "headless" Curtiss, probably either Lincoln Beachey or Charles Hamilton; they both flew Curtisses.

Beachey had supposedly run into a fence one time and knocked the front boom off and discovered that the plane flew better without it. It was a good story. In any case, most biplanes now were "headless." Even the Wright Company had dispensed with the elevator in front.

Grover Loening had gone to work for the Wrights, he'd heard, after his graduation from Columbia. Had he had something to do with the new design? God, how long ago that day on Governors Island seemed.

It promised to be an excellent flying day. Even at this early hour some scores of spectators where on hand, both in the bleachers and along the perimeter fences. More were to stream in during the morning, and the road leading to the field would be jammed with automobiles and carriages and the nearby bay would be filled with small boats from the Savin Hill Yacht Club.

Now that the real competition was about to begin the pilots were no longer concerned about the Aero Club's prohibition; that was management's problem. They had come to Squantum to fly and they were going to, no matter what. Already there was an air of expectancy on the field.

Ominously, two ambulances were parked near the fence. Would there be a different expectancy among the spectators, Willy wondered, remembering Beachey's cynical remark—the expectancy (perhaps the hope?) that they might see the ambulances put to use?

He checked his plane again, then went into the office to sign up for the first of the day's events, a series of closed-circuit speed races around the field scheduled to begin at noon. Then he waited for Harriet.

He had done a lot of thinking during the sleepless night, nothing but thinking, playing and replaying every word of what she had said, what he had said. In daylight he still had arrived at no decision about her, except that marriage was totally out of the question now. That much was certain, even if she agreed to it.

When Harriet and Leo walked into the headquarters building he saw there were faint circles under her eyes, making her if anything more attractive. She had not slept last night either. Her eyes went soft for an instant when she saw Willy, but when he merely inclined his head to her, not smiling, they clouded over and her greeting was no more than she would make to any stranger. Simply: "Hello."

For the first time since he had met this woman, a thousand years ago, Willy felt that he was in control of things.

Leo was too preoccupied with other concerns to notice this odd reserve between two people who supposedly were in love, or at least one of whom was. Both Willards, father and son, were there and in answer to Leo's immediate question the former affirmed that the Aero Club had not lifted its prohibition but that events were going to go forward anyway.

"You're asking the pilots to put their licenses on the line," Leo said. "Not only that but as I understand it there is no assurance they will receive any prize money."

"All contracts will be honored," Willard said, chopping his right arm up and down, repeating what Willy had heard him say before. "Whether or not individual fliers elect to compete in an event is their decision."

"Well, Miss Quinlan will not be competing. As her manager I can't permit her to risk losing her license. I want it clearly understood that she will be doing demonstration flights only. And I told you I want your check in advance for the amount agreed upon."

"I have it right here," Willard said. "Four thousand dollars." He started looking among the papers on the desk.

Willy whistled silently. *Four thousand dollars*. He would earn no money at all unless he placed in one of the competitions. Even then he would probably wind up in the hole, what with fuel costs and tips to mechanics and ground crewmen and all the other incidental expenses. Good for you, he wanted to say to Harriet. But she wasn't looking at him.

"Oh I intend to fly all right," she said to Willard. "As long as I can beat Grahame-White's record to Boston Light and back, I don't care if it's official or not."

"Splendid," said Willard. "I'm looking forward to accompanying you—me and my hundred and ninety pounds of bulk. It will have to be later this afternoon, however, after today's competitions are concluded. I'll have to be here on the ground until then."

"I'm looking forward to it too," Harriet said.

"On one condition," Leo said to Willard. "And that is that you give me your word that you will sit perfectly immobile in the aeroplane and under no circumstances shift your weight forward toward Harriet. Her machine is delicately balanced. Any sudden shift could upset it. I know you to be a man of sudden, I might almost say excitable, movements."

Willard waved away the caution. "I perfectly understand. You have my assurance that I'll sit tight and won't move a muscle."

"My father has flown with my brother," the younger Willard said irritatedly. "I was Miss Quinlan's passenger on Saturday and found her machine quite stable. Your remarks are unwarranted, Mr. Stevens."

Willy looked at Harry Willard. Although it was not he but his brother Charles who was the famous pilot, Willy still was a little overawed with the realization that he was actually here in Squantum and was going to compete with, or at least fly in the company of, some of the country's best airmen, of whom Charles Willard had been one. He had been the hit of the Los Angeles meet two years before—the first aviation meet in America—by taking off and landing within a twenty-foot square on the ground. It was he who had first used the term "holes" in the air.

With so many famous pilots at Squantum, Willy couldn't believe the Aero Club would actually take away their licenses simply because not enough prize money had been deposited. The club would have to back down.

This was neither the time nor the place to talk to Harriet. She was engaged in the conversation with the Willards and he didn't know what he wanted to say to her, or if he wanted to say anything at all. He left the office and went out to his plane and spent the rest of the morning checking and rechecking it and wandering around among the other aircraft and chatting with their pilots while he waited for the speed contest.

It was no contest as far as he was concerned. Midway through the second of three low-level racing events held that afternoon around two pylons erected at either end of the field his Anzani failed again, sputtering to a stop instead of suddenly as it had that time with Carole over New York City. It happened as he was banking into the near turn, but fortunately he had enough speed to maneuver out of the path of the course and bring the plane to a dead-stick landing directly in front of the bleachers. He sat there, disgusted and humiliated—until he heard the swell of enthusiastic applause from the spectators.

Most people still knew little about aeroplanes, but they could recognize expert piloting when they saw it.

Even though the number of competitors had been reduced by the departure of several aviators who had decided not to challenge the Aero Club's prohibition, he had finished next to last in the first race and been well behind the leaders in the second, not exactly giving them a run for the money—assuming there would be any money. The reconditioned Anzani had tried its best, but he had taken a lot out of it in the flight from Long Island and it did not have what you needed for speed in any case. Nor for all the skill he had acquired in the previous few months could he handle a plane like Beachey. The man cut his turns in nearly vertical banks, his lower wingtip mere inches above the ground.

This time it *was* the fuel line, he discovered: a loosened fitting where two lengths of tubing joined. Easily repaired. He would be flying again tomorrow. He would do better in the distance and altitude events, he was sure.

He stood by the plane waiting for the engine to cool so he

could begin work on the fuel line. He looked across the field at Harriet's hangar.

It wasn't fair to her not to say a word to her, to let her think he hated her.

Hate her? Hate her? Even now, after everything, he still must love her, else why would his heart be aching this way? That hadn't changed, even though everything had changed.

Or was it only aching for himself, for the dream smashed, for the might-have-been?

How in all ordinary prudence and common sense could he still think of marrying her? Yet how could he *not* think of it? What kind of relationship could there be for them without marriage, even if it would be doomed to be a sterile, childless one?

So many, many times he had told himself how impossible it was to dream that Harriet could love him and that they would spend the rest of their lives with each other. Yet now that she had told him she did love him, everything was even more impossible. The greatest happiness he had ever imagined in fantasy had become in reality the greatest agony.

Life was worse than a tale told by an idiot. It was a pointless play directed by a mad marionettist who delighted in tormenting his hapless puppets, manipulating them together into absurd postures, then cruelly flinging them apart.

A roar from the crowd made him look up. Somebody in a monoplane was performing a fancy maneuver over the field.

He ought to warn Harriet about the Blériot. He was a better flier than she was. A year ago he would never have imagined he could rival her as an aviator. But he had become a better flier that she was; he knew that now. He ought to tell her what had happened when he had flown her plane, tell her what he had done to recover control. If he didn't warn her, and the same thing happened to her and she wasn't prepared . . .

Then, from some dark hidden shameful corner of his soul, unbidden and instantly repented, sprang the thought:

That would be one way out, wouldn't it? That would solve everything, wouldn't it?

❧ ❧

It was late afternoon, nearing the time for Harriet's flight with Willard. He started walking toward her hangar, and as he walked he observed that the crowd was really smaller than he had thought it would be, certainly smaller than the promoters had hoped for. But the meet was to last all week. No doubt attendance would pick up on succeeding days.

Again in the hangar other people were monopolizing Harriet's attention. She was talking animatedly with two women who evidently were reporters because they were jotting things down in notebooks. One of them, possibly the woman she'd said she'd promised to take up for a ride, fingered the fabric of the famous flying costume on the sleeve of Harriet's extended arm. The hangar was open in the rear with wire netting across it to allow spectators to look in but not to enter, and a group of people had their noses against it.

"Is it true, Miss Quinlan," he heard one of the reporters ask, "that some people have suggested you name your aeroplane the 'Pankhurst' in honor of the English suffragette leader?"

"Yes," Harriet laughed. "But if I were to name it anything it would be 'Genevieve,' after the patron saint of aviators in France."

Or (the thought came to Willy out of nowhere) "Harriet's Chariot." How gauche. She would not appreciate it.

"What are your views on women's suffrage, Miss Quinlan?"

A suffragette, the saying went, was a woman who was no longer a lady but had not yet become a gentleman. He turned away before he had any more asinine thoughts.

Hardy was wiping off the engine of the aeroplane. Willy greeted him and ran his fingers along a bracing wire between the cowling and one wing, testing its tension.

"The machine is in perfect condition," Hardy said defensively. "I have checked every wire, every fitting, every control."

Willy knew he had. But the plane had been in perfect condition yesterday too.

He went around to the tail and looked at the horizontal stabilizer, and as he did a foreboding came over him.

The two reporters seemed to have no end of questions. He waited as long as he could, then waved his hand at Harriet urgently. She made a few quick last replies to the women.

He beckoned her to the other side of the plane, out of view of the people peering into the back of the hangar.

"What is it, William?"

He knew then how terribly cruelly he had treated her all day. Her voice was lifeless and colorless. A moment before, with the reporters, her eyes had been sparkling. Now they were dull, even as she looked directly into his eyes.

Oh dear God how painfully breathtakingly beautiful she was. How fetching in her costume, with the hood thrown back behind her graceful neck. She was wearing a cape that day in matching plum color.

She was the same Harriet as before. He did still love her. Yet somehow he could not bring himself to say the words.

"I understand you had some bad luck in the speed event," she said.

"Just a problem with the fuel feed. Nothing serious."

"It may be just as well. Since you didn't finish maybe the Aero Club won't consider you to have been a competitor."

"I'll be competing tomorrow, and the rest of the week."

She was so lovely. He felt the sweet familiar pain in his chest. She looked like a little girl lost. How could he have been such an utter ass? He loved her. Now and for always. Nothing mattered but that.

Yet he could not bring himself to say the words.

"Harriet, I want you to do something for me. I want you to wear a strap when you fly your plane."

"Why? And where am I going to get one?"

He chose his words carefully, not wanting to alarm her. But it was important that she know. Important to him.

"Something happened on Sunday when I flew your plane. I still don't know what it was. Maybe it was something I did, but it suddenly pitched down on its nose. That kid and I were almost thrown out."

"Oh William! I didn't see that! When?"

She *was* alarmed—for *him*. Her eyes had come to life. The most beautiful woman in the world loved him. All he had to do was tell her that he still wanted her love.

He threw away the precious chance.

"Just before we landed," he said. "Fortunately I was able to roll it out of the dive. But it was more dumb luck than anything else."

He glanced around the hangar. "I'll speak to Hardy. He should be able to rig something up."

They were back where they were. The aliveness in her eyes faded.

"I've never had a problem with the plane, William. And don't forget, I still have this." She touched the Aztec head hanging in front of her chest.

"Just do it for me, Harriet."

Hardy was not receptive to the idea, but at Willy's insistence and with Harriet's approval he agreed to make a strap if he could find something to use, a length of leather or webbing. But there was nothing like that in the hangar. They went to search separately in the other hangars. Willy had no luck in the first one he tried, but when he emerged he saw Hardy carrying something out of another hangar down the line. It was a thin strip of leather, four or five feet long, with a buckle at one end, he saw when Hardy showed it to him. The other end was broken. It was part of a strap from a carriage harness. What anyone had been using it for he couldn't guess. Not only was it thinner than he would have liked but hard and stiff, and when they looped it under and over the seat the two ends barely overlapped. But it would do. It would have to.

The leather was so brittle that Hardy had difficulty boring a hole with an awl at the broken end for the buckle prong. He muttered to himself in French and looked at Willy dubiously.

"It'll do," Willy said.

It would have to do. At least it would be better than nothing.

When the strap was buckled it stretched nearly straight across the seat with no more than a few inches between it and the back support. Far too constricting for a man but Harriet, thank God, was a slender woman.

He told her to climb in and try it. "It's too tight," she said when she managed to cinch it together. "It's cutting into me. I can hardly breathe. It's hard for me to reach the wheel. I can't fly like this."

"Yes you can. Once you're in the air you won't even notice it."

"Oh William, is this really necessary?"

"Please, Harriet. I know it's too tight but it's the best we can do. After today we'll get you a proper strap. There's at least one company I know of that makes them."

She drew in her breath as far as she could and unbuckled the strap and exhaled with relief.

"I don't know if I can stand it all the way to Boston Light and back."

She giggled. "But I always did want a wasp waist."

What was he trying to do? The strap was little better than useless.

He put his hands on the cockpit rim. "Harriet—I don't want you to fly today. Postpone your flight with Willard. I don't want you to fly the plane until I take it up again and see if I can figure out what might have happened or what might be wrong with it and how it can be fixed."

"Don't be ridiculous, William. Everything's ready to go. It's already been announced. We can't very well reschedule at the last minute. I know this plane and there's nothing the matter with it. Hardy has checked it over completely a dozen times today."

She started to get out, but when she saw the look on his face she settled back down into the seat.

"William, do you really think there might be something wrong? I'll do whatever you say. I'll tell Willard I want to re-schedule."

Another chance, the last one.

He stared at his fingers that still gripped the coaming, the knuckles white. He averted his eyes from hers. He was aware of

Hardy watching them and shaking his head, of Harriet studying his face.

Maybe they were right. There was nothing the matter with the plane. It was something he had done. Or just a freak occurence. It wouldn't happen again.

"No . . ," he said slowly, reassuring himself. "It'll be okay. Just don't do anything abruptly. Just be cautious and careful."

"I always am, William."

In place of foreboding Willy now felt something else almost as disturbing, yet strangely calming: a sense of surrender to inevitability. To fate.

He had done what he could. He had warned her. It was out of his hands now.

7

IT WAS NEARLY six o'clock. The sky was still bright and crystal clear, as it had been all that day. There was only a little wind.

Willy's mind was also calm. If some vagrant action or peculiarity of the air had had anything to do with his loss of control in Harriet's plane on Sunday—a sudden gust, Leo's freak downdraft or updraft, one of Charles Willard's "holes," some of Harriet's "rarefied air"—he could not have wished for better conditions for her.

He had done what he could. It was out of his hands now.

The Blériot was rolled out and positioned at the end of the getaway. A small stepladder was placed beside the forward cockpit. Harriet came out of her hangar, surrounded by reporters. At the foot of the ladder she unfastened the cape she had been wearing and handed it to an admirer. Then, just like the queen of the air that she was, she regally mounted the steps.

Another entourage accompanied the two Willards as they walked from the headquarters building. Willard *père* shook hands with Harriet and climbed into the rear seat. A photographer snapped his picture.

Willy heard Leo warning Willard again that he must not under any circumstances move around in his seat, and heard Willard assuring Leo again that he understood perfectly.

Willy crouched on the plywood on top of the fuselage between the two cockpits and reached over Harriet's shoulders to help her fasten the strap. She drew her torso up very straight to lessen the pressure against her middle.

He started to tell her: if the plane suddenly dives don't try to pull out of it. Push the wheel all the way forward and do a roll with full left warp and rudder.

But did he really know that that was what had saved him? It might be the worst possible thing she could do. The plane wasn't going to dive anyway.

He jumped down and grabbed the rim of her cockpit. Hardy put his hands on the propeller. Harriet signaled to him.

"*I love you!*" Willy yelled. "*Nothing's changed!*"

But he had waited too long. She did not hear him above the roar of the engine. Her eyes were watching the winding tachometer. Willard was sitting well back in his seat as he had been told to do, his arms extended along the sides of the shuddering fuselage.

At Harriet's signal the mechanics holding the plane let go and it started down the getaway.

The voice of Tom Coffee, the meet announcer, boomed over the electric megaphones:

"*Miss Harriet Quinlan, the first licensed aviatrix in America and the first woman to fly the English Channel, is taking off, ladies and gentlemen. Today she is flying a two-seater Blériot with the manager of the meet William A. P. Willard as her passenger on a flight around Boston Light and back.*"

It was a beautiful takeoff. For all the familiarity with aeroplanes he had gained in the past year, Willy felt a sense of astonishment, almost the same unbelief as when he had watched Wilbur Wright on Governors Island, as the contrivance of struts and wires and shiny cloth climbed into the sky. And for all the flying the people in the stands had witnessed that day, they felt it too. He heard gasps and cries. How was it possible that such a thing could actually lift itself into the air?

In an ascending circle over the field in her white bird Harriet reached an altitude of about a thousand feet and then headed out over the bay toward Boston Light some fifteen miles away.

And again, as the plane shrank in size as it steadily gained altitude and distance from him, eventually becoming a mere speck, Willy thought about the silly, puzzling phenomenon of diminishment with distance. Everything he loved in life was contained in that dot in the sky. In a moment more you couldn't see the plane at all. Harriet was an atom, but still the same size in relation to herself, with all the atoms of her physical being unchanged, yet microscopic now to him with distance.

Another aeroplane was getting ready to take off.

"That's Miss Blanche Stuart Scott you see being positioned on the getaway, folks," Coffee informed the crowd. *"She is flying a Curtiss pusher biplane and will attempt to set a women's endurance record."*

Willy watched this takeoff. Harriet Quinlan—*his* Harriet— had paved the way for Blanche Scott and Ruth Law and every other American woman who would ever fly.

He and Leo stood waiting, both of them scanning the sky where the speck had vanished. Harry Willard was nearby, talking with one of the reporters, occasionally looking up toward the east in the direction of Boston Light. Blanche Stuart Scott was circling over the field. It seemed like hours to Willy but it was only about twenty minutes later when the speck reappeared.

Willy grinned at Leo and slapped his shoulder.

"She made the light!"

The Blériot was still at a great height but in a few more minutes its shape could be discerned.

"Harriet Quinlan is returning from Boston Light, ladies and gentlemen."

Willy was aware that he was shaking Leo's shoulders, that he was dancing on his toes in his impatience and anticipation. How could he have been such an absolutely goddamned asinine fool that he had been that day? When she landed he was going to run up to her and before God and the whole damned world tell her.

Tell her.

The Blériot rapidly grew larger as Harriet held it in a steady descent. She had to be doing at least eighty-five miles an hour.

Please, darling. Not too steep. Not too fast.

But her control of the craft seemed complete. The dangerous part of the flight was over. All that remained was a routine landing. Willy was almost able to relax.

A minute later Harriet sped over the field at some two thousand feet, banked around the far end and crossed the field again, still in a rapid descent. Sunlight shining through the fabric made the Blériot's wings translucent. There was spontaneous applause from the stands.

"She's like a great gossamer dragonfly," Leo said with awe in his voice. "This is the most beautiful flight I've ever seen her make."

Out over the water once more, only a thousand feet up now, Harriet began the final turn for the landing approach.

Suddenly—

Suddenly the nose dipped. The tail rose nearly vertically. A large dark object shot out of the rear cockpit and described an arc in the air.

Feet first, his body rigid, William A. P. Willard hurtled toward the water of Dorchester Bay.

The Blériot immediately righted itself. But only for an instant. Before Willy could begin to thank himself and Hardy and whatever God there was that he had made Harriet use a strap, the nose dipped again, even more perpendicularly, and the plane turned over on its back, flinging Harriet out into space. Her small form turned over and over as it fell.

Both bodies hit near the shore long before the plane did. Its balance regained, and three hundred pounds lighter, it righted itself again and floated down in flat circles to an almost gentle meeting with the water of the bay. There was a splash from the wheels as the water caught them and the plane turned over onto its back.

Willy did not see that. When Harriet was flung out of her cockpit and he saw her falling and knew that she was gone his eyes had closed and he had turned away. He stood immobile, his mind again strangely calm, hardly conscious of the screams from the crowd, of Leo's "*My God, my God, my God!*", of Harry Willard's cry, "*My father! My father!*"

According to Zeno's paradox, Achilles can never win the race against the tortoise, no matter how fast he runs. He covers half the distance in a given time, and half the remaining distance in another given time, and half of that half, and half of the next half—on and on in ever smaller increments unto infinity. He can never reach the end, you see, because an infinitesimal distance will always remain.

It was the same with a falling body, wasn't it? A falling body could never reach the ground. In each split-split-split second there still remained an infinitesimal distance yet to go.

There had to be.

He groaned in anguish, hating himself for his stupid thoughts, hating the laws of physics and the everyday experience that proved Zeno wrong, the mathematics of—what was it, calculus?—that had solved the paradox.

Races *were* won. Falling bodies *did* strike the ground.

Or the water.

Leo would have collapsed if Willy hadn't been gripping his arm. They were both supporting each other.

"*Oh my God she's gone*," Leo gasped.

She was gone. There was no possible way she could have survived. But she had hit shallow water close to the shore. Soft mud underneath. Maybe. Maybe.

Oh God . . . please.

It was not until they ran to the shore along with dozens of

others and he saw a man splashing through the water with Harriet's limp body that Willy allowed himself to accept the truth that she was gone.

Harriet was dead, instantaneously killed, all the beauty of her body and her being instantaneously crushed forever. Beyond retrieval.

Harriet's chariot had a great fall, and there was nothing any-body could do about it at all.

It wasn't the fall that killed the man, said the coroner. It was the sudden stop.

Some people insisted that a person falling to his death died during the fall. How stupid. What had Harriet thought in her last seconds, the brain that conceived thoughts still intact, still thinking, until the very last split second? Terror? Puzzlement? Disbelief?

Or what he was thinking:

Now it's done. Now it truly is finished.

Oh stop it, stop it!

He ran to the water's edge. Farther out people in motorboats were retrieving Willard's body. A distance away the damned Blériot floated serenely on its back and other boats were circling around it. He saw Earle Ovington climb out of one of them onto the fuselage.

The man carrying Harriet's body reached dry ground. Who was that man? What right had he to hold her in his arms like that? The way he was carrying her, draped upside down in front of him, the left leg of her costume was pulled up out of the boot exposing the back of her thigh. No one had the right to see her this way.

Several men pushed past him with a stretcher as he stood on the sand, two of them in white coats, the others in business suits, one wearing a straw boater, a pipe in his mouth.

They laid Harriet on the stretcher. Someone removed her helmet. He caught a glimpse of her face. There was only a little mud on it. Then the surging crowd blocked his view. A doctor carrying his bag hurried up and shoved people aside. He knelt by the body and made a quick determination. The bearers lifted the stretcher and started toward the field. An ambulance with siren screaming was trying to reach the scene, scattering people out of the way.

Women and men were reaching around the stretcher-bearers to touch the body as the bearers pushed through them. Some of them were trying to remove parts of Harriet's costume. A souvenir.

Ghouls.

"Get those people away from her!" Willy cried at a mounted Signal Corps officer riding up.

The man and horse advanced against the people blocking the stretcher. Intimidated by the rearing beast they fell back.

They were not all ghouls. There was genuine anguish on the faces around him. People were crying, sobbing, looking at each other helplessly. Had it really happened? Were they both really dead? A mother, tears running down her cheeks, held a little girl against her protectively, held her head against her waist so that she could not see more than she had already seen.

The band had struck up some ridiculous tune. The greater part of the crowd was still in the stands. Hundreds of people were not fully aware as yet of the tragedy that had occurred.

Willy and Leo followed the stretcher-bearers as close behind as the crush of people would allow. A woman came running up to them, a distraught look on her face. She was dressed in boots and pantaloons and carried a helmet and goggles.

"I saw it happen!" Blanche Scott said. "I almost fainted in the air. I didn't think I'd be able to land. God, how awful. What a terrible thing."

She looked as if she might faint right there. Willy reached out a hand to steady her.

"Wait here," Leo said. "I've got to find out where they're taking her."

He ran toward the ambulance, forcing people to make way. The attendants had loaded the stretcher inside and were closing the doors.

"Are they both dead?" Blanche said.

It was an expression of disbelieving hope, not a question.

"Miss Scott," someone said breathlessly. One of the two newspaper reporters Willy had seen in the hangar was running up, notebook in hand.

"Elizabeth Elliot, Boston Herald American," she clipped. "I understand you saw the accident from your aeroplane, Miss Scott. What do you think happened?"

Blanche Scott shook her head.

"I was the last reporter to interview Miss Quinlan." (A good subhead for the story she would write, Willy thought.) "Did you know her very well? What did you think of her flight? I mean, before—"

Scott was polite. "She was a courageous lady. She made one of the most dangerous flights anyone has ever made. I wouldn't have dared it myself, over water and those little islands and no place to land." She turned away from the reporter.

"Any other thoughts, Miss Scott?"

Blanche Scott looked at Willy and shrugged.

"The game needs the sacrifices."

The reporter wrote it down.

Epilogue:
New York City
1912

B OTH BODIES were taken to Quincy Hospital, where official death was pronounced, thence to Hall's undertaking parlor. The examination of Harriet Quinlan found that she had suffered a fractured skull, compound fracture of the right leg, crushed chest, bones in both arms broken, and a slight bruise under the left eye.

As of July 1912 she was the fourth woman in aviation's brief history to be killed in an aeroplane, one French, three American.

As of July 1912 hers was the one hundred fifty-fourth death by aeroplane since that of Lieutenant Selfridge in 1908.

The game needed the sacrifices.

The next day Willy and Leo accompanied Harriet's remains on a train to New York. Willy left his plane at Squantum, with no plans for retrieving it. He didn't care if he ever saw it or any other aeroplane again.

For long miles they sat together in silence, opposite each other in the coach. Willy tried to close his eyes. Every time he did all he saw was Harriet's body hurtling down. Would he ever be able to close his eyes again and not see it? Not in the exhausted sleep that had finally, mercifully, claimed him the night before, but to close his eyes in wakefulness and not see her tiny form falling . . . falling . . . falling . . .

Eventually both men realized it was foolish to try to keep their grief inside. That only made it harder to bear.

Dispassionately, almost clinically, they began discussing the accident in a flood of words, each spilling out what was in his mind as much for his own benefit as for the other's, each speaking as much to himself as to the other.

"It was Willard," Leo said. "Earle Ovington examined the wreckage and he told me he found one of the rudder wires looped over the end of the control column and that was the cause. He's crazy. That wouldn't have made the plane stand on end. Furthermore, Paul Peck pointed out that the plane wouldn't have glided down like it did if a rudder wire had been caught. And it wasn't a gust of wind like some people are saying. And it certainly wasn't Harriet fainting, like that bastard Beachey claims. It was Willard. I know it. He was an impulsive man. Many times I've been talking to him and he'd suddenly lean forward or leap out of his chair to say something that flashed in his mind. He must have done that in the plane. I think he was probably exuberant about the flight and forgot the danger and leaned forward to try to say something to Harriet, maybe congratulate her. Exactly what I told him not to do."

"I strapped her in," Willy said. "I thought she would be all right. How could she have been thrown out? The strap was tight."

"I don't know. Maybe the strain broke it when the plane somersaulted. Or maybe she undid it sometime during the flight. It wouldn't have mattered either way. Without Willard's weight in the rear she couldn't have recovered control, even if she was still in her seat. No aviator could have, and she was one of the best. She still would have crashed."

"There was hardly any damage to the plane, Leo. If she had stayed strapped in she could have ridden down with it. She might have been hurt, but not . . . She told me the strap was too tight. If it didn't break she must have unbuckled it. That's the only explanation. It was just a makeshift. I shouldn't have let her go up until we found something better."

"We'll never know what really happened, Willy. You can't

blame yourself. If there's any blame it's mine for letting her take Willard up in it. Or ultimately Blériot's for designing it so poorly in the first place. Even if she had come down with the plane she might have been knocked unconscious and drowned in the water. I'd rather she died the way she did than like that."

It was not much to choose between, but Willy silently agreed with Leo. If Harriet had come down with the plane and drowned, the helpless agony inside him would be all the greater. He would just be tormenting himself with different thoughts: if only she had landed rightside up . . . if only she had come down near one of the boats in the bay and someone had rescued her immediately . . . if only she hadn't been knocked unconscious and been able to swim out from under the plane . . .

Or worse: if she were still conscious, underwater, struggling to free herself from the strap . . .

No, better that it had been quick and clean. She could not have felt any pain.

"There's no use speculating," Leo said finally. "At least we have the consolation of knowing that there is nothing neither you nor I nor anyone else could have done to prevent her death."

Unless it had been to strap Willard in instead of her, Willy thought. Or have insisted she cancel the flight when she had offered him the chance.

Or better yet—to have crashed the damned plane himself the day he took it up.

His mind wandered. How strange that Blanche Scott should have said what she did. Her words were almost an echo of those of Otto Lilienthal, killed in his glider years before the Wrights flew: *Opfer mussen gebracht werden.* Sacrifices must be made.

"I've got to go see Mr. and Mrs. Quinlan as soon as we get to New York," Leo was saying. "I telegraphed them from Quincy. They're all alone now. Even with the money from the meet I don't think Harriet's estate will amount to more than fourteen thousand dollars. But wisely invested, it should take care of them as long as they live."

Leo saw the tears suddenly streaming from Willy's eyes and leaned across and put his hand comfortingly on his shoulder.

"I know, Willy. I know."

But Leo didn't know. He couldn't know and never would know. He didn't know that locked forever in Willy's heart, lodged at the very pit of his soul for as long as his soul would endure, was the thought that had brought the tears; the thought that had sprung into his brain the instant the laws of physics had sprung Harriet from her aeroplane; the terrible guilty punishing thought that would gnaw at his very being each time he closed his eyes and saw her falling:

Now at last it truly is all over. Now we are both free.

And he had been glad. In that dark hidden shameful corner of his soul, he had been glad.

His heart groaned. There was no consolation, no redemption, no freedom for him. Never would there be.

They laid her out in Campbell's funeral home on East Twenty-third Street and on Wednesday evening, July 3, a memorial service was held.

Ellen Reynolds asked Willy if he wanted her and his father to go with him. He told her no.

There were fewer people in attendance than the death of the world's most famous aviatrix should have warranted, Willy thought at first. The entire city should be there. There should be a line outside. But New York's millions were anticipating tomorrow's Glorious Fourth and the world moved on. The sensation-seeking crowd was already forgetting her and directing its expectations to the next spectacle. (And what was her one death compared to the eight hundred deaths of those who had gone down with the *Titanic*, whom the world still mourned?)

Even so, the room was filled to overflowing. Every chair was taken when he arrived and people were still coming in. Nearly the entire editorial staff of *Leslie's Weekly* was there, it seemed; he saw Mr. Sleicher and recognized some of the other people he'd seen that day in Harriet's office. There were numbers of fellow fliers who had known her, three representatives of the Aero Club of Italy who were in the country. The club had made Harriet an honorary member.

Harriet's parents, William and Ursula Quinlan, sat in the middle of the first row facing the flower-surrounded open casket, Mrs. Quinlan all in black and veiled. Helen Vanderbilt was in the chair on the other side of her, holding her hand. Leo stood by the casket to accept condolences from the attendees and to introduce those whom Mr. and Mrs. Quinlan did not know.

Willy went up the aisle between the rows of chairs and waited until a condolence-giver finished speaking with the Quinlans. He told Mrs. Quinlan his name and mumbled a few banal words. She said "Yes" and thanked him but he did not think she remembered him.

Like his wife, William Quinlan looked quite old, at least in his late seventies. He shook Willy's hand limply. Willy was only another of Harriet's many friends he had never met before and would never meet again.

With pathetic anguish in her voice, Mrs. Quinlan said, "Someone took Harriet's necklace, Mr. Reynolds. It wasn't with with her."

She did remember him, and she looked at him as if there was something he could say. What could he possibly say to comfort her? "I loved your daughter, Mrs. Quinlan"? "She was my very life—and I let her die"?

Helen Vanderbilt held out her hand and squeezed his, looking up at him sadly.

"She was my best and dearest friend, William. I just can't believe . . . "

He avoided looking at the body. He went back to the rear and stood beside Ladis Leukowitz, who flew out of Nassau Boulevard. He was another idiot who had decided to take his aeroplane over New York City and had his engine quit on him and lived to tell about it. Even at the back of the room the scent of the flowers was overwhelming.

The Rev. James B. Wasson of St. Thomas's Episcopal Church began the service and proceeded to deliver himself of his own banalities.

" . . . Her name is added to the long list of those who have given their lives in order that the world might be larger and better, in order that life might be greater and greater . . . "

Oh yes, Willy thought. How much larger and better the world was, how greater life. *You ass.* Her death has diminished the world, impoverished it. Life was only a greater and greater joke.

" . . . but in our sorrow tonight, there rests still a joyous note of triumph. For we realize that through this death there has come progress and that, therefore, Miss Quinlan's life was a victory over those very elements which at the end brought on her tragic end. For through such as she was do we reach near and nearer the far-off goal of our hope . . . "

Progress? What "progress" was he talking about? Better designed, safer aeroplanes? What did he know about aeroplanes? What "victory" over the elements? She was killed because she fell out of a machine a thousand feet in the air. It was as simple as that. A mountain climber who fell off a cliff could claim the same kind of "victory."

What a prolonged, barbaric ritual we put ourselves through, he thought. We think we do it in honor of the deceased. We do it for ourselves. Harriet was dead, aware of nothing, nonexistent, as nonexistent as she was before she was born. We do it for ourselves. Because we must. Because there is nothing else we can do.

It was a good standard eulogy. Willy hoped it helped the Quinlans.

Opfer mussen gebracht werden.

Not until Helen Vanderbilt and Mr. Quinlan had assisted the mother to her feet and led her out and everyone else began leaving did he go up to the coffin. The undertaker or one of his staff was about to close it. Willy held up his hand and the man stood away.

He looked down at Harriet. She could have been asleep (a final banality). There was not a mark on her, none at least on her reposed, still beautiful face, except perhaps the faintest trace of a bruise under one eye that the mortician's art had not entirely disguised. Fate had shown her that much kindness. And except for its coldness, the flesh of her clasped hands when he touched them briefly felt the same as it had when last he had touched them. Only forty-eight hours ago this shell, this simulacrum, had been warm and coursing with life.

No—it was more than fifty hours now. Tomorrow, seventy-two hours. Next week . . . next month . . . next year . . .

He clenched his fists until the nails nearly pierced his skin. It was *barbarous* to put her into the ground. He could not bear to know that all this beauty would soon begin to decay, turn hideous. Consume it in a flash of fire and let him take the ashes up and scatter them to the sky she loved.

You will always be young now, my darling.

He looked at the lovely face once more, then bent to kiss her lips one last time. But tears suddenly gushed forth and a droplet fell on her cheek.

Recoiling, he turned and blindly hurried out of the place before he broke down completely.

Interment was next day at Woodlawn Cemetery in upper Manhattan, the coffin accompanied only by family and closest friends. Willy was not asked to attend, nor did he wish to.

On the sixteenth of July seven pilots who had defied the Aero Club of America and flown at Squantum were summoned to appear at the club's offices on Madison Avenue and present themselves before the contest committee: Lincoln Beachey, Glenn L. Martin, Phillips W. Page, Paul W. Peck, Arch Freeman, J. F. Terrill and William Reynolds.

All of them wore black armbands in respect for Harriet Quinlan and William Willard. In his bitterness Willy wondered whether, for some of them, the armbands were also worn in the hope that this reminder of the tragedy that had marred the meet and occasioned universal sorrow in the aviation world would help persuade the committee to go easy on them.

Willy had returned to the world to the extent of sending for his plane to be shipped back to Hempstead Plains—someone would buy it there—and reading the newspapers again. On Tuesday the Quincy police had gone on strike, demanding pay of three dollars a day, leaving the meet temporarily without security. Then on Wednesday the pilots had struck and settled for a percentage of the gate receipts. But the gate was dismally below what the promoters had anticipated. It was a disaster all around.

Plagued with bad luck from the beginning, shadowed by the two deaths, the third Harvard-Boston meet had petered out in more or less complete failure.

They had been summoned by the Aero Club for "trial," but there could not be a trial without some kind of defense, and there was none. They had all been warned. They were there for sentencing, and the sentence was suspension of their licenses until January 1, 1913.

None of the pilots protested. They had fully expected the worst. Suspension was a satisfactory outcome for everyone. The offenders had only been slapped on their wrists, but hard enough to sting for six months, and the Aero Club had made manifest its authority over them and every other licensed aviator in the country.

Lincoln Beachey was the only one who showed no sign of relief when the suspension was announced. He actually made a scoffing sound. The others looked at him sharply, afraid he might get them back into trouble.

For Christ's sake, man, we were lucky.

But it turned out that Beachey was the one pilot who could not have cared less about the decision. Unless it was Willy Reynolds, who no longer cared about anything.

Beachey was standing on the curb trying to flag down a cab when Willy emerged from the building. When Beachey saw him he put two fingers to the bill of his cap. Willy went up to him.

"I was going to retire from flying at the end of the year. Now it's just six months sooner," Beachey said, glancing at Willy between glances in both directions along the street.

"I've had enough of this bloody business, seeing fine fliers like Harriet Quinlan get themselves killed—though that's the way I always wanted to go out myself. I don't mean like her, but crashing down in a plane from thousands of feet in front of the grandstand and making a big splash while the band played the latest rag and everybody saying when they hauled what was left of me away, 'Well, Beachey was certainly flying some.'"

He took out a cigar and bit off the end and Willy held a match to it. Beachey puffed on the cigar and nodded. He peered at Willy.

"I've never been under the delusion that the crowds came just to witness my flying skills, kiddo, and neither should you. I've shaken hands with the Silent Reaper a thousand times. He's given me frights I couldn't describe to anyone who's never flown. Well, today the old fellow and I part as pals."

A cab stopped and as Beachey started to get in he turned and grinned.

"But there's nothing like flying, is there?"

Willy walked down Madison to Twenty-sixth Street and over to Fifth Avenue.

There was her building, squat and solid, built to last forever. People inside it, busily putting together the latest issue of *Leslie's Weekly*. People she had worked with, laughed with, starting to forget her. Their lives went on.

No, that wasn't true. It was his bitterness talking. No one who had known her would ever forget her. They'd said their goodbye to her with a grieving obituary in that week's issue, prominently centered on the editorial page, bordered in black.

It had given her age at death as 27. Harriet's secrets were buried with her in her grave.

Across Fifth Avenue to Broadway. He almost walked in front of a car—so what? Up to Twenty-seventh Street.

The Hotel Victoria was the same as the last time he had seen it. Of course it was. But it was a small building and they would tear it down someday to build something bigger, demolishing one more vestige of Harriet's existence. Maybe not for years, but eventually. New York never stopped building, higher and higher. New York had no time to look back.

The drapes were drawn over the window at which she had sat that day. He crossed over. Why was he doing this to himself?

They had stood here, on this pavement, the night after the theater, walked down this sidewalk at Christmastime coming back from Child's, the day he had kissed her for the first time. Thousands of people had walked where they had walked. Tens of thousands more would. Was there an imprint, some kind of trace, in the insensate concrete, some memory of her? Or would the memory endure only in his mind?

And when his mind ceased?

How could life—no: memory, for what was life but memory?— be so painful and yet so sweet, so sweet . . ?

The Recent Present

THE OLD MAN felt warmth on his face. The sun had lowered beneath the canopy.

He was aware of a droning. The aeroplane, coming back again. The purr of its engine grew louder as it approached out of the sun.

He sat erect and opened his eyes, tried to focus them on what his ears heard.

She's coming back, Leo! I can hear her! She's coming back! Oh God . . . this time . . . this time . . .

The sunlight blinded him. He threw the blanket aside and struggled to get to his feet, to move toward the sound. He pushed against the sides of the cockpit, lifting himself up. Was he in his aeroplane? How did he get in his aeroplane?

God—the pain in his chest. Was it the wheel? Where was the wheel? His feet were tangling with the rudder bar. He lurched forward, felt himself falling . . .

falling . . .

falling . . .

He reached out his arms . . . and embraced infinity.

Marilyn and her mother went through Willy's effects together, what there was of them. No clothes to save for the ragman; he hadn't worn anything but pajamas, bathrobe and slippers for years. Everything else he had ever possessed had long since been dispersed or disposed of in one way or another, at one time or another: the last house he had owned, the furniture, all the books he used to have, albums of photographs—everything.

Poor Willy, Marilyn thought. Poor, poor Willy. She hadn't been able to get the picture of his last moments out of her mind.

"I'm glad you weren't there, Mother. "It was so awful. I was half asleep in a chair on the patio and heard him muttering something. I opened my eyes and he was trying to stand up and before I could do anything he crashed down on the floor and was . . . *gone.*"

"Don't dwell on that, honey," her mother said. "It was his time. Way past his time. I truly think that in the last few years he had simply grown very tired of living. Be glad it was so quick. If he felt any pain it must have been very brief."

"I know. But I'll always wonder what it was that made him suddenly try to get out of the wheelchair."

They began emptying out the drawer of the small cabinet next to Willy's bed. Not much worth saving here either—a packet of old letters and cards from family members, that was about all.

"What's this?" Marilyn said.

In the back of the drawer was an old thin bifold wallet, the discolored leather cracked and brittle. Not an ordinary money wallet though. She sat down on the bed and opened it. There was a little card inside. It looked like some kind of certificate.

"Fédération Aéronautique Internationale," she slowly pronounced the French words aloud. "Aero Club of America."

She held it up to her mother and they both read the paragraph below the names.

"I didn't know Willy was an aviator, Mother. How old is this anyway?"

"Lord, I have no idea. It has to be before he and Grandmother Reynolds were married, and that was back in, oh, Nineteen-nineteen, I think. I remember her mentioning one time that he had been a flier when he was a very young man, one of the earliest ones. But I never heard him talk about it."

"Do you think it would have any value to anyone? Probably not. I'm going to keep it."

"Let me see that again," said her mother. She looked at the certificate closely.

"I just remembered something else. Grandmother Reynolds said that Willy had tried to enlist in the air service in Nineteen-seventeen, during the First World War, but was rejected because he was too old. Imagine—nearly eighty years ago he was too old! But other than that he would never have anything to do with airplanes, even though she said he was always interested in them, subscribing to aviation magazines and things like that. But he wouldn't even fly in a commercial airliner. I asked her why, was he afraid? And all she knew was that at one time he had told her something like, 'This is my punishment.' She could never get him to explain what he meant.

"Isn't that the oddest thing?"

"Punishment for what, I wonder," said Marilyn. "Oh, I wish I'd known all this before, Mother. He must have had some interesting stories to tell if he was one of the first fliers. I wish I had known him longer—before, when he had all his faculties. I think he would have told me. I think he wanted to talk about flying and airplanes the last time, the day he died. I'll always think he wanted to tell me something."

There was something else in the wallet, tucked in a sleeve. Marilyn withdrew it carefully. It was a newspaper clipping, discolored to as dark a brown as the leather. It was so fragile that when she tried to unfold it, it crumbled into pieces.

She retrieved a fragment from her lap and was only able to make out: AVIAT MEET. On a larger fragment were what looked like some kind of caricatures with photographs of peoples' faces, none of them whole or distinct. The fragment fell apart as she touched it.

Oh, well. She brushed the paper bits off her skirt onto the floor and closed the wallet. The license inside would be something to remember Willy by, something to show her children, when and if she had any. Not much. But something. It must have meant a lot to Willy, to have kept it all these years.

When her mother tried to remove the rubber band around the letters it snapped and something fell to the floor. It looked like a large postcard, but there was no writing or stamp on it. If it was a postcard it had never been mailed. She picked it up and turned it over.

"This must be very old too," she said.

Marilyn held it in her hand and looked at it. It was a lithographed drawing of an attractive young woman in a purplish costume standing in front of a funny-looking antique airplane.

"Don't tell me Willy flew in one of those things," she said. "Can you imagine anyone actually going up in something like that?"

The card was in remarkably good condition considering its probable age. The colors were hardly faded. She read the printing at the bottom.

"I wonder who Harriet Quinlan was. I wonder if Willy knew her."

She looked at the picture again and sighed, then slipped the card into the fold of the wallet. She would keep this too.

"Whoever she was, she was very pretty, wasn't she?"

Apologia

READERS familiar with the history of aviation will have recognized at once that "Harriet Quinlan" is a stand-in for Harriet Quimby, America's first licensed female aviator, and have perhaps wondered: why write a novel about a fictitional character and not a straight biography of the actual person she is so transparently based on?

The answer is that a straight biography would have amounted to not much more than a pamphlet, so little is known about Harriet Quimby beyond the limited public record. For that reason, I decided to attempt a novelistic treatment of her life and career—and indeed, when I first began writing this book, the real-life Harriet *was* my heroine. But it became clear to me early on that even this approach faced the obstacle of the dearth of known facts about her.

Microfilmed newspapers and magazines of a bygone era preserve the public writings and aerial exploits of Harriet Quimby, who was not only a well-known New York drama critic and journalist but who, for a brief eleven months between 1911 and 1912, was one of the most prominent members of the world's still-small band of aviation pioneers. It was a time when nearly every venture into the air in the primitive and fragile craft of the day set a new record of some kind—if it did not end in catastrophe.

But except for what can be read (or imagined) between the lines of the many articles she wrote for *Leslie's Illustrated Weekly* and other periodicals, almost nothing is known about Harriet Quimby the private person. She apparently wanted it that way.

There is no full-length biography of her that I know of. There is no listing for Harriet Quimby the aviator in the Library of Congress or the New York Public Library. Her name would stump most "trivia"experts.

Not that Harriet Quimby has been forgotten entirely. Between 1995 and 2000, the Harriet Quimby Research Conference (www.harrietquimby.org/) published a number of papers dealing with her flying career and the known (or conjectured) minutiae of her life. On December 17, 1999, the ninety-sixth anniversary of the Wright Brothers' first flight, she was honored in a ceremony at the Wright memorial at Kitty Hawk, North Carolina.

Her lovely face also graces the fifty-cent air mail stamp. But how many people have a need for or have ever seen a fifty-cent air mail stamp?

As famous as she was in her day, Harriet Quimby never became a household name like that of one female aviator who came two decades after her. She was not even included on a plaque honoring "Early Birds" (those who flew before 1914) in the National Air and Space Museum in Washington, DC when I visited there, while that of Matilde Moisant was.

One can only speculate on what Harriet Quimby might have accomplished in aviation had her career not been so tragically cut short.

Using a fictitious substitute for Harriet Quimby, I decided, would enable me to construct a novel closely based on her record as America's first aviatrix as she might have been seen through the eyes of a fellow flying student (while extensively employing her own words) and at the same time free me of the constraints imposed by the factual void surrounding her private life. More importantly, for novelistic purposes, it would give me license to introduce into the story elements of sexuality and romance— evidence for which in Harriet Quimby's own life is nonexistent.

Whether I have done justice or injustice to Harriet Quimby by this approach I leave to the reader's judgment.

In any event, Harriet Quimby deserves to be remembered as more than a footnote in the history of aviation. I can only hope that she would forgive me for the liberties I have taken with her person in an attempt to bring her to life, even if under a pseudonym. Surely she would forgive me for falling in love with her.

Two final notes:

The minor mystery concerning the cause of Harriet Quimby's death at Squantum, Massachusetts on July 1, 1912 is of little interest to anyone today. But for what it is worth, I believe the explanation advanced by Leo Stevens (who went on to become a successful designer and manufacturer of parachutes) is the likeliest one.

Ursula Quimby died in 1913. William Quimby, who lived until 1922, buried his wife, and reinterred their youngest daughter from Manhattan's Woodlawn Cemetery, in Kensico Cemetery at appropriately named Valhalla, New York. There, on a peaceful, tree-shaded hillside in Westchester County, a small monument and plaque erected by people who admired, loved and could not forget Harriet Quimby mark her resting place today.

D. O.